SOCIETY AND THE VICTORIANS

OUR FRIEND THE CHARLATAN

Other novels by George Gissing also published by Harvester

THE NETHER WORLD
Edited with an introduction by John Goode

THYRZA
Edited with an introduction by Jacob Korg

DEMOS: A STORY OF ENGLISH SOCIALISM
Edited with an introduction by Pierre Coustillas

SLEEPING FIRES
With an introduction by Pierre Coustillas

ISABEL CLARENDON
Edited, in 2 volumes, with an introduction by Pierre Coustillas

IN THE YEAR OF JUBILEE
Edited by P.F. Kropholler, with an introduction by Gillian Tindall

THE UNCLASSED
Edited with an introduction by Jacob Korg

The next volumes in the series will be *The Emancipated, The Crown of Life, the Whirlpool,* and *New Grub Street.*

For these and other Harvester titles see the end of this book.

" Nonsense!   He couldn't hear at that distance."

OUR FRIEND · THE CHARLATAN

George Gissing

Edited with a new introduction and notes by
PIERRE COUSTILLAS
Director, Centre for Victorian Studies,
University of Lille

2 052089

THE HARVESTER PRESS

THE HARVESTER PRESS LIMITED
Publisher: John Spiers
2 Stanford Terrace,
Hassocks, Nr. Brighton,
Sussex, England

SOCIETY & THE VICTORIANS
General Editor: John Spiers

The Harvester Press series 'Society & The Victorians', now comprising nearly 30 titles, makes available again important works by and about the Victorians. Each of the titles chosen has been either out of print and difficult to find, or exceedingly rare for many years. A few titles, although available in the secondhand market, are needed in modern critical editions and the series attempts to meet this demand. Scholars of established reputation provide substantial new introductions, and the majority of titles have textual notes and a full bibliography. Texts are reprinted from the best editions.

'Our Friend the Charlatan'

First published in 1901 by Chapman & Hall

This edition, reproducing the text of the first edition, 1901, first published in 1976 by The Harvester Press

Introduction, Notes etc. © 1976 Pierre Coustillas

'Society & The Victorians' No. 28

ISBN 0 85527 199 X

Printed in England by Redwood Burn Limited
Trowbridge, Wiltshire

Contents

Bibliographical Note

Our Friend the Charlatan, originally entitled 'The Coming Man', was first published in London by Chapman & Hall on May 25, 1901. The hardcover edition in blue cloth gilt was priced at 6 shillings; a two-shilling issue bound in stiff green pictorial wrappers, also dated 1901, probably consisted of sheets of the first edition bound sometime between 1901 and 1903. Both issues had the illustrations by Launcelot Speed. A 'new and cheaper edition', without the illustrations, in the same format in green cloth with black titling, selling at 2s. 6d., appeared in June 1903 under the same imprint. It is undated, and so also is a two-shilling issue bound in stiff green pictorial wrappers, with the original illustrations, and obviously consisting of sheets of the first edition, with a new title page. Lastly Chapman & Hall published a sixpenny reprint in pictorial wrappers in June 1906. Like a number of Gissing's novels of the 1890s, the book was included in Bell's Indian and Colonial Library in 1901. The volume was available in cloth and in paper covers.

The American edition appeared in slate grey cloth under the imprint of Henry Holt in early June 1901, priced at $1.50. According to *Publishers' Weekly* there was a second impression of this late in 1901. No translation of the novel is on record.

The original handwritten manuscript, 116 pages long, was sold in 1913, apparently for 11 guineas, by Algernon Gissing, the author's brother and literary executor, to Frank Redway, the Wimbledon bookdealer. Alexander Turnbull bought it, bound in red morocco by Wallis, from Robson & Co., 23 Coventry Street, Piccadilly, in 1915 for £75. It is now in the Alexander Turnbull Library, Wellington, New Zealand.

The proofs of the English edition, dated by the printers (Richard Clay and Sons Ltd, Bungay) March 18/April 2 1901, are in the possession of Madame Denise Le Mallier, who also holds a copy of the first American edition with corrections in Gissing's hand.

Acknowledgements

The editor wishes to express his thanks to the Librarian of the Alexander Turnbull Library, Wellington, New Zealand, for lending him a microfilm of the manuscript of *Our Friend the Charlatan*. He also acknowledges his gratitude to Dr J.R. Tye for his pioneering work in the study of the manuscript, and to Mr P.F. Kropholler whose notes on the novel have, as on previous occasions, proved extremely useful. Consultation of the proofs of the novel, and of Gissing's copy of the American edition, was possible thanks to the generosity of Mme. Denise Le Mallier. The quotations from the unpublished portions of the manuscript are made with the kind permission of the Alexander Turnbull Library.

P.C.

Introduction

One can say of *Our Friend the Charlatan* what G.W. Stonier said of Gissing in 1958: the trouble is that it is nobody's favourite. The story has obviously suffered from its position in Gissing's career: it belongs neither to the working-class stories, which have received considerable attention in the last 10 years, nor to the solid group of novels devoted to the material, moral and cultural life of the middle classes, on which his reputation largely rests. *Our Friend the Charlatan* belongs to the third part of Gissing's career, when he published not only novels in his own unmistakable manner, but short stories in volume form, criticism on Dickens, and semi-autobiographical essays, and when he thought of publishing historical novels as well as a book on Wakefield in his father's time. Among the later novels it occupies an unpredictable place between *The Crown of Life*, with its optimistic conclusion, and *Will Warburton*, noteworthy for its tender resignation and doleful pity. It has an intellectual neatness and brilliance of its own which contrasts with these two mellow tales of modern life, respectively written under the influence of love and of approaching death. Conceived and composed in France, the story partakes of the French turn of mind. It is mainly the analyst's intellect—not at all his heart—which expresses itself here. If *Our Friend the Charlatan* has predecessors in Gissing's works they are *The Odd Women*, *In the Year of Jubilee* and *The Whirlpool*. But the story does not have the same breadth; its setting, though clearly defined, is not as strongly integrated into the plot. The action, set in drawing-rooms, is for the most part propelled by the dialogue. We do not breathe the atmosphere of the country town as we do in

Denzil Quarrier. True, Hollingford is reminiscent of Polterham, but its reality has vanished into middle ground. We are closer than ever to the type of drawing-room comedy that awaits dramatization, and the satire concerns at once human character and society. Therefore, to the casual observer, the novel may seem atypical, but as we shall see, this is hardly tenable.

I

There is no dearth of information about the circumstances of composition of the story. Gissing set to work in the autumn of 1899, after he had settled in Paris, with Gabrielle Fleury and her mother and brother in their flat at 13 Rue de Siam. *By the Ionian Sea* was then ready, and the anti-jingo *Crown of Life* soon to appear, its publication coinciding, unfortunately, with the outbreak of the Boer War. The new novel was provisionally entitled 'The Coming Man' and bravely begun in an atmosphere which must have been unpropitious to composition, despite the impulse that sprang from his love for Gabrielle. The novelist's diary shows that he started on September 29, and that after various difficulties domestic and professional, he made a new start on October 17. By November 10 his manuscript was about 35 pages long; that is, nearly one third of the novel in its completed state. Then, as had so often happened, he suddenly lost faith in his story and laid it aside. The background (which was nonetheless to play a small enough part in the narrative) was not clear in his mind, and he thought it better to postpone the completion of the story until he had collected some more material in England. This manuscript fragment was certainly destroyed after he had incorporated into the novel whatever passages of it were still usable. At the time he resumed 'The Coming Man'—after writing 'Among the Prophets' from November 19, 1899 to early February 1900, as well as a few of his best short stories, and spending the whole of April 1900 in England[1]—he was living in the French countryside, at St. Honoré-les-Bains, and felt in greatly improved spirits. His manuscript kept him busy for three months, from May 29 to August 29; in addition Sundays, he rested only for a few days which were devoted to other, shorter writings, to reading and some outings. Sometimes, on sitting to work, he would rewrite a page he had penned the day before, but on the whole composition proceeded at a steady pace. It can be followed day by day on the manuscript: it is remarkable that by adding the figures he wrote down in his diary one gets a total of about 119 pages while the manuscript runs to 116 pages plus one page, numbered 36b, done at the end of June when he decided that he must go back to make some changes.

Gissing despatched the novel to his agent James B. Pinker the day after its completion, in order to have it typed, and he then turned to what became the first (unpublished) version of *The Private Papers of Henry Ryecroft*. Typists and the postal service were very efficient in those days, since by September 8 the first half of the typescript was in his hands and by the 17th the whole of it had been returned to Pinker. Author and agent wished for serialization, but no opportunity occurred and Pinker was pressed to find publishers for the book. Henry Holt in America offered an advance of £150 and Chapman & Hall in England offered £350 for seven years' rights. This was more than Gissing had ever received for any book, but it was too good to be quite true. The American firm objected to spring publication and as Gissing thought he could not wait until the autumn, he had to be content with £100 from that quarter. Holt must have rejoiced retrospectively as even this reduced advance was not justified by sales. A second copy of the typescript was corrected by the author for the American publisher in early March 1901, which accounts for some slight differences between the English and the American versions of the novel. It was only then that after many hesitations a title was hit upon which pleased both English and American publishers: *Our Friend the Charlatan*.[2]

The book was warmly reviewed on both sides of the Atlantic. There was some carping at the pessimistic view of human nature implied in it, but the brilliant comic atmosphere blinded some reviewers to the reality below the surface. 'Powerful and uncomfortable', said the *Illustrated London News*, summing up the general impression left by the story upon the 39 reviewers whose pieces are listed in the Bibliography. 'Mr. Gissing is thoroughly original and even amazingly skilful', commented the *Pall Mall Gazette*. 'He has never written a book in which the psychology was truer or the purpose more manful and more honest.' The sales in England, however, were comparatively disappointing and the author once more recorded his disillusion. No accurate figures are available from either Chapman & Hall or Holt, but it is certain

that neither firm, though both were extremely pleased with
the book from the artistic standpoint, made much money out
of it. A technical comparison of the first English edition in
cloth and the subsequent issues from the same plates shows
that the so-called 'new and cheaper edition' issued in June
1903, at a time when *Ryecroft* was bringing many new readers to Gissing, consisted of sheets of the original edition,
bound in cheaper cloth with a cancel title-page. Besides, the
present-day scarcity of the sixpenny reprint of 1906 seems to
indicate that the book did not do well in that form either. No
wonder then that the novel, being very scarce to-day, has not
received much critical attention. Samuel Vogt Gapp, Jacob
Korg and Gillian Tindall have made valuable comments on
it, but quite a few significant aspects of the story remain to be
studied—most of them beyond the scope of an introduction.
No one, for instance, has attempted to place the titular charlatan in the long line of deceivers and self-deceivers with which
the novels and short stories are fraught; or again, no one has
undertaken to study the forms and mechanism of satire in a
novel which is satirical throughout, or the treatment of the
new woman or even the use Gissing made of *La Cité
Moderne*, the doctoral thesis pillaged by Dyce Lashmar.

II

Among Gissing's characters can be distinguished various
types which strongly appealed to him as artistic material: out-
cast intellectuals, spinsters trying to keep up appearances,
idealists perverted by vanity and fashionable social doctrines,
to mention only obvious examples. Charlatans and charlatanism struck him from his school days. In an age when
repressive moralism was a common attitude, a child of keen
intelligence like him could hardly fail to be impressed by the
gap he observed at school, at church or at home, between
what the political and religious authorities promised or
preached and the harsh realities around him, also by the subjects that were never discussed, or were referred to with an
obvious lack of candour. He quickly became aware of a good
deal of sham and humbug in his surroundings. As a boarder
at Lindow Grove School, Alderley Edge, he could watch at
close quarters an educational charlatan—James Wood, the
Principal, a man addicted to gesticulating and posturizing
whom he came to judge severely in adult life. The youth who

wrote an 'Ode to Truth' at Owens College already had a dis-
taste of hypocrisy and insincerity; he was impatient with
bourgeois morality, painfully conscious of all the taboos, religious, ideological and sexual, that burdened the atmosphere
of the time. Conversely the strict discipline enforced by his
mother in the home, his own natural shyness and his eagerness to fulfil the hopes his father placed in him must have
encouraged him to practise dissimulation and secrecy whenever he feared a rebuke. Even as a boy he must often have felt
to the point of discomfort the discrepancy between thought
and speech, between professed ideal and inglorious deed. He
surely often meditated on the relative value of sincerity. The
contrast between the apparent and the hidden aspects of life
was food for his reflection, as it was material for sensational
novelists and playwrights. He was brought by his own
actions to ponder over motivation and early enough in his
career was tempted to explore untapped strata of human psychology.

His soul-searing experience in Manchester precipitated a
tendency which lay dormant in him. It supplied his fiction,
from the very first story he wrote in America, with a theme
which, though as a rule palpably different from charlatanism, is in some cases (notably, that of Godwin Peak in *Born
in Exile*) interwoven with it. This theme was what Gillian
Tindall rightly calls 'the guilty secret'. It accounts, at the
level of plot and characterization, for a number of melodra-
matic elements. Even as late as *Sleeping Fires* (1895) Gissing
was using the device of illicit fatherhood to account for the
banishment of his hero, Edmund Langley. In *The Crown of
Life*, the theme is sparked off by the slightest of
misdemeanours—Piers Otway becomes slightly tipsy in
quite excusable circumstances and is sent away by the girl he
loves. In his last completed novel, *Will Warburton*, the guilty
secret assumes a form reminiscent of the case of Godwin
Peak: ruined by the speculation of a friend to whom he has
entrusted his money, Warburton secretly becomes a grocer.
Like Peak, though with inverted ambition, he assumes a new
personality and shuns his friends until he is discovered accidentally by one of them. Both Peak and Warburton play a part;
yet the theme works in opposite directions—Peak tries to
climb up the social ladder, Warburton is determined to climb
down it. The former's self-seeking contrasts with the latter's
resignation. Both men deceive their circle, pretend to be what

they are not, yet they do not delude themselves; they are charlatans, but clear-headed ones.

Charlatanism in Gissing's work also takes its root in a cog-
nate affinity of his own temperament. Stories about him as a
boy, told after his death by his schoolfellow T.T. Sykes, tes-
tify to a fondness for playing pranks in a harmless way. Readers of his story 'My First Rehearsal' will readily associate the
joke of Gissing at Alderley Edge bewildering local farmers
with the news that their farms were to be destroyed to make
room for railway extensions, with the story of the budding
actor who is eased of all his belongings by the pseudo-
manager of a travelling company. Sometimes, as in two other
early stories, 'A Terrible Mistake' and 'My Clerical Rival', the
theme of double-dealing deviated into that of misunderstanding, and the plot was resolved in a joyous atmosphere of clari-
fication. When in later works he chose to resume that line of
inspiration, he did so in by-plots (*vide* the Malkin-Jacox sub-
plot in *Born in Exile* or the Damerel mystery in *In the Year of
Jubilee*). And, incidentally, it would seem that Gissing's
growing dissatisfaction with *The Town Traveller* was partly
due to his use of a plot of that kind, typical of his prentice
work, in a late novel.

Gradually the theme of delusion and/or self-delusion took
an intellectual turn; it ceased to be a purely mechanical
instrument and was fused with the notions of wishful thinking and careerism in a political, social or religious context.
There is no monotony whatever in the treatment of the
theme; indeed, it is quite possible to read the whole of Gissing's work without noticing it, as other lines of inspiration
are much more salient. It goes through many nice variations
in nature, time and extent. The nature of delusion is always
concerned with the role to be played or that could have been
played by the character in society, but the amount of self-
interest varies a good deal (it is considerable in Mutimer, but
apparently non-existent in Egremont); professional ambition may or may not be linked with the quest for personal
happiness (Mutimer, Peak, and Dyce Lashmar in the present
book combine social ambition with the pursuit of an intellectually and/or financially suitable wife). The charlatans'
thoughts are generally turned towards the future—besides
the names just mentioned could be placed three other major
characters in Gissing's novels: Denzil Quarrier, Bruno Chilvers and Jasper Milvain. But some short stories offer opposite

examples of failed men who are obsessed with their past and see themselves pathetically in retrospect as coming men whose ascension was broken by ill-luck. The hero of 'A Victim of Circumstances' succeeds in convincing himself that his wife's death has cut short his career as an artist while in fact it was his wife, also a painter, who had the greater talent: he does not scruple to declare himself the author of her pictures. In 'The Light on the Tower' a thwarted politician inclined to self-pity comes to see himself as a victim of fate. Both Castledine in the former story and Fleetwood in the latter are men of words who yield to self-pity and play upon their wives' feelings. They are, like most of Gissing's charlatans, men who fail, and Gissing delighted in dissecting their failure, as he enjoyed analysing and debunking the spurious success of such careerists as Bruno Chilvers and Jasper Milvain.

Women always have an important function in the charlatans' lives, but here also the pattern offers considerable variety. The true victims of circumstances are the wives of Castledine and Fleetwood, not Castledine and Fleetwood themselves—they sacrifice their dignity and self-respect. Denzil Quarrier's wife drowns herself to escape persecution by her legal husband, a ne'er-do-well who would not have become her tormentor but for Denzil's political designs and the jealousy they aroused. Women, as often as not, are regarded by the charlatans as stepping-stones in their careers. In different ways, Mutimer, Milvain, Peak and Lashmar consider women indispensable to their social ascent. With Peak, woman is very nearly an end in herself. With Lashmar—a tepid lover like Mutimer and Milvain—she must be a source of income or else is of no interest. Here again the diversity of context and approach blurs the common denominator. Mutimer the proletarian is dazzled by middle-class femininity to the point of forgetting his political principles; Milvain is a cynical fortune-hunter who adjusts his emotions to the aim in sight. Both men are thick-skinned; delicacy of feeling is alien to their nature. On the contrary, Godwin Peak idealizes woman, or rather educated middle-class women with refined feelings. Lashmar the charlatan is akin to Milvain in that he directs his courtship towards the supposedly biggest fortune with marvellous pliability. His cynicism is only implicit, perhaps also unconscious—and this makes him a subtler creation than Milvain, in particular because Gissing's distance from his creation is greater and more constant. In *New Grub Street* we occasionally feel (too strongly, I think) the author's desire to do Milvain justice. Milvain's good and bad points are sharply differentiated—his black and white spots are, as it were, juxtaposed. With Lashmar we do not feel such sharp differentiation between the various elements of his character.

When *Our Friend the Charlatan* was published, stress was laid by several reviewers on Lashmar's egoism. *Literature* observed: 'It is almost impossible, in dealing with...*Our Friend the Charlatan* to avoid a comparison with *The Egoist* of Mr. Meredith. In many points Dyce Lashmar...bears a strong resemblance to the great Sir Willoughby. True, he is not quite the gentleman, and the head of the house of Patterne, with all his faults, was well-bred; he has no chivalry whatsoever, whereas the baronet preserved some touch of the true feeling even in the most adverse circumstances. But both men laboured under a magnified sense of their own importance, both curiously enough, found themselves engaged at different times—once at the same time—to three several ladies; and both ended by marrying, as a last resort, the woman whom they had first ruthlessly sacrificed for the sake of greater attractions.' Meredith's influence can hardly be questioned; Gissing was familiar with *The Egoist* and indeed with the whole of Meredith's work. The cyclic pattern is common to both stories; Dyce, like Sir Willoughby, loops the loop; the last attachment is in each case a counter-apotheosis predictable from the outset. The other Gissing heroes mentioned above are also egoists in their own way, but none of them is a pretender and an egoist with such a strong Meredithian flavour. Indeed, the word 'egoist' appears on p. 259. The female atmosphere in which he moves contributes to create a Meredithian climate: at least Constance Bride and Mrs. Toplady are women of the type that appealed to the Sage of Box Hill. Constance is a new woman, practical and cautious, with little nonsense about her. Of the three women who appear at some time or other as Dyce's potential wife, she is the most level-headed and has some of the moral and intellectual qualities which Meredith prized so highly. Mrs. Toplady, as will be seen in a moment, is a typical Meredithian commentator who points to the fun of the action and does her best to enhance it.

There is one more aspect of the novel which invites a comparison with *The Egoist* or with *The Ordeal of Richard*

Feverel—another novel Gissing thought much of. It is the
country-house setting. Patterne Hall, Raynham Abbey and
Rivenoak are privileged places for the functioning of the
comic spirit. Rivenoak is the headquarters of comedy (few
people of importance in the story remain at a distance from
it, but they are numerous enough to create the illusion of the
outside world.) Lady Ogram, tyrannical and crotchety, commands the situation or imagines she does. Behind the show of
obedience to her caprices and desires, lies a network of
intrigue, but so long as she is alive, Rivenoak is the centre of
action. After her death, with its financial consequences, the
various actors in the comedy go their several ways. All ambi-
guities are clarified and the whole affair ends ironically
except for Constance Bride who has come very near to justifying her name. Together with *Isabel Clarendon, Our Friend
the Charlatan* is the only novel in which country-house
scenes play any significant part. Here they give the action an
air of spaciousness which does a little to cool the hot atmosphere of intrigue. Yet, unlike Meredith, Gissing refrains
from slackening the pace of events with long descriptions (he
no longer had three volumes to fill) as he dispenses with the
many analytic disquisitions which clutter up *The Egoist*.
The country-house is an ideal hotbed for Lashmar's egoism
to grow in. Fanned by flattery, his ambition develops outside
the field of politics into that of love and degenerates into cove-
tousness.

Egoism is indeed a disease which is not limited to the hero.
Lady Ogram's altruism is but a mask for egoism. She
manages to combine to an unusual extent unselfishness and
self-centredness. Hatred of Robb, the conservative Member
for Hollingford, is her main staff in life; her fight with him
does not even stop with death. As she has the advantage of out-
living him she knows that her own will, once executed, shall
secure her definite victory. Her grand-niece, May Tomalin,
harbours similar contradictions. Her philanthropic activities not only betray how raw her mind still is—they are an out-
let for her dissatisfaction. Like Jessica Morgan who (in *In the
Year of Jubilee*) joins the Salvation Army out of bitterness, or
Mrs. Lant who bullies the poor at her nether-world soup-
kitchen, she finds in philanthropy a way to assuage her own
ungratified urges. Even Constance is affected by the atmosphere of greed which prevails at Rivenoak. She agrees to
feign to pledge her faith to Dyce out of submission to Lady

Ogram's inordinate command, and she comes to find the situation more sweet than bitter. Considering her past relationship with Dyce she sees in the oddity of the situation a possibility of revenge. However, such frailty as she may betray for a while is eventually overcome when she has fully understood what a weak, untrustworthy creature Dyce Lashmar is. We leave her in single blessedness and alone in the camp of victory.

She is one of those new women who people pretty thickly the fiction of the period; cycling has entered into her daily existence, the bicycle being not so much a means as a symbol of her emancipation. In a scene which foreshadows the ending, she cycles away, leaving Dyce behind. She is superior to May Tomalin in many ways, yet not quite enough to be free from jealousy towards a new rival. May is the University Extension type of the 'nineties. She cannot open her mouth without displaying her half-baked knowledge. Gissing had depicted the male equivalent with greater leniency in *Thyrza*. Egremont failed all along the line; he did not strike us as a fool, only as an idealist to whom one can't refuse an ounce of intellectual sympathy. May Tomalin has few, if any, redeeming features. She misses a chance of becoming Lady Dymchurch out of sheer stupidity. Clearly in this book no female character finds favour in the author's eyes. Lord Dymchurch exits, cured of all desire to make further acquaintance with womankind, and Gissing in some moods would have approved him. Here autobiographical elements occur side by side with others which make of the book a period piece.

III

One of the novel's main interests is its use of comedy. Comic scenes are not lacking in Gissing's early fiction, but his first attempt at writing a really amusing book did not occur until *The Paying Guest*, a comedy of lower-middle-class daily life without any political implications. *The Town Traveller* described boarding-house manners with some Dickensian overtones and again shunned wider issues. Both stories, however unpretentious, were nevertheless admirably documented pictures, and their documentary value will increase as years go by and the manners and mentalities depicted become less readily understandable by future generations. In

Our Friend the Charlatan Gissing aimed higher and he passed from the comedy of manners to the comedy of character. The author's intellect alone is at work dissecting human motives with consummate skill and rousing the reader's smile all the while. The approach is devoid of passion, there is no personal involvement on the novelist's part. With the sole exception of Lord Dymchurch, the distance between the writer and his characters is much greater than in most of the earlier novels. He obviously enjoys his task. Egoism, a Meredithian subject, is analysed with a Meredithian instrument, the comic spirit, which W.E. Henley defined as 'the missing link between art and nonsense.'[3] Meredith himself explained at length what he meant by the comic spirit in a seminal lecture which he waited 20 years to print in book form. It is an attitude of mind, consisting in intense, acute contemplation of human behaviour. James Moffatt defines it as 'the *ethos* of a calm, curious observer, alive to the pretences and foibles of mankind, yet loving them nonetheless that he is thus acutely sensitive to their untrained opinions, their affectations, pedantries, delusion, inconsistencies, hypocrisies.'[4] The comic spirit is deflationary in essence; though it is never akin to moralizing, it teaches a lesson. Meredith sought for its practisers and found Menander, Terence, Chaucer, Shakespeare, and Molière, who all attempted to cure by laughter—laughter of the head and, less conspicuously, of the heart. On the philosophical level he saw the comic spirit as a factor of human improvement in a society which, however, in order to benefit from it, must have achieved some degree of intellectual development. Comedy, he thought, could only have free play in a society in which woman was allowed to reach an intellectual development equal to man's. Indeed, in his novels the comic spirit partakes of feminine archness tempered by broadmindedness: thus, in *The Ordeal of Richard Feverel*, Lady Blandish, kind-hearted, sensible, ironic, at once in and out of the action, is one of its interpreters, as is, for that matter, that rather portentous youth Adrian Harley, who tends to be as much of a tease as Meredith could be in actual life with some of his friends.

Now, in *Our Friend the Charlatan*, the comedy is very nearly Meredithian. It springs from the invisible yet omniscient author and finds expression through a number of characters on the outskirts of the action. Mrs. Toplady is the main one: Gissing would have hated such a woman by his side and the very fact that he does not criticize her *per se* while he could have portrayed her devastatingly, doubtless indicates that he deliberately limited her role to that of an ironic commentator, close enough to the action to give the wheel of fun an occasional push. She it is who discovers the review of Izoulet's book that darkens Dyce's prestige as a thinker. She is unobtrusive; she is content to watch and ponder and smile roguishly. Her smile matters more than her words. She helps the reader to see more deeply into people's motives. Her point of view is that of high society. She has wit, shrewdness, slyness—yet is not altogether devoid of sympathy, however condescending. Her vast experience enables her to be indulgent. Her first glance at Lashmar tells her what is false without and what is false within. Her strong point is that she belongs to the world into which Dyce and May try to penetrate, but this could turn out to be deceptive as she, too, lives on illusions and is a receptacle of false values. Other commentators, like Martyn Blaydes (who is not unlike old Porteous in Orwell's *Coming Up for Air*), the Reverend Lashmar, and even Kerchever, the solicitor, for a short while fulfil functions which complement that of Mrs. Toplady. Martyn Blaydes passes sharp judgment on modernity, its spuriousness and vanity. His Platonic wisdom seasoned with Old England habits makes him obsolete and quaint, but his warning is worth hearing. The admonitions of Dyce's father are those of a world-weary churchman, whose only firm belief is that the world is going to the dogs: he has married a foolish woman, he has a son who excels only in speciousness and wishful thinking, he has been shaken by the effects of Darwinsim, and, worst of all, he is incapable of coping with the material difficulties that assail him. No more than Martyn Blaydes has he a chance of being heard by Dyce. Their voices are those of reflection and gravity, of experience and disappointment. Mrs. Toplady lightens the atmosphere, she laughs at the foibles of her circle not from an entrenched camp, like Blaydes and the elder Lashmar, but from the very centre of the world at whose gate Dyce stamps so impatiently.

It is clear enough that Gissing's standpoint, as already seen in *The Whirlpool* and in *The Crown of Life*, tends to identify itself with that of the peaceful, lucid observer. In *The Crown of Life*, Irene Derwent visits relations at a country place in Cheshire, two elderly ladies, cousins of her dead mother. They embody virtues, human and philosophical, which Giss-

ing considered more and more his ideal: 'They were in circumstances of simple security, living as honoured
gentlewomen, without display as without embarrassment;
fulfilling cheerfully the natural duties of their position, but
seeking no influence beyond the homely limits; their life a
humanizing example, a centre of charity and peace. . .They
were behind the times only in the sense of escaping, by seclusion, those modern tendencies which vulgarize.'[5] Lord Dymchurch and Ryecroft, both of them readers of Marcus
Aurelius, were already within sight. They do not care for
fame, only for peace in decency. As Samuel Vogt Gapp noted
some 40 years ago, Dymchurch's 'going back to the Old Stoic
is contrasted with the shallow and self-seeking modernism of
Dyce Lashmar. . .[He] comes to think resignedly of death'
upon reading Marcus Aurelius.[6] Dyce is condemned not only
because he is a pretender, a weak-willed, shallow individual
fascinated by what the early Gissing would have called a will-
o'-the-wisp, but because he propagates a theory that the
novelist cannot approve of—namely that it is possible to orga-
nise society on scientific principles. Gissing had started as an
optimist and had for a time been a keen Positivist, but by 1900
he had lost all confidence in the socialist application of evolutionary theory to government. The prefatory note to the
book, read before and after the story, does not quite produce
the same impression. 'Science!' says Irene Derwent to Piers
Otway in *The Crown of Life.* 'We were told, you know, that
science would be religion enough.' To which Piers, reflecting Gissing's opinion, replies: 'There's the pity—the failure
of science as a civilizing force.'[7] Evolutionary principles,
Gissing thought, cannot be applied to the organization of
society because society must promote rational principles of
justice and order for which nature, cosmic, animal or veget-
able, simply does not care. Izoulet's biosociological theory,
attractive though it could be to the Cartesian mind at the turn
of the century, nowadays seems rather puerile in some of its
aspects. 'Just as cells combine to form the sociological unit',
prates Lashmar paraphrasing the French writer, 'so do
human beings combine to form the social-political unit—the
State. . .A cell in itself is blind motion; an aggregate of cells is
a living creature. A man by himself is only an animal with
superior possibilities, men associated produce reason, civilization, the body politic.' The spuriousness of the comparison
is blatant, but Gissing seems to have been at first more struck

by the cleverness of the book than by the showiness of its reasoning. His praise of it to his friend Eduard Bertz in February
1900 has the ring of sincerity.[8]

The original position of *Our Friend the Charlatan* among
its author's twenty-odd novels stems from the image it offers
of a pessimistic thinker with a cheery face. By 1900 Gissing
had few illusions left, but his intellectual powers were undim-
inished. He still admired Meredith, went to the length of
adopting a method which amounted to a tribute to the grand
old man, envied his sanguineness, but less than ever could see
any justification for it. 'The mind which renounces, at once
and for ever, a futile hope, has its compensation in an ever-
growing calm.'[9] Thus speaks his alter ego, Henry Ryecroft,
whose meditations he began to put into shape immediately
after completing *Our Friend the Charlatan*. This will be
equated with defeatism and worth combating as such by the
young and those who have preserved unaltered the spirit of
youth, but whether enthusiasm or lucid pessimism is the best
asset in life is likely to remain a controversial question, doubtless also a futile one. Action need not be supported by blind
faith. By fighting mendaciousness, the tortuous way and foolish optimism, he deliberately opted for a place in a minority.
Our Friend the Charlatan, his last but one novel of modern
life, shows him in a mood neither didactic nor sentimental,
relishing his clever study of human motives, a master in the
art of debunking, a kill-joy whose eyes are never dimmed by
the tenderness and pity which marks and perhaps mars most
of his other late works.

1. Gissing had a very busy month in England in April 1900. He
   visited Lincoln, staying five days at the Saracen's Head, where
   one morning at breakfast he heard the story—reported in *Henry
   Ryecroft* (Summer XXI)—of the man who made his breakfast of
   apples. In the present novel, Dyce Lashmar's headquarters are in
   a hotel which bears the same name.
2. He had suggested before 'The Young Man Eloquent', 'A Man
   with a Future', 'Lashmar the Eloquent', 'A Man of Words', 'The
   Friend of Woman'. The last named would have been unfelicitous
   in view of the main theme of the story.
3. Quoted by Lionel Stevenson, *The Ordeal of George Meredith*,
   New York, Scribners, 1953, p. 233.

4. *George Meredith: A Primer to the Novels*, London, Hodder & Stoughton, 1909. p. 15.
5. *The Crown of Life*, ch. X.
6. *George Gissing, Classicist*, Philadelphia, University of Pennsylvania Press, 1936, p. 110.
7. *The Crown of Life*, ch. XXXIII.
8. *The Letters of George Gissing to Eduard Bertz*, ed. A.C. Young, London, Constable, 1961, pp. 273-74.
9. *The Private Papers of Henry Ryecroft*, Spring XX.

OUR FRIEND
THE CHARLATAN

OUR FRIEND
THE CHARLATAN

By GEORGE GISSING

WITH ILLUSTRATIONS BY LAUNCELOT SPEED

LONDON
CHAPMAN AND HALL, Ld.
1901

PREFATORY NOTE

Suum cuique. The book to which Dyce Lashmar was indebted for his "bio-sociological" theory is *La Cité Moderne,* by M. Jean Izoulet, Professor of Sociology at the Collége de France. I trust that no reader of *Our Friend the Charlatan* will attribute to me any satirical intention with regard to M. Izoulet's remarkable book. Every reference to it in these pages is, of course, toned by the conditions of the story.

G. G.

St. Honoré en Morvan,
    1901.

LIST OF ILLUSTRATIONS

OUR FRIEND THE CHARLATAN

CHAPTER I

As he waited for his breakfast, never served to time,
Mr. Lashmar drummed upon the window-pane, and
seemed to watch a blackbird lunching with much gusto
about the moist lawn of Alverholme Vicarage. But his
gaze was absent and worried. The countenance of the
reverend gentleman rarely wore any other expression,
for he took to heart all human miseries and follies, and
lived in a ceaseless mild indignation against the tenor
of the age. Inwardly, Mr. Lashmar was at this
moment rather pleased, having come upon an article
in his weekly paper which reviewed in a very depressing strain the present aspect of English life. He felt
that he might have, and ought to have, written the
article himself—a loss of opportunity which gave new
matter for discontent.

The Rev. Philip was in his sixty-seventh year; a
thin, dry, round-shouldered man, with bald occiput,
straggling yellowish beard, and a face which notably
resembled that of Darwin. He was proud of this
resemblance, but affected incredulous surprise if any
one drew attention to it. Privately he held the
theory of organic evolution, reconciling it with a very
broad Anglicanism; in his public utterances he touched
upon the Darwinian doctrine with a weary disdain.

Our Friend the Charlatan

This contradiction involved no insincerity; Mr. Lashmar merely held in contempt the common understanding, and declined to expose an esoteric truth to vulgar misinterpretation. At the same time he worried over the dubious position—as he worried over everything.

Nearer causes of disquiet were not lacking to him. For several years the income of his living had steadily decreased; his glebe, upon which he chiefly depended, fell more and more under the influence of agricultural depression, and at present he found himself, if not seriously embarrassed, like to be so in a very short time. He was not a good economist; he despised everything in the nature of parsimony; his ideal of the clerical life demanded bountiful expenditure of money no less than unsparing personal toil. He had generously exhausted the greater part of a small private fortune; from that source there remained to him about a hundred pounds a year—devoted to a private purpose. His charities must needs be restricted; his parish outlay must be pinched; domestic life must proceed on a narrower basis. And all this was to Mr. Lashmar supremely distasteful.

No less so to Mr. Lashmar's wife, a lady ten years his junior, endowed with abundant energies in every direction save that of household order and thrift. Whilst the vicar was still tapping drearily on the window-pane, Mrs. Lashmar entered the room, and her voice sounded the deep, resonant note which announced a familiar morning mood.

"You don't mean to say that breakfast isn't ready! Surely, my dear, you could ring the bell?"

"I have done so," replied the vicar, in a tone of abstracted melancholy.

Mrs. Lashmar rang with emphasis, and for the next five minutes her contralto swelled through the vicarage, rendering inaudible the replies she kept demanding from a half rebellious, half intimidated servant. She was not personally a coarse woman, and her manners did not grossly offend against the convention of good breeding; her nature was self-assertive, she could not brook a semblance of disregard for her authority, yet had no idea of how to rule. The small, round face had once been pretty; now, with its prominent eyes, indrawn lips, and obscured chin, it inspired no sympathetic emotion, rather an uneasiness and an inclination for retreat. In good humour or in ill, Mrs. Lashmar was aggressive. Her smile conveyed an amiable defiance; her look of grave interest alarmed and subdued.

"I have a line from Dyce," remarked the vicar, as at length he sat down to his lukewarm egg and very hard toast. "He thinks of running down."

"When?"

"He doesn't say."

"Then why did he write? I've no patience with those vague projects. Why did he write until he had decided on the day?"

"Really, I don't know," answered Mr. Lashmar feebly. In this mood his wife had a dazing effect upon him.

"Let me see the letter."

Mrs. Lashmar perused the half-dozen lines in her son's handwriting.

"Why, he *does* say!" she exclaimed in her deepest and most disdainful chord. "He says 'before long.'"

"True. But I hardly think that conveys——"

"Oh, please don't begin a sophistical argument! He says when he is coming, and that's all I want to know. Here's a letter, I see, from that silly Mrs. Barker. Her husband has quite given up drink, and earns good wages, and the eldest boy has a place—pooh!"

"All very good news, it seems to me," remarked the vicar, slightly raising his eyebrows.

But one of Mrs. Lashmar's little peculiarities was that, though she would exert herself to any extent for people whose helpless circumstances utterly subjected them to her authority, she lost all interest in them as soon as their troubles were surmounted, and even

viewed with resentment that result of her own efforts.
Worse still, from her point of view, if the effort had
largely been that of the sufferers themselves—as in
this case. Mrs. Barker, a. washerwoman who had
reformed her sottish husband, was henceforth a mere
offence in the eyes of the vicar's wife.

"As silly a letter as ever I read!" she exclaimed,
throwing aside the poor little sheet of cheap note-paper
with its illiterate gratitude. "Oh, here's something
from Lady Susan. Pooh! Another baby. What do
I care about her babies! Not one word about Dyce—
not one word. Now, really!"

"I didn't remember that you expected——" began
the vicar mildly, and then stopped.

Mrs. Lashmar paid no heed to him. With a resentful countenance she had pushed the letters aside, and
was beginning her meal. Amid all the so-called duties
which she imposed upon herself—for, in her own way,
she bore the burden of the world no less than did the
Rev. Philip—Mrs. Lashmar never lost sight of one
great preoccupation, the interests of her son. He,
Dyce Lashmar, only child of the house, now twenty-
seven years old, lived in London, and partly supported
himself as a private tutor. The obscurity of this
existence, so painful a contrast to the hopes his parents
had nourished, so disappointing an outcome of all the
thought that had been given to Dyce's education, and
of the not inconsiderable sums spent upon it, fretted
Mrs. Lashmar to the soul; at times she turned in anger
against the young man himself, accusing him of ungrateful supineness, but more often eased her injured
feelings by accusation of all such persons as, by any
possibility, might have aided Dyce to a career. One
of these was Lady Susan Harrop, a very remote relative
of hers. Twice or thrice a year, for half-a-dozen years
at least, Mrs. Lashmar had urged upon Lady Susan
the claims of her son to social countenance and more
practical forms of advancement; hitherto with no
result—save, indeed, that Dyce dined once every

season at the Harrops' table. The subject was painful
to Mr. Lashmar also, but it affected him in a different
way, and he had long ceased to speak of it.

"That selfish, frivolous woman," sounded presently
from behind the coffee-service, not now in accents of
wrath, but as the deliberate utterance of cold judgment. "Never in all her life has she thought of any
one but herself. What right has such a person to bring
children into the world? What can be expected of
them but meanness and hypocrisy?"

Mr. Lashmar smiled. He had just broken an imperfect tooth upon a piece of toast, and, as usual when
irritated, his temper became ironic.

"Sweet are the uses of disappointment," he observed.
"How it clears one's vision!"

"Do you suppose I ever had any better opinion of
Lady Susan?" exclaimed his wife.

It was a philosophic principle of Mr. Lashmar's never
to argue with a woman. Sadly smiling, he rose from
the table.

"Here's an article you ought to read," he said,
holding out the weekly paper. "It's full of truth, well
expressed. It may even have some bearing on this
question."

The vicar went about his long day's work, and took
with him many uneasy reflections. He had not
thought of it before breakfast, but now it struck him
that much in that pungent article on the men of to-
day might perchance apply to the character and
conduct of his own son. "A habit of facile enthusiasm, not perhaps altogether insincere, but totally
without moral value . . . convictions assumed at will,
as a matter of fashion, or else of singularity . . . the
lack of stable purpose, save only in matters of gross
self-interest . . . an increasing tendency to verbose
expression . . . an all but utter lack of what old-
fashioned people still call principle . . . " these
phrases recurred to his memory with disagreeable
significance. Was that in truth a picture of his son,

of the boy whom he had loved and watched over and so zealously hoped for? Possibly he wronged Dyce, for the young man's mind and heart had long ceased to be clearly legible to him. "Worst, perhaps, of all these frequent traits is the affectation of—to use a silly word—altruism. The most radically selfish of men seem capable of persuading themselves into the belief that their prime motive is to 'live for others.' Of truly persuading themselves—that is the strange thing. This, it seems to us, is morally far worse than the unconscious hypocrisy which here and there exists in professors of the old religion; there is something more nauseous about self-deceiving 'altruism' than in the attitude of a man who, thoroughly worldly in fact, believes himself a hopeful candidate for personal salvation." Certain recent letters of Dyce appeared in a new light when seen from this point of view. It was too disagreeable a subject; the vicar strove to dismiss it from his mind.

In the afternoon he had to visit a dying man, an intelligent shopkeeper, who, while accepting the visit as a proof of kindness, altogether refused spiritual comfort, and would speak of nothing but the future of his children. Straightway Mr. Lashmar became the practical consoler, lavish of kindly forethought. Only when he came forth did he ask himself whether he could possibly fulfil half of what he had undertaken.

"It is easier," he reflected, "to make promises for the world to come. Is it not also better? After all, can I not do it with a clearer conscience?"

He walked slowly, worrying about this and fifty other things, feeling a very Atlas under the globe's oppression. His way took him across a field in which there was a newly bourgeoned copse, and, glancing that way, he remembered to have found, last spring, white violets about the roots of the trees. A desire for their beauty and odour possessed him; he turned across the grass. Yes, the perfume guided him to a certain mossy corner where pale sweet florets nestled amid their leaves. He bent over them, and stretched his hand to pluck, but in the same moment checked himself; why should he act the destroyer in this spot of perfect quietness and beauty?

"Dyce would not care much about them," was another thought that came into his mind.

He rose from his stooping posture with ache of muscles and creaking of joints. Alas for the days when he ran and leapt and knew not pain! Walking slowly away he worried himself about the brevity of life.

By a stile he passed into the high road, at the lower end of the long village of Alverholme. He had an appointment with his curate at the church school, and, not to be unpunctual, he quickened his pace in that direction. At a little distance behind him was a young lady whom he had not noticed; she, recognizing the vicar, pursued with light quick step and soon overtook him.

"How do you do, Mr. Lashmar?"

"Why—Miss Bride!" exclaimed the vicar. "What a long time since we saw you! Have you just come?"

"I'm on a little holiday. How are you? And how is Mrs. Lashmar?"

Miss Bride had a soberly decisive way of speaking, and an aspect which corresponded therewith; her figure was rather short, well-balanced, apt for brisk movement; she held her head very straight, and regarded the world with a pair of dark eyes suggestive of anything but a sentimental nature. Her grey dress, black jacket, and small felt hat trimmed with a little brown ribbon declared the practical woman, who thinks about her costume only just as much as is needful; her dark-brown hair was coiled in a plait just above the nape, as if neatly and definitely put out of the way. She looked neither more nor less than her age, which was eight-and-twenty. Of good looks, judged by the common type, she had none to spare, yet those familiar with her face would hardly have called it plain. At first sight her features struck one as hard and unsympathetic, though tolerably regular; watching her as she talked or listened, one became aware of a mobility which gave large expressiveness, especially in the region of the eyebrows, which seemed to move with her every thought. Her lips were long, and ordinarily compressed in the line of conscious self-control. She had a very shapely neck, the skin white and delicate; her facial complexion was admirably pure and of warmish tint.

"And where are you living, Miss Bride?" asked Mr. Lashmar, regarding her with curiosity.

"At Hollingford—that is to say, near it. I am secretary to Lady Ogram—I don't know whether you ever heard of her?"

"Ogram? I know the name. I am very glad indeed to hear that you have such a pleasant position. And your father? It is very long since I heard from him."

"He has a curacy at Liverpool, and seems to be all right. My mother died about two years ago."

The matter-of-fact tone in which this information was imparted caused Mr. Lashmar to glance at the speaker's face. Though not much of an observer, he was comforted by an assurance that Miss Bride's features were less impassive than her words. Indeed, the cold abruptness with which she spoke was sufficient proof of feeling roughly subdued.

Some six years had now elapsed since the girl's father, after holding a curacy with Mr. Lashmar, accepted a living in another county. The technical term in this case was rich in satiric meaning; Mr. Bride's incumbency quickly reduced him to indigence. At the end of the first twelvemonth in his rural benefice the unfortunate cleric made a calculation that he was legally responsible for rather more than twice the sum of money represented by his stipend and the offertories. The church needed a new roof; the parsonage was barely habitable for long lack of repairs;

8

the church school lost its teacher through default of salary—and so on. With endless difficulty Mr. Bride escaped from his vicarage to freedom and semi-starvation, and deemed himself very lucky indeed when at length he regained levitical harbourage.

These things had his daughter watched with her intent dark eyes; Constance Bride did not feel kindly disposed towards the Church of England as by law established. She had seen her mother sink under penury and humiliation and all unmerited hardship; she had seen her father changed from a vigorous, hopeful, kindly man to an embittered pessimist. As for herself, sound health and a good endowment of brains enabled her to make a way in the world. Luckily she was a sole child; her father managed to give her a decent education till she was old enough to live by teaching. But teaching was not her vocation. Looking round for possibilities, Constance hit upon the idea of studying pharmaceutics and becoming a dispenser; wherein, by dint of steady effort, she at length succeeded. This project had already been shaped whilst the Brides were at Alverholme; Mrs. Lashmar had since heard of Constance as employed in the dispensary of a midland hospital.

"Hollingford?" remarked the vicar, as he walked on. "I think I remember that you have relatives there."

"I was born there, and I have an old aunt still living in the town—she keeps a little baker's shop."

Mr. Lashmar, though a philosopher, was not used to this bluntness of revelation; it caused him a slight shock, evinced in a troublous rolling of the eyes.

"Ha! yes! I trust you will dine with us this evening, Miss Bride?"

"Thank you, I can't dine; I want to leave by an early evening train. But I should like to see Mrs. Lashmar, if she is at home."

"She will be delighted. I must beg you to pardon me for leaving you—an appointment at the schools;

but I will get home as soon as possible. Pray excuse me."

"Why, of course, Mr. Lashmar. I haven't forgotten the way to the vicarage."

She pursued it, and in a few minutes rang the bell. Mrs. Lashmar was in the dining-room, busy with a female parishioner whose self-will in the treatment of infants' maladies had given the vicar's wife a great deal of trouble.

"It's as plain as blessed daylight, mum," the woman was exclaiming, "that this medicine don't agree with her."

"Mrs. Dibbs," broke in the other, severely, "you will allow me to be a better judge—*what* is it?"

The housemaid had opened the door to announce Miss Bride.

"Miss Bride?" echoed the lady in astonishment. "Very well; show her into the drawing-room."

The visitor waited for nearly a quarter of an hour. She had placed herself on one of the least comfortable chairs, and sat there in a very stiff attitude, holding her umbrella across her knees. After a rather nervous survey of the room (it had changed very little in appearance since her last visit of six years ago), she fell into uneasy thoughtfulness, now and then looking impatiently towards the door. When the hostess at length appeared, she rose with deliberation, her lips just relaxed in a half-smile.

"So it is really you!" exclaimed Mrs. Lashmar, in a voice of forced welcome. "I thought you must have altogether forgotten us."

"It's the first time I have returned to Alverholme," replied the other, in a contrasting tone of calmness.

"And what are you doing? Where are you living? Tell me all about yourself. Are you still at the hospital? You did get a place at a hospital, I think? We were told so."

Mrs. Lashmar's patronage was a little more patronizing than usual, her condescension one or two degrees more condescending. She had various reasons for regarding Constance Bride with disapproval, the least of them that sense of natural antipathy which was inevitable between two such women. In briefest sentences Miss Bride made known that she had given up dispensing two years ago, and was now acting as secretary to a baronet's widow.

"A baronet's widow?" repeated the hostess, with some emphasis of candid surprise. "How did you manage that? Who is she?"

"An old friend of my family," was the balanced reply. "Lady Ogram, of Rivenoak, near Hollingford."

"Oh! Indeed! I wasn't aware——"

Mrs. Lashmar thought better of her inclination to be trenchantly rude, and smoothed off into commonplaces. Presently the vicar entered, and found his wife conversing with the visitor more amiably than he had expected.

"You have seen Miss Bride already," said Mrs. Lashmar. "I am trying to persuade her to stay over-night with us. Is it really impossible?"

Constance civilly but decidedly declined. Addressing herself to the vicar, she spoke with more ease and friendliness than hitherto; nevertheless, it was obvious that she counted the minutes dictated by decency for the prolongation of her stay. Once or twice her look wandered to a certain part of the wall where hung a framed photograph—a portrait of Dyce Lashmar at the age of one-and-twenty; she regarded it for an instant with cold fixity, as though it interested her not at all. Just as she was on the point of rising, there came a sound of wheels on the vicarage drive.

"Who's that, I wonder?" said Mrs. Lashmar. "Why —surely it isn't——?"

A voice from the hall had reached her ears; surprise and annoyance darkened her countenance.

"It's certainly Dyce," said the vicar, who for his part recognized the voice with pleasure.

"Impossible! He said he was coming in a week's time."

Mr. Lashmar would not have cared to correct this statement, and remark was rendered superfluous by the opening of the door and the appearance of Dyce himself.

"Afraid I'm taking you rather at unawares," said the young man, in a suave Oxford voice. "Unexpectedly I found myself free——"

His eyes fell upon Constance Bride, and for a moment he was mute; then he stepped towards her, and with an air of peculiar frankness, of comrade-like understanding, extended his hand.

"How do you do, Miss Connie! Delighted to find you here. Mother, glad to see you." He touched Mrs. Lashmar's forehead with his lips. "Well, father, uncommonly pleasant to be at the vicarage again!"

Miss Bride had stood up, and was now advancing towards the hostess.

"You *must* go?" said Mrs. Lashmar, with her most agreeable smile.

"What, going?" exclaimed Dyce. "Why? Are you staying in the village?"

"No. I must catch a train."

"What train?"

"The six forty-five."

"Why, then you have plenty of time! Mother, bid Miss Connie be seated; I haven't had a moment's talk with her, it's absurd. Six forty-five? You needn't leave here for .twenty minutes. What a lucky thing that I came in just now."

For certain ticks of the clock it was a doubtful matter whether Miss Bride would depart or remain. Glancing involuntarily at Mrs. Lashmar, she saw the gloom of resentment and hostility hover upon that lady's countenance, and this proved decisive.

"I'll have some tea, please," cried the young man cheerfully, as Constance with some abruptness resumed

Our Friend the Charlatan

her seat. "How is your father, Miss Connie? Well? That's right. And Mrs. Bride?"

"My mother is dead," replied the girl quite simply, looking away.

A soft murmur of pain escaped Dyce's lips; he leaned forward, uttered gently a "Pray forgive me!" and was silent. The vicar interposed with a harmless remark about the flight of years.

CHAPTER II

In the moments when Dyce Lashmar was neither aware of being observed nor consciously occupied with the pressing problems of his own existence, his face expressed a natural amiability, inclining to pensiveness. The features were in no way remarkable; they missed the vigour of his father's Darwinian type without attaining the regularity which had given his mother a claim to good looks. Such a visage falls to the lot of numberless men born to keep themselves alive and to propagate their insignificance. But Dyce was not insignificant. As soon as his countenance lighted with animation, it revealed a character rich in various possibility, a vital force which, by its bright indefiniteness, made peculiar appeal to the imagination. Sometimes he had the air of a lyric enthusiast; often that of a profound thinker; not seldom there came into his eyes a glint of stern energy which seemed to challenge the world upon some mighty issue. Therewithal, nothing perceptibly histrionic; look or speak as he might, the young man exhaled an atmosphere of sincerity, and persuaded others because he seemed so thoroughly to have convinced himself.

He did not make an impression of high breeding. His Oxford voice, his easy self-control, satisfied the social standard, but left a defect to the finer sense. Dyce had not the self-oblivion of entire courtesy; it seemed probable that he would often err in tact; a certain awkwardness marred his personal bearing, which aimed at the modern ideal of flowing unconstraint. Though well enough built to the middle stature, he

14

had little natural or acquired grace of limb. Athletics did not attract him; physically he was indolent, and he often brought the charge against himself, with pleasure in the frank avowal.

Sipping the cup of tea which his mother had handed to him, Dyce talked at large. Nothing, he declared, was equal to the delight of leaving town just at this moment of the year, when hedge and meadow were donning their brightest garments and the sky gleamed with its purest blue. He spoke in the tone of rapturous enjoyment, and yet one might have felt a doubt whether his sensibility was as keen as he professed or imagined; all the time, he appeared to be thinking of something else. Most of his remarks were addressed to Miss Bride, and with that manner of intimate friendliness which he alone of the family used towards their visitor. He inquired about the events of her life, and manifested a strong interest in the facts which Constance briefly repeated.

"Let me walk with you as far as the station," he said, when the time came for her departure.

"Please don't trouble," Constance replied, with a quick glance at Mrs. Lashmar's face, still resentful under the conventional smile.

Dyce, without more words, took his hat and accompanied her; the vicar went with them to the garden-gate, courteous, but obviously embarrassed.

"Pray remember me to your father," he said. "I should much like to hear from him."

"It's chilly this evening," remarked Dyce, as he and his companion walked briskly away. "Are you going far?"

"To Hollingford."

"But you'll be travelling for two or three hours. What about your dinner?"

"Oh, I shall eat something when I get home."

"Women are absurd about food," exclaimed Dyce, with laughing impatience. "Most of you systematically starve yourselves, and wonder that you get all sorts

15

of ailments. Why wouldn't you stay at the vicarage
to-night? I'm quite sure it would have made no
difference if you had got back to Hollingford in the
morning."

"Perhaps not, but I don't care much for staying at
other people's houses."

Dyce examined his companion's face. She did not
meet his look, and bore it with some uneasiness. In
the minds of both was a memory which would have
accounted for much more constraint between them than
apparently existed. Six years ago, in the days of late
summer, when Dyce Lashmar was spending his vacation
at the vicarage, and Connie Bride was making ready to
go out into the world, they had been wont to see a
good deal of each other, and to exhaust the topics of
the time in long conversations, tending ever to a closer
intimacy of thought and sentiment. The companionship was not very favourably regarded by Mr. Lashmar,
and to the vicar's wife was a source of angry apprehension. There came the evening when Dyce and Constance
had to bid each other good-bye, with no near prospect
of renewing their talks and their rambles together. What
might be in the girl's thought, she alone knew; the
young man, effusive in vein of friendship, seemed never
to glance beyond a safe border-line, his emotions satisfied
with intellectual communion. At the moment of shaking
hands, they stood in a field behind the vicarage; dusk
was falling and the spot secluded. They parted . . .
Constance in a bewilderment which was to last many
a day, for Dyce had kissed her, and without a word
was gone.

There followed no exchange of letters. From that
hour to this the two had in no way communicated.
Mr. Bride, somewhat offended by what he had seen and
surmised of Mr. and Mrs. Lashmar's disposition, held
no correspondence with the vicar of Alverholme; his
wife had never been on friendly terms with Mrs.
Lashmar. How Dyce thought of that singular incident it was impossible to infer from his demeanour;

Constance might well have supposed that he had forgotten all about it.

"Is your work interesting?" were his next words. "What does Lady Ogram go in for?"

"Many things."

"You prefer it to the other work?"

"It isn't so hard, and it's much more profitable."

"By the bye, who *is* Lady Ogram?" asked Dyce, with a smiling glance.

"A remarkable old woman. Her husband died ten years ago; she has no children, and is very rich. I shouldn't think there's a worse-tempered person living, yet she has all sorts of good qualities. By birth, she belongs to the working-class; by disposition she's a violent aristocrat. I often hate her; at other times I like her very much."

Dyce listened with increasing attention.

"Has she any views?" he inquired.

"Oh, plenty!" Constance answered, with a dry little laugh.

"About social questions—that kind of thing?"

"Especially."

"I shouldn't be surprised if she called herself a socialist."

"That's just what she does—when she thinks it will annoy people she dislikes."

Dyce smiled meditatively.

"I should like to know her. Yes, I should very much like to know her. Could you manage it for me?"

Constance did not reply. She was comparing the Dyce Lashmar of to-day with him of the past, and trying to understand the change that had come about in his talk, his manner. It would have helped her had she known that, in the ripe experience of his seven-and-twentieth year, Dyce had arrived at certain conclusions with regard to women, and thereupon had based a method of practical behaviour towards them. Women, he held, had never been treated with elementary justice. To worship them was no less unfair than to hold them in contempt. The honest man, in our day, should regard a woman without the least bias of masculine prejudice; should view her simply as a fellow-being who, according to circumstances, might or not be on his own plane. Away with all empty show and form, the relics of barbarism known as chivalry! He wished to discontinue even the habit of hat-doffing in female presence. Was not civility preserved between man and man without such idle ceremony? Why not, then, between man and woman? Unable, as yet, to go the entire length of his principles in everyday life, he endeavoured at all events to cultivate in his intercourse with women a frankness of speech, a directness of bearing, beyond the usual. He shook hands as with one of his own sex, spine uncrooked; he greeted them with level voice, not as one who addresses a thing afraid of sound. To a girl or matron whom he liked he said, in tone if not in phrase, "Let us be comrades." In Dyce's opinion this tended notably to the purifying of the social atmosphere. It was the introduction of simple honesty into relations commonly marked—and corrupted—by every form of disingenuousness. Moreover, it was the great first step to that reconstruction of society at large which every thinker saw to be imperative and imminent.

But Constance Bride knew nothing of this, and in her ignorance could not but misinterpret the young man's demeanour. She felt it to be brusque; she imagined it to imply a purposed oblivion of things in the past. Taken together with Mrs. Lashmar's way of receiving her at the vicarage, it stirred in her heart and mind (already prone to bitterness) a resentment which, of all things, she shrank from betraying.

"Is Lady Ogram approachable?" Dyce asked, when his companion had walked a few paces without speaking. "Does she care to make new acquaintances?"

"It depends. She likes to know interesting people."

"Well"—Dyce murmured a laugh—"perhaps she

might think me interesting, in a way. Her subject is
mine. I'm working at sociology; have been for a long
time. I'm getting my ideas into shape, and I like to
talk about them."

"Do you write?" asked the girl, without raising her
eyes to his.

"No—people write too much; we're flooded with
print. I've grown out of my old ambitions that way.
The Greek philosophers taught by word of mouth, and
it was better. I want to learn how to talk—to talk
well—to communicate what I have to say in a few
plain words. It saves time and money; I'm convinced,
too, that it carries more weight. Every one now-a-days
can write a book, and most people do; but how many
can talk? The art is being utterly forgotten. Chatter
and gabble and mumble—an abuse of language. What's
your view?"

"I think perhaps you are right."

"Come, now, I'm glad to hear you say that. If I had
time, I would tell you more; but here's the station, and
there's the smoke of the train. We've cut it rather
close. Across the line; you'll have to run—sharp!"

They did so, reaching the platform as the train drew
up. Dyce allowed his companion to open a carriage-
door for herself. That was quite in accord with his
principles, but perhaps he would for once have neglected them had he been sure by which class Miss
Bride would travel. She entered a third.

"You wouldn't care to introduce me to Lady
Ogram?" he said, standing by the window, and looking
straight into the girl's eyes.

"I will if you wish," she answered, meeting his look
with hard steadiness and a frown as of pain.

"Many thanks! Rivenoak, Hollingford, the address?
Suppose I call in a few days?"

"If you like."

The train moved. Dyce bared his head, and, as he
turned away, thought how contemptible was the
practice.

19

Our Friend the Charlatan

Walking briskly against a cold wind, he busied his imagination about Lady Ogram. The picture he made to himself of this wealthy and original old lady was very fertile of suggestion; his sanguine temper bore him to heights of brilliant possibility. Dyce Lashmar had a genius for airy construction; much of his time was spent in deducing imaginary results from some half presented opportunity. As his fancy wrought, he walked faster and faster, and he reached the vicarage in a physical glow which corresponded to his scintillating state of mind.

Of Constance Bride he thought hardly at all. She did not interest him; her proximity left him cold. She might be a useful instrument; apart from his method, that was the light in which he regarded all the women he knew. Experience had taught him that he possessed a certain power over women of a certain kind; it seemed probable that Constance belonged to the class; but this was a fact which had no emotional bearing. With a moment's idle wonder he remembered the circumstances of their former parting. He was then a boy, and who shall account for a boy's momentary impulses? Constance was a practical sort of person, and in all likelihood thought no more of that foolish incident than he did.

"Why are you so eccentric in your movements, Dyce?" cried Mrs. Lashmar, irritably, when he entered the drawing-room again. "You write one day that you're coming in a week or two, and on the next here you are. How could you tell that it was convenient to us to have you just now?"

"The Woolstan boy has a cold," Dyce replied, "and I found myself free for a few days. I'm sorry to put you out."

"Not at all. I say that it *might* have done."

Dyce's bearing to his mother was decently respectful, but in no way affectionate. The knowledge that she counted for little or nothing with him was an annoyance, rather than a distress to Mrs. Lashmar. With tender-

Our Friend the Charlatan

ness she could dispense, but the loss of authority wounded her.

Dinner was a rather silent meal. The vicar seemed to be worrying about something even more than usual. When they had risen from table, Mrs. Lashmar made the remark which was always forthcoming on these occasions.

" So you are still doing nothing, Dyce ? "

" I assure you, I'm very busy," answered the young man, as one indulgent to an inferior understanding.

" So you always say. When did you see Lady Susan ? "

" Oh, not for a long time."

" What vexes me is, that you don't make the slightest use of your opportunities. It's really astonishing that, with your talents, you should be content to go on teaching children their A B C. You have no energy, Dyce, and no ambition. By this time you might have been in the diplomatic service, you might have been in parliament. Are you going to waste your whole life ? "

" That depends on the view one takes of life," said Dyce, in a philosophical tone which he sometimes adopted—generally after dinner. " Why should one always be thinking about ' getting on ' ? It's the vice of the time. Why should I elbow and hustle in a vulgar crowd ? A friend of mine, Lord Dymchurch——"

" What ! You have made friends with a lord ? " cried Mrs. Lashmar, her face illumined.

" Why not ? I was going to say that Dymchurch, though he's poor, and does nothing at all, is probably about the most distinguished man in the peerage. He is distinguished by nature, and that's enough for him. You'd like Dymchurch, father."

The vicar looked up from a fit of black brooding, and said, " Ah ! no doubt." Mrs. Lashmar, learning the circumstances of Lord Dymchurch, took less pride in him, but went on to ask questions. Had his lordship

no interest which might serve a friend? Could he
not present Dyce to more influential people?

"I should be ashamed to hint that kind of thing to
him," answered Dyce. "Don't be so impatient, mother.
If I am to do anything—in your sense of the word—
the opportunity will come. If it doesn't, well, fate has
ordered it so."

"All I know is, Dyce, that you might be the coming
man, and you're content to be nobody at all."

Dyce laughed.

"The coming man! Well, perhaps I *am;* who
knows? At all events it's something to know that you
believe in me. And it may be that you are not the
only one."

Later, Dyce and his father went into the study to
smoke. The young man brought with him a large
paper-backed volume which he had taken out of his
travelling-bag.

"Here's a book I'm reading. A few days ago I happened to be at Williams and Norgate's. This caught
my eyes, and a glance at a page or two interested me
so much that I bought it at once. It would please
you, father."

"I've no time for reading now-a-days," sighed the
vicar. "What is it?"

He took the volume, a philosophical work by a
French writer, bearing a recent date. Mr. Lashmar
listlessly turned a few pages, whilst Dyce was filling
and lighting his pipe.

"It's uncommonly suggestive," said Dyce, between
puffs. "The best social theory I know. He calls
his system Bio-sociology; a theory of society founded
on the facts of biology—thoroughly scientific and convincing. Smashing socialism in the common sense—
that is, social democracy; but establishing a true
socialism in harmony with the aristocratic principle.
I'm sure you'd enjoy it. I fancy it's just your view."

"Yes—perhaps so."

"Here's the central idea. No true sociology could

be established before the facts of biology were known, as the one results from the other. In both, the ruling principle is that of association, with the evolution of a directing power. An animal is an association of cells. Every association implies division of labour. Now, progress in organic development means the slow constitution of an organ—the brain—which shall direct the body. So in society—an association of individuals, with slow constitution of a directing organ, called the Government. The problem of civilization is to establish government on scientific principles—to pick out the fit for rule—to distinguish between the Multitude and the Select, and at the same time to balance their working. It is nonsense to talk about Equality. Evolution is engaged in *cephalizing* the political aggregate, as it did the aggregate of cells in the animal organism. It makes for the differentiation of the Chosen and of the Crowd—that is to say, towards Inequality."

"Very interesting," murmured the vicar, who listened with an effort whilst mechanically loading his pipe.

"Isn't it? And the ideas are well marked out; first the bio-sociological theory, then the psychology and ethics which result from it. The book has given me a stronger impulse than anything I've read for years. It carries conviction with it. It clears one's mind of all sorts of doubts and hesitations. I always kicked at the democratic idea; now I know that I was right."

"Ah! Perhaps so. These questions are very difficult. By the bye, Dyce, I want to speak to you about a matter that has been rather troubling me of late. Let us get it over now, shall we?"

Dyce's animated look faded under a shadow of uneasiness. He regarded the vicar steadily, with eyes which gathered apprehension.

"It's very disagreeable," pursued Mr. Lashmar, after puffing at a pipe unlit. "I'm afraid it'll be no less so to you than to me. I've postponed the necessity as

23

Our Friend the Charlatan

long as I could. The fact is, Dyce, I'm getting pinched in my finances. Let me tell you just how matters stand."

The son listened to an exposition of his father's difficulties; he had his feet crossed, his head bent, and the pipe hanging from his mouth. At the first silence he removed his pipe, and said quietly:

"It's plain that my allowance must stop. Not another word about that, father. You ought to have spoken before; I've been a burden to you."

"No, no, my dear boy! I haven't felt it till now. But, as you see, things begin to look awkward. Do you think you can manage?"

"Of course I can. Don't trouble about me for a moment. I have my hundred and fifty a year from Mrs. Woolstan, and that's quite enough for a bachelor. I shall pick up something else. In any case, I've no right to sponge on you! I've done it too long. If I had had the slightest suspicion——"

A sense of virtue lit up Dyce's countenance again. Nothing more rejoiced him than to utter generous sentiments. Having reassured his father, he launched into a larger optimism.

"Don't suppose that I have taken your money year after year without thinking about it. I couldn't have gone on like that if I hadn't felt sure that some day I should pay my debt. It's natural enough that you and mother should feel a little disappointment about me. I seem to have done nothing, but, believe me, I am not idle. Money-making, I admit, has never been much in my mind; all the same, I shall have money enough one of these days, and before very long. Try to have faith in me. If it were necessary, I shouldn't mind entering into an obligation to furnish such and such a sum yearly by when I am thirty years old. It's a thing I've never said to any one, but I know perfectly well that a career, perhaps rather a brilliant one, is opening before me. I know it, just as one knows that one is in good health; it's an intimate sense, needing no support of argument."

24

Our Friend the Charlatan

"Of course I'm glad to hear you speak like that," said the vicar, venturing only a glance at his son's face.

"Don't, I beg, worry about your affairs," pursued Dyce, with kindling eye. "Cut off my supplies, and go quietly on." He stretched out a soothing hand, palm downwards. "The responsibility for the future is mine; from to-night I take it upon myself."

Much more in the same vein did Dyce pour forth, obviously believing every word he said, and deriving great satisfaction from the sound of his utterances. He went to bed, at length, in such a self-approving frame of mind that no sooner had he laid his head on the pillow than sweet sleep lapped him about, and he knew nothing more till the sunlight shimmered at his window.

A letter awaited him at the breakfast table; it had been forwarded from his London address, and he knew at a glance that it came from Mrs. Woolstan, the mother of his pupil. The lady, dating from a house at West Hampstead, wrote thus:

"Dear Mr. Lashmar,

"You will be surprised to hear from me so soon again. I particularly want to see you. Something has happened which we must talk over at once. I shall be alone to-morrow afternoon. Do come if you possibly can.

"Sincerely yours,
"Iris Woolstan."

Dyce had come down in a mood less cheerful than that of over-night. As happened sometimes, he had slept too soundly; his head was not quite clear, and his nerves felt rather unsteady. This note from Mrs. Woolstan, he knew not why, caused him uneasiness; a vague prevision of ill was upon him as he read.

He had intended passing the day at Alverholme, and, on the morrow, travelling to Hollingford. Now he felt no inclination to hazard a call upon Lady Ogram; he would return to London forthwith.

"No bad news, I hope?" said his father, when this purpose was proclaimed.

"Mrs. Woolstan wants me back sooner than I expected, that's all."

His mother's lip curled disdainfully. To be at the beck and call of a Mrs. Woolstan, the widow of a man of no account, and left in but moderate circumstances, seemed to her an ignoble thing. However, she had learnt the tenor of Dyce's discourse of the evening before, and tried once more to see a radiance in his future.

CHAPTER III

HAIR the hue of an autumn elm-leaf; eyes green or blue as the light fell upon them; a long thin face, faintly freckled over its creamy pallor, with narrow arch of eyebrow, indifferent nose, childlike lips and a small pointed chin—thus may one suggest the portrait of Iris Woolstan. When Dyce Lashmar stepped into her drawing-room, she had the air of one who has been impatiently expectant. Her eyes widened in a smile of nervous pleasure; she sprang up, and offered her hand before the visitor was near enough to take it.

"So kind of you to come! I was half afraid you might have gone out of town—not that it would have mattered. I did really want to see you as soon as possible, but Monday would have done just as well."

She spoke rapidly, in a high, but not shrill, voice, with a drawing in of the breath before and after her speech, and a nervous little pant between the sentences, her bosom fluttering like that of a frightened bird.

"As a matter of fact," cried Lashmar, with brusque cordiality, dropping into a chair before his hostess was seated, "I *had* gone out of town. I got your letter at Alverholme, and came back again sooner than I intended."

"Oh! oh!" panted Mrs. Woolstan, on her highest note, "I shall never forgive myself! Why *didn't* you telegraph—or just do nothing at all, and come when you were ready! Oh! When there wasn't the least hurry."

"Then why did you write as if something alarming had happened?" cried the other, laughing, as he crossed his legs and laid his silk hat aside.

"Oh, did I? I'm sure I didn't mean to. There's nothing alarming at all—at least—that is to say— well, it's something troublesome and disagreeable and very unexpected, and I'm rather afraid you won't like it. But we've plenty of time to talk about it. I'm at home to nobody else. It was really unkind of you to come back in a hurry! Besides, it's against your principles. You wouldn't have done that if I had been a man."

"A man would have said just what he meant," replied Dyce, smiling at her with kindly superiority. "He wouldn't have put me in doubt."

"No, no! But did I really write like that? I thought it was just a plain little business-like note— indeed I did! It will be a lesson to me—indeed it will! And how did you find your people? All well, I hope?"

"Well, in one way; in another—but I'll tell you about that presently."

Dyce had known Mrs. Woolstan for about a couple of years; it was in the second twelvemonth of their acquaintance that he matured his method with regard to women, and since then he had not only practised it freely, but had often discussed it, with her. Iris gave the method her entire approval, and hailed it as the beginning of a new era for her sex. She imagined that her own demeanour was no less direct and unconstrained than that of the philosopher himself; in reality, the difference was considerable. Though several years older than Dyce—her age being thirty-four—she showed nothing of this seniority in her manner towards him, which, for all its impulsiveness, had a noticeable deference, at moments something of subdued homage.

"You don't mean to say you have bad news?" she exclaimed, palpitating. "You too?"

Our Friend the Charlatan

"Why, then *you* have something of the same kind to tell me?" said Dyce, gazing at her anxiously.

"Tell me yours first—please do!"

"No. It's nothing very important. So say what you've got to say, and be quick about it, come!"

Mrs. Woolstan's bosom rose and fell rapidly as she collected her thoughts. Unconventional as were the terms in which Lashmar addressed her, they carried no suggestion of an intimacy which passed the limits of friendship. When his eyes turned to her, their look was unemotional, purely speculative, and in general he spoke without looking at her at all.

"It's something about Mr. Wrybolt," Iris began, with a face of distress. "You know he is my trustee —I told you, didn't I? I see him very seldom, and we don't take much interest in each other; he's nothing but a man of business, the kind I detest; he can't talk of anything but money and shares and wretched things of that sort. But you know him— you understand."

The name of Wrybolt set before Dyce's mind a middle-aged man, red-necked, heavy of eyelid, with a rather punctilious bearing and an authoritative mode of speech. They had met only once, here at Mrs. Woolstan's house.

"I'm sure I don't know why, but just lately he's begun to make inquiries about Len, and to ask when I meant to send him to school. Of course I told him that Len was doing very well indeed, and that I didn't see the slightest necessity for making a change—at all events just yet. Well, yesterday he came, and said he wanted to see the boy. Len was in bed, he's in bed still, though his cold's much better, and Mr. Wrybolt would go up to his room, and talk to him. When he came down again—you know I'm going to tell you the whole truth, and of course you won't mind it—he began talking in a very nasty way, he *has* a nasty way when he likes. 'Look here, Mrs. Woolstan,' he said, 'Leonard doesn't seem to me to be doing well

29

Our Friend the Charlatan

at all. I asked him one or two questions in simple
arithmetic, and he couldn't answer.' 'Well,' I said,
'for one thing Len isn't well, and it isn't the right
time to examine a boy; and then arithmetic isn't his
subject at all; he hasn't that kind of mind.' But he
wouldn't listen, and the next thing he said was still
nastier. 'Do you know,' he said, 'that the boy is
being taught *atheism?*' Well, what could I answer?
I got rather angry, and said that Len's religious teaching was my own affair, and I couldn't see what *he* had
to do with it; and besides, that Len *wasn't* being
taught atheism, but that people who were not in the
habit of thinking philosophically couldn't be expected
to understand such things—I think that was rather
good, wasn't it? Didn't I put it rather well?"

Iris panted in expectation of approval. But merely
a nod was vouchsafed to her.

"Go on," said Dyce dryly.

"You're not vexed, I hope? I'm going to be quite
frank, you know, just as you like people to be. Well,
Mr. Wrybolt went on, and would have it that Len was
badly taught and altogether led in the wrong way, and
that he'd grow up an immoral and an irreligious man.
'You must remember, Mr. Wrybolt,' I said, rather
severely, 'that people's ideas about morality and
religion differ very much, and I can't think you have
sufficiently studied the subject to be capable of understanding my point of view.' It was rather severe,
wasn't it? But I think it was rather well put."

"Go on," said Dyce, with another nod.

"Well now, I'm quite sure you'll understand me.
We *do* generally understand each other. You see, I
was put into a most difficult position. Mr. Wrybolt is
my trustee, and he has to look after Len—though he's
never given a thought to him till now—and he's a man
of influence; that is to say, in his own wretched, vulgar
world; but unfortunately it's a kind of influence one's
obliged to think about. Len, you know, is just eleven,
and one has to begin to think about his future, and it

30

isn't as if he was going to be rich and could do as he liked. I'm sure you'll understand me. With a man like Mr. Wrybolt——"

"Not so many words," interposed the listener, smiling rather disdainfully. "I see the upshot of it all. You promised to send Len to school.

Mrs. Woolstan panted and fluttered and regarded Lashmar with eyes of agitated appeal.

"If you think I ought to have held out—please say just what you think—let us be quite frank and comrade-like with each other—I can write to Mr. Wrybolt."

"Tell me plainly," said Dyce, leaning towards her. "What was your reason for giving way at once ? You really think, don't you, that it will be better for the boy ? "

"Oh, how *could* I think so, Mr. Lashmar ! You *know* what a high opinion——"

"Exactly. I am quite ready to believe all that. But you will be easier in mind with Len at school, taught in the ordinary way ? Now be honest—make an effort."

"I—perhaps—one has to think of a boy's future——"

The pale face was suffused with rose, and for a moment looked pretty in its half-tearful embarrassment.

"Good. That's all right. We'll talk no more of it."

There was a brief silence. Dyce looked slowly about him. His eyes fell on nothing of particular value, nothing at all unusual in the drawing-room of a small house of middle-suburb type. Round about hung autotypes and etchings and photographs ; there was good, comfortable furniture ; the piano stood for more than mere ornament, as Mrs. Woolstan had some skill in music. Iris's widowhood was of five years' duration. At two-and-twenty she had married a government-office clerk, a man nearly twice her age, exasperated by routine and lack of advancement ; on her part it was a marriage of generosity ; she did not love the man, but was touched by his railing against fate, and fancied she might be able to aid his ambitions. Woolstan talked of a possible secretaryship under the chief of his department; he imagined himself gifted for diplomacy, lacking only the chance to become a power in statecraft. But when Iris had given herself and her six hundred a year, she soon remarked a decline in her husband's aspiration. Presently Woolstan began to complain of an ailment, the result of arduous labour and of disillusion, which might make it imperative for him to retire from the monotonous toil of the Civil Service; before long he withdrew to a pleasant cottage in Surrey, where he was to lead a studious life and compose a great political work. The man had, in fact, an organic disorder, which proved fatal to him before he could quite decide whether to write his book on foolscap or on quarto paper. Mrs. Woolstan devoted herself to her child, until, when Leonard was nine, she entrusted him to a tutor very highly spoken of by friends of hers, a young Oxford man, capable not only of instructing the boy in the most efficient way, but of training whatever force and originality his character might possess. She paid a hundred and fifty pounds a year for these invaluable services—in itself not a large stipend, but large in proportion to her income. And Iris had never grudged the expenditure, for in Dyce Lashmar she found, not merely a tutor for her son, but a director of her own mind and conscience. Under Dyce's influence she had read—or tried to read—many instructive books; he had fostered, guided, elevated her native enthusiasm, he had emancipated her soul. These, at all events, were the terms in which Iris herself was wont to describe the results of their friendship, and she was eminently a sincere woman, ever striving to rise above the weakness, the disingenuousness, of her sex.

"If you knew how it pains me!" she murmured, stealing a glance at Lashmar. "But, of course, it won't make any difference—between us."

"Oh, I hope not. Why should it?" said Dyce

absently. "Now I'll tell you something that has happened since I saw you last."

"Yes—yes—your own news! Oh, I'm afraid it is something bad!"

"Perhaps not. I rather think I'm at a crisis in my life—probably *the* crisis. I shouldn't wonder if everything proves to have happened just at the right time. My news is this. Things are going rather badly down at the vicarage. There's serious diminution of income, which I knew nothing about. And the end of it is, that I mustn't count on any more supplies, they have no more money to spare for me. You see, I am thoroughly independent."

He laughed; but Mrs. Woolstan gazed at him in dismay.

"Oh! oh! How very serious! What a dreadful thing!"

"Pooh! Not at all. That's your feminine way of talking."

"I'm afraid it is. I didn't mean to use such expressions. But really—what are you going to do?"

"That'll have to be thought about."

Iris, with fluttering bosom, leaned forward.

"You'll talk it over with me? You'll treat me as a real friend—just like a man friend? You know how often you have promised to."

"I shall certainly ask your advice."

"Oh! that's kind, that's good of you! We'll talk it over *very* seriously."

How many hours had they spent in what Iris deemed "serious" conversation? When Dyce stayed to luncheon, as he did about once a week, the talk was often prolonged to tea-time. Subjects of transcendent importance were discussed with the most hopeful amplitude. Mrs. Woolstan could not be satisfied with personal culture; her conscience was uneasy about the destinies of mankind; she took to herself the sorrows of the race, and burned with zeal for the great causes of civilization. Vast theories were tossed about between them; they surveyed the universe from the origin to the end of all things. Of course it was Dyce who led the way in speculation; Iris caught at everything he propounded with breathless fervour and a resolute liberality of mind, determined to be afraid of no hypothesis. Oh, the afternoons of endless talk! Iris felt that this was, indeed, living the higher life!

"By the bye," fell from Lashmar musingly, "did you ever hear of a Lady Ogram?"

"I seem to know the name," answered Mrs. Woolstan, keenly attentive. "Ogram? Yes, of course; I have heard Mrs. Toplady speak of her; but I know nothing more. Who is she? What about her?"

A maidservant entered with the tea-tray. Dyce lay back in his chair, gazing vacantly, until his hostess offered him a cup of tea. As he bent forward to take it, his eyes for a moment dwelt with unusual intentness on the face and figure of Iris Woolstan. Then, as he sipped, he again grew absent-minded. Iris, too, was absorbed in thought.

"You were speaking of a Lady Ogram," she resumed gently.

"Yes. A friend of mine down at Alverholme knows her very well, and thought I might like to meet her. I half think I should. She lives at Hollingford; a rich old woman, going in a good deal for social questions. A widow, no children. Who knows?" he added, raising his eyebrows and looking straight at Iris. "She might interest herself in—in my view of things."

"She might," replied the listener, as if overcoming a slight reluctance. "Of course it all depends on her own views."

"To be sure, I know very little about her. It's the vaguest suggestion. But, you see, I'm at the moment when any suggestion, however vague, has a possible value. One point is certain; I shan't take any more pupils. Without meaning it, you have decided this question for me; it's time I looked another way."

"I *felt* that!" exclaimed Mrs. Woolstan, her eyes

brightening. "That was what decided me; I see now that it was—though, perhaps, I hardly understood myself at the time. No more pupils! It is time that your serious career began."

Lashmar smiled, nodding in reflective approval. His eyes wandered, with an upward tendency; his lips twitched.

"Opportunity, opportunity," he murmured. "Of course it will come. I'm not afraid."

"Oh, it will come!" chanted his companion. "Only make yourself known to people of influence, who can appreciate you."

"That's it." Dyce nodded again. "I must move about. For the present I have read and thought enough; now I have to make myself felt as a force."

Mrs. Woolstan gazed at him in a rapture of faith. His countenance wore its transforming light; he had passed into a dream of conquest. By constitution very temperate in the matter of physical indulgence, Lashmar found exciting stimulus even in a cup of tea. For the grosser drinks he had no palate; wine easily overcame him; tea and coffee were the chosen aids of his imagination.

"Yes, I think I shall go down to Hollingford."

"Who," asked Iris, "is the friend who promised to introduce you?"

There was a scarce perceptible pause before his reply.

"A parson—once my father's curate," he added, vaguely. "A liberal-minded man, as so many parsons are now-a-days."

Iris was satisfied. She gave the project her full approval, and launched into forecast of possible issues.

"But it's certain," she said presently, in a lower voice, "that after this I shall see very little of you. You won't have time to come here."

"If you think you are going to get quite rid of me so easily," answered Dyce, laughing—his laugh seldom sounded altogether natural—" you're much mistaken.

But come now, let us talk about Len. Where are you going to send him? Has Wrybolt chosen a school?"

During the conversation that followed Dyce was but half attentive. Once and again his eyes fell upon Mrs. Woolstan with peculiar observancy. Not for the first time he was asking himself what might be the actual nature and extent of her pecuniary resources, for he had never been definitely informed on that subject. He did not face the question crudely, but like a civilized man and a philosopher; there were one or two reasons why it should interest him just now. He mused, too, on the question of Mrs. Woolstan's age, regarding which he could arrive at but a vague conclusion; sometimes he had taken her for hardly more than thirty, sometimes he suspected her of all but ten years more. But, after all, what were these things to him? The future beckoned, and he persuaded himself that its promise was such as is set only before fortune's favourites.

Before leaving, he promised to come and lunch in a day or two, for the purpose of saying good-bye to Leonard. Yet what, in truth, did he care about the boy? Leonard was a rather precocious child, inclined to work his brain more than was good for a body often ailing. Now and then Dyce had been surprised into a feeling of kindly interest, when Len showed himself peculiarly bright, but on the whole he was tired of his tutorial duties, and not for a moment would regret the parting.

"I'm sorry," he said, in a moved voice; "I hoped to make a man of him, after my own idea. Well, well, we shall often see each other again, and who knows whether I mayn't be of use to him some day?"

"What a fine sensibility he has, together with his great intelligence!" was Iris Woolstan's comment in her heart. And she reproached herself for not having stood out against Wrybolt.

As he walked away from the house Dyce wondered why he had told that lie about the friend at Alver-

Our Friend the Charlatan

holme. Would it not have been better, from every point of view, to speak plainly of Connie Bride? Where was the harm? He recognized in himself a tortuous tendency, not to be overcome by reflection and moral or utilitarian resolve. He could not, much as he desired it, be an entirely honest man. His ideal was honesty, even as he had a strong prejudice in favour of personal cleanliness. But occasionally he shirked the cold tub; and, in the same way, he found it difficult at times to tell the truth.

CHAPTER IV

In the morning he had a letter from Mrs. Woolstan. Opening it hurriedly, he was pleased, but not surprised, to discover a cheque folded in the note-paper. Iris wrote that she wished to pay at once what was owing to him in respect of his tutorial engagement so abruptly brought to an end. "Even between friends one must be business-like. You ought, of course, to have received a quarter's notice, and, as it is now nearly the end of April, you must allow me to reckon my debt as up to the quarter-day in September. If you say a word about it, I shall be angry, so *no nonsense, please !*"

The phrase underlined was a quotation from Dyce himself, who often used it, in serio-joking tone, when he had occasion to reprove Mrs. Woolstan for some act or word which jarred with his system. He was glad to have the cheque, and knew quite well that he should keep it, but a certain uneasiness hung about his mind all the morning. Dyce had his ideal of manly independence ; it annoyed him that circumstances made the noble line of conduct so difficult. He believed himself strong, virile, yet so often it happened that he was constrained to act in what seemed rather a feeble and undignified way. But, after all, it was temporary ; the day of his emancipation from paltry necessities would surely come, and all the great qualities latent in him would have ample scope.

Plainly, he must do something. He could live for the next few months, but, after that, had no resources to count upon. Such hopes as he had tried to connect with the name of Lady Ogram might be the veriest dream, but for the moment no suggestion offered in any other quarter. It would be better, perhaps, to write to Connie Bride before going down to Hollingford. Yes, he would write to Connie.

Having breakfasted, he stood idly at the window of his sitting-room. His lodgings were in Upper Woburn Place, nearly opposite the church of St. Pancras. He had read, he knew not where, that the crowning portion of that remarkable edifice was modelled on the Temple of the Winds at Athens, and, as he gazed at it this morning, he suffered from the thought of his narrow experience in travel. A glimpse of the Netherlands, of France, of Switzerland, was all he could boast. His income had only just covered his expenditure; the holiday season always found him more or less embarrassed, and unable to go far afield. What can one do on less than three hundred a year? Yet he regretted that he had not used a stricter economy. He might have managed in cheaper rooms; he might have done without this and the other little luxury. To have travelled widely would now be of some use to him; it gave a man a certain freedom in society, added an octave to the compass of his discourse. Acquaintance with books did not serve the same end; and, though he read a good deal, Dyce was tolerably aware that not by force of erudition could he look for advancement. He began to perceive it as a misfortune that he had not earlier in life become clear as to the nature of his ambition. Until a couple of years ago he had scarcely been conscious of any aim at all, for the literary impulses which used to inspire his talk with Connie Bride were merely such as stir in every very young man of our time; they had never got beyond talk, and, on fading away, left him without intellectual motive. Now that he knew whither his desires and his abilities tended, he was harassed by consciousness of imperfect equipment. Even academically he had not distinguished himself; he had made no attempt at journalism; he had not brought himself into useful contact with any political group. All he could claim for encouragement was a personal something which drew attention, especially the attention of women, in circles of the liberal-minded—that is to say, among people fond of talking more or less vaguely about very large subjects. For talk he never found himself at a loss, and his faculty in this direction certainly grew. But as yet he had not discovered the sphere which was wholly sympathetic and at the same time fertile of opportunity.

Among the many possibilities of life which lie before a young and intelligent man, one never presented itself to Dyce Lashmar's meditation. The thought of simply earning his living by conscientious and useful work, satisfied with whatever distinction might come to him in the natural order of things, had never entered his mind. Every project he formed took for granted his unlaborious pre-eminence in a toiling world. His natural superiority to mankind at large was, with Dyce, axiomatic. If he used any other tone about himself, he affected it merely to elicit contradiction; if in a depressed mood he thought otherwise, the reflection was so at conflict with his nature that it served only to strengthen his self-esteem when the shadow had passed.

The lodgings he occupied were like any other for which a man pays thirty shillings a week. Though he had lived in them for two or three years, there was very little to show that they did not belong to some quite ordinary person. Dyce spent as little time at home as possible, and, always feeling that his abode in such poor quarters must be transitory, he never troubled himself to increase their comfort, or in any way to give character to his surroundings. His library consisted only of some fifty volumes, for he had never felt himself able to purchase books ; Mudie, and the shelves of his club, generally supplied him with all he needed. The club, of course, was an indispensable luxury ; it gave him a West-end address, enabled him to have a friend to lunch or dine in decent circumstances without undue expense, and supplied him with very good stationery for his correspondence. Moreover, it pleasantly enlarged his acquaintance. At the club he had got to know Lord Dymchurch, a month or two ago, and this connection he did not undervalue. His fellow members, it is true, were not, for the most part, men of the kind with whom Dyce greatly cared to talk; as yet, they did not seem much impressed with his conversational powers; but Lord Dymchurch promised to be an exception, and of him Dyce had already a very high opinion.

After an hour or so of smoking and musing and mental vacillation, he sat down to write his letter. "Dear Miss Connie," he began. It was the name by which he addressed Miss Bride in the old days, and it seemed good to him to preserve their former relations as far as possible; for Constance, though a strange sort of girl, now-a-days decidedly cold and dry, undeniably had brains, and might still be capable of appreciating him. "Yesterday I had to come back to town in a hurry, owing to the receipt of some disagreeable news, so of necessity I postponed my visit to Hollingford. It occurs to me that I had better ask whether you were serious in your suggestion that Lady Ogram might be glad to make my acquaintance. I know nothing whatever about her, except what you told me on our walk to the station, so cannot be sure whether she is likely to take any real interest in my ideas. Our time together was too short for me to explain my stand-point; perhaps I had better say a word or two about it now. I am a Socialist—but not a Social-democrat; democracy (which for the rest has never existed) I look upon as an absurdity condemned by all the teachings of modern science. I am a Socialist, for I believe that the principle of association is the only principle of progress."

Here he paused, his pen suspended. He was on the point of referring to the French book which he had read with so much profit of late, and which now lay on the table before him. It might interest Constance; she might like to know of it. He mused for some moments, dipped his pen, and wrote on.

"But association means division of labour, and that labour may be efficient there must be some one capable of directing it. What the true socialism has to keep in view is a principle of justice in the balance of rights and duties between the few who lead and the multitude who follow. In the history of the world hitherto, the multitude has had less than its share, the ruling classes have tyrannized. At present it's pretty obvious that we're in danger of just the opposite excess—Demos begins to roar alarmingly, and there'll be a poor look-out for us if he gets all he wants. What we need above all things is a reform in education. We are teaching the people too much and too little. The first duty of the State is to make citizens, and that can only be done by making children understand from the beginning what is meant by citizenship. When every child grows up in the knowledge that neither the State can exist without him, nor he without the State—that no individual can live for himself alone—that every demand one makes upon one's fellow men carries with it a reciprocal obligation—in other words, when the principle of association, of solidarity, becomes a part of the very conscience, we shall see a true State and a really progressive civilization.

"I could point out to you the scientific (biological and zoological) facts which support this view, but very likely your own knowledge will supply them."

He paused to smile. That was a deft touch. Constance, he knew, took pride in her scientific studies.

"We shall talk all this over together, I hope. Enough at present to show you where I stand. Is this attitude likely to recommend itself to Lady Ogram? Do you think she would care to hear more about it? Write as soon as you have time, and let me know your opinion."

On re-reading his letter Dyce was troubled by only

one reflection. He had committed himself to a definite theory, and, should it jar with Lady Ogram's way of thinking, there would probably be little use in his going down to Hollingford. Might he not have left the matter vague? Was it not enough to describe himself as a student of sociology? In which case——

He did not follow out the argument. Neither did he care to dwell upon the fact that the views he had been summarizing were all taken straight from a book which he had just read. He had thoroughly adopted them; they exactly suited his temper and his mind— always premising that he spoke as one of those called by his author *l'Élite*, and by no means as one of *la Foule*. Indeed, he was beginning to forget that he was not himself the originator of the bio-sociological theory of civilization.

Economy being henceforth imposed upon him, he lunched at home on a chop and a glass of ale. In the early afternoon, not knowing exactly how to spend his time, he walked towards the busy streets, and at length entered his club. In the library sat only one man, sunk in an easy-chair, busied with a book; Dyce had to walk across the room to get a view of him, and the reader proved to be Lord Dymchurch; at Lashmar's approach he looked up, smiled, and rose to take the offered hand.

" I disturb you," said Dyce.

" There's no denying it," was the pleasant answer, " but I am quite ready to be disturbed. You know this of course ? "

He showed Spencer's *The Man versus the State.*

" Yes," answered Dyce; "and I think it a mistake from beginning to end."

" How so ? "

Lord Dymchurch was a man of thirty, slight in build, rather languid in his movements, conventionally dressed but without any gloss or scrupulous finish, and in manners peculiarly gentle. His countenance, natur- ally grave, expressed the man of thought rather than of action; its traits, at the same time, preserved a curious youthfulness, enhanced by the fact of his wearing neither moustache nor beard; when he smiled, it was with an almost boyish frankness, irresistible in its appeal to the good-will of the beholder. Yet the corners of his eyes were touched with the crow's foot, and his hair began to be brindled, tokens which found their confirmation on brow and lip as often as he lost himself in thought. He had a soft voice, habitually subdued. His way of talking inclined to the quietly humorous, and was as little self-assertive as man's talk can be; but he kept his eyes fixed on any one who conversed with him, and that clear, kindly gaze offered no encouragement to pretentiousness or any other idle characteristic. Dyce Lashmar, it might have been noticed, betrayed a certain deference before Lord Dymchurch, and was not wholly at his ease; however decidedly he spoke, his accent lacked the imperturbable confidence which usually distinguished it.

"The title itself I take to be meaningless," was his reply to the other's question. "How can there possibly be antagonism between the individual and the aggregate in which he is involved? What rights or interests can a man possibly have which are apart from the rights and interests of the body politic without which he could not exist? One might just as well suppose one of the cells which make up an organic body asserting itself against the body as a whole."

Lord Dymchurch reflected, playing, as he commonly did, with a seal on his watch-guard.

"That's suggestive," he said.

Dyce might have gone on to say that the suggestion, with reference to this very book of Herbert Spencer's, came from a French sociologist he had been reading; but it did not seem to him worth while.

"You look upon the State as an organism," pursued Lord Dymchurch. "A mere analogy, I suppose?"

"A scientific fact. It's the final stage of evolution. Just as cells combine to form the physiological unit,

Our Friend the Charlatan

so do human beings combine to form the social-political unit—the State. Did it ever occur to you that the science of biology throws entirely new light on sociological questions? The laws operating are precisely the same in one region as in the other. A cell in itself is blind motion; an aggregate of cells is a living creature. A man by himself is only an animal with superior possibilities; men associated produce reason, civilization, the body politic. Could reason ever have come to birth in a man alone?"

Lord Dymchurch nodded and mused. From his look it was plain that Lashmar interested and, at the same time, puzzled him. In their previous conversations, Dyce had talked more or less vaguely, throwing out a suggestion here, a criticism there, and, though with the air of one who had made up his mind on most subjects, preserving an attitude of liberal scepticism; to-day he seemed in the mood for precision, and the coherence of his arguments did not fail to impress the listener. His manner in reasoning had a directness, an eagerness, which seemed to declare fervid conviction; as he went on from point to point, his eyes gleamed and his chin quivered; the unremarkable physiognomy was transformed as though from within, illumined by unexpected radiance, and invested with the beauty of intellectual ardour. Very apt for the contagion of such enthusiasm, Lord Dymchurch showed in his smile that he was listening with pleasure, yet he did not wholly yield himself to the speaker's influence.

"One objection occurs to me," he remarked, averting his eyes for a moment. "The organic body is a thing finished and perfect. Granted that evolution goes on in the same way to form the body politic, the process, evidently, is far from complete—as you began by admitting. Won't the result depend on the nature and tendency of each being that goes to make up the whole? And, if that be so, isn't it the business of the individual to assert his individuality, so as to make the

45

State that he's going to belong to the kind of State he would wish it to be? I express myself very awkwardly."

"Not at all, not at all! In that sense, individualism is no doubt part of the evolutionary scheme. I quite agree with you. What I object to is the idea, conveyed in Spencer's title, that the man as a man can have interests or rights opposed to those of the State as a State. Your thorough individualist seems to me to lose sight of the fact that, but for the existing degree of human association, he simply wouldn't be here at all. He speaks as if he had made himself, and had the right to dispose of himself; whereas it is society, civilization, the State—call it what you will—that has given him everything he possesses, except his physical organs. Take a philosopher who prides himself on his detachment from vulgar cares and desires, duties and troubles, and looks down upon the world with pity or contempt. Suppose the world—that is to say, his human kind— revenged itself by refusing to have anything whatever to do with him, however indirectly; the philosopher would soon find himself detached with a vengeance. And suppose it possible to go further than that; suppose the despised world could demand back from him all it had given, through the course of ages, to his ancestors in him; behold Mr. Philosopher literally up a tree—a naked anthropoid, with a brain just capable of supplying his stomach and—perhaps—of saving him from wild beasts."

Lord Dymchurch indulged a quiet mirth.

"You've got hold of a very serviceable weapon," he said, stretching his legs before him, and clasping his hands behind his head. "I, for one, would gladly be convinced against individualism. I'm afraid it's my natural point of view, and I've been trying for a long time to get rid of that old Adam. Go on with your idea about the organization of society. What ultimate form do you suppose nature to be aiming at?"

Dyce seemed to reflect for a moment. He asked

himself, in fact, whether Lord Dymchurch was at all likely to come upon that French work which, pretty certainly, he had not yet read. The probability seemed slight. In any case, cannot a theory be originated independently by two minds?

His eye lighting up with the joy of clear demonstration—to Dyce it was a veritable joy, his narrow, but acute, mind ever tending to sharp-cut system—he displayed the bio-sociological theory in its whole scope. More than interested, and not a little surprised, Lord Dymchurch followed carefully from point to point, now and then approving with smile or nod. At the end, he was leaning forward, his hands grasping his ankles, and his head nearly between his knees; and so he remained for a minute when Dyce had ceased.

" I like that!" he exclaimed at length, the smile of boyish pleasure sunny upon his face. "There's something satisfying about it. It sounds helpful."

Help amid the confusing problems of life was what Lord Dymchurch continually sought. In his private relations one of the most blameless of men, he bore about with him a troubled conscience, for he felt that he was living to himself alone, whereas, as a man, and still more as member of a privileged order, he should have been justifying his existence and his position by some useful effort. At three-and-twenty he had succeeded to the title, and to very little else; the family had been long in decline; a Lord Dymchurch who died early in the nineteenth century practically completed the ruin of his house by an attempt to form a Utopia in Canada, and since then a rapid succession of ineffectual peers, *fruges consumere nati*, had steadily reduced the dignity of the name. The present lord—Walter Erwin de Gournay Fallowfield—found himself inheritor of one small farm in the county of Kent, and of funded capital which produced less than a thousand a year; his ancestral possessions had passed into other hands, and, excepting the Kentish farm-house, Lord Dymchurch had not even a dwelling he could call his own. Two sisters were his surviving kin; their portions being barely sufficient to keep them alive, he applied to their use a great part of his own income; unmarried, and little likely to change their condition, these ladies lived together very quietly, at a country house in Somerset, where their brother spent some months of every year with them. For himself, he had rooms at Highgate Grove, not unpleasant lodgings in a picturesque old house, where he kept the books which were indispensable to him, and a few pictures which he had loved from boyhood. All else that remained from the slow Dymchurch wreck was down in Somerset.

He saw himself as one of the most useless of mortals. For his sisters' sake he would have been glad to make money, and one way of doing so was always open to him; he had but to lend his name to Company promoters, who again and again had sought him out with tempting proposals. This, however, Lord Dymchurch disdained; he was fastidious in matters of honour, as on some points of taste. For the same reason he remained unmarried; a penniless peer in the attitude of wooing seemed to him ridiculous, and in much danger of becoming contemptible. Loving the life of the country, studious, reserved, he would have liked best of all to withdraw into some rustic hermitage, and leave the world aside; but this he looked upon as a temptation to be resisted; there must be duties for him to discharge, if only he could discover them. So he kept up his old acquaintances, and—though rarely—made new; he strove to interest himself in practical things, if perchance his opportunity might meet him by the way; and always he did his best to obtain an insight into the pressing questions of the time. Though in truth of a very liberal mind, he imagined himself a mass of prejudices; his Norman blood (considerably diluted, it is true) sometimes appeared to him as a hereditary taint, constituting an intellectual, perhaps a moral, disability; in certain moods he felt hopelessly out of touch with his age. To any one who spoke

48

Our Friend the Charlatan

confidently and hopefully concerning human affairs, Lord Dymchurch gave willing attention. With Dyce Lashmar he could not feel that he had much in common, but this rather loquacious young man certainly possessed brains, and might have an inkling of truths not easily arrived at. To-day, at all events, Lashmar's talk seemed full of matter, and it was none the less acceptable to Lord Dymchurch because of its anti-democratic tenor.

"Not long ago," he remarked quietly, "I was reading Marcus Aurelius. You will remember that the idea of the community of human interests runs through all his thought. He often insists that a man is nothing apart from the society he belongs to, and that the common good should be our first rule in conduct. When you were speaking about individualism a sentence of his came into my mind. 'What is not good for the beehive cannot be good for the bee.'"

"Yes, yes!" cried Dyce eagerly. "Thank you very much for reminding me. I had quite forgotten it."

They were no longer alone in the library, two other men had strolled in and were seated reading; on this account Lord Dymchurch subdued his voice even more than usual, for he had a horror of appearing to talk pretentiously, or of talking at all when his words might fall upon indifferent ears. Respectful of this recognized characteristic, Lashmar turned the conversation for a minute to lighter themes, then rose and moved away. He felt that he had made an impression, that Lord Dymchurch thought more of him than hitherto, and this sent him forth in buoyant mood. That evening, economy disregarded, he dined well at a favourite restaurant.

On the third day after posting his letter to Constance Bride, he received her reply. It was much longer than he had expected. Beginning with a rather formal expression of interest in Dyce's views, Constance went on to say that she had already spoken of him to Lady Ogram, who would be very glad to make his

49

acquaintance. He might call at Rivenoak whenever
he liked. Lady Ogram generally had a short drive in
the morning, but in the afternoon she was always at
home. The state of her health did not allow her to
move much; her eyes forbade much reading, consequently, talk with interesting people was one of her
chief resources.

"I say with *interesting* people, and use the word
advisedly. Anything that does *not* interest her she
will not endure. Being frankness itself, she says
exactly what she thinks, without the least regard for
others' feelings. If talk is—or seems to her—dull, she
declares that she has had enough of it. I don't think
there is any need to warn you of this, but it may be as
well that you should know it.

"Whilst I am writing, I had better mention one or
two other peculiarities of Lady Ogram. At the first
glance you will see that she is an invalid, but woe to
you if you show that you see it. She insists on being
treated by every one (I suppose, her doctor excepted,
but I am not sure) as if she were in perfect health.
You will probably hear her make plans for great
journeys, for drives, rides, even walks about the
country, and something more than mere good breeding
must rule your features as you listen. Occasionally
her speech is indistinct; you must manage never to
miss a word she says. She is slightly—very slightly—
deaf; you must speak in your natural voice, yet never
oblige her to be in doubt as to what you say. She
likes a respectful manner, but if it is overdone the
indiscretion soon receives a startling reproof. Be as
easy as you like in her presence provided that your
ease is natural; if it strikes Lady Ogram as self-
assertion—beware the lash! From time to time she
will permit herself a phrase or an exclamation, which
reminds one that her birth was not precisely aristocratic;
but don't imagine that any one else is allowed to use a
too racy vernacular; you must guard your expressions,
and the choicer they are the better she is pleased.

Our Friend the Charlatan

"As you may wish to speak of politics, I will tell you that, until a year or two ago, Lady Ogram was a stout Conservative; she is now on the Liberal side, perhaps for the simple reason that she has quarrelled with the Conservative member for Hollingford, Mr. Robb. I need not go into the details of the affair; sufficient that the name of Robb excites her fury, and that it is better to say nothing about the man at all, unless you know something strongly to his disadvantage, and, in *that* case, you must take your chance of being dealt with as a calumniator or a sycophant; all depends on Lady Ogram's mood of the moment. Detesting Mr. Robb, she naturally aims at ousting him from his Parliamentary seat, and no news could be more acceptable to her than that of a possible change in the political temper of Hollingford. The town is Tory, from of old. Mr. Robb is sitting in his second Parliament, and doubtless hopes to enter a third. But he is nearly seventy years old, and we hear that his constituents would not be sorry if he gave place to a more active man. The hope that Hollingford may turn Liberal does not seem to me to be very well founded, and yet I don't regard the thing as an impossibility. Lady Ogram has persuaded herself that a thoroughly good man might carry the seat. For that man she is continually seeking, and she carries on a correspondence on the subject with party leaders, whips, caucus directors, and all manner of such folk. If she lives until the next general election, heaven and earth will be moved against Mr. Robb, and I believe she would give the half of her substance to any one who defeated him."

This epistle caused a commotion in Lashmar's mind. The last paragraph opened before him a vista of brilliant imaginings. He read it times innumerable; he could think of nothing else. Was not here the occasion for which he had been waiting? Had not fortune turned a shining face upon him?

If only he had still been in enjoyment of his

little competence. There, indeed, was a troublesome
reflection. He thought of writing to his father, of
laying before him the facts of his position, and asking
seriously whether some financial arrangement could
not be made, which would render him independent for
a year or two. Another thought occurred to him—but
he did not care to dwell upon it for the present.
Twenty-four hours' consideration decided him to go
down to Hollingford without delay. When he had
talked with Lady Ogram, he would be in a better
position for making up his mind as to the practical
difficulty which beset him.

He deemed it very friendly on Connie Bride's part
to have written such a letter of advice. Why had she
taken the trouble? Notwithstanding the coldness of
her language, Connie plainly had his interests at heart,
and gave no little thought to him. This was agreeable, but no matter of surprise; it never surprised
Lashmar that any one should regard him as a man of
importance; and he felt a pleasant conviction that the
boyish philandering of years ago would stand him in
good stead now that he understood what was due to
women—and to himself.

CHAPTER V

So next morning he packed his bag, drove to Euston, and by mid-day was at Hollingford. The town, hitherto known to him only by name, had little charm of situation or feature, but Dyce, on his way to a hotel, looked about him with lively interest, and persuaded himself that the main streets had a brisk progressive air; he imagined Liberalism in many faces, and noted cheerfully the publishing office of a Liberal newspaper. If his interview with Lady Ogram proved encouraging, he would stay here over the next day, and give himself time to become acquainted with the borough.

At his hotel, he made inquiry about the way to Rivenoak—a name respectfully received. Lady Ogram's estate was distant some two miles and a half from the edge of the town; it lay hard by the village of Shawe, which was on the highroad to—places wherewith Dyce had no concern. Thus informed, he ordered his luncheon, and requested that a fly might be ready at three o'clock to convey him to Rivenoak. When that hour arrived, he had studied the local directory, carefully looked over the town and county newspapers, and held a little talk with his landlord, who happened to be a political malcontent, cautiously critical of Mr. Robb. Dyce accepted the fact as of good augury. It was long since he had felt so light-hearted and sanguine.

Through an unpleasant quarter, devoted to manufactures, his vehicle bore him out of Hollingford, and then along a flat, uninteresting road, whence at moments he had glimpses of the river Holling, as it flowed between level fields. Presently the country

became more agreeable; on one hand it rose gently to
wooded slopes, on the other opened a prospect over a
breezy common, yellow with gorse. At the village
named Shawe, the river was crossed by a fine old bridge,
which harmonized well with grey cottages and an
ancient low-towered church; but the charm of all this
had been lamentably injured by the recent construction
of a large paper-mill, as ugly as mill can be, on what
was once a delightful meadow by the waterside. Dyce
eyed the blot resentfully; but he had begun to think
of his attitude and language at the meeting with Lady
Ogram, and the gates of Rivenoak quickly engaged his
attention.

The drive wound through a pleasant little park, less
extensive, perhaps, than the visitor had preconceived
it, and circled in front of a plain Georgian mansion,
which, again, caused some disappointment. Dyce had
learnt from the Directory that the house was not very
old, but it was spoken of as "stately"; the edifice
before him he would rather have described as "com-
modious." He caught a glimpse of beautiful gardens,
and had no time to criticize any more, for the fly
stopped and the moment of his adventure was at hand.
When he had mechanically paid and dismissed the
driver, the folding doors stood open before him; a man-
servant, with back at the reverent angle, on hearing
his name at once begged him to enter. Considerably
more nervous than he would have thought likely, and
proportionately annoyed with himself, Dyce passed
through a bare, lofty hall, then through a spacious
library, and was ushered into a room so largely con-
structed of glass, and containing so much verdure, that
at first glance it seemed to be a conservatory. It was,
however, a drawing-room, converted to this purpose
after having served, during the late baronet's lifetime,
for such masculine delights as billiards and smoking.
Here, when his vision had focussed itself, Dyce became
aware of three ladies and a gentleman, seated amid a
little bower of plants and shrubs. The hostess was

easily distinguished. In a very high-backed chair, made rather throne-like by the embroidery and gilding upon it, sat, much huddled together, a meagre lady clad in black silk, with a silvery-grey shawl about her shoulders, and another of the same kind across her knees. She had the aspect of extreme age and of out-worn health; the skin of her face was like shrivelled parchment; her hands unpleasantly suggested those of a skeleton; and one might have supposed her on the point of sinking across the arm of her chair for very feebleness. But in the whitish-yellow visage shone a pair of eyes which had by no means lost their vitality; so keen were they, so darkly lustrous, that to meet them was to forget every other peculiarity of Lady Ogram's person. Regarding the eyes alone, one seemed to have the vision of a handsome countenance, with proud lips and carelessly defiant smile. The illusion was aided by a crown of hair such as no woman of Lady Ogram's age ever did, or possibly could, possess in her own right; hair of magnificent abundance, of rich auburn, plaited and rolled into an elaborate coiffure.

Before this remarkable figure, Dyce Lashmar paused and bowed. Pale and breathing uneasily, he bore as well as he could the scrutiny of those dark eyes for what seemed to him a minute or two of most uncom-fortable time. Then, with the faintest of welcoming smiles, Lady Ogram—who had slowly straightened her-self—spoke in a voice which startled the hearer, so much louder and firmer was it than he had expected.

"I am glad to see you, Mr. Lashmar. Pray sit down."

Without paying any attention to the rest of the company, Dyce obeyed. His feeling was that he had somehow been admitted to the presence of a sovereign, and that any initiative on his own part would be utterly out of place. Never in his life had he felt so little and so subdued.

"You have come down from town this morning?" pursued his hostess, still closely examining him.

Our Friend the Charlatan

"This morning—yes."

Lady Ogram turned to the lady sitting near her right hand, and said abruptly:

"I don't agree with you at all. I should like to see as many women doctors as men. Doctoring is mostly humbug, and if women were attended by women there'd be a good deal less of that. Miss Bride has studied medicine, and a very good doctor she would have made."

Dyce turned towards Constance, of whose proximity he had been aware, though he had scarcely looked at her, and, as she bent her head smiling, he rose and bowed. The lady whom their hostess had addressed—she was middle-aged, comely, good-humoured of countenance, and plainly attired—replied to the blunt remarks in an easy, pleasant tone.

"I should have no doubt whatever of Miss Bride's competence. But——"

Lady Ogram interrupted her, seeming not to have heard what she said.

"Let me introduce to you Mr. Dyce Lashmar, who has thought a good deal more about this kind of thing than either you or me.—Mrs. Gallantry, Mr. Gallantry."

Again Dyce stood up. Mr. Gallantry, a tall, loose-limbed, thinly thatched gentleman, put on a pair of glasses to inspect him, and did so with an air of extreme interest, as though profoundly gratified by the meeting. This was his habitual demeanour. Seldom breaking silence himself, he lent the most flattering attention to any one who spoke, his brows knitted in the resolve to grasp and assimilate whatever wisdom was uttered.

"Did you walk out from Hollingford?" asked Lady Ogram, who again had her eyes fixed on the visitor.

"No, I drove—as I didn't know the way."

"You'd have done much better to walk. Couldn't you ask the way? You look as if you didn't take enough exercise. Driving, one never sees anything. When I'm in new places, I always walk. Miss Bride and I are going to Wales this summer, and we shall

Dyce introduced to Lady Ogram.

walk a great deal. Do you know Brecknock? Few
people do, but they tell me it's very fine. Perhaps you
are one of the people who always go abroad? I prefer
my own country. What did you think of the way from
Hollingford?"

To this question she seemed to expect an answer,
and Dyce, who was beginning to command himself, met
her gaze steadily as he spoke.

"There's very little to see till you come to Shawe.
It's a pretty village—or rather, it was, before some one
built that hideous paper-mill."

Scarcely had he uttered the words when he became
aware of a change in Lady Ogram's look. The gleam
of her eyes intensified; the wrinkles multiplied on her
forehead, and all at once two rows of perfect teeth
shone between the pink edges of her shrivelled lips.

"Hideous paper-mill, eh?" she exclaimed, on a half-
laughing note of peculiar harshness, "I suppose you
don't know that *I* built it?"

A shock went through Dyce's blood. He sat with
his eyes fixed on Lady Ogram's, powerless to stir or
to avert his gaze. Then the courage of despair suddenly
possessed him.

"If I had known that," he said, with much deliberation, "I should have kept the thought to myself. But
I'm afraid there's no denying that the mill spoils the
village."

"The mill is the making of the village," said Lady
Ogram, emphatically.

"In one sense, very likely. I spoke only of the
picturesqueness of the place."

"I know you did. And what's the good of picturesqueness to people who have to earn their living? Is
that your way of looking at things? Would you like
to keep villages pretty and see the people go to the
dogs?"

"Not at all. I'm quite of the other way of thinking,
Lady Ogram. It was by mere accident that I made
that unlucky remark. If any one with me had said

such a thing, it's more than likely I should have replied with your view of the matter. You must remember that this district is quite strange to me. Will you tell me something about it? I am sure you had excellent reasons for building the mill; be so kind as to explain them to me."

The listeners to this dialogue betrayed approval of the young man's demeanour. Constance Bride, who had looked very grave indeed, allowed her features to relax; Mrs. Gallantry smiled a smile of conciliation, and her husband drew a sigh as if supremely edified.

Lady Ogram glanced at her secretary.

"Miss Bride, let him know my 'excellent reasons,' will you?"

"For a long time," began Constance, in clear, balanced tones, "the village of Shawe has been anything but prosperous. It was agricultural, of course, and farming about here isn't what it used to be; there's a great deal of grass and not much tillage. The folk had to look abroad for a living; several of the cottages stood empty; the families that remained were being demoralized by poverty; they wouldn't take the work that offered in the fields, and preferred to scrape up a living in the streets of Hollingford, if they didn't try their hand at a little burglary and so on. Lady Ogram saw what was going on, and thought it over, and hit upon the idea of the paper-mill. Of course most of the Shawe cottagers were no good for such employment, but some of the young people got taken on, and there was work in prospect for children growing up, and, in any case, the character of the village was saved. Decent families came to the deserted houses, and things in general looked up."

"Extremely interesting," murmured Mr. Gallantry, as though he heard all this for the first time, and was beyond words impressed by it.

"Very interesting indeed," said Lashmar, with his frankest air. "I hope I may be allowed to go over the mill; I should like nothing better."

"You shall go over it as often as you like," said Lady Ogram, with a grin. "But Miss Bride has more to tell you."

Constance looked inquiringly.

"Statistics?" she asked, when Lady Ogram paid no heed to her look.

"Don't be stupid. Tell him what I think about villages altogether."

"Yes, I should very much like to hear that," said Dyce, whose confidence was gaining ground.

"Lady Ogram doesn't like the draining of the country population into towns; she thinks it a harmful movement, with bad results on social and political life, on national life from every point of view. This seems to her to be the great question of the day. How to keep up village life?—in face of the fact that English agriculture seems to be doomed. At Shawe, as Lady Ogram thinks, and we all do, a step has been taken in the right direction. Lots of the young people who are now working here in wholesome surroundings would by this time have been lost in the slums of London or Liverpool or Birmingham. Of course, as a mill-owner, she has made sacrifices; she hasn't gone about the business with only immediate profits in view; children and girls have been taught what they wouldn't have learnt but for Lady Ogram's kindness."

"Admirable!" murmured Mr. Gallantry. "True philanthropy, and true patriotism!"

"Beyond a doubt," agreed Dyce. "Lady Ogram deserves well of her country."

"There's just one way," remarked Mrs. Gallantry, "in which, it seems to me, she could have deserved better. Don't be angry with me, Lady Ogram; you know I profit by your example in saying just what I think. Now, if, instead of a mill, you had built a training institution for domestic service——"

"Bah!" broke in the hostess. "How you harp on that idea! Haven't you any other?"

"One or two more, I assure you," replied Mrs.

Gallantry, with the utmost good-humour. "But I particularly want to interest you in this one. It's better that girls should work in a mill in the country than go to swell the population of slums; I grant you that. But how much better still for them to work in private houses, following their natural calling, busy with the duties of domestic life. They're getting to hate that as much as their men-folk hate agricultural labour; and what could be a worse symptom or a greater danger?"

"Pray," cried Lady Ogram, in her grating voice, "how would a servant's school have helped the village?"

"Not so quickly, perhaps, but in time. With your means and influence, Lady Ogram, you might have started an institution which would be the model of its kind for all England. Every female child in Shawe would have had a prospect before her, and the village would have attracted decent poor families, who might somehow have been helped to support themselves——"

Lady Ogram waved her hand contemptuously.

"Somehow! That's the way with you conservative-reform women. Somehow! Always vague, rambling notions."

"Conservative-reform!" exclaimed Mrs. Gallantry, showing a little pique, though her face was pleasant as ever. "Surely your own ideas are to a great extent conservative."

"Yes, but there's a liberal supply of common-sense in them!" cried the hostess, so delighted to have made a joke that she broke into cackling laughter, and laughed until failure of breath made her gasp and wriggle in her chair, an alarming spectacle. To divert attention, Constance began talking about the mill, describing the good effect it had wrought in certain families. Dyce listened with an air almost as engrossed as that of Mr. Gallantry, and, when his moment came, took up the conversation.

"Mrs. Gallantry's suggestion," he said, "is admirable,

Our Friend the Charlatan

and the sooner it's carried out, not merely in one place, but all over England, the better. But I rather think that, in the given circumstances, Lady Ogram took the wisest possible step. We have to look at these questions from the scientific point of view. Our civilization is concerned, before all things, with the organization of a directing power; the supreme problem of science, and at the same time the most urgent practical question of the day, is how to secure initiative to those who are born for rule. Anything which serves to impress ordinary minds with a sense of social equilibrium—to give them an object lesson in the substitution of leadership for anarchy—must be of immense value. Here was a community falling into wreck, cut loose from the orderly system of things, old duties and obligations forgotten, only hungry rights insisted upon. It was a picture in little of the multitude given over to itself. Into the midst of this chaos, Lady Ogram brings a directing mind, a beneficent spirit of initiative, and the means, the power, of re-establishing order. The villagers have but to look at the old state of things and the new to learn a lesson which the thoughtful among them will apply in a wider sphere. They know that Lady Ogram had no selfish aim, no wish to make profit out of their labour; that she acted purely and simply in the interests of humble folk—and of the world at large. They see willing industry substituted for brutal or miserable indolence; they see a striking example of the principle of association, of solidarity—of perfect balance between the naturally superior and the naturally subordinate."

"Good, very good!" murmured Mr. Gallantry. "Eloquent!"

"I admit the eloquence," said Mrs. Gallantry, smiling at Lashmar with much amiability, "but I really can't see why this lesson couldn't have been just as well taught by the measure that I proposed."

"Let me show you why I think not," replied Dyce, who was now enjoying the sound of his own periods,

61

and felt himself inspired by the general attention. "The idea of domestic service is far too familiar to these rustics to furnish the basis of any new generalization. They have long ceased to regard it as an honour or an advantage for their girls to go into the house of their social superiors; it seems to them a kind of slavery; what they aim at is a more independent form of wage-earning, and that's why they go off to the great towns, where there are factories and public-houses, work-rooms and shops. To establish here the training institution you speak of would have done many sorts of good, but not, I think, that particular good, of supreme importance, which results from Lady Ogram's activity. In the rustics' eyes, it would be merely a new device for filling up the ranks of good cooks and housemaids, to the sole advantage of an upper class. Of course that view is altogether wrong, but it would be held. The paper-mill, being quite a novel enterprise, excites new thoughts. It offers the independence these people desire, and yet it exacts an obvious discipline. It establishes a social group corresponding exactly to the ideal organism which evolution will some day produce—on the one hand ordinary human beings understanding their obligations and receiving their due; on the other, a superior mind, reciprocally fulfilling its duties, and reaping the nobler advantage which consists in a sense of worthy achievement."

"Very striking indeed!" fell from Mr. Gallantry.

"You seem to have made out a fair case, Mr. Lashmar," said his wife, with a good-natured laugh. "I'm not sure that I couldn't debate the point still, but at present I'll be satisfied with your approval of my scheme."

Lady Ogram, leaning more firmly against the back of her chair than before her attack of breathlessness, had gazed at the young man throughout his speeches. A grim smile crept over her visage; her lips were pressed together, her eyes twinkled with subdued satisfaction. She now spoke abruptly.

Our Friend the Charlatan

"Do you remain at Hollingford to-night, Mr. Lashmar?"

"Yes, Lady Ogram."

"Very well. Come here to-morrow morning at eleven, go over the mill, and then lunch with us. My manager shall be ready for you."

"Thank you very much."

"Miss Bride, give Mr. Lashmar your Report. He might like to look over it."

Mr. and Mrs. Gallantry were rising to take leave, and the hostess did not seek to detain them; she stood up, with some difficulty, exhibiting a figure unexpectedly tall.

"We'll talk over your idea," she said, as she offered her hand to the lady. "There's something in it, but you mustn't worry me about it, you know. I cut up rough when I'm worried."

"Oh, I don't mind a bit!" exclaimed Mrs. Gallantry gaily.

"But I do," was Lady Ogram's rejoinder, which again made her laugh, with the result that she had to sink back into her chair, waving an impatient adieu as Mr. Gallantry's long, loose figure bowed before her.

Constance Bride had left the room for a moment; she returned with a thin pamphlet in her hand, which, after taking leave of Mr. and Mrs. Gallantry, she silently offered to Lashmar.

"Ah, this is the Report," said Dyce. "Many thanks."

He stood rustling the leaves with an air of much interest. On turning towards his hostess, about to utter some complimentary remark, he saw that Lady Ogram was sitting with her head bent forward and her eyes closed; but for the position of her hands, each grasping an arm of the chair, one would have imagined that she had fallen asleep. Dyce glanced at Constance, who had resumed her seat, and was watching the old lady. A minute passed in absolute silence, then the hostess gave a start, recovered herself, and fixed her look upon the visitor.

"How old are you?" she asked, in a voice which had become less distinct, as if through fatigue.

"Seven-and-twenty, Lady Ogram."

"And your father is a clergyman?"

"My father is vicar of Alverholme, in Northampton-shire."

She added a few short, sharp questions concerning his family and his education, which Dyce answered succinctly.

"Would you like to see something of Rivenoak? If so, Miss Bride will show you about."

"With pleasure," replied the young man.

"Very well. You lunch with us to-morrow. Be at the mill at eleven o'clock."

She held out her skeleton hand, and Dyce took it respectfully. Then Constance and he withdrew.

"This, as you see, is the library," said his companion, when they had passed into the adjoining room. "The books were mostly collected by Sir Spencer Ogram, father of the late baronet; he bought Rivenoak, and laid out the grounds. That is his portrait—the painter has been forgotten."

Dyce let his eyes wander, but paid little attention to what he saw. His guide was speaking in a dry, un-interested voice, she, too, seeming to have her thoughts elsewhere. They went out into the hall, looked into one or two other rooms, and began to ascend the stairs.

"There's nothing of interest above," said Constance, "except the view from the top of the house. But Lady Ogram would like you to see that, no doubt."

Observing Constance as she went before him, Dyce was struck with a new dignity in her bearing. Not-withstanding her subordinate position at Rivenoak, and the unceremonious way in which Lady Ogram exercised authority over her, Constance showed to more advantage here than on her recent visit to Alverholme; she was more naturally self-possessed, and seemed a freer, happier person. The house garb, though decorous rather than ornamental, became her better than her walking-costume.

Our Friend the Charlatan

Her well-shaped head, and thoughtful, sensitive, controlled features, had a new value against this background of handsome furniture and all the appointments of wealth. She moved as if breathing the air that suited her.

From the terrace on the roof, their eyes commanded a wide and beautiful prospect, seen at this moment of the year in its brightest array of infinitely varied verdure. Constance, still in an absent tone, pointed out the features of the landscape, naming villages, hills, and great estates. Hollingford, partly under a canopy of smoke, lay low by its winding river, and in that direction Dyce most frequently turned his eyes.

"I felt very much obliged to you," he said, "for your carefully written letter. But wasn't there one rather serious omission?"

Speaking, he looked at Constance with a humorous twinkle of the eye. She smiled.

"Yes, there was. But, after all, it did no harm."

"Perhaps not. I ought to have used more discretion on strange ground. By the bye, do you take an interest in the mill?"

"A good deal of interest. I think that what you said about it was, on the whole, true—though such an obvious improvisation."

"Improvisation? In one sense, yes; I had to take in the facts of the case very quickly. But you don't mean that you doubt my sincerity?"

"No, no. Of course not."

"Come, Miss Connie, we must understand each other—— "

She interrupted him with a look of frank annoyance.

"Will you do me the kindness not to call me by that name? It sounds childish—and I have long outgrown childhood."

"What shall I call you? Miss Bride?"

"It is the usual form of address."

"Good. I was going to say that I should like you to be clear about my position. I have come here, not

65

in the first place with a hope of personal advantage, but to see if I can interest Lady Ogram in certain views which I hold and am trying to get accepted by people of influence. It happened that this affair of the mill gave me a good illustration of the theory I generally have to put in an abstract way. Your word 'improvisation' seems to hint that I shaped my views to the purpose of pleasing Lady Ogram—a plain injustice, as you will see if you remember the letter I wrote you."

Constance was leaning on a parapet, her arms folded.

"I'm sorry you so understood me," she said, though without the accent of penitence, for in truth she seemed quietly amused. "All I meant was that you were admirably quick in seizing an opportunity of beginning your propaganda."

"I don't think you meant only that," remarked Dyce coolly, looking her in the eyes.

"Is it your habit to contradict so grossly?" asked Constance, with a cold air of surprise.

"I try to make my talk, especially with women, as honest as I can. It seems mere justice to them, as well as to myself. And please observe that I did *not* grossly contradict you. I said that you *seemed* to me to have another thought in your mind beyond the one you admitted. Tell me, please, do you exact courtiership from men? I imagined you would rather dislike it."

"You are right—I do."

"Then it's clear that you mustn't be annoyed when I speak in my natural way. I see no reason in the world why one shouldn't talk to a woman—about things in general—exactly as one does to a man. What is called chivalry is simply disguised contempt. If a man bows and honeys to a woman, he does so because he thinks she has such a poor understanding that this kind of thing will flatter and please her. For my own part, I shall never try to please a woman by any other methods than those which would win the regard and friendship of a man."

Our Friend the Charlatan

Constance wore a look of more serious attention.

"If you stick to that," she said, with a frank air, "you'll be a man worth knowing."

"I'm very glad to hear you say so. Now that we've cleared the air, we shall get on better together. Let me tell you that, whatever else I may fall short in, I have the virtue of sincerity. You know well enough that I am naturally ambitious, but my ambition has never made me unprincipled. I aim at distinction, because I believe that nature has put it within my reach. I don't regard myself as an average man, because I can't; it would be practising hypocrisy with myself. There is—if you like—the possibility of self-deception. Perhaps I am misled by egregious conceit. Well, it is honest conceit, and, as it tends to my happiness, I don't pray to be delivered from it."

Constance smiled.

"This is very interesting, Mr. Lashmar. But why do you honour me with such confidence?"

"Because I think you and I are capable of understanding each other, which is a rare thing between man and woman. I want you as an advocate of my views, and, if I succeed in that, I hope you will become a supporter of my ambitions."

"What are they, just now?"

"Your letter contained a suggestion; whether you intended it or not, I don't know. Why shouldn't I be the man Lady Ogram is looking for—the future Liberal member for Hollingford?"

His companion gazed at a far point of the landscape.

"That is perhaps not an impossible thing," she said, meditatively. "More unlikely things have come to pass."

"Then it does seem to you unlikely?"

"I think we won't discuss it just now. You see from here the plan of the gardens and the park. Perhaps you would like to walk there a little before going back to Hollingford?"

This was a dismissal, and Dyce accepted it. They

went down-stairs together, and in the hall parted, with more friendliness on Constance's side than she had hitherto shown. Dyce did not care to linger in the grounds. He strolled awhile about the village, glancing over the pamphlet with its report of last year's business at the mill, and the local improvements consequent upon it, then returned on foot to Hollingford, where he arrived with an excellent appetite for dinner.

CHAPTER VI

WIND and rain interfered with Lashmar's project for the early morning. He had meant to ramble about the town for an hour before going out to Shawe. Unable to do this, he bought half-a-dozen newspapers, and read all the leading articles and the political news with close attention. As a rule, this kind of study had very little attraction for him; he was anything but well-informed on current politics; he understood very imperfectly the British Constitution, and had still less insight into the details of party organization and conflict. All that kind of thing he was wont to regard as unworthy of his scrutiny. For him, large ideas, world-embracing theories, the philosophies of civilization. Few Englishmen had a smaller endowment of practical ability; few, on the other hand, delighted as he did in speculative system, or could grasp and exhibit in such lucid entirety hypothetical laws. Much as he talked of science, he was lacking in several essentials of the scientific mind; he had neither patience to collect and observe facts, nor conscientiousness in reasoning upon them; prejudice directed his every thought, and egotism pervaded all his conclusions. Excelling in speciousness, it was natural that he should think success as a politician within his easy reach; possessed by a plausible theory of government, he readily conceived himself on the heights of statesmanship, ruling the nation for its behoof. And so, as he read the London and provincial papers this morning, they had all at once a new interest for him; he probed questions, surveyed policies, and whilst smiling at the intellectual poverty of average man, gravely marked for himself a shining course amid the general confusion and ineptitude.

At ten o'clock there shot a glint of promise across the heavy-clouded sky; the rain had ceased, the wind was less boisterous. Feeling a need of exercise, Lashmar set forth on foot, and walked to Shawe, where he arrived in good time for his appointment. The manager of the mill, a dry but very intelligent Scotchman, conscientiously showed him everything that was to be seen, and Dyce affected great interest. Real interest he felt little or none ; the processes of manufacture belonged to a world to which he had never given the slightest thought, which in truth repelled him. But he tried to persuade himself that he saw everything from a philosophical point of view, and found a place for it in his system. The folk employed he regarded attentively, and saw that they looked healthy, well cared for.

"This must be all very gratifying to Lady Ogram," he remarked, in a voice which struck just the right note of dignified reflection.

"I understand that it is," replied the manager. "And to Miss Bride also, no doubt."

"Does Miss Bride take an active interest in the mill ? "

"In the hands, she does. She is an uncommon sort of young lady, and, I should say, makes her influence felt."

As this was the most direct statement to which the Scotchman had committed himself during their hour together, it correspondingly impressed Lashmar. He went away thinking of Constance, and wondering whether she was indeed such a notable woman. Must he really regard her as an equal, or something like it ? For it is needless to say that Dyce at heart deemed all women his natural inferiors, and only by conscious effort could entertain the possibility that one or other of their sex might view and criticize him with level eyes. Six years ago Connie Bride had looked up to him; he, with his university culture, held undoubted superiority over a country girl striving hard to educate herself and to find a place in the world. But much had changed since then, and Dyce was beginning to feel that it would not do to reckon on any dulness, or wilful blindness, in Constance with regard to himself, his sayings and doings. Their talk on the roof yesterday had, he flattered himself, terminated in his favour; and that, because he took the attitude of entire frankness, a compliment to the girl. That he had been, in the strict sense of the word, open-hearted, it did not occur to him to doubt. Dyce Lashmar's introspection stopped at a certain point. He was still but a young man, and circumstance had never yet shown him an austere visage.

The sun was shining, the air exquisitely fresh. Lady Ogram had not named the hour of luncheon, but it seemed to Dyce that he could hardly present himself at Rivenoak before one o'clock; so, instead of directing his steps towards the lodge, he struck off into a by-road, where the new-opened leafage of the hawthorn glistened after the morning showers. Presently there came speeding towards him a lady on a bicycle, and he was sure that it was Constance. She did not slacken her pace; clearly she would not stop.

"Good-morning!" sounded cheerfully from her, as she drew near. "Have you seen the mill? Come up to the house as soon as you like."

She had swept past, leaving in Dyce a sense of having been cavalierly treated.

He turned, and followed towards Rivenoak. When he reached the house, Constance was walking among the flower-beds, in her hand a newspaper.

"Do you cycle?" she asked.

"No. I never felt tempted."

"Lady Ogram is having her drive. Shall we stay in the garden, as the sun is so bright?"

They strolled hither and thither. Constance had a

glow in her cheeks, and spoke with agreeable animation. For a few minutes they talked of the mill, and
Dyce repeated the manager's remark about Miss
Bride's influence; he saw that it pleased her, but she
affected to put it carelessly aside.

"How long have you known Lady Ogram?" he
inquired.

"A good many years. My father was once a friend of
hers—long ago, when he was a curate at Hollingford."

The circumstances of that friendship, and how it
came to an end, were but vaguely known to Constance.
She remembered that, when she was still a child, her
mother often took her to Rivenoak, where she enjoyed
herself in the gardens or the park, and received
presents from Lady Ogram, the return journey being
often made in their hostess's carriage. In those days
the baronet's wife was a vigorous adherent of the
Church of England, wherein she saw the hope of the
country and of mankind. But her orthodoxy discrim-
inated; ever combative, she threw herself into the
religious polemics of the time, and not only came to be
on very ill terms with her own parish clergyman, but
fell foul of the bishop of the diocese, who seemed to
her to treat with insufficient consideration certain
letters she addressed to him. Then it was that, hearing by chance a sermon by the Rev. Mr. Bride in an
unfashionable church at Hollingford, and finding in it a
forcible expression of her own views, she straightway
selected Mr. Bride from all the Hollingford clergy as
the sole representative of Anglicanism. She spoke of
him as a coming man, prophesied for him a brilliant
career, and began to exert herself on his behalf.
Doubtless she would have obtained substantial pro-
motion for the curate of St. John's, had not her own
vehemence and Mr. Bride's difficult character brought
about a painful misunderstanding between them. The
curate was not what is known as a gentleman by
birth; he had the misfortune to count among his near
kinsfolk not only very poor, but decidedly ungenteel,

Our Friend the Charlatan

persons. His only sister had married an uneducated man, who, being converted to some nondescript religion, went preaching about the country, and, unluckily, in the course of his apostolate, appeared at Hollingford. Here he had some success; crowds attended his open-air sermons. It soon became known that the preacher's wife, with him always, was a sister of Mr. Bride of St. John's, and great scandal arose in orthodox circles. Mr. Bride took quite another view of the matter, and declared that, in doing so, he was behaving simply as a Christian. The debate exasperated Lady Ogram's violent temper, and fortified Mr. Bride in a resentful obstinacy. After their parting, in high dudgeon, letters were exchanged, which merely embittered the quarrel. It was reported that the Lady of Rivenoak had publicly styled the curate of St. John's "a low-born and ill-bred parson"; whereto Mr. Bride was alleged to have made retort that, as regards birth, he suspected that he had somewhat the advantage of Lady Ogram, and, as for his breeding, it at all events forbade him to bandy insults. Not long after this, St. John's had another curate. A sequel of the story was the ultimate settling at Hollingford of Mr. Bride's sister and her husband, where, to this day, the woman, for some years a widow, supported herself by means of a little bakery.

"I hadn't seen Lady Ogram for a long time," Constance went on, "and when I got my place of dispenser at Hollingford hospital, I had no idea of recalling myself to her memory. But ˙ one day my friend Dr. Baldwin told me that Lady Ogram had spoken of me, and wished to see me. 'Very well,' said I, 'then let Lady Ogram invite me to come and see her.' 'If I were you,' said the doctor, 'I think I shouldn't wait for that.' 'Perhaps not, doctor,' I replied, 'but you are not me, and I am myself.' The result of which was that Dr. Baldwin told me I had as little grammar as civility, and we quarrelled—as we regularly did once a week."

Dyce listened with amusement.

" And she did invite you," he added.

" Yes. A month afterwards she wrote to the hospital, and, as the letter was decent, though very dry, I went to Rivenoak. I could not help a kindly feeling to Lady Ogram, when I saw her ; it reminded me of some of the happiest days of my childhood. All the same, that first quarter of an hour was very dangerous. As you know, I have a certain pride of my own, and more than once it made my ears tingle. I dare say you can guess Lady Ogram's way of talking to me ; we'll call it blunt good-nature. ' What are you going to do ? ' she asked. ' Mix medicines all your life ? ' I told her that I should like to pass my exams., and practise, instead of mixing medicines. That seemed to surprise her, and she pooh'd the idea. ' I shan't help you to that,' she said. ' I never asked you, Lady Ogram.' It was a toss-up whether she would turn me out of the house or admire my courage : she is capable of one or the other. Her next question was, where did I live ? I told her I lodged with my aunt, Mrs. Shufflebotham ; and her face went black. Mrs. Shufflebotham, I have been told, was somehow the cause of a quarrel between my father and Lady Ogram. That was nothing to me. My aunt is a kind and very honest woman, and I wasn't going to disown her. Of course I had done the wise, as well as the self-respecting, thing ; I soon saw that Lady Ogram thought all the better of me because I was not exactly a snob."

" This is the first I have heard of your aunt," remarked Dyce.

" Is it ? Didn't your father let you know of the shocking revelation I made to him the other day ? "

" He told me nothing at all."

Constance reflected.

" Probably he thought it too painful. Mrs. Shufflebotham keeps a little shop, and sells cakes and sweetmeats. Does it distress you ? "

Distress was not the applicable word, for Lashmar

had no deep interest in Constance or her belongings. But the revelation surprised and rather disgusted him. He wondered why she made it, thus needlessly, and, as it were, defiantly.

"I should be very stupid and conventional," he answered, with his indulgent smile, "if such things affected me one way or another."

"I don't mind telling you that, when I first knew about it, I wished Mrs. Shufflebotham and her shop at the bottom of the sea." Constance laughed unmelodiously. "But I soon got over that. I happen to have been born with a good deal of pride, and, when I began to think about myself—it was only a few years ago—I found it necessary to ask what I really had to be proud of. There was nothing very obvious—no wealth, no rank, no achievements. It grew clear to me that I had better be proud of *being* proud, and a good way to that end was to let people know I cared nothing for their opinion. One gets a good deal of satisfaction out of it."

Lashmar listened in a puzzled and uneasy frame of mind. Theoretically, it should have pleased him to hear a woman talking thus, but the actual effect upon him was repellent. He did not care to look at the speaker, and it became difficult for him to keep up the conversation. Luckily, at this moment the first luncheon-bell sounded.

"Lady Ogram has returned," said Constance. They had wandered to the rear of the house, and thus did not know of the arrival of the carriage. "Shall we go in?"

She led the way into a small drawing-room, and excused herself for leaving him alone. A moment later there appeared a page, who conducted him to a chamber where he could prepare for luncheon. When he came out again into the hall, he found Lady Ogram standing there, reading a letter. Seen from behind, her masses of elaborately dressed hair gave her the appearance of a young woman; when she turned at

Our Friend the Charlatan

the sound of a footfall, the presentation of her yellow parchment visage came as a shock. She looked keenly at the visitor, and seemed to renew her approval of him.

"How do you do?" was her curt greeting, as she gave her hand. "Have you been over the mill?"

"Greatly to my satisfaction, Lady Ogram."

"I'm glad to hear it. We'll talk about that presently. I'm expecting a gentleman to lunch whom you'll like to meet—Mr. Breakspeare, the editor of our Liberal paper. Ah, here he comes."

A servant had just opened the hall-door, and there entered a slight man in a heavy overcoat.

"Well, Mr. Breakspeare!" exclaimed the hostess, with some heartiness. "Why must I have the trouble of inviting you to Rivenoak? Is my conversation so wearisome that you keep away as long as you can?"

"Dear lady, you put me to shame!" cried Mr. Breakspeare, bending low before her. "It's work, work, I assure you, that forbids me the honour and the delight of waiting upon you, except at very rare intervals. We have an uphill fight, you know."

"Pull your coat off," the hostess interrupted, "and let us have something to eat. I'm as hungry as a hunter, whatever *you* may be. You sedentary people, I suppose, don't know what it is to have an appetite."

The editor was ill-tailored, and very carelessly dressed. His rather long hair was brushed straight back from the forehead, and curved up a little at the ends. Without having exactly a dirty appearance, he lacked freshness, seemed to call for the bath; his collar fitted badly, his tie was all askew, his cuffs covered too much of the hand. Aged about fifty, Mr. Breakspeare looked rather younger, for he had a very smooth high forehead, a clear eye, which lighted up as he spoke, and a pink complexion answering to the high-noted and rather florid manner of his speech.

Walking briskly forward—she seemed more vigorous to-day than yesterday—the hostess led to the dining-room, where a small square table received her and her

Our Friend the Charlatan

three companions. Lady Ogram's affectation of appetite lasted but for a few minutes; on the other hand, Mr. Breakspeare ate with keen gusto, and talked very little until he had satisfied his hunger. Whether by oversight, or intentional eccentricity, the hostess had not introduced him and Lashmar to each other; they exchanged casual glances, but no remark. Dyce talked of what he had seen at the mill; he used a large, free-flowing mode of speech, which seemed to please Lady Ogram, for she never interrupted him and had an unusual air of attentiveness. Presently the talk moved towards politics, and Dyce found a better opportunity of eloquence.

"For some thirty years," he began, with an air of reminiscence, "we have been busy with questions of physical health. We have been looking after our bodies and our dwellings. Drainage has been a word to conjure with, and athletics have become a religion —the only one existing for multitudes among us. Physical exercise, with a view to health, used to be the privilege of the upper class; we have been teaching the people to play games and go in for healthy sports. At the same time there has been considerable æsthetic progress. England is no longer the stupidly inartistic country of early Victorian times; there's a true delight in music and painting, and a much more general appreciation of the good in literature. With all this we have been so busy that politics have fallen into the background—politics in the proper sense of the word. Ideas of national advance have been either utterly lost sight of, or grossly confused with mere material gain. At length we see the Conservative reaction in full swing, and who knows where it will land us? It seems to be leading to the vulgarest and most unintelligent form of chauvinism. In politics our need now is of *brains*. A stupid routine, or a rowdy excitability, has taken the place of the old progressive Liberalism, which kept ever in view the prime interests of civilization. We want men with *brains*."

77

"Exactly," fell from Mr. Breakspeare, who began to eye the young man with interest. "It's what I've been preaching, in season and out of season, for the last ten years. I heartily agree with you."

"Look at Hollingford," remarked the hostess, smiling grimly.

"Just so!" exclaimed the editor. "Look at Hollingford! True, it was never a centre of Liberalism, but the Liberals used to make a good fight, and they had so much intelligence on their side that the town could not sink into utter dulness. What do we see now?" He raised his hand and grew rhetorical. "The crassest Toryism sweeping all before it, and everywhere depositing its mud—which chokes, and does *not* fertilize! We have athletic clubs, we have a free library, we are better drained and cleaner and healthier and more bookish, withal, than in the old times; but for politics—alas! A base level of selfish and purblind materialism—personified by Robb!"

At the name of the borough member, Lady Ogram's dark eyes flashed.

"Ah, Robb," interjected Lashmar. "Tell me something about Robb. I know hardly anything of him."

"Picture to yourself," returned the editor, with slow emphasis, "a man who at his best was only a stolid country banker, and who now is sunk into fatuous senility. I hardly know whether I dare trust myself to speak of Robb, for I confess that he has become to me an abstraction rather than a human being—an embodiment of all the vicious routine, the foul obscurantism, the stupid prejudice, which an enlightened Liberalism has to struggle against. There he sits, a satire on our parliamentary system. He can't put together three sentences; he never in his life had an idea. The man is a mere money-sack, propped up by toadies and imbeciles. Has any other borough such a contemptible representative? I perspire with shame and anger when I think of him!"

Dyce asked himself how much of this vehemence

was genuine, how much assumed to gratify their hostess. Was Mr. Breakspeare inwardly laughing at himself and the company? But he seemed to be an excitable little man, and possibly believed what he said.

"That's very interesting," Dyce remarked. "And how much longer will Hollingford be content with such representation?"

"I think," replied Breakspeare gravely, "I really think that at the next election we shall floor him. It is the hope of my life. For that I toil; for that I sacrifice leisure and tranquillity and most of the things dear to a man philosophically inclined. Can I but see Robb cast down, I shall withdraw from the arena and hum (I have no voice) my *Nunc dimittis.*"

Was there a twinkle in the editor's eye as it met Lashmar's smile? Constance was watching him with unnaturally staid countenance, and her glance ran round the table.

"I'm only afraid," said Lady Ogram, "that he won't stand again."

"I think he will," cried Breakspeare, "I think he will. The ludicrous creature imagines that Westminster couldn't go on without him. He hopes to die of the exhaustion of going into the lobby, and remain for ever a symbol of thick-headed patriotism. But we will floor him in his native market-place. We will drub him at the ballot. Something assures me that, for a reward of my life's labours, I shall behold the squashing of Robb!"

Lady Ogram did not laugh. Her sense of humour was not very keen, and the present subject excited her most acrimonious feelings.

"We must get hold of the right man," she exclaimed, with a glance at Lashmar.

"Yes, the right man," said Breakspeare, turning his eyes in the same direction. "The man of brains, and of vigour; the man who can inspire enthusiasm; the man, in short, who has something to say, and knows

79

how to say it. In spite of the discouraging aspect of things, I believe that Hollingford is ready for him. We leading Liberals are few in number, but we have energy and the law of progress on our side."

Lashmar had seemed to be musing whilst he savoured a slice of pine-apple. At Breakspeare's last remark, he looked up and said:

"The world moves, and always has moved, at the impulse of a very small minority."

"Philosophically, I am convinced of that," replied the editor, as though he meant to guard himself against too literal or practical an application of the theorem.

"The task of our time," pursued Dyce, with a half absent air, "is to make this not only understood by, but acceptable to, the multitude. Political education is our pressing need, and political education means teaching the People how to select its Rulers. For my own part, I have rather more hope of a constituency such as Hollingford, than of one actively democratic. The fatal thing is for an electorate to be bent on choosing the man as near as possible like unto themselves. That is the false idea of representation. Progress does not mean guidance by one of the multitude, but by one of nature's elect, and the multitude must learn how to recognize such a man."

He looked at Lady Ogram, smiling placidly.

"There's rather a Tory sound about that," said the hostess, with a nod, "but Mr. Breakspeare will understand."

"To be sure, to be sure!" exclaimed the editor. "It is the aristocratic principle rightly understood."

"It is the principle of nature," said Lashmar, "as revealed to us by science. Science—as Mr. Breakspeare is well aware—teaches, not levelling, but hierarchy. The principle has always been dimly perceived. In our time, biology enables us to work it out with scientific precision."

Mr. Breakspeare betrayed a little uneasiness.

Our Friend the Charlatan

" I regret," he said diffidently, " that I have had very little time to give to natural science. When we have floored Robb, I fully intend to apply myself to a study of all that kind of thing."

Lashmar bestowed a gracious smile upon him.

" My dear sir, the flooring of Robb—Robb in his symbolic sense—can only be brought about by assiduous study and assimilation of what I will call bio-sociology. Not only must we, the leaders, have thoroughly grasped this science, but we must find a way of teaching it to the least intelligent of our fellow-citizens. The task is no trifling one. I'm very much afraid that neither you nor I will live to see it completed."

" Pray don't discourage us," put in Constance. " Comprehensive theories are all very well, but Mr. Breakspeare's practical energy is quite as good a thing."

The editor turned his eyes upon Miss Bride, their expression a respectful gratitude. He was a married man, with abundant offspring. Mrs. Breakspeare rose every morning at half-past six, and toiled at her domestic duties, year in year out, till ten o'clock at night; she was patient as laborious, and had never repined under her lot. But her education was elementary; she knew nothing of political theories, nothing of science or literature, and, as he looked at Constance Bride, Breakspeare asked himself what he might not have done, what ambition he might not have achieved, had it been his fate to wed such a woman as *that!* Miss Bride was his ideal. He came to Rivenoak less often than he wished, because the sight of her perturbed his soul and darkened him with discontent.

" Discourage you ! " cried Lashmar. " Heaven forbid ! I'm quite sure Mr. Breakspeare wouldn't take my words in that sense. I am all for zeal and hopefulness. The curse of our age is pessimism, a result and a cause of the materialistic spirit. Science, which really involves an infinite hope, has been misinterpreted by socialists in the most foolish way, until we get a

Our Friend the Charlatan

miserable languid fatalism, leading to decadence and despair. The essential of progress is Faith, and Faith can only be established by the study of Nature."

"That's the kind of thing I like to hear," exclaimed the editor, who, whilst listening, had tossed off a glass of wine. (The pink of his cheeks was deepening to a pleasant rosiness, as luncheon drew to its end.) "*Hoc signo vinces!*"

Lady Ogram, who was regarding Lashmar, said abruptly, "Go on! Talk away!" And the orator, to whose memory happily occurred a suggestion of his French sociologist, proceeded meditatively.

"Two great revolutions in knowledge have affected the modern world. First came the great astronomic discoveries, which subordinated our planet, assigned it its place in the universe, made it a little rolling globe amid innumerable others, instead of the one inhabited world for whose behalf were created sun and moon and stars. Then the great work of the biologists, which put man into his rank among animals, dethroning him from a fantastic dignity, but at the same time honouring him as the crown of nature's system, the latest product of æons of evolution. These conquests of science have put modern man into an entirely new position, have radically changed his conception of the world and of himself. Religion, philosophy, morals, politics, all are revolutionized by this accession of knowledge. It is no exaggeration to say that the telescope and the microscope have given man a new heart and soul. *But*"—he paused, effectively—"how many are as yet really aware of the change? The multitude takes no account of it—no conscious account; the average man lives under the heaven of Joshua, on the earth of King Solomon. We call our age scientific. So it is—for a few score human beings."

Reflecting for a moment, Dyce felt that it would be absurd to charge him with plagiarism, so vastly more eloquent was he than the author to whom he owed his

ideas. Conscience did not trouble him in the least.
He marked with satisfaction the attentiveness of his
audience.

"Politics, to be a living thing, must be viewed in
this new, large light. The leader in Liberalism is the
man imbued with scientific truth, and capable of
applying it to the every-day details of government.
Science, I said, teaches hierarchic order—that is, the
rule of the few by the select, the divinely appointed.
But this hierarchy is an open order—open to the
select of every rank; a process of perpetual renewal
will maintain the health of the political organism.
The true polity is only in slow formation; for,
obviously, human reason is not yet a complete development. As yet, men come to the front by accident;
some day they will be advanced to power by an
inevitable and impeccable process of natural selection.
For my own part"—he turned slightly towards the
hostess—"I think that use will be made of our existing
system of aristocracy; in not a few instances, technical
aristocracy is justified by natural pre-eminence. We
can all think of examples. Personally, I might
mention my friend Lord Dymchurch—a member of the
true aristocracy, in every sense of the word."

"I don't know him," said Lady Ogram.

"That doesn't surprise me. He leads an extremely
retired life. But I am sure you would find him a very
pleasant acquaintance."

Lashmar occasionally had a fine discretion. He
knew when to check the flood of his eloquence: a
glance at this face and that, and he said within himself: *Sat prata biberunt.* Soon after this, Lady Ogram
rose, and led the company into her verdurous drawing-
room. She was beginning to show signs of fatigue;
seated in her throne-like chair, she let her head lie
back, and was silent. Constance Bride, ever tactful,
began to take a more prominent part in the conversation, and Breakspeare was delighted to talk with
her about ordinary things. Presently, Lashmar, in

reply to some remark, mentioned that he was returning to London this evening, whereupon his hostess asked :

" When are you coming back again ? "

" Before long, I hope, Lady Ogram. The pleasure of these two days——"

She interrupted him.

" Could you come down in a fortnight ?"

" Easily, and gladly."

" Then do so. Don't go to Hollingford your room will be ready for you here. Just write and let me know when you will arrive."

In a few minutes both men took their leave, and went back to Hollingford together, driving in a fly which Breakspeare had ordered. For the first minutes they hardly talked ; they avoided each other's look, and exchanged only insignificant words. Then the editor, with his blandest smile, said in a note of sudden cordiality :

" It has been a great pleasure to me to meet you, Mr. Lashmar. May I, without indiscretion, take it for granted that we shall soon be fighting the good fight together ? "

" Why, I think it likely," answered Dyce, in a corresponding tone. " I have not *quite* made up my mind——"

" No, no. I quite understand. There's just one point I should like to touch upon. To-day we have enjoyed a veritable symposium—for me, I assure you, a high intellectual treat. But, speaking to you as to one who does not know Hollingford, I would suggest to you that our Liberal electors are perhaps hardly ripe for such a new and bracing political philo-sophy——"

Dyce broke into gay laughter.

" My dear sir, you don't imagine that I thought of incorporating my philosophy in an electioneering address ? Of course one must use common-sense in these matters. Practical lessons come before the theory. If I stand for Hollingford "—he rolled the

words, and savoured them—" I shall do so as a very
practical politician indeed. My philosophical creed
will of course influence me, and I shall lose no opportunity of propagating it—but have no fear of my
expounding bio-sociology to Hollingford shopkeepers
and artisans."

Breakspeare echoed the speaker's mirth, and they
talked on about the practical aspects of the next
election in the borough.

Meanwhile, Lady Ogram had sat in her great chair,
dozing. Constance, accustomed to this, read for half-
an-hour, or let her thoughts wander. At length, overcoming her drowsiness, Lady Ogram fixed an unwonted
look upon Miss Bride, a gaze of benevolent meditation.

" We shall have several letters to write to-morrow
morning," she said presently.

" Political letters ? " asked Constance.

" Yes. By the bye, do you know anything about
Lord Dymchurch ? "

" Nothing at all."

" Then find out about him as soon as possible.
What are Mr. Lashmar's means ? "

" I really can't tell you," answered Constance,
slightly confused by the unexpected question. " I
believe his father is very well-to-do; I have heard him
spoken of as a man of private fortune."

" Then our friend is independent—or at all events
not pinched. So much the better."

Again Lady Ogram fell into musing ; the countless
wrinkles about her eyes, eloquent as wrinkles always
are, indicated that her thoughts had no disagreeable
tenor.

" Mr. Lashmar impresses you favourably ? " Constance at length ventured to ask.

Lady Ogram delayed her answer for a moment, then,
speaking thickly in her tired voice, said with slow
emphasis :

" I'm glad to know him. Beyond a doubt he is the
coming man."

CHAPTER VII

On his return, Lashmar found a letter from Mrs. Woolstan awaiting him at Upper Woburn Place. The lady wrote in rather an agitated strain; she had to report that Leonard was already packed off to school, the imperious Wrybolt having insisted on sending him away as soon as he had recovered from his cold, the pretence being that the boy ought not to lose any part of the new term. "It is really very hard on me, don't you think? I know nothing whatever about the school, which is a long way off, right away in Devonshire. And it does so grieve me that you couldn't say good-bye to the poor little fellow. He says he shall write to you, and it would be *so* kind, dear Mr. Lashmar, if you could find a moment to answer him. I know how grateful dear Len would be. But we will *talk* about these things, for of course you will come and lunch all the same, at least I hope you will. Shall we say Thursday? I am not at all pleased with Mr. Wrybolt's behaviour. Indeed it seems to me very high-handed, very! And I told him very plainly what I thought. You can have no idea how galling is a woman's position left at the mercy of a trustee—a stranger too. And now that I am quite alone in the house—but I know you don't like people who complain. It's all very well for *you*, you know. Ah! if I had your independence! What I would make of my life!— Till Thursday, then, and don't, please, be bored with my letters."

This Mrs. Woolstan wrote and posted before luncheon. At three o'clock in the afternoon, just when she was

86

Our Friend the Charlatan

preparing to go out, the servant made known to her that Mr. Wrybolt had called. What, Mr. Wrybolt again ! With delay which was meant to be impressive, she descended to the drawing-room, and coldly greeted the gentleman of the red neck and heavy eyelids. Mr. Wrybolt's age was about five-and-forty; he had the well-groomed appearance of a flourishing City man, and presented no sinister physiognomy; one augured in him a disposition to high-feeding and a masculine self-assertiveness. Faces such as his may be observed by the thousand round about the Royal Exchange ; they almost invariably suggest degradation, more or less advanced, of a frank and hopeful type of English visage; one perceives the honest, hearty school-boy, dimmed beneath self-indulgence, soul-hardening calculation, debasing excitement and vulgar routine. Mr. Wrybolt was a widower, without children ; his wife, a strenuous sportswoman, had been killed in riding to hounds two or three years ago. This afternoon he showed a front all amiability. He had come, he began by declaring, to let Mrs. Woolstan know that the son of a common friend of theirs had just, on his advice, been sent to the same school as Leonard ; the boys would be friends, and make each other feel at home. This news Mrs. Woolstan received with some modification of her aloofness ; she was very glad; after all, perhaps it had been a wise thing to send Leonard off with little warning ; she would only have made herself miserable in the anticipation of parting with him. That, said Mr. Wrybolt, was exactly what he had himself felt. He was quite sure that in a few days Mrs. Woolstan would see that all was for the best. The fact of the matter was that Len's tutor, though no doubt a very competent man, had been guilty of indiscretion in unsettling the boy's ideas on certain very important subjects. Well, admitted the mother, perhaps it was so; she would say no more; Mr. Wrybolt, as a man of the world, probably knew best. And now, as he was here, she would use the oppor-

tunity to speak to him on a subject which had often
been in her mind of late. It was a matter of business.
As her trustee was aware, she possessed a certain little
capital which was entirely at her own disposal. More
than once Mr. Wrybolt had spoken to her about it—
had been so kind as to express a hope that she managed
that part of her affairs wisely, and to offer his services
if ever she desired to make any change in her invest-
ments. The truth was, that she had thought recently
of trying to put out her money to better advantage,
and she would like to talk the matter over with him.
This they proceeded to do, Mr. Wrybolt all geniality
and apt suggestiveness. As the colloquy went on, a
certain change appeared in the man's look and voice;
he visibly softened, he moved his chair a little nearer,
and all at once, before Mrs. Woolstan had had time to
reflect upon these symptoms, Wrybolt was holding her
hand and making her an offer of marriage.

Never was woman more genuinely surprised. That
this prosperous financier, who had already made one
advantageous marriage and might probably, if he
wished, wed another fortune—that such a man as Mr.
Wrybolt would think of *her* for his wife, was a thing
which had never entered her imagination. She was
fluttered, and flattered, and pleased, but not for a
moment did she think of accepting him. Her eyes
fell in demurest sadness. Never, never could she
marry again; the past was always with her, and the
future imposed upon her the most solemn of duties.
She lived for the memory of her husband and for
the prospects of her child. Naturally, Mr. Wrybolt
turned at first an incredulous ear; he urged his suit,
simply and directly, with persuasion derived partly
from the realm of sentiment, partly from Lombard Street
—the latter sounding the more specious. But Mrs.
Woolstan betrayed no sign of wavering; in truth, the
more Wrybolt pleaded, the firmer she grew in her
resolve of refusal. When decency compelled the man
to withdraw, he was very warm of countenance, and

Our Friend the Charlatan

lobster-hued at the back of his neck; an impartial observer would have thought him secretly in a towering rage. His leave-taking was laconic, though he did his best to smile.

Of course Mrs. Woolstan soon sat down to write him a letter, in which she begged him to believe how grateful she was, how much honoured by his proposal and how deeply distressed at not being able to accept it. Surely this would make no difference between them? Of course they would be friends as ever—nay, more than ever? She could never forget his nobly generous impulse. But let him reflect on her broken life, her immutable sadness; he would understand how much she would have wronged such a man as he in taking advantage of that moment's heroic weakness. To this effusive epistle came speedily a brief response. Of course all was as before, wrote Wrybolt. He was wholly at her service, and would do anything she wished in the matter of her money. By all means let her send him full particulars in writing, and he would lose no time; the yield of her capital might probably be doubled.

Mrs. Woolstan, after all, went no further in that business. She had her own reasons for continuing to think constantly of it, but for the present felt she would prefer not to trouble Mr. Wrybolt. Impatiently she looked forward to Thursday and the coming of Dyce Lashmar.

He came, with a countenance of dubious import. He was neither merry nor sad, neither talkative nor taciturn. At one moment his face seemed to radiate hope; the next, he appeared to fall under a shadow of solicitude. When his hostess talked of her son, he plainly gave no heed; his replies were mechanical. When she asked him for an account of what he had been doing down in the country, he answered with broken scraps of uninteresting information. Thus passed the quarter of an hour before luncheon, and part of luncheon itself; but at length Dyce recovered his more natural demeanour. Choosing a moment when the parlour-maid was out of the room, he leaned towards Mrs. Woolstan, and said, with the smile of easy comradeship:

"I have a great deal to tell you."

"I'm so glad!" exclaimed Iris, who had been sinking into a disheartened silence. "I began to fear nothing interesting had happened."

"Have patience. Presently."

After that, the meal was quickly finished; they passed into the drawing-room, and took comfortable chairs on either side of the hearth. May had brought cold, clammy weather; a sky of billowing grey and frequent gusts against the window made it pleasant here by this bright fireside. Lashmar stretched his legs, smiled at the gimcracks shelved and niched above the mantelpiece, and began talking. His description of Lady Ogram was amusing, but not disrespectful; he depicted her as an old autocrat of vigorous mind and original character, a woman to be taken quite seriously, and well worth having for a friend, though friendship with her would not be found easy by ordinary people.

"As luck would have it, I began by saying something which might have given her mortal offence." He related the incident of the paper-mill. "Nothing could have been better. She must be sickened with toadyism, and I could see she found my way a refreshing contrast. It made clear to her at once that I met her in a perfectly independent spirit. If we didn't like each other, good-bye, and no harm done. But, as it proved, we got on very well indeed. In a fortnight's time I am to go down and stay at Rivenoak."

"Really? In a fortnight? She must have taken to you wonderfully."

"My ideas interested the old lady—as I thought perhaps they might. She's very keen on political and social science. It happens, too, that she's looking about for a Liberal candidate to contest Hollingford at the next election."

Dyce added this information in a very quiet, matter-of-fact voice, his eyes turned to the fire. Upon his hearer they produced no less an effect than he anticipated.

"A Liberal candidate!" echoed Iris, quivering with delighted astonishment. "She wants you to go into Parliament!"

"I fancy she has that idea. Don't make a fuss about it; there's nothing startling in the suggestion. It was probably her reason for inviting me to Rivenoak."

"Oh, this is splendid—magnificent!"

"Have the goodness to be quiet," said Dyce. "It isn't a thing to scream about, but to talk over quietly and sensibly. I thought you had got out of that habit."

"I'm very sorry. Don't be cross. Tell me more about it. Who is the present Member?"

Dyce gave an account of the state of politics at Hollingford, sketching the character of Mr. Robb on the lines suggested by Breakspeare. As she listened, Mrs. Woolstan had much ado to preserve outward calm ; she was flushed with happiness; words of enthusiasm trembled on her lips.

"When will the election be?" she asked in the first pause.

"Certainly not this year. Possibly not even next. There's plenty of time."

"Oh, you are *sure* to win! How can a wretched old Tory like that stand against you? Go and make friends with everybody. You only need to be known. How I should like to hear you make a speech! Of course I must be there when you do. How does one get to Hollingford? What are the trains?"

"If you leave Euston by the newspaper train to-morrow morning," said Dyce, with cold jocularity, "you may be just in time to hear the declaration of the poll. Meanwhile," he added, "suppose we think for a moment of the trifling fact that my income is just nothing a-year. How does that affect my chances in a political career, I wonder?"

Mrs. Woolstan's countenance fell.

"Oh—but—it's impossible for that to stand in your way. You said yourself that you didn't seriously trouble about it. Of course you will get an income— somehow. Men who go in for public life always do— don't they?"

She spoke timidly, with downcast eyes, a smile hovering about her lips. Dyce did not look at her. He had thrust his hands into his trouser's-pockets, and crossed his legs; he smiled frowningly at the fire.

"Does Lady Ogram know your circumstances?" Iris asked, in a lower voice.

"I can't be sure. She may have heard something about them from—my friend. Naturally I didn't tell her that I was penniless."

"But—if she is bent on having you for a candidate —don't you think she will very likely make some suggestion? A wealthy woman——"

The voice failed; the speaker had an abashed air.

"We can't take anything of that kind into account," said Lashmar, with blunt decision. "If any such suggestion were made, I should have to consider it very carefully indeed. As yet I know Lady Ogram very slightly. We may quarrel, you know; it would be the easiest thing in the world. My independence is the first consideration. You mustn't imagine that I *clutch* at this opportunity. Nothing of the kind. It's an opening, perhaps; but in any case I should have found one before long. I don't even know yet whether Hollingford will suit me. It's a very unimportant borough; I may decide that it would be better to look to one of the large, intelligent constituencies. I'm afraid"—he became rather severe—"you are inclined to weigh my claims to recognition by the fact that I happen to have no money."

"Oh, Mr. Lashmar! Oh, don't!" exclaimed Iris, in a pained voice. "How can you be so unkind—so unjust!"

Our Friend the Charlatan

"No, no; I merely want to guard myself against misconception. The very freedom with which I speak to you might lead you to misjudge me. If I thought you were ever tempted to regard me as an adventurer——"

"Mr. Lashmar!" cried Iris, almost tearfully. "This is dreadful. How could such a thought enter my mind? Is *that* your opinion of me?"

"Pray don't be absurd," interposed Dyce, with an impatient gesture. "I detest this shrillness, as I've told you fifty times."

Iris bridled a little.

"I'm sure I wasn't *shrill*. I spoke in a very ordinary voice. And I don't know why you should attribute such thoughts to me."

Lashmar gave way to nervous irritation.

"What a feminine way of talking! Is it impossible for you to follow a logical train of ideas? I attributed no thought whatever to you. All I said was, that I must take care not to be misunderstood. And I see that I had very good reason; you have a fatal facility in misconceiving even the simplest things."

Mrs. Woolstan bridled still more. There was a point of colour on her freckled cheeks, her lower lip showed a tooth's pressure.

"After all," she said, "you must remember that I am a woman, and if women don't express themselves quite as men do, I see no great harm in it. I don't think mannishness is a very nice quality. After all, I am myself, and I can't become somebody else, and certainly should not care to, if I could."

Dyce began to laugh forbearingly.

"Come, come," he said, "what's all this wrangling about? How did it begin? That's the extraordinary thing with women; one gets so easily off the track, and runs one doesn't know where. What was I saying? Oh, simply that I couldn't be sure, yet, whether Hollingford would suit me. Let us keep to the higher plane. It's safer than too familiar detail."

Our Friend the Charlatan

Iris was not to be so easily composed. She remarked a change in her friend since he had ceased to be Leonard's tutor; he seemed to hold her in slighter esteem, a result, no doubt, of the larger prospects opening before him. She was jealous of old Lady Ogram, whose place and wealth gave her such power to shape a man's fortunes. For some time now, Iris had imagined herself a power in Lashmar's life, had dreamed that her influence might prevail over all other. In marrying, she had sacrificed herself to an illusory hope; but she was now an experienced woman, able to distinguish the phantasmal from the genuine, and of Lashmar's abilities there could be no doubt. Her own judgment she saw confirmed by that of Lady Ogram. Sharp would be her pang if the aspiring genius left her aside, passed beyond her with a careless nod. She half accused him of ingratitude.

"I'm not at all sure," she said, rather coldly, " that you think me capable of rising to the higher plane. Perhaps the trivial details are more suited to my intelligence."

Dyce had relieved himself of a slight splenetic oppression, and felt that he was behaving boorishly. He brightened and grew cordial, admitted a superfluous sensitiveness, assured his companion that he prized her sympathy, counted seriously upon her advice; in short, was as amiable as he knew how to be. Under his soothing talk, Mrs. Woolstan recovered herself; but she had a preoccupied air.

"If you regard me as a serious friend," she said at length with some embarrassment, "you can easily prove it, and put my mind at ease."

"How?" asked Dyce, with a quick, startled look.

"You have said more than once that a man and woman who were really friends should be just as men are with each other—plain-spoken and straightforward and—and no nonsense."

"That's my principle. I won't have any woman for a friend on other terms."

Our Friend the Charlatan

"Then—here's what I want to say. I'm your friend —call me Jack or Harry, if you like—and I see a way in which I can be of use to you. It happens that I have rather more money than I want for my own use, I want to lend you some until your difficulties are over— just as one man would to another."

Her speech had become so palpitant that she was stopped by want of breath; a rosy shamefacedness subdued her; trying to brave it out she achieved only an unconscious archness of eye and lip which made her for the moment oddly, unfamiliarly attractive. Dyce could not take his eyes from her; he experienced a singular emotion.

"That's uncommonly good of you, Iris," he said, with all the directness at his command. "You see, I call you by your name, just to show that I take our friendship seriously. If I could borrow from any one, I would from you. But I don't like the idea. You're a good fellow"—he laughed—"and I thank you heartily."

Iris winced at the "good fellow."

"Why can't you consent to borrow?" she asked, in a note of persistency. "Would you refuse if Lady Ogram made such a suggestion?"

"Oh, Lady Ogram! That would depend entirely——"

"But you must have money from somewhere," Iris urged, her manner becoming practical. "I'm not rich enough to lend very much, but I could help you over a year, perhaps. Wouldn't you rather go back to Rivenoak with a feeling of complete independence? I see what it is. You don't really mean what you say; you're ashamed to be indebted to a woman. Yes, I can see it in your face."

"Look at the thing impartially," said Dyce, fidgeting in his chair. "How can I be sure that I should ever be able to pay you back? In money matters there *is* just that difference: a man can go to work and earn; a woman generally can't do anything of the kind. That's why it seems simply unjust to take a woman's money; that's the root of all our delicacy in the matter. Don't trouble about my affairs; I shall pull through the difficult time."

"Yes," exclaimed Iris, "with somebody else's help. And *why* should it be somebody else? I'm not in such a position that I should be ruined if I lost a few hundred pounds. I have money I can do what I like with. If I want to have the pleasure of helping you, why should you refuse me? You know very well—at least, I hope you do—that I should never have hinted at such a thing if we had been just ordinary acquaintances. We're trying to be more sensible than everyday people. And just when there comes a good chance of putting our views into practice, you draw back, you make conventional excuses. I don't like that! It makes me feel doubtful about your sincerity. Be angry, if you like. I feel inclined to be angry too, and I've the better right!"

Again her panting impulsiveness ended in extinction of voice; again she was rosily self-conscious, though, this time, not exactly shamefaced; and again the young man felt a sort of surprise at he gazed at her.

"In any case," he said, standing up and taking a step or two, "an offer of this kind couldn't be accepted straight away. All I can say now is that I'm very grateful to you. No one ever gave me such a proof of friendship, that's the simple fact. It's uncommonly good of you, Iris——"

"It's not uncommonly good of *you*," she broke in, still seated, and her arms crossed. "Do as you like. You said disagreeable things, and I felt hurt, and when I ask you to make amends in a reasonable way——"

"Look here," cried Lashmar, standing before her with his hands in his pockets, "you know perfectly well—*perfectly well*—that, if I accept this offer, you'll think the worse of me."

Iris started up.

"It isn't true! I shall think the worse of you if you go down to Lady Ogram's house, and act and speak as if you were independent. What sort of face will you have when it comes at last to telling her the truth?"

Dyce seemed to find this a powerful argument. He raised his brows, moved uneasily, and kept silence.

"I shall *not* think one bit the worse of you," Iris pursued, impetuously. "You make me out, after all, to be a silly, ordinary woman, and it's horribly unjust. If you go away like this, please never come here again. I mean what I say. Never come to see me again!"

Lashmar seemed to hesitate, looked uncomfortable, then stepped back to his chair and sat down.

"That's right!" said Iris, with quiet triumph.

And she, too, resumed her chair.

CHAPTER VIII

Under the roof at Rivenoak was an attic which no one ever entered. The last person to do so was Sir Quentin Ogram; on a certain day in 1850—something, the baronet locked the door and put the key into his pocket, and during the more than forty years since elapsed the room had remained shut. It guarded neither treasure nor dire secret; the hidden contents were merely certain essays in the art of sculpture, sundry shapes in clay or in marble, the work of Sir Quentin himself when a very young man. Only one of these efforts had an abiding interest, that was a marble bust representing a girl, or young woman, of remarkable beauty, the head proudly poised, the eyes disdainfully direct, on the lips a smile which seemed to challenge the world's opinion. Not a refined or nobly suggestive face, but stamped with character, alive with vehement self-consciousness; a face to admire at a distance, not without misgiving as one pictured the flesh and blood original. Young Quentin had made a fine portrait. The model was his mistress, and, soon after the bust was finished, she became his wife.

Naturally, Sir Spencer and Lady Ogram were not bidden to the wedding; in fact, they knew nothing about it until a couple of years after, when, on the birth to him of a son and heir, Quentin took his courage in both hands and went down to Rivenoak to make the confession. He avowed somewhat less than the truth, finding it quite task enough to mitigate the circumstances of Mrs. Ogram's birth and breeding.

Our Friend the Charlatan

The exhibiting of portraits paved his way. This superbly handsome creature, adorned as became her present and prospective station, assuredly gave no shock at the first glance. By some freak of fate she had for parents a plumber and a washerwoman—"poor but very honest people," was Quentin's periphrase; their poverty of late considerably relieved by the thoughtful son-in-law, and their honesty perhaps fortified at the same time. Arabella (the beauty's baptismal name) unfortunately had two brothers; sisters, most happily, none. The brothers, however, were of a roaming disposition, and probably would tend to a colonial life. Quentin had counselled it, with persuasions which touched their sense of the fitting. So here was the case stated; Sir Spencer and his lady had but to reflect upon it, with what private conjectures might chance to enter their minds. Quentin was an only child; he had provided already for the continuance of the house; being of mild disposition, the baronet bowed his head to destiny, and, after a moderate interval, Arabella crossed the threshold of Rivenoak.

Of course there were one or two friends of Quentin's who knew all the facts of the case; these comrades he saw no more, having promised his wife never again to acknowledge or hold any intercourse with them. With his bachelor life had ended the artistic aspirations to which he had been wont to declare that he should for ever devote himself; Mrs. Ogram (she had been for a year or two a professional model) objected to that ungentlemanly pursuit with much more vigour and efficacy than the young man's parents, who had merely regretted that Quentin should waste his time and associate with a class of persons not regarded as worthy of much respect. Whether the dismissed cronies would talk or keep silence, who could say? Sir Spencer affected to believe that Arabella, when his son came to know her, was leading the life of a harmless, necessary sempstress, and that only by long entreaty, and under

Our Friend the Charlatan

every condition of decorum, had she been induced to
sit for her bust to the enthusiastic sculptor. Very
touching was the story of how, when the artist became
adorer and offered marriage, dear Arabella would not
hear of such a thing; how, when her heart began to
soften, she one day burst into tears and implored Mr.
Ogram to prove his love, not by wildly impossible
sacrifice, but simply by sending her to school, so that
she might make herself less unworthy to think of him
with pathetic devotion, and from a great distance, to
the end of her days. To school, in very deed, she had
been sent; that is to say, she had all manner of teachers,
first in England and then abroad, during the couple of
years before the birth of her child; and by this instruction Arabella profited so notably, that her language
made no glaring contrast to that of the civilized world,
and her mind seemed if anything more acute, more
circumspective, than women's generally in the sphere
to which she was now admitted. Sir Spencer and
Lady Ogram did not love her; they made no pretence
of doing so; and it may be feared that the lives of both
were shortened by chagrin and humiliation. At the
age of thirty or so, Quentin succeeded to the baronetcy.
In the same year his son died. No other offspring had
blessed, or was to bless, the romantic union.

Behold Arabella, erst of Camden Town, installed as
mistress of a house in Mayfair, and reigning over
Rivenoak. Inevitably, legends were rife about her;
where the exact truth was not known, people believed
worse. Her circle of society was but a narrow one;
but for two classes of well-dressed people, the unscrupulous snob and the cheerily indifferent, her
drawing-room would have been painfully bare. Some
families knew her because Sir Quentin was one of the
richest men in his county; certain persons accepted
her invitations because she was not exactly like other
hostesses, and could talk in rather an amusing way.
The years went on; scandal lost its verdure; Lady
Ogram was accepted as a queer woman with a queer

100

Our Friend the Charlatan

history, a rather vulgar eccentric, whose caprices and enterprises afforded agreeable matter for gossip. No one had ever ventured to assail her post-matrimonial reputation; she was fiercely virtuous, and would hold no terms with any woman not wholly above reproach. It had to be admitted that she bore herself with increasing dignity; moreover, that she showed a disposition to use her means and influence for what are called good ends. Towards the year 1870, the name of Lady Ogram began to be mentioned with respect.

Then her husband died. Sir Quentin had doubtless fallen short of entire happiness; before middle-age he was a taciturn, washed-out sort of man, with a look of timid anxiety. Perchance he regretted the visions of his youth, the dreams of glory in marble. When he became master of Rivenoak, and gave up his own London house, Arabella wished him to destroy all his sculpture, that no evidence might remain of the relations which had at first existed between them, no visible relic of the time which she refused to remember. Sir Quentin pleaded against this condemnation, and obtained a compromise. The fine bust, and a few other of his best things, were to be transferred to Rivenoak, and there kept under lock and key. Often had the baronet felt that he would like to look at the achievements of his hopeful time, but he never summoned courage to mount to the attic. His years went by in a mouldering inactivity. Once or twice he escaped alone to the Continent, and wandered for weeks about the Italian sculpture-galleries, living in the sunny, ardent past; he came back nerve-shaken and low in health. His death was sudden; "failure of the heart's action," said doctors, in their indisputable phrase; and Lady Ogram shut herself up for a time that she might not have the trouble of grieving before witnesses.

The baronet had behaved very generously to her in his last will and testament. Certain sums went to kinsfolk, to charities, to servants; his land and the bulk of his personal estate became Lady Ogram's own. She was a most capable and energetic woman of affairs; by her counsel, Sir Quentin had increased his wealth, and doubtless it seemed to him that no one had so good a right as she to enjoy its possession. The sacrifice he had made for her, though he knew it a blight upon his life, did but increase the power exercised over him by his arbitrary spouse; he never ceased to feel a certain pride in her,—pride in the beauty of her face and form, pride in the mental and moral vigour which made her so striking an exception to the rule that low-born English girls cannot rise above their native condition. Arabella's family had given him no trouble; holding it a duty to abandon them, she never saw parents or brothers after her marriage, and never spoke of them. Though violent of temper, she had never made her husband suffer from this characteristic; to be sure, Sir Quentin was from the first submissive, and rarely gave her occasion for displeasure. Over the baronet's grave in the little churchyard of Shawe she raised a costly monument. Its sole inscription was the name of the deceased, with the dates of his birth and death; Lady Ogram knew not, indeed, what else to add.

Fully another ten years elapsed before the widow's health showed any sign of failing. It was whilst passing a winter in Cornwall that she suffered a slight paralytic attack, speedily, in appearance, overcome, but the beginning of steady decline. Her intellectual activity had seemed to increase as time went on. Outgrowing various phases of orthodox religious zeal, outgrowing an unreasoned Conservatism in political and social views, she took up all manner of novel causes, and made Rivenoak a place of pilgrimage for the apostles of revolution. Yet the few persons who enjoyed close acquaintance with her knew that, at heart, she still nourished the pride of her rank, and that she had little if any genuine sympathy with democratic principles. Only a moral restlessness, a perhaps half-conscious lack of adaptation to her circumstances, accounted for the antinomianism which took hold upon her. Local politics found her commonly on the Conservative side, and, as certain indiscreet inquirers found to their cost, it was perilous to seek Lady Ogram's reasons for this course. But there came at length a schism between her and the Hollingford Tories; it dated from the initial stage of her great quarrel with their representative, Mr. Robb.

Lady Ogram, who was on the look-out in these latter years for struggling merit or talent which she could assist, interested herself in the son of a poor woman of Shawe, a boy who had won a scholarship at Hollingford School, and seemed full of promise. Being about sixteen, the lad had a great desire to enter a bank, and Lady Ogram put his case before the senior partner in the chief Hollingford banking-house, who was no other than Mr. Robb himself. Thus recommended, the boy soon had his wish; he was admitted to a clerkship. But less than six months proved him so unsuitable a member of the establishment, that he received notice of dismissal. Not till after this step had been taken did Lady Ogram hear of it. She was indignant at what seemed to her a lack of courtesy; she made inquiries, persuaded herself that her *protégé* had been harshly dealt with, and wrote a very pungent letter to the head of the firm. Mr. Robb did not himself reply, and the grave arguments urged by his subordinate served nothing to mitigate Lady Ogram's wrath. Insult had been added to injury; her ladyship straightway withdrew an account she kept at the bank, and dispatched to the M.P. a second letter, so forcible in its wording that it remained altogether without response.

Never half-hearted in her quarrels, Lady Ogram made known to all her acquaintances in the neighbourhood the opinion she had of Mr. Robb, and was in no wise discouraged when it came to her ears that the banker M.P. spoke of taking legal proceedings against her. It happened that Mr. Robb about this time addressed an

Our Friend the Charlatan

important meeting of his constituents. His speech was not brilliant, and Lady Ogram made great fun of the newspaper report. He reminded her, she said, of a specially stupid organ-grinder, grinding all out of time the vulgarest and most threadbare tunes. Henceforth, applying the name of a character in Dickens, she spoke of Hollingford's representative as Robb the Grinder; which, when Mr. Robb heard of it, as of course he did very soon, by no means sweetened his disposition towards "the termagant of Rivenoak"—a phrase he was supposed to have himself invented. "I'll grind her!" remarked the honourable gentleman, in the bosom of his family, and before long he found his opportunity. In the next parliamentary recess, he again spoke at Hollingford, this time at a festal meeting of the Conservative Club, where the gentility of town and district was well represented. His subject was the British Aristocracy, its glories in the past, its honours in the present, and the services it would render in a future dark with revolutionary menace. The only passage which had any particular meaning, or to which any one listened, ran pretty much thus :

"Ladies and gentlemen—ha—hum—we pride ourselves on the fact that—ha—our aristocracy is recruited from the choice representatives of the middle class—hum. The successful in every—that is to say in all the respectable branches of activity—ha—see before them the possibility, I would say the glorious possibility, of taking a seat in that illustrious Upper Chamber, which is the balance of our free Constitution. May the day never come, ladies and gentlemen, when—ha—the ranks of our nobility suffer intrusion from the unworthy —hum. And I would extend this remark to the order below that of peers, to the hereditary dignity which often rewards—ha—distinguished merit. May those simple titles, so pleasant—hum—to our ears, whether applied, I say, to man or woman—ha—hum—ha— never be degraded by ignoble bearers, by the low born —ha—by the tainted in repute—ha—in short by any

"You shall pay for this, you old hag!" shrieked the injured woman.

of those unfit, whether man or woman—ha—hum—
who, like vile weeds, are thrown up to the surface by
the, shall I say, deluge of democracy."

Every hearer saw the application of this, and Lady
Ogram had not long to wait before she read it in print.
Her temper that day was not mild. She had occasion
to controvert a friend, a Conservative lady, on some
little point of fact in an innocent gossip, and that lady
never again turned her steps to Rivenoak.

But worse was to come. Rarely had Lady Ogram
any trouble with her domestics; she chose them very
carefully, and kept them for a long time; they feared
her, but respected her power of ruling, the rarest gift
in women of whatever rank. Now it befell that the
maid in personal attendance upon her left to be married,
and in her engagement of a successor Lady Ogram
(perhaps because of her turbid state of mind just now)
was less circumspect than usual; she did not ascertain,
for instance, that the handmaid had a sister attached in
like capacity to the person of Mrs. Robb, nor did she note
certain indications of a temper far too closely resembling
her own. Before many days had passed, mistress and
attendant found themselves on cool terms, and from
this to the extremity of warmth was a step as fatally
easy as that from the sublime to the ridiculous. Lady
Ogram gave an order; it was imperfectly obeyed.
Lady Ogram, her eyes blazing with wrath, demanded
an explanation of this neglect; met with inadequate
excuses, she thundered and lightened. Any ordinary
domestic would have been terror-stricken, but this
handmaid echoed storm with storm; she fronted the
lady of Rivenoak as no one had ever dared to do.
The baronet's widow, losing all command of herself,
caught up the nearest missile—a little ivory-framed
hand-mirror—and hurled it at her antagonist, who was
struck full on the forehead, and staggered.

" You shall pay for this, you old hag," shrieked the
injured woman. " I'll pull you up before the Hollingford magistrates, and I'll tell them where you got your

manners. I know now that it's true, what Mrs. Robb told my sister, that you began life as a "—Saxon mono-syllable—" on London streets! "

Some minutes later, a servant sent to Lady Ogram's room by the retreating combatant found her mistress lying unconscious. For a day or two the lady of Riven-oak was thought to be near her end; but the struggle prolonged itself, hope was seen, and in three months' time the patient went about her garden and park in a bath-chair. Doctors opined that she would never walk again; yet, before six months were out, Lady Ogram was down in Cornwall, taking the air very much as of old. But her aspect had greatly changed; her body had shrunk, her face had become that of an old, old woman. Then it was that she renewed her falling locks, and appeared all at once with the mag-nificent crown of auburn hair which was henceforth to astonish beholders.

More than two years had now elapsed since that serious illness. Lady Ogram's age was seventy-nine. Medical science declared her a marvel, and prudently held it possible that she might live to ninety.

What to do with her great possessions had long been a harassing subject of thought with Lady Ogram. She wished to use them for some praiseworthy pur-pose, which, at the same time, would perpetuate her memory. More than twenty years ago she had in-structed her solicitor, Mr. Kerchever, to set on foot an inquiry for surviving members of her own family. The name was Tomalin. Search had gone on with more or less persistence, and Tomalins had come to light, but in no case could a clear connection be established with the genealogical tree, which, so far as Arabella had knowledge of it, rooted in the per-son of John Tomalin of Hackney, her grandfather, by trade a cabinet-maker, deceased somewhere about 1840. Since her illness, Lady Ogram had fallen into the habit of brooding over the days long gone by. She revived the memory of her home in Camden

Our Friend the Charlatan

Town, of her life as a not-ill-cared-for child, of her experiences in a West-end workroom, her temptations, multiplied as she grew to the age of independence, her contempt of girls who " went wrong," those domestic quarrels and miseries which led to her breaking away and becoming an artists' model. How remote it all was! Had she not lived through it in a prior existence, with re-birth to the life of luxury and command which alone seemed natural to her ? All but sixty years had passed since she said good-bye for ever to Camden Town, and for thirty years at least, the greater part of her married life, she had scarce turned a thought in that direction. Long ago her father and mother were dead ; she knew of it only from Mr. Kerchever, who, after the death of Sir Quentin, gave her a full account of the baronet's pecuniary relations with the Tomalin household. No blackmailing had ever been practised; the plumber and his wife were content with what they received (Arabella felt a satisfaction in remembering that of her own accord she had asked her husband to do something for them, when she might very well have disregarded them altogether), and the two brothers, who were supposed to have left England, had never been heard of again. The failure to discover any one named Tomalin whom she could regard as of her own blood was now a disappointment to Lady Ogram ; sometimes she even fretted about it. Mr. Kerchever had it in charge to renew the inquiry, to use every possible means, and spare no outlay. The old woman yearned for kinsfolk, as a younger sometimes does for offspring of her own.

The engagement of Constance Bride as resident secretary resulted no doubt from this craving in the old lady's mind for human affection. Perhaps she felt that she had behaved with less than justice to the girl's father; moreover, Constance as a little child had greatly won her liking, and in the girl she perceived a capability, an independence, which strongly appealed to

Our Friend the Charlatan

her. Thus far they had got on very well together, and
Lady Ogram began to think that she had found in
Constance what she had long been looking for—one of
her own sex equal to the burden of a great responsibility and actuated by motives pure enough to make
her worthy of a high privilege.

Had her girlhood fallen into brutal hands, Arabella's
native savagery would doubtless have developed strange
excesses in a life of social outlawry. The companionship of Quentin Ogram, a mild idealist, good-
naturedly critical of the commonplace, though it often
wearied her and irritated her primitive instincts, was
a civilizing influence, the results of which continued
to manifest themselves after the baronet's death. On
the æsthetic side she profited not at all; to the beautiful she ever presented a hard insensibility, and in
latter years she had ceased even to affect pleasure in
the things of nature or art which people about her
admired. Her flowery and leafy drawing-room indicated
no personal taste; it came of a suggestion by her
gardener when she converted to her own use the former
smoking-room; finding that people admired and
thought it original, she made the arrangement a
permanence, anxious only that the plants exhibited
should be rarer and finer than those possessed by
her neighbours. On the other hand, her moral life
from the first showed capacity of expansion, and held
at its service an intellect, of no very fine quality indeed,
but acute and energetic. In all practical affairs she
was greatly superior to the average woman, adding to
woman's meticulous sense of interest and persistent
diplomacy a breadth of view found only in exceptional
males; this faculty the circumstances of her life richly
fostered, and, by anomaly, advancing years enlarged,
instead of contracting, the liberality of her spirit.
After fifty years told, when ordinary mortals have long
since given their measure in heart and brain, Lady
Ogram steadily advanced. Solitary possessor of wealth,
autocrat over a little world of her own, instead of

108

Our Friend the Charlatan

fossilizing in dull dignity she proved herself receptive of many influences with which the time was fraught. She cast off beliefs, or what she had held as such, and donned others ; she exchanged old prejudices for new forms of zeal ; above all, she chose to be in touch with youth and aspiration rather than with disillusioned or retrospective age. Only when failing health shadowed the way before her did she begin to lose that confident carriage of the mind which, together with her profound materialism, had made worry and regret and apprehension things unknown to her. Thus, when aged, but by no means senile, she began to suffer a disquiet of conscience (so common in our day), which had nothing to do with spiritual perceptiveness, but came of habitual concentration on every-day cares and woes, on the life of the world as apart from that of the soul. Through sleepless nights, Lady Ogram brooded over the contrast between her own exaltation and the hopeless level of the swinking multitude. What should she do with her money ? The question perturbed her with a sense of responsibility which could have had no meaning for her in earlier years. How could she best use the vast opportunity for good which lay to her hand ?

Endless were the projects she formed, rejected, took up again. Vast was the correspondence she held with all manner of representative people, seeking for information, accumulating reports, lectures, argumentative pamphlets, theoretic volumes, in mass altogether beyond her ability to cope with ; now-a-days, her secretary read and digested and summarized with tireless energy. Lady Ogram had never cared much for reading ; she admired Constance's speed and intelligence and power of grappling with printed matter. But that she had little faith in the future of her own sex, she would have been tempted to say, " There is the coming woman." Miss Bride's companionship was soon indispensable to her ; she had begun to dread the thought of being left alone with her multiplying solicitudes and uncertainties.

Her great resource in these days was her savage

hatred of Mr. Robb and his family and all in any way
adhering to him. Whenever she fixed her mind on
that, all wider troubles fled into space, and she was the
natural woman of her prime once more. Since making
the acquaintance of Dyce Lashmar, she had thought
of little but this invigorating theme. At last she had
found the man to stand against Robb the Grinder, the
man of hope, the political and moral enthusiast who
would sweep away that mass of rotten privilege and
precedent encumbering the borough of Hollingford.
She wrote to all her friends, at Hollingford and throughout the county, making known that the ideal candidate
in the Liberal cause had at last been discovered. And
presently she sent out invitations to a dinner, on a day
a fortnight ahead, which should assemble some dozen
of her faithful, to meet and hear the eloquent young
philosopher.

Excitement was not good for Lady Ogram's health ;
the doctors agreed in prescribing tranquillity, and she
had so far taken their advice as to live of late in com-
parative retirement. Her observant companion noticed
that the conversations with Lashmar had been followed
by signs of great fatigue ; an agitated manner, a temper
even more uncertain than usual, and physical symptoms
which Constance had learnt to look for, proved during
the ensuing days that the invalid was threatened with
another crisis. Acting on her own responsibility,
Constance addressed a note to Dr. Baldwin, who
presently, as if making a casual call, dropped in to see
his patient. The doctor knew how to comport himself
with Lady Ogram. He began by remarking cheerfully
how well she looked, and asking whether she had settled
the details of her summer holiday. Dull and rather
sullen of air, Lady Ogram replied with insignificant
brevities ; then, as the doctor chatted on about local
matters, her interest gradually awoke.

"Anything more been done about the new hospital ? "
she asked.

"Oh, there are promises, but nothing really import-

ant. It'll cost far more money than there seems any
chance as yet of getting. We ought to buy that bit of
land I told you about on Burgess Hill. The price is
high, but it's a perfect situation, and I'm afraid it'll
be going to the builders if something isn't soon done."

Lady Ogram would have purchased the site in
question long since, for it was her purpose to act
decisively in this matter of the much-needed hospital,
but it happened that the unspeakable Robb was the
man who had first drawn public attention to the suit-
ability of Burgess Hill, and Lady Ogram was little
inclined to follow where Robb had led. She hoped to
find a yet better site, and by undertaking at once both
purchase of land and construction of the building, with
a liberal endowment added, to leave in the lurch all
philanthropic rivals. For years she had possessed plans
and pictures of "The Lady Ogram Hospital." She
cared for no enterprise, however laudable, in which she
could only be a sharer; the initiative must be hers, and
hers the glory.

Discreetly, Dr. Baldwin worked round to the subject
of his patient's health. He hoped she was committing
no imprudence in the way of excessive mental exertion.
It seemed to him—perhaps he was mistaken—that talk
agitated her more than usual. Quiet and repose—quiet
and repose.

That afternoon Lady Ogram was obliged to lie down,
a necessity she always disliked in the daytime, and for
two or three days she kept her room. Constance now
and then read to her, but persuaded her to speak as
little as possible of exciting subjects. She saw no one
but this companion. Of late she had been in the habit
of fixing her look upon Constance, as though much
occupied with thoughts concerning her. When she
felt able to move about again, they sat together one
morning on the terrace before the house, and Lady
Ogram, after a long inspection of the other's countenance,
asked suddenly :

" Do you often hear from your father ? "

" Not often. Once in two months, perhaps."

" I suppose you are not what is called a good daughter ? "

Constance found the remark rather embarrassing, for it hit a truth of which, though at long intervals, she had been uneasily aware.

" Father and I have not much in common," she replied. " I respect him, and I hope he isn't quite without some such feeling for me. But we go such different ways."

" Does he believe what he pretends to ? "

" He has never made any pretences at all, Lady Ogram. That's his character, and I try to think that it's mine too."

" Well—well," exclaimed the old lady, " I suppose you're not going to quarrel with me because I ask a simple question ? You have a touchy temper, you know. If I had had a temper like yours, I should have very few friends at my age."

Constance averted her eyes, and said gravely :

" I try to correct myself by your example."

" You might do worse. By the bye—if you won't snap my nose off—I suppose your father isn't very well to do ? "

" He's very poor. Such men always are."

Lady Ogram lay back and mused. She had no affection for Constance, yet felt more kindly disposed to her than to any other girl or woman she knew. Consciously or not, she had come to feel a likeness between her own mind and that of the clergyman's daughter; she interpreted Constance's thoughts by her own. Indeed, there was a certain resemblance, both mental and moral. In one regard it showed itself strikingly, the contempt for their own sex which was natural to both. As a mere consequence of her birth, Arabella Tomalin had despised and distrusted womanhood; the sentiment is all but universal in low-born girls. Advancing in civilization, she retained this instinct, and confirmed the habit of mind by the results of her experience; having always sought for meanness and incapacity in the female world, she naturally had found a great deal of it. By another way, Constance Bride had arrived at very much the same results; she made no friends among women, and desired none. Lady Ogram and she agreed in their disdain for all " woman " movements; what progress they aimed at concerned the race at large, with merely a slighting glance towards the special circumstances of its sex-burdened moiety. Moreover, the time-worn woman perceived in her young associate a personal ambition which she read by the light of her own past. She divined in Constance a hunger for things at once substantial and brilliant, a smouldering revolt against poverty and dependence. Not for the first time did she remark and study such a disposition; the symptoms were very well known to Lady Ogram; but never before had she met it in combination with genuine ability and other characteristics which she held in esteem.

"Let us talk about our future Member," were her next words.

They talked of Dyce Lashmar.

CHAPTER IX

IT was natural that Lady Ogram should from the beginning have suspected Miss Bride of a peculiar interest in Dyce Lashmar. When first she introduced her friend's name, Constance a little exaggerated the tone of impartiality, and in subsequent conversation she was never quite herself on this topic. Evidently she thought of Lashmar more often than she cared to have it known; a sort of subdued irritation now and then betrayed itself in her when she assented to a favourable comment regarding him, and a certain suspense of judgment—quite unlike her familiar mental attitude—always marked her agreement in hopes for his future. The old woman of the world interpreted this by her own lights. At moments it vexed her, for she did not like to be mystified; at others, it touched a chord of sympathy in some very obscure corner of her being. And, as no practical problem could be put before her without her wishing to solve it autocratically, Lady Ogram soon formed a project with regard to these two persons, a project which took firmer consistence, and pleased her more, the more she pondered it.

On the appointed day, Lashmar arrived at Rivenoak. He was allowed to spend an hour in reposeful solitude ere being admitted to his hostess's presence. Conducted at length to the green drawing-room, he found Lady Ogram alone. She scrutinized him with friendly but searching eye, gave him her hand, and bade him be seated near her.

"I have another visitor coming from London to-day; an old friend of mine, Mrs. Toplady."

Our Friend the Charlatan

Where had Dyce heard that name? Somewhere, certainly. He tried hard to remember, but without success.

"I think you will like her," pursued Lady Ogram, "and she will perhaps be useful to you. She tries to know everybody who is, or is going to be, somebody. She'll ask you, no doubt, to her house in Pont Street, where you'll meet a great many fools and some reasonable people. She herself, I may tell you, is no fool; but she has a good deal more patience with that sort than I ever had, and so, of course, has many more friends. She's what they call a leader of Society, yet she doesn't grudge leaving London for a day or two in the beginning of the Season to do me a service."

"I seem to know her name," said Dyce.

"Of course you do, if you ever read about what Society is doing."

Lady Ogram always uttered the word with a contemptuous lip, but plainly she did not dislike to have it understood that Society, in certain of its representatives, took respectful account of her.

"And now," she continued, "I want to tell you about some other friends of mine you're to meet at dinner to-morrow. Most of them belong to Hollingford, and you will have to know them."

Very pungently did she sketch these personages. When her listener showed amusement, Lady Ogram was pleased; if he seemed to find the picture too entertaining, she added—"But he—or she—is not a fool, remember that." So did the talk go on, until a servant entered to announce the arrival of Mrs. Toplady, who had gone to her room, and being rather tired, would rest there till dinner-time.

"Where is Miss Bride?" asked Lady Ogram.

"Miss Bride has just returned from Hollingford, my lady."

"I remember," said the hostess to her guest. "She had an appointment with Mrs. Gallantry, who has her eye on a house for the training-school. I suppose we must set the thing going; there's no harm in it."

Our Friend the Charlatan

Constance entered in a few minutes, greeted Lashmar as if she saw him every day, and began to talk about Mrs. Gallantry's project.

When, a couple of hours later, Dyce came down dressed for dinner, Mrs. Toplady was already in the drawing-room. He heard her voice, a well-modulated contralto which held the ear, and looking in that direction, saw a tall, dark-robed woman, of middle age, with a thin face, its lines rather harsh, but in general effect handsome, and a warm complexion, brightly red upon the prominent cheek-bones. Jewellery sparkled in her hair, from her white throat, and on her fingers. As Lashmar came forward, she finished what she was saying, and turned her eyes upon him with expectant interest; a smile at the corner of her lips had a certain mischievousness, quite good-humoured but a little perturbing to one who encountered it, together with the direct dark gaze, for the first time. Introduction having been performed with Lady Ogram's wonted carelessness, Mrs. Toplady said at once:

"I know a friend of yours, Mr. Lashmar,—Mrs. Woolstan. Perhaps she has spoken to you of me?"

"She has," Dyce replied, remembering now that it was from Mrs. Woolstan he had heard her name.

"Why, how's that?" exclaimed the hostess. "You never told me about it, Mr. Lashmar."

Dyce had much ado to conceal his annoyed embarrassment. He wondered whether Mrs. Woolstan had made known the fact of his tutorship, which he did not care to publish, preferring to represent himself as having always held an independent position. With momentary awkwardness he explained that Mrs. Toplady's name had but once casually passed Mrs. Woolstan's lips in his hearing, and that till now he had forgotten the circumstance.

"I saw her yesterday," said the lady of the roguish lips. "She's in trouble about parting with her little boy—just been sent to school."

"Ah—yes."

Our Friend the Charlatan

" Very sweet face, hasn't she ? Is the child like her?
I never saw him—perhaps *you* never did, either ? "

Mrs. Toplady had a habit, not of looking steadily at
an interlocutor, but of casting a succession of quick
glances, which seemed to the person thus inspected
much more searching than a fixed gaze. Though vastly
relieved by the assurance that Mrs. Woolstan had used
discretion concerning him, Dyce could not become at
ease under that restless look ; he felt himself gauged
and registered, though with what result was by no
means discernible in Mrs. Toplady's countenance.
Those eyes of hers must have gauged a vast variety
of men; her forehead told of experience and meditation
thereon. Of all the women he could remember, she
impressed him as the least manageable according to
his method. Compared with her, Lady Ogram seemed
mere ingenuousness and tractability.

" And, pray, *who* is Mrs. Woolstan ? " the hostess was
asking, with a blunt insistence.

" A charming little woman," replied Mrs. Toplady,
sincerity in look and voice. " I knew her before her
marriage, which, perhaps, was not quite—but the poor
man is dead. A sister of hers married into my
husband's family. She plays beautifully—an exquisite
touch."

They were summoned to dinner. At table it was
Mrs. Toplady who led the conversation, but in such a
way as to assume no undue prominence, rather she
seemed to be all attention to others' talk, and, her smile
notwithstanding, to listen with the most open-minded
interest to whatever was said. Her manner to Lady
Ogram was marked with deference, at times with something like affectionate gentleness; to Miss Bride she
paid the compliment of amiable gravity ; and towards
Lashmar she could not have borne herself more
respectfully—at all events in language—if he had
been in the Cabinet; every word which fell from him
she seemed to find suggestive, illuminative, and to
treasure it in her memory. After dinner, Dyce received

from her his cue for drawing-room oratory; he was led into large discourse, and Mrs. Toplady's eyes beamed the most intelligent sympathy. None the less did roguery still lurk at the corner of her lips, so that from time to time the philosopher fidgeted a little, and asked himself uneasily what that smile meant.

At nine o'clock next morning, Lashmar and Constance sat down to breakfast alone. Mrs. Toplady rarely showed herself much before noon.

"If the sky clears," said Constance, "Lady Ogram will drive at eleven, and you are invited to accompany her."

"And you?" asked Dyce.

"I have work for two or three hours."

Lashmar chipped at an egg, a thoughtful smile upon his countenance.

"Can you tell me anything about Mrs. Toplady?" he inquired.

"Only what I have heard from Lady Ogram."

Constance sketched a biography. The lady had been twice married, first in early youth to a man who had nothing, and who became consumptive; during his illness they suffered from dire poverty, and, at her husband's death, the penniless widow received great kindness from Lady Ogram, whose acquaintance she had made accidentally. Two years afterwards, she married a northern manufacturer of more than twice her age; an instance, said the story-teller, of natural reaction. It chanced that a royal personage, on a certain public occasion, became the guest of the manufacturer, who had local dignities; and so well did Mrs. Toplady play her part of hostess that royalty deigned to count her henceforth among its friends. Her husband would have received a title, but an inopportune malady cut short his life. A daughter of the first marriage still lived; she had wedded into the army, and was little heard of. Mrs. Toplady, a widow unattached, took her ease in the world.

"She has seven or eight thousand a year," said

Constance, "and spends it all on herself. Naturally she is a very polished and ornamental person."

"Something more than that, I fancy," returned Dyce, musing.

"Oh, as Lady Ogram would say, she is not a fool."

Dyce smiled, and let the topic pass. He was enjoying his breakfast; certain dainties flattered his palate, and, under this genial influence, he presently felt moved to intimate speech.

"You live very comfortably here, don't you? You have no objection on principle to this kind of thing?" —his waving hand indicated the well-spread table.

"I? Certainly not. Why should I object to civilization?"

"I'm not quite sure that I have got at your point of view yet," answered Dyce good-humouredly. "You know mine. The tools to him who can use them. A breakfast such as this puts us at an advantage over the poorer world for the rest of the day. But the advantage isn't stolen. How came we here? Is it merely the cost of the railway ticket that transports me from my rasher in a London lodging to reindeer's tongue and so on in the breakfast-room at Rivenoak? I fancy not."

He paused. Was it wise to hint before Constance that he had lived rather poorly? He hoped, and believed, that she knew nothing definite as to his circumstances.

"Why, no," she assented, with a smile. "I, for example, have perhaps some part in it."

Dyce gazed at her, surprised at this frankness.

"You certainly have. And it reminds me that I may seem very ungrateful; I have hardly said thank you. Shake hands, and believe that I am *not* ungrateful."

She hesitated. Not till the hand had been extended to her for an appreciable moment, did she give her own. In doing so, she wore a hard smile.

"So this evening," went on Dyce, "I meet my sup-

119

Our Friend the Charlatan

porters. Lady Ogram gave me an account of them yesterday. Tell me what you think. May I be myself with these people? Or must I talk twaddle? I dislike twaddle, as you know, but I don't want to spoil my chances. You understand how I look at this business? My object in life is to gain influence, that I may spread my views. Parliament, I take it, is the best means. Considering the nature of the average elector, I don't think one need worry about the means one uses to get elected. I won't tell lies; that goes against the grain with me. But I must be practical."

Constance watched him, and seemed to weigh his remarks.

"As for twaddle," she said, "I shouldn't advise much of it in Mrs. Toplady's hearing."

"You are right. That would never do. I suppose that woman may be of use to me?"

"Yes, I think so," replied Constance seriously. "You are, of course, aware that a man doesn't become parliamentary candidate by just walking into a town and saying—'Behold me! your votes!' There is such a thing as party organization."

Dyce looked at her with involuntary respect. He reminded himself that "twaddle" was as little likely to have weight with Miss Bride as with Mrs. Toplady.

"She knows political people?" he asked.

"She knows everybody—or can know. I confess I don't understand why. In any case, it'll be well for you to have her good word. Lady Ogram can do a good deal here, but I'm not sure that she could make your acceptance by the Liberals a certain thing."

"Of course, I have thought of that," said Dyce. Then, thinking he had spoken in too off-hand a way, he added graciously, "I needn't say that I regard your advice as valuable. I shall often ask for it."

Constance was mute.

"I suppose I may take it for granted that you wish for my success?"

"To be sure. I wish for it because Lady Ogram does."

Our Friend the Charlatan

Dyce felt inclined to object to this, but Constance's face did not invite to further talk on the point.

"At all events," he continued, "it seems no other candidate has been spoken of. The party isn't sanguine; they look upon Robb as unassailable—*sedet in æternumque sedebit*. But we shall see about it. Presently I should like to talk over practical details with you. I suppose I call myself Unionist? These questions of day-to-day politics, how paltry they are! Amazing that men can get excited about them. I shall have to look on it as a game, and amuse myself for certain hours of the day—a relaxation from serious thought and work. You haven't told me, by the bye, what you think of my bio-sociological system."

"I've been considering it. How was it suggested to you?"

Constance asked the question so directly, and with so keen a look, that she all but disconcerted the philosopher.

"Oh, it grew out of my reading and observation—grew bit by bit—no armed Pallas leaping to sudden life."

"You have worked it out pretty thoroughly."

"In outline, yes."

Dyce read the newspapers, and walked a little in the garden. Punctually at eleven Lady Ogram descended. The carriage was at the door.

This stately drive, alone with the autocrat of Rivenoak, animated the young man. He felt that the days of his insignificance were over, that his career—the career so often talked about—had really begun. A delightful surprise gave piquancy to his sensations; had he cared to tell himself the truth, he would have known that, whatever his self-esteem, he had never quite believed in the brilliant future which he liked to imagine. It is one thing to merit advancement, quite another to secure it. Yet here he was, driving with a great lady, his friend, his admirer; driving towards the excitement of political contest, perhaps towards a seat in Parliament, and who could say what subsequent distinctions? Lady Ogram was not the woman to aid half-heartedly where her feelings were interested. Pretty surely he could count upon large support, so long as he did not disappoint his benefactress. For the present he had no anxieties—thanks to another woman, of whom, in truth, he thought scarcely once in twenty-four hours. He lived gloriously at ease; his faculties were expanding under this genial sunshine of prosperity. Even in aspect he was a man of more importance than a few weeks ago; his cheeks had coloured, his eyes rested with a new dignity on all they saw.

They returned, and as Lady Ogram was entering the hall, a servant made a respectful announcement.

"Mr. Kerchever is here, my lady."

"Mr. Kerchever? Indeed?"

With an unusually quick step she moved towards the library. There, occupied with a newspaper, sat a man whose fifty years still represented the prime of life, a tall, athletically-built man, his complexion that of a school-boy after summer holidays, his brown hair abundant and crisp, spring and stay declared in every muscle of his limbs and frame. Lightly he arose, gracefully he swung forward, with the bow and smile of one who knows not constraint. Mr. Kerchever followed the law, but he also, whenever a chance offered, followed the hounds, and with more gusto. At school and university he had won palms; that his place in academic lists was less glorious mattered little to one who had a comfortable seat awaiting him in the paternal office.

"And what brings you here?" asked Lady Ogram, unable to subdue an agitation which confused her utterance.

"I have made a discovery which will interest you," replied Mr. Kerchever, in a voice which sounded very strong and melodious by contrast.

"What is it? Don't keep me waiting."

Our Friend the Charlatan

"I have found a grand-daughter of your brother Joseph Tomalin."

The listener drew a deep, tremulous sigh.

"Can't you go on?", she exclaimed thickly, just as the lawyer was resuming.

"I'll tell you how I came upon her track——"

"I don't care anything about that!" cried the old lady, with violent irritation. "*What* is she? *Where* is she?"

"Miss May Tomalin is twenty-five years old. Her parents are dead. She lives with relatives of her mother in the town of Northampton. She has been well educated, well brought up altogether. And she possesses an income of something less than a hundred a year."

Again Lady Ogram drew a deep breath. Her face was hotly flushed; her hands trembled; a great joy shone from the transformed countenance.

"Thank goodness!" broke from her hoarsely. "Thank goodness!" Then, with sudden alarm, "I suppose you're making no idiotic mistake?"

"That kind of mistake, Lady Ogram," responded Mr. Kerchever, with a tolerant motion of the eyebrows, "is not quite in my way. Indeed, I'm not in the habit of making mistakes of any kind. You may be sure I have taken every precaution before coming here with such news as this."

"All right! What are you angry about? Lawyers and doctors and parsons—there's no talking with them, they're so touchy. Can't you go on? Here's a girl falls out of the clouds, and I'm to show no curiosity about her! You drive me crazy with your roundabout nonsense. Go *on*, can't you!"

Mr. Kerchever eyed his client curiously. He was not offended, for he had known Lady Ogram long, and had received traditions regarding her from a time before he was born; but he could not help being struck with her face and manner; they made him uneasy.

123

Our Friend the Charlatan

"I will tell you everything forthwith," he resumed, "but I must beg you to control yourself, Lady Ogram. I do so out of regard for your health. Emotion is natural, but now that you know the news is all good, your excellent sense should tranquillize you. Pray let us talk quietly."

Lady Ogram glanced at him, but nodded acquiescence.

"I'm as cool as you are. Talk as much as you like."

"A few days ago I had occasion to look through the lists of a London university calendar. My eye fell on the name Tomalin, and, of course, I was interested. May Tomalin matriculated at London three years ago. I could find no further record of her, but inquiries were easy, and they guided me to Northampton. There I made the acquaintance of a Mr. Rooke, a manufacturer, in whose house Miss Tomalin is resident, and has been for a good many years; to be precise, since she was nine years old. Without trouble I discovered the girl's history. Her grandfather, Joseph Tomalin, died in Canada forty-seven years ago——"

"How do you know it was Joe—my brother?" asked the listener sharply.

"All these things you can follow out for yourself in detail in the papers I will leave with you. This Joseph had a brother Thomas, and his age corresponds very well with that of your own brother Joseph. Thomas Tomalin has left no trace, except the memory of his name preserved by the wife of Joseph, and handed on to her son, who, in turn, spoke of Thomas to his wife, who has been heard by Mrs. Rooke (her sister) to mention that fact in the family history. What is more, I find a vague tradition that a sister of Joseph and Thomas made a brilliant marriage."

"How is it that your advertisements were never seen by these people—these Rookes?"

"So it happened, that's all one can say. I have known many such failures.—May Tomalin was born at Toronto, where her father, also a Joseph, died in '80.

124

Our Friend the Charlatan

Her mother, an Englishwoman, came back to England in '81, bringing May, the only child; she settled at Northampton, and, on her death in the following year, May passed into the care of the Rookes. She has no surviving relative of her own name. Her father, a builder, left a little money, which now provides the young lady with her income."

From a state of choleric flurry Lady Ogram was passing into irritable delight.

"Better late than never," she exclaimed, "but I can't see why you didn't find the girl ages ago."

"We only knew that your brothers went to Australia. Thomas, no doubt, died there. The story of Joseph's wanderings is irrecoverable; we must be content to have satisfactory evidence of his death, and of this girl's descent from him."

"Well, and why haven't you brought her?"

"I saw no need for such precipitancy. Miss Tomalin has not yet been informed of what is going on. Of course she is her own mistress, free to accept any invitation that may be offered her. The Rookes seem to be quiet, decent people, in easy circumstances; no trouble of any kind is to be feared from them. You may act at your leisure. Here is the address. Of course if you would like me to return to North-ampton——"

"She must come at once!" said Lady Ogram, starting up. "Would the Crows understand a telegram?"

"The Rookes? I think it would be better to write. Naturally, I have not let them know your name. At first I found Mr. Rooke rather disposed to stand upon his dignity; but a firm of Northampton solicitors vouched for my *bona-fides*, and then things were smoother. No, I don t think I would telegraph."

"Then go to Northampton and bring the girl back with you."

"If you wish it."

"When is there. a train? Oh, there's the luncheon-bell. Of course you must eat. Come and eat. I have some one staying here that I should like you to know —our Liberal candidate at the next election."

" Oh, so you have found one ? "

"Of course I have. Didn't I write to tell you? A lot of people dine here this evening to meet him. Perhaps you could stay over night ? Yes, now I come to think of it, I should like you to dine with us. You shall go to Northampton to-morrow. Write to Rooky this afternoon." Lady Ogram grew sportive. " Prepare him. Come along, now, to lunch ; you look hungry."

" Just one word. You are quite sure it will be wise to bring this young lady at once to Rivenoak ? "

" You say she knows how to behave herself ! "

" Certainly. But the change in her position will be rather sudden, don't you think ? And—if I may venture—how can you be sure that Miss Tomalin will recommend herself to you ? "

" Isn't she of my own blood ? " cried Lady Ogram, in a high croak of exasperation. " Isn't she my brother's grandchild—the only creature of my own blood living ? "

" I merely urge a little prudence."

" Is the girl a fool ? "

" I have no reason to think so. But she has led a quiet, provincial life."

" Come and eat ! " cried Lady Ogram. " We'll talk again afterwards."

Mrs. Toplady joined them in the dining-room, as she seated herself. " Everybody's late to-day. Mr. Kerchever—Mr. Lashmar—I want you to know each other. Mr. Lashmar, what have you been doing all the morning ? Why, of course, you had a drive with me—I had forgotten ! Do sit down and let us eat. If every one's as hungry as I am ! "

For all that, she satisfied her appetite with one or two mouthfuls, and talked on in a joyously excited strain, to the astonishment of Constance, who saw that Mr. Kerchever must have brought some very important

Our Friend the Charlatan

news. Lashmar, also exhilarated, kept up conversation with Mrs. Toplady. It was a vivacious company, Miss Bride being the only person who spoke little. She was commonly silent amid general talk, but her eyes travelled from face to face, reading, commenting.

Mr. Kerchever consented to stay over night. In the afternoon he had a stroll with Lashmar, but they did not much enjoy each other's society. Dyce took no interest whatever in sports or games, and the athletic lawyer understood by politics a recurring tussle between two parties, neither of which had it in its power to do much good or harm to the country; of philosophy and science (other than that of boxing) he knew about as much as the woman who swept his office. Privately, Mr. Kerchever opined that this young man was a conceited pedant, who stood no chance whatever of being elected to Parliament. When questioned by Lady Ogram, he inquired whether Mr. Lashmar had means.

" Oh, he has money enough," was the careless answer. " But it's his brains that we count upon."

" I never heard that they went for much in politics," said Mr. Kerchever.

CHAPTER X

THE dinner went off very well indeed.

It was not merely her animus against Mr. Robb
which supported Lady Ogram's belief in the future
of the Liberals at Hollingford. A certain restiveness
could be noted in the public mind, heretofore so
obedient to the long Tory tradition. Mr. Breakspeare's paper certainly had an increasing sale, and
an allusion to Mr. Robb in public gatherings other
than political was not so sure of cordial response as
formerly. This might only imply a personal dissatisfaction with the borough's representative, who of late
had been very visibly fossilizing; it would be difficult
to explain a marked reaction in Hollingford against
the tendencies of the country at large. Still, a
number of more or less active and intelligent persons
had begun to talk of stoutly contesting the Tory seat,
and with these the lady of Rivenoak had active communication. They gathered about her this evening;
enjoyed the excellent meal provided for them; inspected Mr. Dyce Lashmar, and listened attentively
even to his casual remarks. Mr. Lashmar might or
might not prove to be the candidate of their choice;
there was plenty of time to think about that; in the
meantime, no one more suitable stood before them,
and, having regard to Lady Ogram's social authority,
considerable from one point of view, they were very
willing to interest themselves in a man of whom she
thought so highly. Very little was definitely known
about him. He was understood to be a gentleman of
means and erudite leisure, nor did his appearance

128

Our Friend the Charlatan

conflict with this description. Now and then Dyce's talk had an impressive quality; he spoke for the most part in brief, pregnant sentences, which seemed the outcome of solid thought and no little experience. Constance Bride, observing him studiously, often admired his grave, yet easy, bearing, his facile, yet never careless, speech. Herself in doubt as to his real weight, whether as man or politician, she carefully watched the impression he produced on others; on the whole it seemed to be favourable, and once or twice she caught a remark decidedly eulogistic. This pleased her. Like everybody else this evening, she was in good spirits.

Mrs. Toplady, much observed and courted, but seemingly quite indifferent to homage, watched the scene with her eyes of placid good-humour, the roguish smile ever and again appearing on her lips. She lost no opportunity of letting fall a laudatory word concerning Dyce Lashmar. Her demeanour with humdrum persons was courteous amiability almost in excess; to the more intelligent she behaved with a humorous frankness which was very captivating. At a certain moment of the evening, she found occasion to sit down by Constance Bride, and Constance would have been more than human had she altogether resisted the charm of that fine contralto modulating graceful compliments. Mrs. Toplady had read the report of the social work at Shawe; it interested her keenly; she could not sufficiently admire the philanthropic energy which had been put into this undertaking—in so great a part, as she heard, due to Miss Bride's suggestions.

"I am glad to hear from Lady Ogram," she said, "that there is a probability of your being in town before long. If so, I hope you will let me have a long talk with you, about all sorts of things. One of them, of course, must be Mr. Lashmar's candidature."

Saying this, Mrs. Toplady beamed with kindness. Constance noted the words and the look for future reflection. At this moment, she was occupied with the news that Lady Ogram thought of going to London, no hint of any such intention having before this reached her ear.

In the course of the afternoon, Lady Ogram had held private colloquy with her guest from the brilliant world, a conversation more intimate on her part than any that had ever passed between them. Such expansion was absolutely necessary to the agitated old lady, and she deemed it good fortune that a confidante in whom she put so much trust chanced to be near her. Speaking of Lashmar, she mentioned his acquaintance with Lord Dymchurch, and inquired whether Mrs. Toplady knew that modest peer.

"He is only a name to me," was the reply, "and I should rather like to see him in the flesh. Mr. Lashmar must bring him to Pont Street—if he can."

"That's what I'm a little doubtful about," said Lady Ogram. "I have been thinking it might help us if a real live lord happened to walk about Hollingford with our candidate. We have to use means, you know."

The old lady grimaced her scorn, and the leader of Society was very roguish indeed about the lips. One thing Mrs. Toplady had learnt which interested her, that her autocratic friend's faith in Dyce Lashmar as the "coming man" was unaffected and sturdy. She mused upon this. Rivenoak had often supplied entertainment to her sportive mind; now, as shadows of night were gathering over it, there seemed to be preparing in this corner of the human stage a spectacle of unforeseen piquancy.

Also with Mr. Kerchever the old lady had had an afternoon talk. Her emotion being now more under command, she could listen to the solicitor's advice, which dissuaded from abrupt action with reference to Miss Tomalin. Mr. Kerchever thought it would be unwise to reveal all the interest she felt in this late-discovered representative of her family. Had he not better write to Mr. Rooke, saying that his client, a widowed lady living at her country house, hoped to have the pleasure of making her young relative's acquaintance, and would shortly address a letter to Miss Tomalin? This course finally met with Lady Ogram's approval; she agreed to let a week pass before taking the next step.

Whatever the ultimate effect of her joyous agitation, for the present it seemed to do her nothing but good. She walked with lighter step, bore herself as though she had thrown off years, and, all through the evening, was a marvel of cheerfulness and cordiality. The reaction came when she found herself at liberty to feel weary, but no eye save that of the confidential maid beheld her collapse. Even whilst being undressed like a helpless infant, the old lady did not lose her temper. Even whilst gulping an unpleasant draught, well aware that she was not likely to sleep until dawn, if then, she smiled at her thoughts. The maid wondered what it all meant.

Dyce Lashmar was abundantly satisfied with himself. "Am I doing it well?" he quietly asked of Constance, somewhere about ten o'clock, and on receiving the reply, "Very well," he gave his friend a more benignant smile than he had bestowed upon her since the old days of semi-sentimental intimacy. He would much have liked to talk over the evening with her before he went to bed; as that was impossible, he pressed her hand very warmly at leave-taking, looked her steadily in the eyes, and said in a low voice:

"To-morrow."

He was greatly satisfied with himself, and, in consequence, felt overflowing with kindliness towards all the sons and daughters of men. One by one he reviewed the persons with whom he had conversed. How pleasant they were! How sensible and well-meaning! What excellent material for the formation of a really civilized state! They had evidently been impressed with him, and, on going home, would make him the subject of their talk. To-morrow his name

would sound frequently in several houses, and with
complimentary adjunct. The thought made his pulses
throb. To be talked of, to be admired, was the
strongest incentive known to Dyce.

Of Lady Ogram he thought with affection; to the
end of his life he would revere her memory. Constance
Bride he esteemed as a loyal friend; never would he
fail in gratitude to her; she should have his confidence,
and he would often seek her counsel; a good, able
girl of the best modern type. Last of all there came
into his mind the visage of a small, impulsive woman,
with freckled oval face, and hair the colour of an
autumn elm-leaf. Iris Woolstan; to her, too, how
much he was beholden. Good, foolish, fidgety Iris
Woolstan! Never again could he be impatient with
her. Of course he must pay back her money as soon
as possible. Brave little creature, light-heartedly
sending him her cheque for three hundred pounds;
why, there was something heroic in it. Yes, he
acknowledged himself lucky in his woman friends; few
men could be so fortunate. To be sure, it was the
result of his rational views, of his straightforward,
honest method. He saw his way to do noble service
in the cause of womanhood, and that by following the
path of mere common-sense—all sentimental and so-
called chivalrous humbug cast aside, all exaggerated
new conceptions simply disregarded. His bosom
swelled with glorious faith in his own future and in
that of the world.

Among the guests had figured Mr. Breakspeare,
looking a trifle fresher than usual in his clean linen
and ceremonial black. Hearing that Lashmar was
to spend a couple of days more at Rivenoak, he asked
him to dine on the following evening, Lady Ogram
readily permitting the invitation.

"I say dine; sup would be the better word, for I
can offer you only simple entertainment. We shall
be alone; I want the full advantage of your talk.
Afterwards, if you approve, we will look in upon an

old friend of mine who would have great satisfaction in exchanging ideas with you. Something of an original, at all events you will find him amusing."

To this relaxation Dyce looked forward with pleasure. Nearly the whole of the next day he spent in solitude, for Lady Ogram did not appear until the afternoon, and then only for an hour; Mrs. Toplady took her leave before mid-day. Miss Bride showed herself only at breakfast and luncheon, when she was friendly, indeed, but not much disposed for talk. Dyce had anticipated a growth of intimacy with Constance; he was prepared for long, confidential gossip in the library or the garden; but his friend briefly excused herself. She had a lot of reading and extracting to do.

" You have told me very little about yourself," he remarked, when she rose to withdraw after luncheon.

" What's there to tell ? "

" It would interest me to know more of your own thoughts—apart from the work you are engaged in."

" Oh, those are strictly for home consumption," said Constance, with a smile; and went her way.

So Dyce paced the garden by himself, or read newspapers and reviews, or lolled indolently in super-comfortable chairs. He had promised to write to Mrs. Woolstan, and in the morning said to himself that he would do so in the afternoon ; but he disliked letter-writing, shrank at all times, indeed, from use of the pen, and ultimately the duty was postponed till to-morrow. His exertions of the evening before had left a sense of fatigue ; it was enough to savour the recollection of triumph. He mused a little, from time to time, on Constance, whose behaviour slightly piqued his curiosity. That she was much occupied with the thought of him, he never doubted, but he could not feel quite sure of the colour of her reflections—a vexatious incertitude. He lazily resolved to bring her to clearer avowal before quitting Rivenoak.

At evening, the coachman drove him to Hollingford, where he alighted at Mr. Breakspeare's newspaper office. The editor received him in a large, ill-kept, barely-furnished room, the floor littered with journals.

"How will that do, Mr. Lashmar?" was his greeting, as he held out a printed slip.

Dyce perused a leading article, which, without naming him, contained a very flattering sketch of his intellectual personality. So, at least, he understood the article, ostensibly a summing of the qualifications which should be possessed by an ideal Liberal candidate. Large culture, a philosophical grasp of the world's history, a scientific conception of human life; again, thorough familiarity with the questions of the day, a mind no less acute in the judgment of detail than broad in its vision of principles; moreover, genuine sympathy with the aspirations of the average man, yet no bias to sentimental weakness; with all this, the heaven-sent gift of leadership, power of speech, calm and justified self-confidence. Lashmar's face beamed as he recognized each trait. Breakspeare, the while, regarded him with half-closed eyes in which twinkled a world of humour.

"A little too generous, I'm afraid," Dyce remarked at length, thoughtfully.

"Not a bit of it!" cried the editor, scratching the tip of his nose, where he had somehow caught a spot of ink. "Bald facts; honest portraiture. It doesn't displease you?"

"How could it? I only hope I may be recognized by such of your readers as have met me."

"You certainly will be. I shall follow this up with a portrait of the least acceptable type of Conservative candidate, wherein all will recognize our parliamentary incubus. Thus do we open the great campaign! If you would care to, pray keep that proof; some day it may amuse you to look at it, and to recall these early days of our acquaintance. Now I will take you to my house, which, I need not say, you honour by this visit. You are a philosopher, and simplicity will not offend you."

Our Friend the Charlatan

They walked along one or two main streets, the
journalist, still ink-spotted on the nose, nodding now
and then to an acquaintance, and turned at length
into a by-way of dwelling houses, which did not,
indeed, suggest opulence, but were roomy and decent.
At one of the doors Breakspeare paused, turned the
handle, and ushered in his guest.

Almost immediately Dyce was presented to his
hostess, on whose thin but pleasant face he perceived
with satisfaction a reverential interest. Mrs. Breakspeare had few words at her command, and was
evidently accustomed to be disregarded; she knew
that her husband admired intellectual women, and
that he often privately lamented his mistake in
marriage; but none the less was she aware that he
enjoyed the comfort of his home—to her a sufficient
recompense. Like many a man, Breakspeare would
have been quite satisfied with his wife, if, at the same
time, he could have had another. He heartily approved
the domestic virtues; it would have exasperated him
had the mother of his children neglected home duties
for any intellectual pursuit; yet, as often as he thought
of Miss Bride, contemptuous impatience disturbed his
tranquillity. He desired to unite irreconcilable things.
His practical safeguard was the humour which, after
all, never allowed him to take life too seriously.

A boy of sixteen, the eldest of seven children, sat
down to table with them. Breakspeare made a slight
apology for his presence, adding genially, "*Meminisse
juvabit.*" The meal was more than tolerable; the
guest thoroughly enjoyed himself, talking with as little
affectation as his nature permitted, and, with a sense of
his own graciousness, often addressing to Mrs. Breakspeare a remark on the level of her intelligence.

"When you come down to Hollingford," said the
journalist, "I suppose you will generally stay at Lady
Ogram's?"

"Possibly," was the reply. "But I think I had
better decide which is to be my hotel, when I

have need of one. Will you advise me in that matter ? "

Breakspeare recommended the house which Lashmar already knew, and added hints concerning the political colour of leading tradesfolk. When they rose, the host reminded Dyce of his suggestion that they should go and see an old friend of his, one Martin Blaydes.

" We shall find him smoking his pipe, with a jug of beer at his elbow. Martin is homely, but a man of original ideas, and he will appreciate your visit."

So they set forth, and walked for a quarter of an hour towards the outskirts of the town. Mr. Blaydes, who held a small municipal office, lived alone in a very modest dwelling, his attendant a woman of discreet years. As Breakspeare had foretold, he was found sitting by the fireside—the evening was cool enough to make a fire agreeable—a churchwarden between his lips, and a brown jug of generous capacity on the table beside him. As the door opened, he turned a meditative head, and blinked myopically at his visitors before rising. His movements were very deliberate; his smile, which had the odd effect of elevating one eyebrow and depressing the other, made him look as if he were about to sneeze. Not without ceremony Breakspeare presented his companion, whom the old man (his years touched on seventy) greeted in the words of Belshazzar to Daniel.

" I have heard of thee, that the spirit of the gods is in thee, and that light and wisdom and excellent understanding are found in thee. Be seated, Mr. Lashmar, be seated. Friend Breakspeare, put your toes on the fender. Mr. Lashmar, my drink is ale; an honest tap which I have drunk for some three score years, and which never did me harm. Will you join me ? "

" With pleasure, Mr. Blaydes."

A touch upon the bell summoned the serving woman.

" Mrs. Ricketts, another jug of the right amber, and

two beakers. I know not if you smoke, Mr. Lashmar? Why, that's right. Two yards of Broseley also, Mrs. Ricketts."

Breakspeare had produced his pouch, which he opened and held to Martin.

"Here's a new mixture, my own blending, which I should like you to try. I see your pipe is empty."

"Gramercy," replied the other, with a wave of the hand. "I stick to my own mundungus; any novelty disturbs my thoughts. Offer it to Mr. Lashmar, who might find this weed of mine a trifle rank. Here comes the foaming jug. What say you to that for a head, Mr. Lashmar? A new nine-gallon, tapped before breakfast this morning, now running clear and cool as a mountain burn. What would life be without this? Elsewhere our ale degenerates; not many honest brewers are left. Druggist's wine and the fire of the distilleries will wreck our people. Whenever you have a chance, Mr. Lashmar, speak a word for honest ale. Time enough is wasted at Westminster; they may well listen to a plea for the source of all right feeling and right thinking—amber ale."

Dyce soon understood that here, at all events, he was not called upon for eloquence or disquisition. Martin Blaydes had become rather dull of ear, and found it convenient to do most of the talking himself. Now and then he turned his sneeze-menacing smile this way or that, and a remark always claimed his courteous attention, but in general his eyes were fixed on the glow of the fireplace, whilst he pursued a humorous ramble from thought to thought, topic to topic. Evidently of local politics he knew nothing, and recked not at all; he seemed to take for granted that Lashmar was about to sit in Parliament for Hollingford, and that the young man represented lofty principles rarely combined with public ambition.

"You may do something; I don't know, I don't know. Things are bad, I fear, and likely to be worse. We had hopes, Mr. Lashmar, when the world and I

Our Friend the Charlatan

were young. In those days there was such a thing as zeal for progress—and progress didn't necessarily mean money. You know my view of the matter, friend Breakspeare. Two causes explain the pass we've come to—the power of women and the tyranny of finance. How does that touch you, Mr. Lashmar?"

"Finance—yes," Dyce replied. "It's the curse of the modern world. But women?"

"Yes, yes, the 'monstrous regiment of women,' as the old writer hath it. Look at the diseases from which we are suffering—materialism and hysteria. The one has been intensified and extended, the other has newly declared itself, since women came to the front. No materialist like a woman; give her a voice in the control of things, and good-bye to all our ideals. Hard cash, military glory, glittering and clanging triumph—there be the gods of a woman's heart. Thought and talk drowned by a scream; nerves worried into fiddle-strings. We had our vain illusion; we were generous in our manly way. 'Open the door! Let the women come forth and breathe fresh air! Justice for wives, an open field for those who will not or cannot wed!' We meant well, but it was a letting out of the waters. There's your idle lady with the pretty face, who wants to make laws for the amusement of breaking them. 'As a jewel of gold in a swine's snout, so is a fair woman without discretion.' There's your hard-featured woman, who thinks that nobody in the world but she has brains. And our homes are tumbling about our heads, because there's no one to look after them. 'One man among a thousand have I found, but a woman among all those have I not found.' Back with them to nursery and kitchen, pantry and herb-garden! Back with them, or we perish."

Dyce wore a broad smile. He knew that he himself would have spoken thus had he not been committed to another way of talking. Breakspeare, too, smiled, but with only half-assent; he reserved his bigamous

138

Our Friend the Charlatan

alternative. Martin Blaydes took a long draught from his beaker, puffed half-a-dozen rings of smoke, and pursued his diatribe in the same good-natured growl.

"The fury to get rich—who is so responsible for it as the mass of indolent, luxurious, and vain women? The frenzy to become notorious—almost entirely women's work. The spirit of reckless ambition in public life—encouraged by the sex which has never known the meaning of responsibility. Decay of the arts—inevitable result of the predominance of little fools who never admired anything but art in millinery. Revival of delight in man-slaying—what woman could ever resist a uniform?—Let them be; let them be. Why should they spoil our ale and tobacco? Friend Breakspeare, how's your wife? Now there, Mr. Lashmar, there is a woman such as I honour! 'She will do him good and not evil all the days of her life.' A woman of the by-gone day—gentle but strong, silent and wise. 'Give her of the fruit of her hands, and let her own works praise her in the gates!' Mr. Lashmar, your beaker stands empty. So, by the bye, does the jug. Mrs. Ricketts!"

The little room contained many books, mostly old and such as had seen long service. As his habit was when a friend sat with him, Mr. Blaydes presently reached down a volume, and, on opening it, became aware of a passage which sent him into crowing laughter.

"Ha, ha, friend Breakspeare, here's something for thee! Thou art the sophist of our time, and list how the old wise man spoke of thy kind. 'They do but teach the collective opinion of the many; 'tis their wisdom, forsooth. I might liken them to a man who should study the temper or the desires of a great strong beast, which he has to keep and feed; he learns how to approach and handle the creature, also at what times and from what causes it is dangerous, or the reverse, what is the meaning of its several cries, and by what sounds it may be soothed or infuriated.

139

Furthermore, when, by constantly living with the huge brute, he has become perfect in all this, he calls it philosophy, and makes a system or art of it, which forthwith he professes. One thing he names honourable, another base; this good, that evil; this just, that unjust; all in accordance with the tastes and wants of the great animal, which he has studied from its grunts and snarls.' Ha, ha, friend Breakspeare! Does it touch thee? 'Comes it not something near?' Nay, nay, take it not in dudgeon! 'Tis old Plato who speaks."

"What, I?" cried the journalist gaily. "I'm infinitely obliged to you. The passage shall do me yeoman's service—turned against the enemy. For it is not I who speak for the many at Hollingford, as well you know. We Liberals are the select, the chosen spirits. The mighty brute is Toryism."

Only the fear of reaching Rivenoak at too late an hour constrained Lashmar to rise at length and take his leave.

"I hope you will let me come and see you again, Mr. Blaydes," he exclaimed heartily, as he grasped the old man's hand.

"Here you will commonly find me, Mr. Lashmar, after eight o'clock, and if you bear with my whimsies I shall thank you for your company. This ale, I try to believe, will last my time. If a company corrupt it, I forswear all fermented liquor, and go to the grave on mere element—'honest water which ne'er left man i' the mire.' But I hope better things—I hope better things."

"And what do you think of Martin?" asked the journalist, as he and Lashmar walked to the nearest place where a vehicle could be obtained for the drive to Rivenoak.

"A fine old cynic!" answered Dyce. "I hope often to drink ale with him."

"Luckily, it doesn't compromise you. Martin belongs to no party, and gives no vote. I could tell you a good story about his reception of a canvasser—a lady, by Jove!—at the last election; but I'll keep it till we meet again, as you are in a hurry. You have put me in spirits, Mr. Lashmar; may it not be long before I next talk with you. Meanwhile, I dig the trenches!"

Ale and strong tobacco, to both of which he was unaccustomed, wrought confusingly upon Dyce's brain as he was borne through the night. He found himself murmuring the name of Constance, and forming a resolve to win her to intimacy on the morrow. Yes, he liked Constance, after all. Then came a memory of Martin Blaydes' diatribe, and he laughed approvingly. But Constance was an exception, the best type of modern woman. After all, he liked her.

Again they two breakfasted together. Dyce gave a mirthful description of his evening, and gaily reported Mr. Blaydes' eloquence on the subject of woman.

"On the whole, I agree with him," said Constance. "And I know, of course, that you do."

"Indeed! You agree with him?"

"So does every sensible person. But the subject doesn't interest me. I hate talk about *women*. We've had enough of it; it has become a nuisance—a cant, like any other. A woman is a human being, not a separate species."

"Why, of course!" cried Lashmar. "Just what I am always saying."

"Say it no more," interrupted his companion. "There are plenty of other things to talk about."

Whereupon, she finished her cup of coffee, nodded a leave-taking, and went at a brisk pace from the room. Dyce continued his meal, meditative, a trifle wounded in self-esteem.

Later in the morning he saw Constance wheeling forth her bicycle. He ran, and gained her side before she had mounted.

"As you are going out, why shouldn't we have a walk together? Give up your ride this morning."

141

Our Friend the Charlatan

"I'm very sorry I can't," Constance answered pleasantly. "The exercise is necessary for me."

"But just this once."

"Impossible! The morning is too fine and the roads too good."

She sprang into the saddle and was off—much to Dyce's mortification. He had not dreamt that she could refuse his request. And he had meant to talk with such generous confidence, such true comradeship; it was even his intention to tell Constance that he looked more for her sympathy and aid than for that of any one else. Surely this would have been very gratifying to her; she could not but have thanked him with real feeling.

At luncheon Miss Bride was obviously unrepentant. One would have said that it amused her to notice the slight coldness which Lashmar put into his manner towards her. She had never seemed in better spirits.

In the afternoon Dyce was summoned to a private interview with Lady Ogram. It took place in an up-stairs room he had not yet entered. His hostess sat before a wood-fire (though the day was warm), and her face now and then had a look of suffering, but she spoke cheerfully, and in a tone of much kindness.

"Well, have you enjoyed your stay with me? You must come down again presently; but, in the mean-time, you'll be busy. Go and see Mrs. Toplady, and get to know all the useful people you can. We shall be working here for you, of course. Miss Bride will keep you posted about everything."

The dark eyes, at this moment pain-troubled, were reading his countenance.

"I needn't tell you," Lady Ogram continued, "that Miss Bride has my entire and perfect confidence. I don't think I'm easily deceived in people, and—even before she spoke to me of you—I had made up my mind that, in some way or other, she must be given a chance of doing something in life. You know all about her ways of thinking—perhaps better than I do."

Our Friend the Charlatan

In the pause which followed Dyce was on the point of disclaiming this intimacy; but the drift of Lady Ogram's talk, exciting his curiosity, prevailed to keep him silent. He bent his look, and smiled modestly.

"She's one of the few women," went on his friend, "who do more than they promise. She'll never be what is called brilliant. She won't make much of a figure in the drawing-room. But, give her a chance, and she'll do things that people will talk about. She has powers of organizing; I don't know whether you understand how well she is getting to be known by serious workers in the social reform way. There's not one of them can write such good letters—tell so much in few words. But we must give her a chance—you and I together."

Dyce was startled. His smile died away, and, involuntarily, he turned a look of surprise on the speaker.

"You mean," said Lady Ogram, as though answering a remonstrance, "that you know all about that, without my telling you. Don't be touchy; you and I can understand each other well enough, if we like. What I want to let you know is, that I consider she has a claim upon me. Not in the ordinary sense. Perhaps I'm not quite an ordinary woman, and I see things in a way of my own. She has a claim upon me, because she's one of the few women who have nothing of the baby or the idiot in them, and I've been looking out for that sort all my life. If Constance Bride"—the voice became slower, as if for emphasis—"is put into a position of trust, she'll do all that is expected of her. There's no particular hurry; she's young enough still. And as for you, you've got your hands full."

Dyce felt so puzzled that he could not shape a word. One thing was growing clear to him; but what did the old woman mean by a "position of trust"? How was Constance to be given her "chance"? And what, exactly, was she expected to do?

"Well, we've had our talk," said the old lady,
143

moving as if in pain and weariness. "Go back to town to-night or to-morrow morning, as you like. Write to me, mind, as well as to Miss Bride, and let me know of all the acquaintances you make. It's just possible I may be in London myself next month; it depends on several things."

She became dreamy. Dyce, though he would have liked to say much, knew not how to express himself; it was plain, moreover, that his hostess had little strength to-day. He rose.

"I think I shall catch the evening train, Lady Ogram."

"Very well. A pleasant journey!"

She gave her hand, and Dyce thought it felt more skeleton-like than ever. Certainly her visage was more cadaverous in line and hue than he had yet seen it. Almost before he had turned away Lady Ogram closed her eyes, and lay back with a sigh.

So here were his prospects settled for him! He was to marry Constance Bride—under some vague conditions which perturbed him almost as much as the thought of the marriage itself. Impossible that he could have misunderstood. And how had Lady Ogram hit upon such an idea? It was plain as daylight that the suggestion had come from Constance herself. Constance had allowed it to be understood that he and she were, either formally or virtually, affianced.

He stood appalled at this revelation in a sphere of knowledge which he held to be particularly his own.

CHAPTER XI

It was a week after the departure of Dyce Lashmar. Lady Ogram had lived in agitation, a state which she knew to be the worst possible for her. Several times she had taken long drives to call upon acquaintances, a habit suspended during the past twelvemonth; it exhausted her, but she affected to believe that the air and movement did her good, and met with an outbreak of still more dangerous choler the remonstrances which her companion at length ventured to make. On the day following this characteristic scene, Constance was at work in the library, when the door opened, and Lady Ogram came in. Walking unsteadily, a grim smile on her parchment visage, she advanced and stood before the writing-table.

"I made a fool of myself yesterday," sounded in a hollow voice, of tremulous intonation. "Is it enough for me to say so?"

"Much more than I like to hear you say, Lady Ogram," answered Constance, hastening to place a chair for her. "I have been afraid that something had happened which troubled you."

"Nothing at all. The contrary. Look at that photo, and tell me what you think of it."

It was the portrait of a girl with features finely outlined, but rather weak in expression; a face pleasant to look upon, and at the first glance possessing a quality of distinction, which tended however to fade as the eye searched for its constituents, and to lose itself in an ordinary prettiness.

"I was going to say," began Constance, "that it seemed to remind me of——"

She hesitated.

"Well? Of what?"

"Of your own portrait in the dining-room. Yes, I think there is a resemblance, though far-away."

Lady Ogram smiled with pleasure. The portrait referred to was a painting made of her soon after her marriage, when she was in the prime of her beauty; not good as a work of art, and doing much less than justice to the full-blooded vigour of the woman as she then lived, but still a picture that drew the eye and touched the fancy.

"No doubt you are right. This girl is a grand-niece of mine, my brother's son's daughter. I only heard of her a week ago. She is coming to see me."

Constance now understood the significance of Mr. Kerchever's visit, and the feverish state of mind in which Lady Ogram had since been living. She felt no touch of sympathetic emotion, but smiled as if the announcement greatly interested her; and in a sense it did.

"I can quite understand your impatience to see her."

"Yes, but one shouldn't make a fool of oneself. An old fool's worse than a young one. Don't think I build my hopes on the girl. I wrote to her, and she has written to me, not a bad sort of letter; but I know nothing about her, except that she has been well enough educated to pass an examination at London University. That means something, I suppose, doesn't it?"

"Certainly it does," answered Constance, noting a pathetic self-subdual in the old lady's look and tone. "For a girl, it means a good deal."

"You think so?" The bony hands were restless and tremulous; the dark eyes glistened. "It isn't quite ordinary, is it? But then, of course, it tells nothing about her character. She is coming to stay for a day or two—coming on Saturday. If I don't like her, no harm's done. Back she goes to her people, that's all—

her mother's family—I know nothing about them, and care less. At all events, she looks endurable, don't you think?"

"Much more than that," said Constance. "A very nice girl, I should imagine."

"Ha! You mean that? Of course you do, or you wouldn't say it. But then, if she's only a 'nice girl!'— pooh! She ought to be more than that. What's the use of a photograph? Every photo ever taken of me made me look a simpering idiot."

This was by no means true, but Lady Ogram had always been a bad sitter to the camera, and had destroyed most of its results. The oil painting in the dining-room she regarded with a moderate complacency. Many a time during the latter years of withering and enfeeblement her memory had turned to that shining head in marble, which was hidden away amid half a century's dust under the roof at Rivenoak. There, and there only, survived the glory of her youth, when not the face alone, but all her faultless body, made the artist's rapture.

"Well," she said abruptly, "you'll see the girl. Her name is May Tomalin. You're not obliged to like her. You're not obliged to tell me what you think of her. Most likely I shan't ask you.—By the bye, I had a letter from Dyce Lashmar this morning."

"Indeed?" said the other, with a careless smile.

"I like his way of writing. It's straightforward and sharp cut, like his talk. A man who means what he says, and knows how to say it; that's a great deal now-a-days."

Constance assented with all good-humour to Lady Ogram's praise.

"You must answer him for me," the old lady continued. "No need, of course, to show me what you write; just put it into a letter of your own."

"I hardly think I shall be writing to Mr. Lashmar," said Miss Bride, very quietly.

"Do you mean that?"

Our Friend the Charlatan

Their eyes met, and Constance bore the other's gaze without flinching.

"We are not such great friends, Lady Ogram. You will remember I told you that I knew him but slightly."

"All right. It has nothing to do with me, whether you're friends or not. You can answer as my secretary, I suppose?"

And Lady Ogram, with her uncertain, yet not undignified, footfall, went straightway from the room. There was a suspicion of needless sound as the door closed behind her.

Constance sat for a minute or two in a very rigid attitude, displeasure manifest on her lips. She did not find it easy to get to work again, and when the time came for her bicycle ride, she was in no mind for it, but preferred to sit over a book. At luncheon Lady Ogram inclined to silence. Later in the day, however, they met on the ordinary terms of mutual understanding, and Constance, after speaking of other things, asked whether she should write Lady Ogram's reply to Mr. Lashmar.

"Mr. Lashmar? Oh, I have written to him myself," said the old lady, as if speaking of a matter without importance.

Three days went by, and it was Saturday. Lady Ogram came down earlier than usual this morning, but did not know how to occupy herself; she fretted at the rainy sky which kept her within doors; she tried to talk with her secretary of an important correspondence they had in hand (it related to a projected society for the invigoration of village life), but her thoughts were too obviously wandering. Since that dialogue in the library, not a word regarding Miss Tomalin had escaped her; all at once she said:

"My niece is due here at four this afternoon."

Constance smiled attentively.

"I want you to be with me when she comes into the room. You won't forget that?"

148

Our Friend the Charlatan

Never before had Constance seen the old autocrat suffering from nervousness; it was doubtful whether any one at any time had enjoyed the privilege. Strange to say, this abnormal state of things had no ill-effect upon Lady Ogram's temper; she was remarkably mild, and for once in her life seemed to feel it no indignity to stand in need of moral support. Long before the time for Miss Tomalin's arrival, she established herself on her throne amid the drawing-room verdure. Constance tried to calm her by reading aloud, but this the old lady soon found unendurable.

"I wonder whether the train will be late?" she said. "No doubt it will; did you ever know a train punctual? It may be half-an-hour late. The railways are scandalously managed. They ought to be taken over by the Government."

"I don't think that would improve matters," said the secretary, glad of a discussion to relieve the tedium. She, too, was growing nervous.

"Nonsense! Of course it would."

Constance launched into argument, and talked for talking's sake. She knew that her companion was not listening.

"It's four o'clock," exclaimed Lady Ogram presently. "There may be an accident with the brougham. Leggett sometimes drives very carelessly"—no more prudent coachman existed—"and the state of the roads about here is perfectly scandalous"—they were as good roads as any in England. "What noise was that?"

"I heard nothing."

"I've often noticed that you are decidedly dull of hearing. Has it always been so? You ought to consult a —— what are the men called who see to one's ears?"

Lady Ogram was growing less amiable, and with much ado Constance restrained herself from a tart reply. Three minutes more, and the atmosphere of the room would have become dangerously electric.

Our Friend the Charlatan

But before two minutes had elapsed, the door opened, and a colourless domestic voice announced:

"Miss Tomalin."

There entered very much the kind of figure that Constance had expected to see; a young lady something above the middle height, passably, not well, dressed, moving quickly and not ungracefully, but with perceptible lack of that self-possession which is the social testimonial. She wore a new travelling costume, fawn-coloured, with a slightly inappropriate hat (too trimmy) and brown shoes which over-asserted themselves. Her collar was of the upright sort, just turned down at the corners; her tie, an ill-made little bow of red. About her neck hung a pair of eye-glasses; to her waist were attached a silver pencil-case and a small ivory paper-knife. The face corresponded fairly well with its photographic presentment so long studied by Lady Ogram, and so well remembered by Constance Bride; its colour somewhat heightened, and the features mobile under nervous stress, it offered a more noticeable resemblance to that ancestral portrait in the dining-room.

Lady Ogram had risen; she took a tremulous step or two from the throne, and spoke in a voice much more senile than its wont.

"I am glad to see you, May—glad to see you. This is my friend and secretary, Miss Bride, whom I mentioned to you."

Constance and the new-comer bowed, hesitated, shook hands. Miss Tomalin had not yet spoken; she was smiling timidly, and casting quick glances about the room.

"You had an easy journey, I hope," said Miss Bride, aware that the old lady was sinking breathless and feeble into her chair.

"Oh, yes. Such a short distance!"

Miss Tomalin's utterance was not markedly provincial, but distinct from that of the London drawing-room; the educated speech of the ubiquitous middle-

class, with a note of individuality which promised to
command itself better in a few minutes. The voice
was agreeable, soft and clear.

"You had no difficulty in finding the carriage?" said
Lady Ogram, speaking with obvious effort.

"Oh, none whatever, thank you! So kind of you to
send it for me."

"I wanted to see you for a moment, as soon as you
arrived. Now they shall take you to your room. Come
down again as soon as you like; we will have tea."

"Thank you; that will be very nice."

Miss Tomalin stood up, looked at the plants and
flowers about her, and added in a voice already more
courageous:

"What a charming room! Green is so very good
for the eyes."

"Are your eyes weak?" inquired Lady Ogram,
solicitously.

"Oh, not really weak," was the rapid answer. (Miss
Tomalin spoke more quickly as she gained confidence.)
"I use glasses when I am studying or at the piano,
but they're not *actually* necessary. Still, I have been
advised to be careful. Of course I read a great deal."

There was a spontaneity, a youthful vivacity, in her
manner, which saved it from the charge of conceit.
She spoke with a naïve earnestness pleasantly relieved
by the smile in her grey eyes, and by something in the
pose of her head which suggested latent modesty.

"I know you are a great student," said Lady Ogram,
regarding her amiably. "But run and take off your
hat, and come back to tea."

She and Constance sat together, silent. They did
not exchange glances.

"Well?" sounded at length from the throne, a
tentative monosyllable.

Constance looked up. She saw that Lady Ogram
was satisfied, happy.

"I'm glad Miss Tomalin was so punctual," was all
she could find to say.

Our Friend the Charlatan

"So am I. But we were talking about your deafness: you must have it seen to. Young people now-a-days! They can't hear, they can't see, they have no teeth——"

"Miss Tomalin, I noticed, has excellent teeth."

"She takes after me· in that. Her eyes, too, are good enough, but she has worn them out already. She'll have to stop that reading; I'm not going to have her blind at thirty. She didn't seem to be deaf, did she?"

"No more than I am, Lady Ogram."

"You are not deaf? Then why did you say you were?"

"It was you, not I, that said so," answered Constance, with a laugh.

"And what do you think of her?" asked Lady Ogram sharply.

"I think her interesting," was Miss Bride's reply, the word bearing a sense to her own thought not quite identical with that which it conveyed to the hearer.

"So do I. She's very young, but none the worse for that. You think her interesting, so do I."

Constance noticed that Lady Ogram's talk to-day had more of the characteristics of old age than ordinarily, as though, in her great satisfaction, the mind relaxed and the tongue inclined to babble. Though May was absent less than a quarter of an hour the old lady waxed impatient.

"I hope she isn't a looking-glass girl. But no, that doesn't seem likely. Of course young people must think a little about dress. Oh, here she comes at last."

Miss Tomalin had made no change of dress, beyond laying aside her hat and jacket. One saw now that she had plenty of light-brown hair, naturally crisp and easily lending itself to effective arrangement. It was coiled and plaited on the top of her head, and rippled airily above her temples. The eyebrows were darker of hue, and accentuated the most pleasantly expressive part of her physiognomy, for when she smiled it was much more the eyes than the lips which drew attention.

"Come and sit here, May," said Lady Ogram, indicating a chair near the throne. " You're not tired ? You don't easily get tired, I hope ? "

"Oh, not very easily. Of course I make a point of physical exercise; it is a part of rational education."

"Do you cycle ?" asked Constance.

"Indeed I do ! The day before yesterday I rode thirty miles. Not scorching, you know; that's weak-minded."

Lady Ogram seemed to be reflecting as to whether she was glad or not that her relative rode the bicycle. She asked whether May had brought her machine.

"No," was the airy reply; "I'm not a slave to it."

The other nodded approval, and watched May as she manipulated a tea-cup. Talk ran on trivialities for a while. The new-comer still cast curious glances about the room, and at moments stole a quick observation of her companions. She was not entirely at ease; self-consciousness appeared in a furtive change of attitude from time to time; it might have been remarked, too, that she kept a guard upon her phrasing and her pronunciation, emphasizing certain words with a sort of academic pedantry. Perhaps it was this which caused Lady Ogram to ask at length whether she still worked for examinations.

"No, I have quite given that up," May replied, with an air of well-weighed finality. "I found that it led to one-sidedness—to narrow aims. It's all very well when one is *very* young. I shouldn't like to restrict my study in that way now. The problems of modern life are so full of interest. There are so many books that it is a duty to read—a positive duty; and one finds so much practical work."

"What sort of work ? "

"In the social direction. I take a great interest in the condition of the poor."

"Really !" exclaimed Lady Ogram. "What do you do ? "

Our Friend the Charlatan

"We have a little society for extending civilization among the ignorant and the neglected. Just now we are trying to teach them how to make use of the free library, to direct their choice of books. I must tell you that a favourite study of mine is Old English, and I'm sure it would be so good if our working-classes could be brought to read Chaucer and Langland and Wyclif and so on. One can't expect them to study foreign languages, but these old writers would serve them for a sort of philological training, which has such an excellent effect on the mind. I know a family— shockingly poor, living, four of them, in two rooms— who have promised me to give an hour every Sunday to 'Piers the Plowman'; I have made them a present of the little Clarendon Press edition, which has excellent notes. Presently I shall set them a little examination paper, very simple of course."

Miss Bride's countenance was a study of subdued expression. Lady Ogram, who probably had never heard of 'Piers the Plowman,' glanced inquiringly at her secretary, and seemed to suspend judgment.

"We, too, take a good deal of interest in that kind of thing," she remarked. "I see that we shall understand each other. Do your relatives, Mr. and Mrs. Rooke, work with you?"

"They haven't quite the same point of view," said Miss Tomalin, smiling indulgently. "I'm afraid they represent rather the old way of thinking about the poor—the common-sense way they call it; it means, as far as I can see, not thinking much about the poor at all. Of course I try to make them understand that this is neglect of duty. We have no right whatever to live in enjoyment of our privileges and pay no heed to those less fortunate. Every educated person is really a missionary, whose duty it is to go forth and spread the light. I feel it so strongly that I could not, simply *could* not, be satisfied to pursue my own culture; it seems to me the worst kind of selfishness. The other day I went, on the business of our society, into a

154

dreadfully poor home, where the people, I'm sure, often suffer from hunger. I couldn't give money—for one thing I have very little, and then it's so demoralizing, and one never knows whether the people will be offended—but I sat down and told the poor woman all about the Prologue to the Canterbury Tales, and you can't think how interested she was, and how grateful! It quite brightened the day for her. One felt one had done *some* good."

There was silence. Lady Ogram looked admiringly at the girl. If any one else had talked to her in this way no vehemence of language would have sufficed to express her scorn; but in May Tomalin such ideals seemed to her a very amiable trait. She was anxious to see everything May said or did in a favourable light.

" Have you tried the effect of music ? " asked Constance gravely, when Miss Tomalin chanced to regard her.

"Oh, we haven't forgotten that. Next winter we hope to give a few concerts in a school-room. Of course it must be really good music; we shan't have anything of a popular kind, at least we shan't if my view prevails. It isn't our object to *amuse* people; it would be really humiliating to play and sing the kind of things the ignorant poor like. We want to train their intelligence. Some of our friends say it will be absurd to give them classical music, which will weary and discontent them. But they must be made to understand that their weariness and discontent is *wrong*. We have to show them how bad and poor their taste is, that they may strive to develop a higher and nobler. I, for one, shall utterly decline to have anything to do with the concerts if the programme doesn't consist exclusively of the really great—Bach and Beethoven and so on. Don't you agree with me ? "

" In principle," replied Lady Ogram, " certainly. We shall have lots of things to talk about, I see."

" I delight in talking about serious things," cried May. But Lady Ogram's physical strength was not equal to the excitement she had gone through. Long before dinner-time her voice utterly failed, and she had no choice but to withdraw into privacy, leaving Constance Bride to play the hostess. Alone with a companion of not much more than her own age Miss Tomalin manifested relief; she began to move about, looking at things with frank curiosity, and talking in a more girlish way. The evening was cloudy, and did not tempt forth, but May asked whether they could not walk a little in the garden.

"This is a beautiful place. I shall enjoy myself here tremendously! And it's all so unexpected. Of course you know, Miss Bride, that I had never heard of Lady Ogram until a few days ago?"

"Yes, I have heard the story."

"Do let us get our hats and run out. I want to see everything."

They went into the garden, and May, whilst delighting in all she saw, asked a multitude of questions about her great-aunt. It was only in the intellectual domain that she evinced pretentiousness and grew grandiloquent; talking of her private affairs she was very direct and simple, with no inclination to unhealthy ways of thought. She spoke of her birth in Canada, and her childish recollections of that country.

"I used to be rather sorry that we had come back to England, for the truth is I don't much care for Northampton, and I have never been quite comfortable with my relatives there. But now, of course, everything is different. It seems a great pity that I should have had such a relative as Lady Ogram and known nothing about it, doesn't it? Strange how the branches of a family lose sight of each other. Can you tell me Lady Ogram's age?"

Constance replied that it was not far from eighty.

"Really I should have taken her for older still. She seems very nice; I think I shall like her. I wonder whether she will ask me often to Rivenoak? Do you know whether she means to?"

Our Friend the Charlatan

When she came down after dressing for dinner, Constance found Miss Tomalin in the dining-room, standing before her great-aunt's portrait.

"Surely that isn't—*can* that be Lady Ogram?" exclaimed the girl.

"Yes; more than fifty years ago."

"Do you know, I think she was rather like *me!*"

Constance smiled, and said that there was certainly a family resemblance. It appeared more strongly in the girl's face, attired as she now was, her neck at liberty from the white linen collar, and her features cast into relief by a dress of dark material. Having felt a little apprehensive about the young lady's evening garb, Constance was surprised to find that it erred if anything on the side of simplicity. Though, for several reasons, not at all predisposed to like Miss Tomalin, she began to feel her prejudice waning, and by the end of dinner they were conversing in a very friendly tone. May chatted of her friends at Northampton, and several times mentioned a Mr. Yabsley, whom it was evident she held in much esteem. Mr. Yabsley, it appeared, was the originator of the society for civilizing the ignorant poor; Mr. Yabsley lectured on very large subjects, and gave readings from very serious authors; Mr. Yabsley believed in the glorious destinies of the human race, especially of that branch of it known as Anglo-Saxon.

"He is an elderly gentleman?" asked Constance, with a half-smile of mischief.

"Old! oh, dear no! Mr. Yabsley is only about thirty—not quite that, I think."

And May suddenly turned to talk of Browning, whom she felt it a "positive duty" to know from end to end. Had Miss Bride really mastered 'Sordello'?"

"I never tried to," Constance answered. "Why should I worry about unintelligible stuff that would give me no pleasure even if I could understand it?"

"Oh! oh! *don't* speak like that!" cried the other distressfully. "I'm sure you don't mean it!"

157

Our Friend the Charlatan

"I care very little for poetry of any kind," said Constance, in all sincerity.

"Oh, how I grieve to hear that! But then, of course, we all have our special interests. Yours is science, I know. I've worked a good deal at science; of course one can't possibly neglect it; it's a simple duty to make oneself as many-sided as possible, don't you think? Just now I'm giving half-an-hour before breakfast every day to Huxley's book on the Crayfish. Mr. Yabsley suggested it to me. Not long ago he was in correspondence with Huxley about something, I don't quite know what, but he takes a great interest in Evolution. Of course you know that volume on the Crayfish?"

"I'm afraid I don't. You arrange your day, I see, very methodically."

"Oh, without method *nothing* can be done. Of course I have a time-table. I try to put in a great many things, but I'm sure it's no use sitting down to any study for less than half-an-hour, do you think so? At present I can only give half-an-hour to Herbert Spencer—I think I shall have to cut out my folk-lore to make more time for him. Yet folk-lore *is* so fascinating! Of course you delight in it?"

"I never had time for it at all," replied Constance.

"Just now I'm quite excited about ghost-worship. Mr. Yabsley doesn't think it is sufficient to explain the origin of religious ideas."

"Mr. Yabsley," remarked Constance, "has pronounced opinions on most things?"

"Oh, he is very wide, indeed. Very wide, and very thorough. There's no end to the examinations he has passed. He's thinking of taking the D.Litt. at London; it's awfully stiff, you know."

When they parted, about eleven o'clock, Miss Tomalin went up-stairs humming a passage from a Beethoven sonata; she declared herself enchanted with her room, and hoped she might wake early to make the coming day all the longer.

Our Friend the Charlatan

At ten next morning Constance was summoned to the up-stairs room, where Lady Ogram sometimes sat when neither so unwell as to stay in bed nor quite well enough to come down. A bad night had left the old lady with a ghastly visage, but she smiled with grim joyfulness as her secretary entered.

"Come, I want you to tell me what you talked about. Where is she now? What is she doing?"

"Miss Tomalin is in the library, rejoicing among the books."

"She is very intellectual," said Lady Ogram. "I never knew any one so keen about knowledge. But what did you talk about last night?"

"Of very many things. Canada and Northampton, religion and crayfish, Huxley and—Yabsley."

"Yabsley? Who's Yabsley?"

"A gentleman of Northampton, a man of light and leading, a great friend of Miss Tomalin's."

"An old man, I suppose?" asked Lady Ogram, sharply.

"Not quite thirty."

"But married? Of course married?"

"I didn't ask; but I fancy not."

Lady Ogram flushed, and fell into extreme agitation. Why had she not been told about this Yabsley? Why had not that ass, that idiot Kerchever made inquiries and heard about him? This very morning she would write him a violent letter. What, May was engaged? To a man called Yabsley?

Constance, as soon as interposition was possible, protested against this over-hasty view of the matter. She did not for a moment think that May was engaged, and, after all, Mr. Yabsley *might* even be married.

"Then why," cried Lady Ogram, furiously, "did you begin by terrifying me? Did you do it on purpose? If I thought so, I would send you packing about your business this moment!"

Constance, who had not yet taken a seat, drew back a few steps. Her face darkened. With hands clasped behind her back, she regarded the raging old autocrat coldly and sternly.

"If you wish it, Lady Ogram, I am quite ready to go."

Their eyes encountered. Lady Ogram was quivering, mumbling, gasping; her look fell.

"Sit down," she said, imperatively.

"I am afraid," was Miss Bride's reply, "we had better not talk whilst you are feeling so unw'll."

"Sit down, I tell you. I wasn't unwell at all till you made me so. Who is this Yabsley? Some low shopkeeper? Some paltry clerk?"

The old lady knew very well that Constance Bride would never tremble before her. It was this proudly independent spirit, unyielding as her own, and stronger still in that it never lost self-command, which had so established the clergyman's daughter in her respect and confidence. Yet her domineering instinct now and then prompted her to outrage the dignity she admired, and her invariable defeat was a new satisfaction when she calmly looked back upon it.

"You mustn't mind me," she said presently, when Constance had quietly refused to make conjectures about the subject under discussion. "Isn't it natural enough that I should be upset when I hear such news as this? I wanted to have a talk with May this morning, but now——"

She broke off, and hung her head gloomily.

"In your position," said Constance, "I should find out by a simple inquiry whether Miss Tomalin is engaged or likely to be. She will answer, I am sure, readily enough. She doesn't seem to be at all reticent."

"Of course I shall do so; thank you for the advice all the same. Would you mind bringing her up here? If you prefer it I will ring."

Scrupulousness of this kind always followed when Lady Ogram had behaved ill to her secretary. The smile with which Constance responded was a ratification of peace. In a few minutes the old lady and May

Our Friend the Charlatan

were chatting together, alone, and without difficulty the great doubt was solved.

"I'm thinking of going to London for a week or two"—thus Lady Ogram approached the point—"and I should rather like to take you with me."

"It's very kind of you," said May, with joy in her eyes.

"But I want to know whether you are quite independent. Is there any one, besides Mr. and Mrs. Rooke, that you would have to consult about it?"

"No one whatever. You know that I am long since of age, Lady Ogram."

"If you like, address me as your aunt. It's simpler, you know."

"Certainly I will. I am quite free, aunt."

"Good. I may take it for granted, then, that you have formed no ties of any kind?"

May shook her head, smiling as though at a thought which the words suggested, a thought not unpleasing, but not at all difficult to dismiss. Thereupon Lady Ogram began to talk freely of her projects.

"I shall go up to town in a fortnight—at the end of this month. Of course you must have some things, dresses and so on. I'll see to that; it's my affair. Before we leave Rivenoak I should like you to meet a few people, my friends at Hollingford particularly, but in a very quiet way; I shall ask them to lunch with us, most likely. Shall you want to go back to Northampton before leaving for London?"

"Oh, it isn't at all necessary," answered May, with sprightliest readiness. "I haven't brought many things with me, but I could send——"

"As for clothing, don't trouble; that's my affair. Then we'll settle that you stay on with me for the present. And now tell me—how do you like Miss Bride?"

"Oh, very much indeed! I'm sure we shall soon quite understand each other."

"I'm glad to hear that; I hope you will. I may tell you that I have a very high opinion indeed of Miss
161

Our Friend the Charlatan

Bride, and that there's no one in whom I put more
confidence."

"Will she go to London with us?"

"Certainly. I couldn't get on without her help."

May was delighted. The prospect of living alone
with her great-aunt, even in London, had mingled a
little uneasiness with her joyful anticipation. Now
she abandoned herself to high spirits, and talked until
Lady Ogram began to have a headache. For an hour
before luncheon they drove out together, May still
gossiping, her aged relative now and then attentive,
but for the most part drowsily musing.

That afternoon, when an hour or two of sleep had
somewhat restored her, Lady Ogram sketched several
letters for her secretary to write. Pausing at length,
she looked at Miss Bride, and for the first time
addressed her by her personal name.

"Constance."

The other responded with a pleased and gratified smile.

"From Mr. Lashmar's talk of him, what sort of idea
have you formed of Lord Dymchurch?"

"Rather a vague one, I'm afraid. I have heard him
only casually mentioned."

"But Mr. Lashmar has a high opinion of him? He
thinks him a man of good principles?"

"Undoubtedly. A very honourable man."

"So I hear from other sources," said Lady Ogram.
"It's probably true. I should rather like to know
Lord Dymchurch. He would be an interesting man to
know, don't you think?"

As not infrequently happened, their eyes met in a
mute interchange of thought.

"Interesting—yes," replied Constance, slowly. And
she added, pressing the nib of her pen on her finger-
nail, "They say he doesn't marry just because he is
poor *and* honourable."

"It's possible," Lady Ogram rejoined, and, after a
moment's reflection, said in an absent voice that the
day's correspondence was finished.

162

CHAPTER XII

THOUGH Mrs. Toplady seldom rose much before mid-day, it was not the mere luxury of repose that kept her in her chamber. As a rule she awoke from excellent sleep at eight o'clock. A touch on the electric button near her hand summoned a maid, who appeared with tea, the morning's post, and a mass of printed matter: newspapers, reviews, magazines, volumes, which had arrived by various channels since noon on the previous day. Apparatus of perfected ingenuity, speedily attached to the bed, enabled her to read or write in any position that she found easiest. First of all she went through her letters, always numerous, never disquieting—for Mrs. Toplady had no personal attachments which could for a moment disturb her pulse, and her financial security stood on the firmest attainable basis. Such letters as demanded a reply she answered at once, and with brevity which in her hands had become an art. Appeals for money, public or private, she carefully considered, responding with a cheque only when she saw some distinct advantage—such as prestige or influence—to be gained by the pecuniary sacrifice. Another touch on the button, and there entered a graceful woman of discreet visage, with whom Mrs. Toplady held colloquy for half-an-hour; in that time a vast variety of concerns, personal, domestic, mundane, was discussed and set in order. Left to herself again, Mrs. Toplady took up the news-papers; thence she passed to the bulkier periodicals; lastly, to literature in volume. Her manner of reading betokened the quick-witted woman who sees at a glance

163

Our Friend the Charlatan

the thing she cares for, and refuses to spend a moment on anything not immediately attractive. People marvelled at the extent of her acquaintance with current writing; in truth, she never read a book, but skimmed the pages just sufficiently for her amusement and her social credit. In the world of laborious idleness Mrs. Toplady had a repute for erudition; she was seriously spoken of as a studious and learned woman, and this estimate of herself she inclined to accept. Having daily opportunity of observing the fathomless ignorance of polite persons, she made it her pride to keep abreast with the day's culture. Genuine curiosity, too, supplied her with a motive, for she had a certain thin, supple, restless intelligence, which took wide surveys of superficial life, and was ever seeking matter for mirth or scorn in the doings of men.

Her first marriage was for love. It cost her seven years of poverty and wretchedness; it cost her, moreover, all the ideals of her youth, and made her a scheming cynic. Having, by natural power and great good fortune, got the world at her feet, she both enjoyed and despised what seemed to her to have been won so easily. The softer emotions were allowed no place in her nature; by careful self-discipline she had enabled herself wholly to disregard the unhappy side of life, to pass without the least twinge of sympathy all human sorrows and pains. If reminded of them against her will, she hardened herself with the bitter memory of her early years, when, as she said, she had suffered quite enough for one lifetime. The habit of her mind was to regard existence as an entertaining spectacle. She had a most comfortable seat, and flattered herself that few people could appreciate so well as she the comedy going on before her. When she found an opportunity for intervention; when, with little or no trouble to herself, she could rearrange a scene or prepare a novel situation, so much the better was she pleased, and all the more disdain did she feel for the fussy, pompous mortals who were so easily manipulated.

Our Friend the Charlatan

At present she had her eyes upon a personage who amused her considerably. He answered to the name of Dyce Lashmar, and fell under the general description of charlatan. Not for a moment had Mrs. Toplady been in doubt as to this classification; but Dyce Lashmar was not quite an ordinary charlatan, and seemed to be worth the observing. She meant to know him thoroughly, to understand what he really aimed at—whether he harboured merely a gross design on Lady Ogram's wealth, or in truth believed himself strong enough to win a place among those grave comedians who rule the world. He was a very young man; he had not altogether got rid of youth's ingenuousness; if his ideas were his own (she doubted it) he had evidently a certain mental equipment, which would aid him—up to a certain point; in any case, he excelled in intellectual plausibility. Perhaps he might get into Parliament; for the amusement of the thing, she would try to help him in that direction. And, on returning from Rivenoak, she had at once begun to spread rumours of a " coming man," a new light in the political world, that it behoved one to keep an eye on. So seldom did Mrs. Toplady risk her reputation by rash prophecy, that those who heard of Mr. Lashmar were disposed to take him with all seriousness. Certain of Mrs. Toplady's intimates begged, and were promised, the privilege of meeting him. To that end, a ceremonious evening was appointed in Pont Street.

Meanwhile, Lashmar had called, and met with a very gracious reception. He was bidden to luncheon on a day in the same week. On arriving, he found with surprise that he was the sole guest.

" I wanted to have a real talk with you," said the hostess, as she received him in her magnificent drawing-room. " I have been thinking a great deal about things you said at Rivenoak."

Her fire of glances perceived that the young man, though agreeably touched and full of expectancy, was

165

to a certain extent on his guard. He, too, no doubt, had power of reading faces, of discerning motives. She did not desire him to be too facile a victim of cajolery; it would take from the interest she felt in his ambitions. At table they talked at first of bio-sociology, Mrs. Toplady, with the adroitness which distinguished her, seeming thoroughly to grasp a subject of which she knew nothing, and which, if she had tried to think about it, would have bored her unspeakably. But she soon diverged to things personal, spoke of people whom she wished Lashmar to meet, and asked whether a date she had in mind would suit his convenience.

" I think you know Lord Dymchurch ? "

" Very well," answered Dyce blandly.

"I should like to meet him. I have heard he is most interesting."

" He certainly is," said Lashmar, " but no man is so hard to get hold of. I never ventured to try to take him anywhere; he very much dislikes meeting strangers."

" Tell me about him, will you ? "

Dyce could speak only of Lord Dymchurch's personal and mental characteristics; of his circumstances he knew nothing more than could be gathered from rumour.

"Let me make a suggestion," said Mrs. Toplady, with a flatteringly intimate air. " Suppose you give a quiet little dinner to a few of your friends, say at one of the restaurants. Don't you think Lord Dymchurch might be willing to come ? If I may propose myself—" The roguish smile was lost in a radiant archness. " Half-a-dozen of us—just to talk over the political situation."

Lashmar looked delighted. In reality he was seized with anxious thought as to whom he could invite for such an important occasion. As is commonly the case with men of great self-esteem and modest resources, he had made friends with the poorer and less ambitious of his acquaintances, and these were not the sort of people

Our Friend the Charlatan

to present either to Mrs. Toplady or to Lord Dymchurch.
However, he knew a man pretty well placed in the
Home Office. He knew also——

"Would you like to ask our friend Mrs. Woolstan?"
let fall the hostess, shooting one swift glance at his busy
forehead.

"Yes—certainly."

"She's charming," pursued Mrs. Toplady, with her
kindest air, "and I'm sure your views interest her."

"Mrs. Woolstan has spoken of them?"

"Oh, yes! She called here, as I told you, the day
before I went down to Rivenoak, and, as we were
talking, I happened to mention where I was going.
'Oh, then,' she said, 'you'll see my friend Mr. Lashmar!' I told her that Lady Ogram had specially
asked me to meet you. Of course it delighted me to
hear that you knew each other so well. I have always
thought Mrs. Woolstan a very clever little woman.
And she looks at things from such a high point of
view—a thorough idealist. Do let us have her. Then,
if I might propose another guest—— ?"

She paused, as if afraid of presuming on Lashmar's
good-nature.

"Pray do! I couldn't possibly have a better
adviser."

Dyce was trying to strike his note of easy comradeship, but found it very difficult. Mrs. Toplady had so
vast an advantage of him in manner, in social resources,
and, for all her amiability, must needs regard him from
higher ground.

"It's very nice of you to say that," she resumed. "I
was thinking of Mr. Roach, the member for Belper.
You don't happen to know him? Oh, that doesn't
matter. He's delightful; about your own age, I think.
Come and meet him here at five o'clock on Sunday;
have a talk, and then send him your invitation. He,
too, is a thorough idealist; you're sure to like him."

Before Lashmar left the house, all the details of this
little dinner were neatly settled, the only point neces-

sarily left uncertain being whether Lord Dymchurch
could be counted upon. Of course Mrs. Toplady had
dictated everything, even to the choice of restaurant
and the very room that was to be engaged; Lashmar
would have the pleasure of ordering the dinner, and of
paying the bill. He thanked his stars again for Mrs.
Woolstan's cheque.

On the strength of that same cheque he had quitted
his rooms near St. Pancras Church, and was now
lodging, with more dignity, but doubtful advantage as
to comfort, in Devonshire Street, Portland Place. The
address, he felt, sounded tolerably well. Only in the
vaguest way had he troubled to compute his annual
outlay on this new basis. He was become an adventurer,
and in common self-respect must cultivate the true
adventurous spirit. Once or twice he half reproached
himself for not striking out yet more boldly into the
currents of ambition, for it was plain that a twelvemonth must see him either made or ruined, and
probably everything depended on the quality of his
courage. Now, he began to wonder whether Mrs.
Toplady's favour would be likely to manifest itself in
any still more practical way; but of this his reflection
offered him no assurance. The probability was that in
Lady Ogram lay his only reasonable hope. On the
spur of such feeling, he addressed a letter to Rivenoak,
giving an account of his luncheon in Pont Street, and
thanking the old autocrat more fervently than he yet
had done for all her good offices.

Since his return from Rivenoak, he had not met
Lord Dymchurch. He might, of course, write his
invitation, but he fancied that it would have more
chance of being accepted if he urged it orally, and, as
he could not call upon the peer (whose private address,
in books of reference, was merely the house in Somerset),
he haunted the club with the hope of encountering him.
On the second day fortune was propitious. Lord
Dymchurch sat in his usual corner of the library, and,
on Lashmar's approach, smiled his wonted greeting.

After preliminary gossip, Dyce commanded himself to courageous utterance.

"I have been asked to come forward as Liberal candidate for a little borough in the Midlands—Hollingford. It's a Tory seat, and I don't know whether I shall stand any chance, but local people want to fight it, and they seem to think that I may be the man for them."

As he spoke, he felt that he wore an expression new to his visage, a sort of smile which his lips had not the habit of framing. Quite unconsciously, indeed, he had reproduced the smile of Mrs. Toplady; its ironic good-humour seemed to put him at ease, and to heighten his personal effectiveness.

"Hollingford?" Lord Dymchurch reflected. "I only know the name."

He looked at Lashmar with a new interest. Constantly worrying about his own inactive life, and what he deemed his culpable supineness as a citizen, the pinched peer envied any man to whom the Lower House offered its large possibilities.

"The idea is quite novel to me," Lashmar continued. "You know something of my views—my cast of mind; do you think I should do well to go in for practical politics?"

"I think any man does well who goes in for anything practical," was Lord Dymchurch's answer. "Stand, by all means, and I wish you success. Parliament isn't overcrowded with men of original views."

"That's very kind of you. I don't want to presume upon your good-nature, but I wonder whether I could persuade you to dine with me, to meet a few friends of mine who are so good as to interest themselves in this matter? Quite an informal little dinner; one or two ladies—the member for Belper—a Home Office man—people who see things rather in my own way."

He added place and date; then, with Mrs. Toplady's smile still on his lips, awaited the response. That Lord Dymchurch would much have preferred to excuse himself was visible enough in the pleasant, youthful-looking countenance, little apt for dissembling; but no less evident was the amiability which made it difficult for him to refuse a favour, and which, in this instance, allied itself with something like a sense of duty. Lord Dymchurch had been considerably impressed by Lashmar's talk; the bio-sociological theory and all its consequences appealed alike to his reason and his imagination; he had mused over this new philosophy, and the opportunity of being ever so little helpful to such a man as its originator should, he felt, be regarded as a privilege. That he could not altogether *take to* Lashmar was nothing to the point. How often had he rebuked himself for his incrustation of prejudices, social and personal, which interfered between him and the living, progressing world! Fie upon his finical spirit, which dwelt so vulgarly on a man's trivial defects!

"With pleasure," he replied; and, as if feeling it insufficient, he added, "with great pleasure!"

Dyce's lips forgot Mrs. Toplady; he smiled his own smile of genial satisfaction, and, as his way was when pleased, broke into effusive talk. He told of Lady Ogram, of the political situation at Hollingford, of editor Breakspeare, of the cantankerous Robb, and to all this Lord Dymchurch willingly lent ear.

"I should uncommonly like you to go down with me some day. You might find it amusing. Lady Ogram is, undeniably, a very remarkable woman."

No sooner was this conversation finished than Lashmar wrote off to Mrs. Toplady half-a-dozen exultant lines, announcing his success. No more wavering, he said to himself. Fate was on his side. He had but to disregard all paltry obstacles, and go straight on.

Yet one obstacle, and that not altogether paltry, continually haunted his mind. He could not forget Lady Ogram's obvious intention that he should marry Constance Bride; and such a marriage was altogether out of harmony with his ambition. If it brought him money—that is to say, a substantial fortune—he might be content to accept it, but it could not be more than a compromise; he had aimed at a very different sort of alliance. Moreover, he knew nothing of Lady Ogram's real intentions with regard to Constance; her mysterious phrases merely perplexed and annoyed him as often as he thought of them. To marry Constance *without* a substantial fortune—that were disaster indeed! And what if Lady Ogram's favour depended upon it?

But he had his little dinner to think of. He wrote to Mrs. Woolstan, who by return of post blithely accepted his invitation, begging him, at the same time, to come and see her before then, if he could possibly spare an hour. Dyce threw the letter aside impatiently. On Sunday he was in Pont Street, where he met the Parliamentary Mr. Roach, a young man fairly answering to Mrs. Toplady's description; an idealist of a mild type, whose favourite talk was of " altruism," and who, whilst affecting close attention to what other people said, was always absorbed in his own thoughts. Before Lashmar had been many minutes in the drawing-room, there entered Mrs. Woolstan, and she soon found an occasion for brief exchange of words with him.

" Why haven't you been to see me yet ? "

" I'm so terribly busy. Of course I ought to have come. I thought of to-morrow—but now that we've met here, and you are coming to dine on the 27th——"

" Oh, I know you *must* be busy ! " conceded Iris, with panting emphasis and gladness. " How splendidly everything's going ! But I want to hear about it all, you know. Your letter about Rivenoak only made me eager to know more."

" We'll have an afternoon presently. Ask Mrs. Toplady to introduce Mr. Roach—he dines with us on the 27th."

To make sure of the M.P., Lashmar invited him verbally, and received a dreamy acceptance—so dreamy that he resolved to send a note to remind Mr. Roach of the engagement.

Our Friend the Charlatan

"So you are to be one of us at Mr. Lashmar's dinner," said the hostess to Mrs. Woolstan. "A delightful evening, won't it be!"

And she watched the eager little face with eyes which read its every line remorselessly: her smile more pitiless in ironic mischief even than of wont.

On the morning of May the 28th, Lashmar wrote a full letter to Rivenoak. It told of a dinner successful beyond his hopes. Mrs. Toplady had surpassed herself in brilliant graciousness; Lord Dymchurch had broken through his reserve, and talked remarkably—most remarkably. "As for the host, why, he did what in him lay, and Mrs. Toplady was good enough to remark, as he handed her into her carriage, 'A few more dinners such as this, and all London will want to know the——' I won't finish her sentence. Joking apart, I think my friends enjoyed themselves, and they were certainly very encouraging with regard to our project."

At the same hour, Mrs. Toplady, propped with pillows, was also writing to Rivenoak.

"It came off very well indeed, and I see that we must take serious account of Mr. Lashmar. You knew that, of course, and I didn't doubt your judgment, but intellectual distinction doesn't always go together with the qualities necessary to a political career. Beyond a doubt he is our coming man! And now let me know when to expect you in London. I look forward to the delight of seeing you, and of making the acquaintance of your niece, who must be *very* interesting. How lucky you are to have discovered at the same time two such brilliant young people! By the bye, I have not mentioned Miss Tomalin to any one; it occurred to me that silence in this matter was perhaps discretion. If I have been needlessly reticent, pray say so. Of course at a word from you, I can speak to the right people, but possibly you had rather nothing at all were said until the young lady has been seen. Myself, I see no reason whatever for explanations."

Our Friend the Charlatan

As she closed this letter, Mrs. Toplady's smile all but became a chuckle. Nothing had so much amused her for a twelvemonth past.

Lashmar had no reply from Rivenoak. This silence disappointed him. Ten days having elapsed, he thought of writing again, but there arrived a letter addressed in Miss Bride's hand, the contents a few lines in tremulous but bold character, signed " A. Ogram." He was invited to lunch, on the next day but one, at Bunting's Hotel, Albemarle Street.

This same afternoon, having nothing to do, he went to call upon Mrs. Woolstan. It was his second visit since the restaurant dinner, and Iris showed herself very grateful for his condescension. She regarded him anxiously; made inquiries about his health; was he not working too hard? His eyes looked rather heavy, as if he studied too late at night. Dyce, assuming the Toplady smile, admitted that he might have been rather over-zealous at his constitutional history of late—concession to practicality had led him to take up that subject; in his thoughts, he reproached himself for a freak of the previous evening, a little outbreak of folly, of no grave importance, which had doubtless resulted from the exciting tenor of his life recently. On the whole, it might serve a useful purpose, reminding him to be on guard against certain weaknesses of his temperament, likely to be fostered by ease and liberty.

" Lady Ogram is in town," he announced. " I lunch with her to-morrow."

The news agitated Mrs. Woolstan.

" Will she be alone ? "

" I suppose so—except for her secretary, who of course is always with her."

Iris desired to know all about the secretary, and Lashmar described a neutral-tinted, pen-wielding young woman, much interested in social reforms.

" Perhaps I shall come to know Lady Ogram," said Iris modestly. " I may meet her at Mrs. Toplady's.

173

That would be delightful! I should be able to follow everything much better."

"To be sure," was the rather dry response. "But I shall be surprised if the old lady stays long or sees many people. Her health is of the shakiest, and London life would be a dangerous experiment, I should say. I don't at all know why she's coming, unless it is to see doctors."

"Oh, I *do* hope she'll be careful," panted Iris. "What a terrible thing it would be if she died suddenly—terrible for you, I mean. She ought to have some one to look well after her, indeed she ought. I wish "—this with a laugh—" she would take me as companion. Oh, wouldn't I have a care of her precious health !"

When Dyce drove to Bunting's Hotel, he had no thought of seeing any one but Lady Ogram and Constance ; the possibility that there might be other guests at luncheon did not enter his mind. Led up to a private drawing-room on the first floor, he became aware, as the door opened, of a handsome girl in animated conversation with his two friends ; she seemed so very much at home that he experienced a little shock, as of the unaccountable, the disconcerting, and his eyes with difficulty turned from this new face to that of the venerable hostess. Here again a surprise awaited him ; Lady Ogram looked so much younger than when he took leave of her at Rivenoak, that he marvelled at the transformation. Notwithstanding her aspect she spoke in a strained, feeble voice, often indistinct ; one noticed, too, that she was harder of hearing. Having pressed his hand—a very faint pressure, though meant for cordial—Lady Ogram turned a look upon the bright young lady near her, and said, with a wheezy emphasis :

"Let me introduce you to my niece, Miss Tomalin."

Never had Lashmar known her so ceremonious ; never had she appeared so observant of his demeanour during the social formality. Stricken with astonishment at what he heard, he bowed stiffly, but sub-

missively. Here, he saw at once, was no opportunity
for the *sans-gêne* favoured by his "method." The
autocrat watched him with severe eyes, and only when
his salute was accomplished did the muscles of her
visage again relax. Mechanically, he turned to bow
in the same way to Miss Bride, but she at once offered
her hand with a friendly, "How do you do?"

"My niece, Miss Tomalin." Where on earth did this
niece spring from? Everybody understood that Lady
Ogram was alone in the world. Constance had expressly affirmed it—yet here was she smiling in the
most natural way possible, as if nieces abounded at
Rivenoak. Dyce managed to talk, but he heard not a
word from his own lips, and his eyes, fixed on Lady
Ogram's features, noted, as if independently, the in-
dubitable fact that her complexion was artificial. This
astounding old woman, at the age of four score, had
begun to paint! So confused was Dyce's state of mind
that, on perceiving the truth of the matter, he all but
uttered an exclamation. Perhaps only Miss Tomalin's
voice arrested him.

"My aunt has told me all about your new socialism,
Mr. Lashmar. You can't think how it has put my mind
at rest! One has so felt that one *ought* to be a socialist,
and yet there were so many things one couldn't accept.
It's delightful to see everything reconciled—all one
wants to keep and all the new things that *must* come!"

May had been developing. She spoke with a confidence which, on softer notes, emulated that of her
aged relative; she carried her head with a conscious
stateliness which might have been—perhaps had been
—deliberately studied after the portrait in the Rivenoak dining-room. Harmonious with this change was
that in her attire; fashion had done its best to trans-
form the aspiring young provincial into a metropolitan
Grace; the result being that Miss Tomalin seemed
to have grown in stature, to exhibit a more notable
symmetry, so that she filled more space in the observer's
eye than heretofore. For all that, she looked no older;

Our Friend the Charlatan

her self-assertion, though more elaborate, was not a bit
more impressive, and the phrases she used, the turn of
her sentences, the colour of her speech, very little
resembled anything that would have fallen from a
damsel bred in the modish world. Her affectation was
shot through with spontaneity; her impertinence had
a juvenile seriousness which made it much more
amusing than offensive; and a feminine charm in her,
striving to prevail over incongruous elements, made
clear appeal to the instincts of the other sex.

"That is very encouraging," was Lashmar's reply.
"If one's thoughts can be of any help to others——"

"What time is it?" broke in Lady Ogram. "Why
doesn't that man come? What business has he to keep
us waiting?"

"It's only just half-past one," said Miss Bride.

"Then he ought to be here." She turned to Lashmar.
"I'm expecting a friend you've heard of—Sir William
Amys. How long are we to sit here waiting for him, I
wonder?"

"What do you think of Herbert Spencer, Mr.
Lashmar?" inquired May.

Dyce's reply was rendered doubly unnecessary by the
opening of the door, and the announcement of the
awaited guest.

"Willy! Willy!" cried Lady Ogram, with indulgent
reproof. "You always used to be so punctual."

The gentleman thus familiarly addressed had grey
hair and walked with a stoop in the shoulders. His
age was sixty, but he looked rather older. Lady Ogram,
who had known him as a boy, still saw him in that light.
His pleasant face, full of intelligence and good-humour,
wore a gently deprecating smile as he stepped forward,
and—whether intentionally or not—he smoothed with
one hand his long, grizzled beard.

"This is military!" he exclaimed. "Are not a few
minutes' grace granted to a man of peace, when he
comes to eat your salt?—And how are you, my dear
lady? How are you?"

Our Friend the Charlatan

"Never was better in my life, Willy!" shrilled Lady Ogram, her voice slipping out of control in her excitement. "Do you know who this is?"

"I could make a guess. The face speaks for itself."

"Ha! You see the likeness!—May, shake hands with Sir William, and make friends with him; he and I knew each other a lifetime before you were born. And this is Mr. Lashmar, our future member for Hollingford."

"If the voters are as kind to me as Lady Ogram," said Dyce, laughing.

The baronet gave his hand, and regarded the young man with shrewd observation. Sir William had no part in public life, and was not predisposed in favour of parliamentary ambitions; he lived quietly in a London suburb, knowing only a few congenial people, and occupying himself with the history of art, on which he was something of an authority. His father had been one of those friends of Sir Quentin Ogram who knew not Arabella's history, and thus arose his early familiarity with the lady of Rivenoak.

They went to table in an adjoining room, and for a few minutes there was talk between the hostess and Sir William about common acquaintances. Lashmar, the while, kept turning his look towards Miss Tomalin. With his astonishment had begun to mingle feelings of interest and attraction. He compared Miss Tomalin's personal appearance with that of Constance Bride, and at once so hardened towards the latter that he could not bring his eyes to regard her again. At the same time he perceived, with gratification, that Lady Ogram's niece was not heedless of his presence; once at least their looks came to the encounter, with quick self-recovery on the young lady's part, and a conscious smile. Dyce began to think her very good-looking indeed. Sir William's remark recurred to him, and he saw an undeniable resemblance in the girl's features to those of Lady Ogram's early portrait. He grew nervously desirous to know something about her.

Our Friend the Charlatan

Presently conversation directed itself towards the subject with which Lashmar was connected. Sir William appeared by no means eager to discuss political or social themes, but May Tomalin could not rest till they were brought forward, and her aunt, who seemed to have no desire but to please her and put her into prominence, helped them on.

"Are you going to stand as a Socialist?" the baronet inquired of Lashmar, with some surprise, when May's talk had sufficiently confused him.

Dyce quietly explained (a shadow of the Toplady smile about his lips) that his Socialism was not Social-democracy.

"For my own part," declared Sir William, "I want to hear a little more of men, and a little less of government. That we're moving into Socialism of one kind or another is plain enough, and it goes against the grain with me. I'm afraid we're losing our vigour as individuals. It's all very well to be a good citizen, but it's more important, don't you think, to be a man?"

"I quite see your point, Sir William," said Lashmar, his eyes brightening as they always did when he found his opportunity for borrowed argument and learning. "Clearly there's an excess to be avoided; individuality mustn't be lost sight of. But I can see absolutely no distinction between the terms Man and Citizen. To my mind they are synonymous, for Man only came into being when he ceased to be an animal by developing the idea of citizenship. In my view, the source of all our troubles is found in that commonly accepted duality. It didn't exist in the progressive ancient world. The dualism of Man and State began with the decline of Græco-Roman civilization, and was perpetuated by the teaching of Christianity. The philosophy of Epicurus and of Zeno—an utter detachment from the business of mankind—prepared the way for the spirit of the Gospels. So, at length, we get our notion of Church and State—a separation ruinous to religion and making impossible anything like perfection in politics; it has

Our Friend the Charlatan

thoroughly rooted in people's mind that fatal distinction between Man as a responsible soul and Man as a member of society. Our work is to restore the old monism. Very, very slowly, mankind is working towards it. A revolution greater than any of those commonly spoken of—so wide and deep that it isn't easily taken in even by students of history—a revolution which is the only hope of civilization, has been going on since the close of the thirteenth century. We are just beginning to be dimly conscious of it. Perhaps in another century it will form the principle of Liberalism."

The baronet heard all this with wonder; he had not been prepared for such solidity of doctrine from Lady Ogram's candidate, and at the luncheon table. As for May Tomalin, she had listened delightedly. Her lips savoured the words "dualism" and "monism," of which she resolved to make brave use in her own argumentative displays. The first to speak was Constance.

"We are getting on very quickly," she said, in her driest and most practical tone, "towards one ideal of socialism. Look at the way in which municipalities are beginning to undertake, and sometimes monopolize, work which used to be left to private enterprise. Before long we shall have local authorities engaged in banking, pawnbroking, coal-supplying, tailoring, estate agency, printing—all these, and other undertakings, are already proposed."

May cast a glance of good-natured envy at the speaker. How she wished she could display such acquaintance with public life. But the information was stored for future use.

"Why, there you are!" exclaimed the baronet. "That's just what I'm afraid of. It's the beginning of tyranny. It'll mean the bad work of a monopoly, instead of the good to be had by free competition. You favour this kind of thing, Mr. Lashmar?"

"In so far as it signifies growth of the ideas of citizenship, and of association. But it interests me

179

much less than purely educational questions. Whatever influence I may gain will be used towards a
thorough reconstruction of our system of popular schooling. I believe nothing serious can be done until we
have a truly civic education for the masses of the
people."

This was the outcome of Lashmar's resolve to be
practical whilst adhering to his philosophy. He knew
that it sounded well, this demand for educational reform ;
however vague in reality, it gave the ordinary hearer a
quasi-intelligible phrase to remember and repeat. Sir
William Amys was not proof against the plausibility of
such words ; he admitted that one might do worse than
devote oneself to that question—popular schooling,
heaven knew, being much in need of common-sense
reform. Dyce tactfully pressed his advantage. He
ridiculed the extravagance of educationalism run mad,
its waste of public money, the harm it does from a
social point of view; and, the longer he spoke, the
better pleased was Sir William to hear him. Their
hostess, silent and closely attentive, smiled with satisfaction. Constance, meanwhile, noted the countenance
of May Tomalin, which showed very much the same
kind of pleased approval. Only a day or two ago,
May, speaking on this subject, had expressed views
diametrically opposite.

After luncheon, Lady Ogram held Lashmar in talk,
whilst the two young ladies conversed with the baronet
apart. Dyce had hoped for a little gossip with Miss
Tomalin, but no chance offered; discretion bade him
take leave before Sir William had given sign of rising.

"I don't know how long we shall be in town," said
Lady Ogram, who did not seek to detain him, " but of
course we shall see you again. We shall generally be
at home at five o'clock."

He had hoped for a more definite and a more cordial
invitation. Issuing into Albemarle Street, he looked
vaguely about him, and wondered how he should get
through the rest of the afternoon. A dull sky aided

Our Friend the Charlatan

the failure of his spirits; when, in a few minutes, rain began to fall, he walked on under his umbrella, thoroughly cheerless and objectless. Then it struck him that he would go presently to Pont Street; Mrs. Toplady might help him to solve the mystery of Lady Ogram's niece.

Confound Lady Ogram's niece! Her appearance could not have been more inopportune. The old woman was obviously quite taken up with her, and, as likely as not, would lose all her interest in politics. Here was the explanation of her not having answered his last long letter. Confound Miss—what was her foolish name?—Tomalin!

And yet—and yet—there glimmered another aspect of the matter. Suppose Miss Tomalin followed her aunt's example, and saw in him a coming man, and seriously interested herself in his fortunes? Then, indeed, she would be by no means a superfluous young person; for who could say to what such interest might lead? Miss Tomalin would be his aunt's heiress, or so one might reasonably suppose. And she was a very pretty girl, as well as intelligent.

Could it be that the real course of his destiny was only just beginning to reveal itself?

By this time, he felt better. To pass an hour, he went into his club, read the papers, and looked, vainly, for Lord Dymchurch.

Greatly to his surprise, he found the world-shunning nobleman in Mrs. Toplady's drawing-room; the hostess and he were alone together—it was early—and seemed to have been engaged in rather intimate talk.

"Oh, this is nice!" exclaimed Mrs. Toplady. "What have you to tell us?"

"Little of interest, I'm afraid—except that I have lunched to-day with Lady Ogram, and made the acquaintance of her niece."

"We were speaking of her," said the hostess, with very pronounced mischief at the corner of her lips, and eyes excessively gracious.

181

Our Friend the Charlatan

"You know Miss Tomalin?" Lashmar inquired, rather abruptly, of Lord Dymchurch.

"I have met her once," was the colourless reply.

Dyce wished to ask where and when, but of course could not. He resented this advantage of Lord Dymchurch.

"She is very clever," the hostess was saying, "and quite charming. A Canadian, you know, by birth. Such a fresh way of looking at things; so bright and——"

Other callers were announced. Lord Dymchurch looked his desire to escape, but sat on. You would have thought him a man with a troubled conscience.

CHAPTER XIII

A FEW days later Lashmar found on his breakfast-table a copy of the *Hollingford Express*, blue-pencilled at an editorial paragraph which he read with interest. The leaded lines announced that Hollingford Liberalism was at length waking up, that a campaign was being quietly but vigorously organized, and that a meeting of active politicians would shortly be held for the purpose of confirming a candidature which had already met with approval in influential circles. The same post brought a letter from Mr. Breakspeare. "Will you," asked the editor, "name a convenient date for meeting your friends and supporters? Say, about the 20th of this month. I am working up enthusiasm. We shall take the public room at the Saracen's Head. Admission to be by invitation card. I write to Lady Ogram, and no doubt you will consult with her."

This looked like business. Dyce reflected rather nervously that he would have to make a speech—a practical speech; he must define his political attitude; philosophical generalities would not serve in the public room at the Saracen's Head. Well, he had a fortnight to think about it. And here was an excuse for calling on Lady Ogram, of which he would avail himself at once.

In the afternoon he went to Bunting's Hotel, but Lady Ogram was not at home. He inquired for Miss Bride, and was presently led up to the private drawing-room, where Constance sat writing. As they shook hands, their eyes scarcely met.

" Can you spare me a few minutes ? " asked the visitor.
" There's something here I wanted to show Lady Ogram ;
183

but I shall be still more glad to talk it over with you."

Constance took the newspaper and Breakspeare's note. As she read, her firm-set lips relaxed a little. She handed the papers back with a nod.

" Has Lady Ogram heard ? " Dyce asked.

" Yes ; she had a letter this morning, and I have answered it. She was pleased. So far, so good. You have had Mrs. Toplady's card for the evening of the 13th ? "

" I have."

" One of the Liberal whips will be there—an opportunity for you."

Every time he saw her Constance seemed to be drier and more laconic. Their intercourse promised to illustrate to the full his professed ideal of relation between man and woman in friendship ; every note of difference in sex would soon be eliminated, if indeed that point were not already attained.

" Won't you sit down ? " asked Miss Bride carelessly ; for Dyce had thrown hat and stick aside, and was moving about with his hands in his pockets.

" But you're busy."

" Not particularly."

" How is our friend ? "

" Lady Ogram ? Pretty well, I think, but overtaxing herself. I don't think she'll be able to stay here long. It certainly wouldn't be wise."

" Of course it's on her niece's account. By the bye "— Dyce paused before Constance's chair—" where has this niece sprung from ? You told me she hadn't a relative in the world."

" So she believed. Miss Tomalin is a recent discovery—the fruit of Mr. Kerchever's researches."

" Ah ! that's rather amusing. Lucky, I imagine, that she is such a presentable person. She might have been——"

He checked himself significantly, and Constance allowed an absent smile to pass over her face.

"I'm afraid," Dyce continued, "this change won't be quite pleasant to you?"

"To me? It makes no difference—none whatever. Will you please sit down? I dislike to talk with any one who keeps fidgeting about."

One might have detected more than discomfort in Miss Bride's look and voice. A sudden flash of something very like anger shone in her eyes; but they were bent and veiled.

"Let us talk about Hollingford," said Lashmar, drawing up a chair. "It begins to look as if things were really in train. Of course I shall go down to talk to the people. Will you help me in putting my programme together?"

"Isn't that already done?"

"Why, no. What do I care about their party questions? I'm sure your advice would be valuable. Could you find time to jot down a few ideas?"

"If you think it any use, certainly. I can't promise to do it this evening, we have people to dine."

Lashmar was secretly offended that Lady Ogram should give a dinner-party in which he had no place.

"Any one coming that I know?" he asked off-hand.

"Let me see. Yes, there's Mrs. Toplady—and Lord Dymchurch——"

Dyce exclaimed.

"What an extraordinary thing! Dymchurch, who never went anywhere, seems all at once to be living in the thick of the world. The other day I found him at Mrs. Toplady's, drinking tea. Was it there he came to know Lady Ogram?"

"Yes," Constance smiled. "Lady Ogram, you remember, much wished to meet him."

"And he dines here? I can't understand it."

"You are not very complimentary," said Constance, with dry amusement.

"You know what I mean. I shouldn't have thought Lady Ogram would have had much attraction for him."

Miss Bride laughed, a laugh of all but genuine gaiety.

"Hadn't we better talk about your programme?" she resumed in an altered voice, as though her humour had suddenly improved. "I should take counsel with Mr. Breakspeare, if I were you. I fancy he likes to be consulted, and his activity will be none the less for it."

Lashmar could not easily fix his thoughts on political tactics. He talked impatiently, all the time absorbed in another subject; and at the first pause he took his leave.

Decidedly it offended him that he was left out from this evening's dinner-party. A suspicion too had broken upon his mind which he found very distasteful and perturbing. Lady Ogram must have particular reasons for thus cultivating Lord Dymchurch's acquaintance; conjecturing what they might be, he perceived how he had allowed himself to shape visions and dream dreams during the last day or two. It was foolish, as he now saw plainly enough; in ambition one must discern the probable, and steady one's course thereby. All at once he felt a strong dislike of Lord Dymchurch, and even a certain contempt. The man was not what he had thought him.

Crossing the street at Piccadilly Circus, he ran before a hansom, and from the hansom was waved a hand, a voice in the same moment calling out his name. As a result of his stopping, he was very nearly run over by another cab; he escaped to the pavement, the hansom pulled up beside him, and he shook hands with Mrs. Woolstan.

"Are you going anywhere?" she asked, her eyes very wide as they gazed at him.

"Nowhere in particular."

"Then do come with me, will you? I have to buy a present for Len's birthday, and I should be so glad of your help in choosing it."

Dyce jumped into the vehicle, and, as his habit was, at once surveyed himself in the little looking-glass conveniently placed for that purpose. The inspection never gratified him, and to-day less than usual. Turning to his companion, he asked:

Our Friend the Charlatan

"Does everybody look ugly in a hansom mirror?"

"What a question! I'm sure I can't tell you."

Iris had coloured a little. Her eyes involuntarily sought the slip of glass at her side of the seat, and the face she saw was not a flattering likeness. With brow knitted, she stared out into the street, and presently asked:

"Have you seen Lady Ogram?"

"Yes."

"I thought you told me that she would have no one with her but her secretary? Why did you say that?"

"Because I didn't know that she had a newly-discovered niece. It seems that you have heard of it. Perhaps you have met her?"

"Not yet. Mrs. Toplady told me."

"And you take it for granted that I had deliberately concealed the niece from you?" said Lashmar, with an amused air. "Pray, why should I have done so?"

"No, no, I thought nothing of the kind," replied Mrs. Woolstan, in a conciliating tone. "Indeed I didn't! It's only that I felt vexed not to have heard the story from you first. I thought you would have told it me as soon as possible—such an interesting thing as that."

Lashmar declared that he had only known of Miss Tomalin's existence for a day or two, and had only heard the explanation of her appearance this very day. His companion asked for a description of the young lady, and he gave one remarkable for splenetic exaggeration.

"You must have seen her in a hansom looking-glass," said Iris, smiling askance at him. "Mrs. Toplady's picture is very different. And the same applies to Miss Bride: I formed an idea of her from what you told me, which doesn't answer at all to that given me by Mrs. Toplady."

"Mrs. Toplady," replied Dyce, his lips reminiscent of Pont Street, "inclines to idealism, I have found. It's an amiable weakness, but one has to be on one's guard against it. Did she say anything about Lord Dymchurch?"

"Nothing. Why?"

Dyce seemed to reflect; then spoke as if confidentially.

"I suspect there is a little conspiracy against the noble lord. From certain things that I have observed and heard, I think it probable that Lady Ogram wants to capture Dymchurch for her niece."

A light shone upon the listener's countenance, and she panted eager exclamations.

"Really? You think so? But I understood that he was so poor. How is it possible?"

"Yes. Dymchurch is poor, I believe, but he is a lord. Lady Ogram is *not* poor, and I fancy she would like above all things to end her life as aunt-in-law (if there is such a thing) of a peer. Her weakness, as we know, has always been for the aristocracy. She's a strong-minded woman in most things. I am quite sure she prides herself on belonging by birth to the lower class, and she knows that most aristocrats are imbeciles; for all that, she won't rest till she has found her niece a titled husband. This is my private conviction; take it for what it is worth."

"But," cried Iris, satisfaction still shining on her face, "do you think there's the least chance that Lord Dymchurch will be—caught?"

"A week ago I should have laughed at the suggestion. Now, I don't feel at all sure of his safety. He goes about to meet the girl. He's dining at their hotel to-night."

"You take a great interest in it," said Mrs. Woolstan, her voice faltering a little.

"Because I am so surprised and disappointed about Dymchurch. I thought better of him. I took him for a philosopher."

"But Mrs. Toplady says the girl is charming, and very clever."

"That's a matter of opinion. Doesn't Mrs. Toplady strike you as something of a busybody—a glorified busybody, of course?"

Our Friend the Charlatan

"Oh, I like her! And she speaks *very* nicely of you."

"I'm much obliged. But, after all, why should she speak otherwise than nicely of me?"

Whilst Iris was meditating an answer to this question, the cab pulled up at a great shop. They alighted; the driver was bidden to wait; and along the alleys of the gleaming bazaar they sought a present suitable for Leonard Woolstan. To Lashmar it was a scarcely tolerable *ennui;* he had even more than the average man's hatred of shopping, and feminine indecision whipped him to contemptuous rage. To give himself something to do, he looked about for a purchase on his own account, and, having made it, told Iris that this was a present from him to his former pupil.

"Oh, how kind of you!" exclaimed the mother, regarding him tenderly. "How very kind of you! Len will be delighted, poor boy."

They left the shop, and stood by the hansom.

"Where are you going to now?" asked Iris.

"Home, to work. I have to address a meeting at Hollingford on the 20th, and I must think out a sufficiency of harmless nonsense."

"Really? A public meeting already? Couldn't I come and hear you?"

Dyce explained the nature of the gathering.

"But I shall see you before then," he added, helping her to enter the cab. "By the bye, don't be indiscreet with reference to what we spoke of just now."

"Why, of course not," answered Iris, her eyes fixed on his face as he drew back saluting.

Though Lashmar had invented his story concerning Lord Dymchurch on the spur of the moment, he now thoroughly believed it himself, and the result was a restlessness of mind which no conviction of its utter absurdity could overcome. In vain did he remember that Lady Ogram had settled his destiny so far as the matter lay in *her* hands, and that to displease the choleric old autocrat would be to overthrow in a moment the edifice of hope reared by her aid. The image of

Our Friend the Charlatan

May Tomalin was constantly before his mind; not that he felt himself sentimentally drawn to her, or in any troublesome degree sensually lured; but she represented an opportunity which it annoyed him to feel that he would not, if he chose, be permitted to grasp. Miss Tomalin by no means satisfied his aspiration in the matter of marriage, whatever wealth she might have to bestow; he had always pictured a very lofty type of woman indeed, a being superb in every attribute, when dreaming of his future spouse. But he enjoyed the sense of power, and was exasperated by a suggestion that any man could have a natural advantage over him. To this characteristic he owed the influence with women which had carried him so far, for there is nothing that better steads a man in his relations with the other sex than amiable egoism serving worldly ambition. This combination of qualities will all but every woman worship. Mrs. Toplady herself, she of the ironic smile and cynic intelligence, felt this magnetic property in Dyce Lashmar's otherwise not very impressive person. On that account did she watch his pranks with so indulgent an eye, and give herself trouble to enlarge the scope of his entertaining activity. She knew, however, that the man was not cast in heroic mould; that he was capable of scruples, inclined to indolence; that he did not, after all, sufficiently believe in himself to go very far in the subjugation of others. Therefore she had never entertained the thought of seriously devoting herself to his cause, but was content to play with it until something more piquant should claim her attention.

Mrs. Toplady had always wished for the coming of the very hero, the man without fear, without qualm, who should put our finicking civilization under his feet. Her god was a compound of the blood-reeking conqueror and the diplomat supreme in guile. For such a man she would have poured out her safe-invested treasure, enough rewarded with a nod of half-disdainful recognition. It vexed her to think that she might pass away before the appearance of that new actor on the human stage; his entrance was all but due, she felt assured. Ah! the world would be much more amusing presently, and she meanwhile was growing old.

Her drawing-rooms on the evening of June 13th were crowded with representatives of Society. Lashmar arrived about ten o'clock, and his hostess had soon introduced him to two or three persons of political note, with whom he exchanged phrases of such appalling banality that he had much ado not to laugh in his interlocutor's face. The swelling current moved him along; he could only watch faces and listen to dialogues as foolish as those in which he had taken part; a dizzying babblement filled the air, heavy with confusion of perfumes. Presently, having circled his way back towards the stair-head, he caught sight of Lord Dymchurch, who had newly entered; their eyes met, but Dymchurch, who wore a very absent look, gave no sign of recognition. Dyce pressed forward.

"I hoped I might meet you here," he said.

The other started, smiled nervously, and spoke in a confused way.

"I thought it likely—of course you know a great many of these people——".

"Oh, a few. I had rather meet them anywhere than in such a crowd, though."

"Wonderful, isn't it?" murmured Dymchurch, with a comical distress in his eyebrows. "Wonderful."

Good-naturedly nodding, he moved away, and was lost to sight. Dyce, holding his place near the entrance, perceived at length another face that he knew—that of a lady with whom he had recently dined at this house; in her company came Constance Bride and May Tomalin. He all but bounded to meet them. Constance looked well in a garb more ornate than Lashmar had yet seen her wearing; May, glowing with pleasure, made a brilliant appearance. Their chaperon spoke with him; he learned that Lady Ogram did not feel quite equal to an occasion such as this, and had stayed at home.

Miss Tomalin, eager to join in the talk, pressed before Constance.

"Have you got your speech ready, Mr. Lashmar?" she asked, with a sprightly condescension.

"Quite. How sorry I am that you won't be able to enjoy that masterpiece of eloquence!"

"Oh, but it will be reported. It must be reported, of course."

The chaperon interposed, presenting to Miss Tomalin a gentleman who seemed very desirous of that honour, and Dyce stifled his annoyance in saying apart to Constance:

"What barbarism this is! One might as well try to converse in the middle of the street at Charing Cross."

"Certainly. But people don't come to converse," was the answer.

"You enjoy this kind of thing, I fancy?"

"I don't find it disagreeable."

The chaperon and Miss Tomalin were moving away; May cast a look at Lashmar, but he was unconscious of it. Constance turned to follow her companions, and Dyce stood alone again.

Half-an-hour later, the circling currents to which he surrendered himself brought him before a row of chairs, where sat the three ladies, and, by the side of Miss Tomalin, Lord Dymchurch. May, flushed and bright-eyed, was talking at a great rate; she seemed to be laying down the law in some matter, and Dymchurch, respectfully bent towards her, listened with a thoughtful smile. Dyce approached, and spoke to Constance. A few moments afterwards, Lord Dymchurch rose, bowed, and gracefully withdrew; whereupon Lashmar asked Miss Tomalin's permission to take the vacant chair. It was granted rather absently; for the girl's eyes had furtively followed her late companion as he moved away, and she seemed more disposed to reflect than to begin a new conversation. This passed, however; soon she was talking politics with an air of omniscience which Lashmar could only envy.

Our Friend the Charlatan

"May I take you to the supper-room?" he asked presently.

The chaperon and Miss Bride were engaged in conversation with a man who stood behind them.

"Yes, let us go," said May, rising. "I'm thirsty."

She spoke a word to the lady responsible for her, and swept off with Lashmar.

"How delightful it is," Dyce exclaimed, "to gather such a lot of interesting people!"

"Isn't it!" May responded. "One feels really alive here You would hardly believe"— she gave him a confidential look—"that this is my first season in London."

"Indeed it isn't easy to believe," said Dyce, in the tone of compliment.

"I always thought of a London season," pursued May, "as mere frivolity. Of course there is a great deal of that. But here one sees only cultured and serious people; it makes one feel how much hope there is for the world, in spite of everything. The common socialists talk dreadful nonsense about Society; of course it's mere ignorance."

"To be sure," Lashmar assented, with inward mirth. "Their views are inevitably so narrow. How long do you stay in town?"

"I'm very much afraid my aunt's health will oblige us to return to Rivenoak very soon. She has been seeing doctors. I don't know what they tell her, but I notice that she isn't quite herself this last day or two."

"Wonderful old lady, isn't she?" Dyce exclaimed.

"Oh, wonderful! You have known her for a long time, haven't you?"

"No, not very long. But we have talked so much, and agree so well in our views, that I think of her as quite an old friend. What can I get you? Do you like iced coffee?"

Dyce seated her, and tended upon her as though no such thing as a "method" with women had ever entered his mind. His demeanour was lamentably old-fashioned. What it lacked in natural grace, Miss Tomalin was not critical enough to perceive.

"How delightful it will be," she suddenly remarked, "when you are in Parliament! Of course you will invite us to tea on the terrace, and all that kind of thing."

"I'm sure I hope I shall have the chance. My election is by no means a certainty, you know. The Tories are very strong at Hollingford."

"Oh, but we're all going to work for you. When we get back to Rivenoak, I shall begin a serious campaign. I could never live without some serious work of the social kind, and I look upon it as a great opportunity for civilizing people. They must be taught that it is morally wrong to vote for such a man as Robb, and an absolute duty of citizenship to vote for you. How I shall enjoy it!"

"You are really very kind!"

"Oh, don't think of it in that way!" exclaimed Miss Tomalin. "I have always thought more of principles than of persons. It isn't in my nature to take anything up unless I feel an absolute conviction that it is for the world's good. At Northampton I often offended people I really liked by what they called my obstinacy when a principle was at stake. I don't want to praise myself, but I really can say that it is my nature to be earnest and thorough and disinterested."

"Of that I am quite sure," said Lashmar, fervently.

"And—do let me tell you—it is such a delight to feel that my opportunities will be so much greater than formerly." May was growing intimate, but still kept her air of dignity, with its touch of condescension. "At Northampton, you know, I hadn't very much scope; now it will be different. What an important thing social position is! What power for good it gives one!"

"Provided," put in her companion, "that one belongs to nature's aristocracy."

"Well—yes—I suppose one must have the presumption to lay claim to that," returned May, with a little laugh.

"Say, rather, the honesty, the simple courage. Self-depreciation," added Dyce, " I have always regarded as a proof of littleness. People really called to do something never lose confidence in themselves, and have no false modesty about expressing it."

"I'm sure that's very true. I heard once that someone at Northampton had called me conceited, and you can't think what a shock it gave me. I sat down, there and then, and asked myself whether I really *was* conceited, and my conscience assured me I was nothing of the kind. I settled it with myself, once for all. Since then, I have never cared what people said about me."

"That's admirable!" murmured Dyce.

"I am sure," went on the girl, with a serious archness, "that you too have known such an experience."

"To tell the truth, I have," the philosopher admitted, bending his head a little.

"I felt certain that you could understand me, or I should never have ventured to tell you such a thing. There is Miss Bride!"

Constance had taken a seat not far from them, and the man who had been talking with her up-stairs was offering her refreshments. Presently, she caught Miss Tomalin's eye, and smiled; a minute or two after, she and her companion came forward to join the other pair, and all ascended to the drawing-rooms together. When he had restored his charge to her chaperon, Lashmar took the hint of discretion and retired into the throng. There-amid, he encountered Iris Woolstan, her eyes wide in search.

"So you *are* here!" she exclaimed, with immediate change of countenance. "I despaired of ever seeing you. What a crush!"

"Horrible, isn't it! I've had enough; I must breathe the air."

"Oh, stay a few minutes. I know so few people. Are Lady Ogram and her niece here?"

Our Friend the Charlatan

"Lady Ogram, I think not. I caught a glimpse of Miss Tomalin somewhere or other, sternly chaperoned."

He lied gaily, for the talk with May had put him into a thoroughly blithe humour.

"I should so like to see her," said Iris. "Don't you think you could point her out, if we went about a little?"

"Let us look for her, by all means. Have you been to the supper-room? She may be there."

They turned to move slowly towards the staircase. Before reaching the door, they were met by Mrs. Toplady, at her side the gentleman who had been Miss Bride's companion down-stairs.

"How fortunate!" exclaimed the hostess to Mrs. Woolstan. "I so want you to know Miss Tomalin, and Mr. Rossendale can take us to her."

Iris expressed her delight, and looked at Lashmar, inviting him to come too. But Dyce stood rigid, an unnatural smile on his features; then he drew back, turned, and was lost to view.

Five minutes later he quitted the house. It was raining lightly. Whilst he looked upward to give the cabman his address, spots fell upon his face, and he found their coolness pleasant.

During the ride home he indulged a limitless wrath against Iris Woolstan. That foolish chatterbox had spoilt his evening, had thrown disturbance into his mind just when it was enjoying the cheeriest hopes. As likely as not she would learn that he had had a long talk with May Tomalin, and, seeing the girl, she would put her own interpretation on the fib he had told her. What a nuisance it was to have to do with these purely feminine creatures, all fuss and impulsiveness and sentimentality! It would not surprise him in the least if she made a scene about this evening. Already, the other day, her tone when she accused him of giving her a false idea of Lady Ogram's niece proved the possibility of nonsensical trouble. The thing was a gross absurdity. Had he not, from the very beginning

196

of their friendship, been careful to adopt a tone as uncompromising as man could use ? Had he not applied to her his " method " in all its vigour ? What right had she to worry him with idiotic jealousies ? Could any one have behaved more honourably than he throughout their intercourse ? Why, the average sensual man——

His debt ? What had that to do with the matter ? The very fact of his accepting a loan of money from her emphasized the dry nature of their relations. That money must quickly be repaid, or he would have no peace. She began to presume upon his indebtedness, he saw that clearly. Her tone had been different ever since.

Deuce take the woman! She had made him thoroughly uncomfortable. What it was to have delicate sensibilities!

CHAPTER XIV

WITH her imperious temper and intelligence purely
practical, it was natural for Lady Ogram to imagine
that, even as she imposed her authority on others in
outward things, so had she sway over their minds—
what she willed that others should think, that, she
took for granted, they thought. Seeing herself as an
entirely beneficent potentate; unable to distinguish
for a moment between her arbitrary impulses and the
well-meaning motives which often directed her; she
assumed as perfectly natural that all within her sphere
of action must regard her with grateful submissiveness.
So, for example, having decided that a marriage between
Dyce Lashmar and Constance Bride would be a very
good thing for both, and purposing large generosity
towards them when the marriage should have come
about, she found it very difficult to conceive that either
of her young friends could take any other view of the
matter. When observation obliged her to doubt the
correctness of her first impressions, she grew only the
more determined that things should be as she wished.
Since the coming of May Tomalin, a new reason—or
rather, emotion—fortified her resolve; seeing a possibility, even a likelihood, that May and Lashmar might
attract each other, and having very different views
with regard to her niece, she was impatient for a
declared betrothal of Constance and the aspiring
politician. Their mutual aloofness irritated her more
than she allowed to be seen, and the moment approached
when she could no longer endure such playing with
her serious purposes.

Our Friend the Charlatan

She knew that she had committed an imprudence in coming to London and entering, however moderately, into the excitements of the season. A day or two sufficed to prove the danger she was incurring; but she refused to take count of symptoms. With a weakness which did not lack its pathos, she had, for the first time in her life, put what she called " a touch of colour" on to her cheeks, and the result so pleased her that she all but forgot the artificiality of this late bloom; each morning, when her maid had wrought the miracle, she viewed herself with high satisfaction, and was even heard to remark that London evidently did her good. Lady Ogram tried to believe that even age and disease were amenable to her control.

She consulted doctors—for the form; behaving with cold civility during their visit, and scornfully satirizing them when they were gone. None the less did she entertain friends at luncheon or dinner, and often talked to them as if years of activity and enjoyment lay before her. " Wonderful old lady!" was the remark of most who left her presence; but some exchanged glances and let fall ominous words.

On the evening when May and Constance were at the crush in Pont Street, she would not go to bed, but lay on a couch in her chamber, occasionally dozing, more often wide-awake and quivering with the agitation of her mind. It was one o'clock when the girls returned, but she had given orders that Miss Tomalin should at once come to see her, and May, rosy, resplendent, entered the dimly-lighted room.

" Well, have you enjoyed yourself?"

The voice was a shock to May's ears. After those to which she had been listening, it sounded sepulchral.

" Very much indeed. A delightful time!"

No token of affection had a place in their greeting. The old autocrat could not bring herself to offer, or ask for, tenderness; but in her eyes, always expressive of admiration when she looked at May, might have been read something like hunger of the heart.

Our Friend the Charlatan

"Sit down, my dear." Even this form of address was exceptional. "Tell me all about it. Who was there?"

"Hundreds of people! I can't remember half of those I was introduced to. Lord Dymchurch——"

"Ha! Lord Dymchurch came? And you had a talk with him?"

"Oh yes. I find he takes a great interest in Old English, and we talked about Chaucer and so on for a long time. He isn't quite so well up in it as I am; I put him right on one or two points, and he seemed quite grateful. He's very nice, isn't he? There's something so quiet and good-natured about him. I thought perhaps he would have offered to take me down to supper, but he didn't. Perhaps he didn't think of it; I fancy he's rather absent-minded."

Lady Ogram knitted her brows.

"Who did go down with you?" she asked.

"Oh, Mr. Lashmar. He was very amusing. Then I talked with——"

"Wait a minute. Did you only have one talk with Lord Dymchurch?"

"Only one. He doesn't care for 'At Homes.' Mrs. Toplady says he hardly ever goes anywhere, and she fancies"—May laughed lightly—"that he came to-night only because *I* was going to be there. Do you think it likely, aunt?"

"Why, I don't think it impossible," replied Lady Ogram, in a tone of relief. "I have known more unlikely things. And suppose it were true?"

"Oh, it's very complimentary, of course."

The old eyes dwelt upon the young face, and with a puzzled expression. Notwithstanding her own character, it was difficult for Lady Ogram to imagine that the girl seriously regarded herself as superior to Lord Dymchurch.

"Perhaps it's more than a compliment," she said, in rather a mumbling voice; and she added, with an effort to speak distinctly, "I suppose you didn't tire him with that talk about Old English?"

Our Friend the Charlatan

"Tire him?" May exclaimed. "Why, he was delighted!"

"But he seems to have been satisfied with the one talk."

"Oh, he went away because Mr. Lashmar came up, that was all. He's very modest; perhaps he thought he oughtn't to prevent me from talking to other people."

Lady Ogram looked annoyed and worried.

"If I were you, May, I shouldn't talk about Old English next time you see Lord Dymchurch. Men don't care to find themselves at school in a drawing-room."

"I assure you, aunt, that is not my only subject of conversation," replied May, amused and dignified. "And I'm perfectly certain that it was just the thing for Lord Dymchurch. He has a serious mind, and I like him to know that mine is the same."

"That's all right, of course. I dare say you know best what pleases him. And I think it very probable indeed, May, that he went to Pont Street just in the hope of meeting you."

"Perhaps so."

May smiled, and seemed to take the thing as very natural; whereupon Lady Ogram again looked puzzled.

"Well, go to bed, May. I'm very glad Lord Dymchurch was there; very glad. Go to bed, and sleep as late as you like. I'm glad you've enjoyed yourself, and I'm very glad Lord Dymchurch was there—very."

The voice had become so senile, so indistinct, that May could hardly catch what it said. She lightly kissed her aunt's cheek—a ceremony that passed between them only when decorum seemed to demand it—and left the room.

On the following morning, Dyce Lashmar received a telegram, couched thus:

"Please call at Bunting's Hotel at three this afternoon."

In order to respond to this summons, he had to break

an engagement; but he did it willingly. Around the
hotel in Albemarle Street circled all his thoughts, and
he desired nothing more than to direct his steps thither.
Arriving with perfect punctuality, he was shown into
Lady Ogram's drawing-room, and found Lady Ogram
alone. Artificial complexion notwithstanding, the
stern old visage wore to-day a look as of nature all but
spent. At Lashmar's entrance, his hostess did not
move; sunk together in her chair, head drooping
forward, she viewed him from under her eyebrows:
even to give her hand when he stood before her seemed
almost too great an effort, and the shrivelled lips scarce
made audible her bidding that he should be seated.

"You are well, I hope?" said Dyce, feeling uncomfortable, but affecting to see nothing unusual in the
face before him.

Lady Ogram nodded impatiently. There was a
moment's silence; then, turning her gaze upon him,
she said abruptly, in a harsh croak:

"What are you waiting for?"

Lashmar felt a cold touch along his spine. He
thought the ghastly old woman had lost her senses,
that she was either mad or delirious. Yet her gaze
had nothing wild; on the contrary, it searched him
with all the wonted keenness.

"Waiting—? I'm afraid I don't understand——"

"Why haven't you done what you know I wish?"
pursued the untuneful voice, now better controlled.
"I'm speaking of Constance Bride."

Relieved on one side, Dyce fell into trouble on the
other.

"To tell you the truth, Lady Ogram," he answered,
with his air of utmost candour, "I have found no
encouragement to take the step of which you are
thinking. I'm afraid I know only too well what the
result would be."

"You know nothing about it."

Lady Ogram moved. As always, a hint of opposition
increased her force. She was suffering acute physical

pain, which appeared in every line of her face, and in the rigid muscles of her arms as she supported herself on the sides of the chair.

"Answer me this," she went on—and her utterance had something which told of those far-off days before education and refined society had softened her tongue. "Will you see Miss Bride this afternoon, and make her an offer of marriage? Are you willing? Just answer me yes or no."

Dyce replied mechanically, and smiled as he spoke.

"I am quite willing, Lady Ogram. I only wish I could feel assured that Miss Bride——"

He was rudely interrupted.

"Don't talk, but listen to me." For a moment the lips went on moving, yet gave no sound; then words came again. "I've told you once already about Constance, what I think of her, and what I intend for her. I needn't go over all that again. As for you, I think I've given proof that I wish you well. I was led to it at first because I saw that Constance liked you; now I wish you well for your own sake, and you may trust me to do what I can to help you on. But till a man's married, no one can say what he'll make of his life. You've plenty of brains, more than most men, but I don't think you've got too much of what I call backbone. If you make a fool of yourself—as most men do—in marriage, it's all up with you. I want to see you safe. Go where you will, you'll find no better wife, better in every way for *you*, than Constance Bride. You want a woman with plenty of common-sense as well as uncommon ability; the kind of woman that'll keep you moving steadily—up—up! Do you understand me?"

The effort with which she spoke was terrible. Her face began to shine with moisture, and her mouth seemed to be parched. Lashmar must have been of much sterner stuff for these vehement and rough-cut sentences to make no impression upon him; he was held by the dark, fierce eye, and felt in his heart that he had heard truths.

Our Friend the Charlatan

"And mind this," continued Lady Ogram, leaning towards him. "Constance's marriage alters nothing in what I had planned for her before I knew you. She'll have her duties quite apart from your interests and all you aim at. I know her; I'm not afraid to trust her, even when she's married. She's honest—and that's what can be said of few women. This morning I had a talk with her. She knows, now, the responsibility I want her to undertake, and she isn't afraid of it. I said nothing to her about *you* ; not a word; but, when you speak to her, she'll understand what was in my mind. So let us get things settled, and have no more bother about them. On Saturday"—it was three days hence—"I go back to Rivenoak; I've had enough of London; I want to be quiet. You are to come down with us. You've business at Hollingford on the twentieth, and you ought to see more of the Hollingford people."

Whatever Lady Ogram had proposed (or rather dictated) Dyce would have agreed to. He was under the authority of her eye and voice. The prospect of going down to Rivenoak, and there, of necessity, living in daily communication with May Tomalin, helped him to disregard the other features of his position. He gave a cheerful assent.

"Now go away for half-an-hour," said Lady Ogram. "Then come back, and ask for Miss Bride, and you'll find her here."

She was at the end of her strength, and could barely make the last words audible. Dyce pressed her hand silently, and withdrew.

After the imposed interval, he returned from a ramble in Piccadilly, where he had seen nothing, and was conducted again to the drawing-room. There Constance sat reading. She was perfectly calm, entirely herself, and, as Lashmar entered, she looked up with the usual smile.

"Have you been out this afternoon?" he began by asking.

Our Friend the Charlatan

" Yes. Why ? "

" You went on business of Lady Ogram's ? "

" Yes. Why ? "

Dyce gave no answer. He laid aside his hat and stick, sat down not far from Constance, and looked at her steadily.

" I have something rather odd to say to you. As we are both rational persons, I shall talk quite freely, and explain to you exactly the position in which I find myself. It's a queer position, to say the least. When I was at Rivenoak, on the last day of my visit, Lady Ogram had a confidential talk with me ; your name came prominently into it, and I went away with certain vague impressions which have kept me, ever since, in a good deal of uneasiness. This afternoon, I have had another private conversation with Lady Ogram. Again your name had a prominent part in it, and this time there was no vagueness whatever in the communication made to me. I was bidden, in plain terms, to make you an offer of marriage."

Constance drooped her eyes, but gave no other sign of disturbance.

" Now," resumed Dyce, leaning forward with hands clasped between his knees, " before I say anything more about this matter as it concerns you, I had better tell you what I think about our friend. I feel pretty sure that she has a very short time to live ; it wouldn't surprise me if it were a question of days, but in any case I am convinced she won't live for a month. What is your opinion ? "

" I fancy you are right," answered the other, gravely.

" If so, this rather grotesque situation becomes more manageable. It is fortunate that you and I know each other so well, and have the habit of straightforward speech. I may assume, no doubt, that, from the very first, our friendship was misinterpreted by Lady Ogram ; reasonable relations between man and woman are so very rare, and, in this case, the observer was no very acute psychologist. I feel sure she is actuated by the

kindest motives; but what seems to her my inexplicable delay has been too much for her temper, and at
last there was nothing for it but to deal roundly with
me. One may suspect, too, that she feels she has not
much time to spare. Having made up her mind that
we are to marry, she wants to see the thing settled.
Looking at it philosophically, I suppose one may admit
that her views and her behaviour are intelligible.
Meanwhile, you and I find ourselves in a very awkward
position. We must talk it over—don't you think ?—
quite simply, and decide what is best to do."

Constance listened, her eyes conning the carpet.
There was silence for a minute, then she spoke.

"What did Lady Ogram tell you about me ?"

"She repeated in vague terms something she had
already said at Rivenoak. It seems that you are to
undertake some great responsibility—to receive some
proof of her confidence which will affect all the rest of
your life. More than that I don't know, but I understand that there has been a conversation between you,
in which everything was fully explained."

Constance nodded. After a moment's reflection she
raised her eyes to Lashmar's, and intently regarded
him; her expression was one of anxiety severely
controlled.

"You shall know what that responsibility is," she
said, with a just perceptible tremor in her voice. "Lady
Ogram, like a good many other people now-a-days,
has more money than she knows what to do with. For
many years, I think, she has been troubled by a feeling
that a woman rich as she, ought to make some extraordinary use of her riches—ought to set an example,
in short, to the wealthy world. But she never could
discover the best way of doing this. She has an
independent mind, and likes to strike out ways for
herself. Ordinary charities didn't satisfy her. To tell the
truth, she wanted not only to do substantial good, but
to do it in a way which should perpetuate her name—
cause her to be more talked about after her death than

she has been in her lifetime. Time went on, and she still could hit upon nothing brilliant; all she had decided was to build and endow a great hospital at Hollingford, to be called by her name, and this, for several reasons, she kept postponing. Then came her meeting with me—you know the story. She was troubling about the decay of the village, and trying to hit on remedies. Well, I had the good luck to suggest the paper-mill, and it was a success, and Lady Ogram at once had a great opinion of me. From that day— she tells me—the thought grew in her mind that, instead of devoting all her wealth, by will, to definite purposes, she would leave a certain portion of it to *me*, to be used by me for purposes of public good. I, in short" —Constance smiled nervously—"was to be sole and uncontrolled trustee of a great fund, which would be used, after her death, just as it might have been had she gone on living. The idea is rather fine, it seems to me; it could only have originated in a mind capable of very generous thought, generous in every sense of the word. It implied remarkable confidence, such as few people, especially few women, are capable of. It strikes me as rather pathetic, too—the feeling that she would continue to live in another being, not a mere inheritor of her money, but a true representative of her mind, thinking and acting as she would do, always consulting her memory, desiring her approval. Do you see what I mean?"

"Of course I do," answered Dyce, meditatively. "Yes, it's fine. It increases my respect for our friend."

"I have always respected her," said Constance, "and I am sorry now that I did not respect her more. Often she has irritated me, and in bad temper I have spoken thoughtlessly. I remember that letter I wrote you, before you first came to Rivenoak; it was silly, and, I'm afraid, rather vulgar."

"Nothing of the kind," interposed Lashmar. "It was very clever. You couldn't be vulgar if you tried."

"Have you the letter still?"

"Of course I have."

"Then do me the kindness to destroy it—will you?"

"If you wish."

"I do seriously. Burn the thing as soon as you get home."

"Very well."

They avoided each other's look, and there was a rather long pause.

"I'll go on with my story," said Constance, in a voice still under studious control. "All this happened when Lady Ogram thought she had no living relative. One fine day, Mr. Kerchever came down with news of Miss Tomalin, and straightway the world was altered. Lady Ogram had a natural heiress, and one in whom she delighted. Everything had to be reconsidered. The great hospital became a dream. She wanted May Tomalin to be rich, very rich, to marry brilliantly. I have always suspected that Lady Ogram looked upon her life as a sort of revenge on the aristocratic class for the poverty and ignorance of her own people—did anything of the kind ever occur to you?"

"Was her family really mean?"

"Every one says so. Mrs. Gallantry tells me that our illustrious M.P. has made laborious searches, hoping to prove something scandalous. Of course she tells it as a proof of Mr. Robb's unscrupulous hatred of Lady Ogram. I dare say the truth is that she came of a low class. At all events, Miss Tomalin, who represents the family in a progressive stage, is to establish its glory for ever. One understands. It's very human."

Lashmar wore the Toplady smile.

"It never occurred to our friend," he said, "that her niece might undertake the great trust instead of you?"

"She has spoken to me quite frankly about that. The trust cannot be so great as it would have been— but it remains with me. Miss Tomalin, it may be hoped, will play not quite an ordinary part in the fashionable world; she has ideas of her own, and "—the

Our Friend the Charlatan

voice was modulated—" some faith in herself. But my position is different and perhaps—my mind. Lady Ogram assures me that her faith in me, and her hopes, have suffered no change. For one thing, the mill is to become my property. Then——"

She hesitated, and her eyes passed over the listener's face. Lashmar was very attentive.

" There's no need to go into details," Constance added quickly. " Lady Ogram told me everything, saying she felt that the time had come for doing so. And I accepted the trust."

" Without knowing, however," said Dyce, " the not unimportant condition which her mind attached to it."

" There was no condition, expressed or reserved."

Constance's tone had become hard again. Her eyes were averted, her lips set in their firmest lines.

" Are you quite sure of that ? "

" Quite," was the peremptory reply.

" How do you reconcile that with what has passed to-day between Lady Ogram and me ? "

" It was between Lady Ogram and *you*," said Constance, subduing her voice.

" I see. You mean that I alone am concerned ; that your position will in no case be affected ? "

" Yes, I mean that," was the quiet reply.

Lashmar thought for a moment, then moved on his chair, and said in a low tone, which seemed addressed to his hearer's sympathy :

" Perhaps you are right. Probably you are. But there is one thing of which *I* feel every assurance. If it becomes plain that her project must come to nothing, Lady Ogram's interest in me is at an end. I may say good-bye to Hollingford."

" You are mistaken," replied Constance, in a voice almost of indifference.

" Well, the question will soon be decided." Lashmar seemed to submit himself to the inevitable. " I shall write to Lady Ogram, telling her the result of our conversation. We shall see how she takes it."

209

He moved as if about to rise, but only turned his chair slightly aside. Constance was regarding him from under her brows. She spoke in her most business-like tone.

"It was this that you came to tell me?"

"Why, no. It wasn't that at all."

"What had you in mind, then?"

"I was going to ask if you would marry me—or rather, if you would promise to—or rather if you would make believe to promise. I thought that, under the circumstances, it was a justifiable thing to do, for I fancied your future, as well as mine, was at stake. Seeing our friend's condition, it appeared to me that a formal engagement between us would be a kindness to her, and involve no serious consequences for us. But the case is altered. You being secure against Lady Ogram's displeasure, I have, of course, no right to ask you to take a part in such a proceeding—which naturally you would feel to be unworthy of you. All I have to do is to thank you for your efforts on my behalf. Who knows? I *may* hold my own at Hollingford. But at Rivenoak it's all over with me."

He stood up, and assumed an attitude of resigned dignity, smiling to himself. But Constance kept her seat, her eyes on the ground.

"I believe you are going down on Saturday?" she said.

"So it was arranged. Well, I mustn't stay——"

Constance rose, and he offered his hand.

"Between us, it makes no difference, I hope?" said Dyce, with an emphasized effort of cheeriness. "Unless you think me a paltry fellow, ready to do anything to get on?"

"I don't think that," replied Constance quietly.

"But you feel that what I was going to ask would have been rather a severe test of friendship?"

"Under the circumstances, I could have pardoned you."

"But you wouldn't have got beyond forgiveness?"

Our Friend the Charlatan

Constance smiled coldly, her look wandering.

" How can I tell ? "

" But—oh, never mind ! Good-bye, for the present."

He pressed her hand again, and turned away. Before he had reached the door, Constance's voice arrested him.

" Mr. Lashmar——"

He looked at her as if with disinterested inquiry.

" Think well before you take any irreparable step. It would be a pity."

Dyce moved towards her again.

" Why, what choice have I ? The position is impossible. If you hadn't said those unlucky words about being so sure——"

" I don't see that they make the slightest difference," answered Constance, her eyebrows raised. " If you had intended a genuine offer of marriage—yes, perhaps. But as all you meant was to ask me to save the situation, with no harm to anybody, and the certainty of giving great pleasure to our friend——"

" You see it in that light ? " cried Lashmar, flinging away his hat. " You really think I should be justified ? You are not offended ? "

" I pride myself on a certain measure of common-sense," answered Constance.

" Then you will allow me to tell Lady Ogram that there is an engagement ? "

" You may tell her so, if you like."

He seized her hand, and pressed his lips upon it. But, scarce had he done so, when Constance drew it brusquely away.

" There is no need to play our comedy in private," she said, with cold reproof. " And I hope that at all times you will use the discretion that is owing to me."

" If I don't, I shall deserve to fall into worse difficulties than ever," cried Lashmar.

" As, for instance, to find yourself under the necessity of making your mock contract a real one—which would be sufficiently tragic."

Our Friend the Charlatan

Constance spoke with a laugh, and thereupon, before Dyce could make any rejoinder, walked from the room.

The philosopher stood embarrassed. "What did she mean by that?" he asked himself. He had never felt on very solid ground in his dealings with Constance; had never felt sure in his reading of her character, his interpretation of her ways and looks and speeches. An odd thing that he should have been betrayed by his sense of triumphant diplomacy into that foolish excess. And he remembered that it was the second such indiscretion, though this time, happily, not so compromising as his youthful extravagance at Alverholme.

What if Lady Ogram, feeling that her end drew near, called for their speedy marriage? Was it the thought of such possibility that had supplied Constance with her sharp-edged jest? If she could laugh, the risk did not seem to her very dreadful. And to him?

He could not make up his mind on the point.

CHAPTER XV

LORD DYMCHURCH was at a critical moment of his life.

Discontent, the malady of the age, had taken hold upon him. No ignoble form of the disease; for his mind, naturally in accord with generous thoughts, repelled every suggestion which he recognized as of unworthy origin, and no man saw more clearly how much there was of vanity and of evil in the unrest which rules our time. He was possessed by that turbid idealism which, in the tumult of a day without conscious guidance, is the peril of gentle souls. Looking out upon the world, he seemed to himself to be the one idle man in a toiling and aspiring multitude; for, however astray the energy of most, activity was visible on every side, and in activity—so he told himself—lay man's only hope. He alone did nothing. Wearing his title like a fool's cap, he mooned in by-paths which had become a maze. Was it not the foolish title that bemused and disabled him? Without it, would he not long ago have gone to work like other men, and had his part in the onward struggle? Discontented with himself, ill at ease in his social position, reproachfully minded towards the ancestors who had ruined him, he fell into that most dangerous mood of the cultured and conscientious man, a feverish inclination for practical experiment in life.

His age was two-and-thirty. A decade ago he had dreamt of distinguishing himself in the Chamber of Peers; why should poverty bar the way of intellect and zeal? Experience taught him that, though money might not be indispensable to such a career as he imagined, the lack of it was only to be supplied by powers such as he certainly did not possess. Abashed at the thought of his presumption, he withdrew altogether from the seat to which his birth entitled him, and at the same time ceased to appear in society. He had the temper of a student, and among his books he soon found consolation for the first disappointments of youth. Study, however, led him by degrees to all the questions rife in the world about him; with the inevitable result that his maturer thought turned back upon things he fancied himself to have outgrown. His time had been wasted. At thirty-two all he had clearly learnt was a regret for vanished years.

He resisted as a temptation the philosophic quietism which had been his strength and his pride. From the pages of Marcus Aurelius, which he had almost by heart, one passage continued to haunt him: "When thou art hard to be stirred up and awaked out of thy sleep, admonish thyself and call to mind that to perform actions tending to the common good is that which thine own proper constitution, and that which the nature of men, do require." Morning and night, the question with him became, what could he do in the cause of civilization? And about this time it chanced that he made the acquaintance of Dyce Lashmar. He listened, presently, to the bio-sociological theory of human life, believing it to be Lashmar's own, and finding in it a great deal that was not only intellectually fruitful, but strong in appeal to his sympathies. Here he saw the reconciliation of his aristocratic prejudices—which he had little hope of ever overcoming—with the humanitarian emotion and conviction which were also a natural part of his being. All this did but contribute to his disquiet. No longer occupied with definite studies, he often felt time heavy on his hands, and saw himself more obnoxious than ever to the charge of idleness. Lashmar, though possibly his ambition had some alloy of self-seeking, gave an example of intellect applied to the world's behoof; especially did his views on education, developed in a recent talk at the club, strike Dymchurch as commendable and likely to have influence. He asked nothing better than an opportunity of devoting himself to a movement for educational reform. The lyrically abstract disgusted him well nigh as much as the too grossly actual. Thus, chancing to open Shelley, he found with surprise that the poet of his adolescence not merely left him cold, but seemed verbose and tedious.

Grave anxiety about his private affairs aided this mental tendency. Some time ago, he had been appealed to by the tenant of his Kentish farm for a reduction of rent, which, on consideration of the facts submitted to him, he felt unable to refuse. The farmer was now dead, and it was not without trouble that the land had been leased again on the same reduced terms; moreover, the new tenant seemed to be a not very satisfactory man, and Dymchurch had to consider the possibility that this part of his small income might become uncertain, or fail him altogether. Now and then he entertained the thought of studying agriculture, living upon his farm, and earning bread in the sweat of his brow; but a little talk with practical men showed him all the difficulties of such an undertaking. So far as his own day-to-day life was concerned, he felt small need of money; but it constantly worried him to think of his sisters down in Somerset, their best years going by, not indeed in actual poverty, but with so little of the brightness or hope natural to ladies of their birth. They did not appear unhappy; like him, they had a preference for the tranquil life; none the less he saw how different everything would have been with them but for their narrow means, and, after each visit to the silent meadow-circled house, he came away reproaching himself for his inertness.

The invitation to Lashmar's restaurant-dinner annoyed him a little, for casual company was by no means to his taste; when it was over, he felt glad that he had come, and more than ever fretted in spirit about his personal insignificance, his uselessness in the scheme of things. He was growing to hate the meaningless symbol which distinguished him from ordinary men; the sight of an envelope addressed to him stirred his spleen, for it looked like deliberate mockery. How if he cast away this empty lordship? Might it not be the breaking down of a barrier between him and real life? In doing so, what duty would he renounce? Who cared a snap of the fingers whether he signed himself " Dymchurch " or " Walter Fallowfield "? It was long enough since the barony of Dymchurch had justified its existence by any public service, and, as most people knew, its private record had small dignity. The likelihood was that he would never marry, and, unless either of his sisters did so, every day a more improbable thing, the title might fall into happy oblivion. What, indeed, did such titles mean now-a-days? They were a silly anachronism, absurdly in contradiction with all teachings of the Science which rules our lives. Lashmar, of course, was right in his demand for a new aristocracy to oust the old, an aristocracy of nature, of the born leaders of men. It might be that he had some claim to a humble position in that spiritual hierarchy, and perhaps the one manifest way to make proof of it was by flinging aside his tinsel privilege—an example, a precedent, to the like-minded of his caste.

Mrs. Toplady had begged him to come and see her. Mrs. Toplady, vaguely known to him by name, would, but a short time ago, have turned him to flight; having talked with her at the restaurant, he inclined to think her a very intelligent and bright-witted woman, the kind of woman who did a service to society by keeping it in touch with modern ideas. After a little uneasy hesitation, he betook himself to Pont Street. Next, he accepted an invitation to dine there, and found himself in the company of an old Lady Ogram, of whom he had never heard, and a girl with an odd name, her niece, who rather amused him. Calling presently in Pont

Our Friend the Charlatan

Street, to discharge his obligation of ceremony, he found Mrs. Toplady alone, and heard from her, in easy, half-confidential chat, a great deal about Lady Ogram and Miss Tomalin, information such as he would never himself have sought, but which, set off by his hostess's pleasant manner, entertained and somewhat interested him. For the young lady and her aged relative shone in no common light as Mrs. Toplady exhibited them. The baronet's widow became one of the most remarkable women of her time, all the more remarkable because of lowly origin; Miss Tomalin, heiress of a great fortune, had pure colonial blood in her veins, yet pursued with delightful zeal the finest culture of an old civilization. As Mrs. Toplady talked thus, the door opened to admit—Mr. Lashmar, and there was an end of confidences for that day.

So far Dymchurch had yielded without much reflection to the friendly pressure which brought him among strangers and disturbed his habits of seclusion. These dinners and afternoon calls had no importance; very soon he would be going down into Somerset, where it might be hoped that he would think out the problems which worried him, and arrive at some clear decision about the future. But when he found himself, reluctantly, yet as it seemed inevitably, setting forth to Mrs. Toplady's "At Home," the reasonable man in him grew restive. Why was he guilty of this weakness? Years had passed since he did anything so foolish as to leave home towards the middle of the night for the purpose of hustling amid a crowd of unknown people in staircases and drawing-rooms. He saw himself as the victim of sudden fatuity, own brother to the longest-eared of fashion's worshippers. Assuredly this should be the last of his concessions.

Inwardly pishing and pshawing, he drifted about the rooms till brought up beside Miss Tomalin. Then his mood changed. This girl, with her queer mixture of naïveté and conceit and examination-room pedantry, decidedly amused him. Was she a type of the young Canadian? He knew nothing of her life at Northampton, and thought she had come over from Canada only a year or two ago. Yes, she amused him. By contrast with the drawing-room young lady, of whom he had always been afraid, she seemed to have so much originality of character, spontaneity of expression. Of course her learning was not exactly profound; the quality of her mind left something to be desired; her breeding fell short of what is demanded by the fastidious; but there was something healthy and genuine about her, which made these deficiencies a matter for indulgence rather than for censure. And then, she was by no means ill-looking. Once or twice he caught an aspect of her features which had no little impressiveness; with mind cast in a more serious mould, she might have become a really beautiful woman.

Just as he had found courage to turn the talk in a personal direction, with an inquiry about Canadian life, he saw the approach of Dyce Lashmar. A glance at Miss Tomalin showed him that she had perceived the young politician, who was looking with manifest interest at her. Abruptly he rose. It had been in his mind to ask the girl to let him take her to the supper-room, but at the sight of Lashmar he did not hesitate for a moment about retreating. And almost immediately he quitted the house.

Dymchurch had never inclined to tender experiences; his life so far was without romance. Women more often amused than interested him; his humorous disposition found play among their lighter characteristics, and on the other hand—natural complement of humour—he felt a certain awe of the mysterious in their nature. Except his own sisters, whom naturally enough he regarded as quite exceptional beings, he had never been on terms of intimacy with any woman of the educated world. Regarding marriage as impracticable—for he had always shrunk from the thought of accepting money with a wife—he gave as little heed as possible to the other sex, tried to leave it altogether out of account in his musings and reasonings upon existence. Frankly he said to himself that he knew nothing about women, and that he was just as likely to be wrong as right in any theory he might form about their place in the world, their dues, their possibilities. By temper, he leaned to the old way of regarding them; women militant, women in the public eye, were on the whole unpleasing to him. But he was satisfied with an occasional laugh at these extravagances, and heard with tolerable patience any-one who pleaded the cause of female emancipation. In brief, women lay beyond the circle of his interests.

The explanation of his abrupt withdrawal on Lash-mar's appearance was simply that he all at once imagined a private understanding between his political friend and Miss Tomalin. The possibility had not hitherto occurred to him; he had given too little thought to Lady Ogram's niece. Now of a sudden it flashed upon him that Lashmar was seeking the girl in marriage, perhaps had already won her favour. Immediately he felt constrained to rise and to depart. The thought that Lashmar might perchance regard him as a rival pricked his pride; not for a moment could he rest under that misconstruction. He left the field clear, and drew breath like a man who has shaken off an embarrassment.

On the way home he saw how natural it was that such a man as Lashmar should woo Miss Tomalin. He might be a little too good for her; yet there was no knowing. That half grim, half grotesque old Lady Ogram had evidently taken Lashmar under her wing, and probably would make no objection to the alliance; perhaps she had even projected it. Utterly without idle self-consciousness, Dymchurch had perceived no particular significance in Mrs. Toplady's social advances to him. The sense of poverty was so persistent in his mind that he never saw himself as a possible object of matrimonial intrigue; nor had he ever come in contact with a social rank where such designs must have been forced on his notice. Well, his "season" was over; he laughed as he looked back upon it. When Lashmar and Miss Tomalin were married, he might or might not see something of them. The man had ideas: it remained to be proved whether his strength was equal to his ambitions.

A few days later Dymchurch heard that one of his sisters was not very well. She had caught a cold, and could not shake it off. This decided him to plan a summer holiday. He wrote and asked whether the girls would go with him to a certain quiet spot high in the Alps, and how soon they could leave home. The answer came that they would prefer not to go away until the middle of July, as a friend was about to visit them, whom they hoped to keep for two or three weeks. Disappointed at the delay, Dymchurch tried to settle down to his books; but books had lost their savour. He was consumed by dreary indolence.

Then came a note from Mrs. Toplady. He knew the writing and opened the envelope with a petulant grimace, muttering, "No, no, no!"

"Dear Lord Dymchurch," wrote his correspondent, "I wonder whether you are going to the performance of 'As You Like It' at Lady Honeybourne's on the 24th? It promises to be very good. If only they have fine weather, the play will be a real delight in that exquisite Surrey woodland. I do so hope we may meet you there. By *we* I mean Miss Tomalin and myself. Lady Ogram has gone back into the country, her health being unequal to London strain, and her niece stays with me for a little. You have heard, no doubt, of the engagement of Mr. Lashmar and Miss Bride. I knew it was coming. They are admirably suited to each other. To-day Mr. Lashmar gives his address at Hollingford, and I hope for good news to-morrow——"

The reader hung suspended at this point. Miss

Bride? Who was Miss Bride? Oh, that lady whom
he had seen once or twice with Lady Ogram; her
secretary, had he not heard? Why, then he was
altogether wrong in his conjecture about Lashmar and
Miss Tomalin. He smiled at the error, characteristic
of such an acute observer of social life!

He had received a card of invitation to Lady Honeybourne's, but had by no means thought of going down
into Surrey to see an amateur open-air performance
of "As You Like It." Yet, after all, was it not a way of
passing an afternoon? And would not Miss Tomalin's
running comment have a piquancy all its own? She
would have "got up" the play, would be prepared
with various readings, with philological and archæo-
logical illustrations. Dymchurch smiled again as he
thought of it, and already was half decided to go.

A copy of the *Hollingford Express*, sent, no doubt,
by Lashmar, informed him that the private meeting
of Liberals at the Saracen's Head had resulted in
acceptance of his friend's candidature. There was a
long report of Lashmar's speech, which he read critically,
but not without envy. Whether he came to be elected
or not, the man was doing something; he knew the joy
of activity, of putting out his strength, of moving others
by the energy of his mind. This morning his lodgings
seemed to Dymchurch a very cave in the wilderness. The
comforts and the graceful things amid which he lived
had lost all meaning—unless, indeed, they symbolized
a dilettant decadence of which he ought to be heartily
ashamed. He ran over the contents of the provincial
newspaper, and in every column found something that
rebuked him. These municipal proceedings, what
zeal and capability they implied! Was it not better,
a thousand times, to be excited about the scheme for
paving "Burgess Lane" than to sit here amid books
and pictures, and do nothing at all but smoke one's
favourite mixture? The world hummed about him
with industry, with triumphant effort; and he alone
of all men could put his hand to nothing.

Our Friend the Charlatan

His thoughts somehow turned upon Miss Tomalin. What was it that he found so piquant in that half-educated, indifferently bred girl? Might it not be that she represented an order of society with which he had no acquaintance, that vague multitude between the refined middle class and the rude toilers, which, as he knew theoretically, played such an important part in modern civilization? Among these people, energy was naked, motives were direct. There the strength and the desires of the people became vocal; they must be studied, if one wished to know the trend of things. Had he not seen it remarked somewhere that from this class sprang nearly all the younger representatives of literature and art, the poets, novelists, journalists of to-day; all the vigorous young workers in science? Lashmar, he felt sure, was but one remove from it. That busy and aspiring multitude would furnish, most likely, by far the greater part of the spiritual aristocracy for which our world was waiting.

From this point of view the girl had a new interest. She was destined, perhaps, to be the mother of some great man. He hoped she would not marry foolishly; the wealth she must soon inherit hardly favoured her chance in this respect; doubtless she would be surrounded by unprincipled money-hunters. On the whole, it seemed rather a pity that Lashmar had not chosen and won her; there would have been a fitness, one felt, in that alliance. At the same time, Lashmar's selection of an undowered mate spoke well for him. For it was to be presumed that Lady Ogram's secretary had no very brilliant prospects. Certainly she did not make much impression at the first glance; one would take her for a sensible, thoughtful woman, nothing more.

After a lapse of twenty-four hours, he replied to Mrs. Toplady. Yes, if the weather were not too discouraging, he hoped to be at Lady Honeybourne's. He added that the fact of Lashmar's engagement had come as news to him.

Our Friend the Charlatan

So, after all, his "season" was not yet over. But perhaps kind Jupiter would send rain, and make the murdering of Shakespeare an impossibility. Now and then he tapped his barometer, which for some days had hovered about "change," the sky meanwhile being clouded. On the eve of Midsummer Day there was every sign of unseasonable weather. Dymchurch told himself, with a certain persistency, that he was glad.

Yet the morrow broke fair, and at mid-day was steadily bright. Throughout the morning Dymchurch held himself at remorseless study, and was rewarded by the approval of his conscience; whence, perhaps, the cheerfulness of resignation with which he made ready to keep his engagement at the Surrey house. And so, with a smile on his meditative face, he went out into the sunshine. He was thinking of Rosalind in Arden.

Lord Honeybourne and he had been school-fellows; they were together at Oxford, but not in the same set, for Dymchurch read, and the other ostentatiously idled. What was the use of exerting oneself in any way— asked the Hon. L. F. T. Medwin-Burton—when a man had only an income of four or five thousand in prospect, fruit of a wretchedly encumbered estate which every year depreciated? Having left the University without a degree—his only notable performance a very amusing speech at the Union, proposing the abolition of the House of Lords—he allied himself with young Sir Evan Hungerford in a journalistic enterprise, and for a year or two the bi-monthly *Skylark* supplied matter for public mirth, not without occasional scandal. Then came his succession to the title, and Viscount Honeybourne, as the papers made known, presently set forth on travel which was to cover all British territory. He came back with an American wife, an incalculable fortune, and much knowledge of Greater Britain; moreover he had gained a serious spirit, and henceforth devoted himself to Colonial affairs. His young wife— she was seventeen at the time of her marriage—straightway took a conspicuous place in English society, her note being intellectual and social earnestness.

The play was to begin at three o'clock. Arriving half-an-hour before, Dymchurch found his hostess in the open-air theatre, beset with managerial cares, whilst her company, already dressed for their parts, sat together under the greenwood tree, and a few guests strayed about the grass. He had met Lady Honeybourne only once, and that a couple of years ago; with difficulty they recognized each other. Lord Honeybourne, she told him, had hoped to be here, but the missing of a steamer (he had run over, just for a day or two, to Jamaica) would make him too late.

"You know Miss Tomalin?" the lady added, with a bright smile. "She has been lunching with me, and we are great friends. I wish I had known her sooner, she would have had a part. There she is, talking with Miss Dolbey. Yes, of course we have had to cut the play down. It's shocking, but there was no choice."

Dymchurch got away from this chatter, and stood aside. Then Miss Tomalin's radiant glance discovered him; she broke from the lady with whom she was conversing, and stepped in his direction with a look of frank pleasure.

"How do you do, Lord Dymchurch! I came early, to lunch with Lady Honeybourne and some of her actors. We have been getting on together splendidly. Let us settle our places. Mrs. Toplady may be a little late; we must keep a chair for her. Which do you prefer?—Isn't it admirably managed? This big tree will give shade all the time. Suppose we take these chairs? Of course we needn't sit down at once. Put your cane across two, and I'll tie my handkerchief on the third. There! Now we're safe.—Did you ever see an open-air play before? Charming idea, isn't it? You don't know Lady Honeybourne very well, I think? Oh, she's very bright, and has lots of ideas. I think we shall be real friends. She must come down to Rivenoak in August."

Our Friend the Charlatan

"I'm sorry," interposed Dymchurch, as soon as there came a pause, "that Lady Ogram had to leave town so soon."

"Oh, it was too much for her. I advised her very seriously, as soon as she began to feel exhausted, not to stay another day. Indeed, I couldn't have allowed it; I'm convinced it was dangerous, in her state of health. I hear from her that she is already much better. Rivenoak is such a delightfully quiet place, and such excellent air. Did you see a report of Mr. Lashmar's speech? Rather good, I thought. Perhaps *just* a little vague. The fault I hoped he would avoid. But, of course, it's very difficult to adapt oneself all at once to electioneering necessities. Mr. Lashmar is theoretical; of course that is his strong point."

Dymchurch listened with an air of respectful, though smiling, attention. The girl amused him more than ever. Really, she had such a pleasant voice that her limitless flow of words might well be pardoned, even enjoyed.

"Lady Honeybourne and I have been talking about the condition of the poor. She has capital ideas, but not much experience. Of course I am able to speak with some authority: I saw so much of the poor at Northampton."

Once or twice Dymchurch had heard mention of Northampton in May's talk, but his extreme discretion had withheld him from putting a question on the subject. Catching his look, she saw inquiry in it.

"You know that I lived at Northampton, before I made my home at Rivenoak? Oh, I thought I had told you all about that."

Acting on her aunt's counsel, approved by Mrs. Toplady, May was careful not to let it be perceived by casual acquaintances that, until a month ago, she had been an absolute stranger to her titled relative. At the same time, it was necessary to avoid any appearance of mystery, and people were given to understand that she had passed some years with her family in the midland town.

Our Friend the Charlatan

" And what work did you take part in ? " asked her companion.

"It was a scheme of my own, mainly educational—I'll tell you all about it, when we have time. What a lot of people all at once! Ah, it's the 2.40 train that brings them. You came by the one before ? There's Mrs. Toplady; so she isn't late, after all."

The audience began to seat itself. A string-band, under a marquee aside from the plot of smooth turf which represented the stage, began to discourse old English music; on this subject, as soon as they were seated side by side, Dymchurch had the full benefit of May's recently acquired learning. How quick the girl was in gathering any kind of information! And how intelligently she gave it forth! Babble as she might (thought the amused peer), her talk was never vulgar; at worst, there was excess of ingenuousness; a fault, after all, in the right direction. She was very young, and had little experience of society; in a year or two these surface blemishes would be polished away. The important thing was that she did sincerely care for things of the mind, and had a mind to apply to them.

He sat on Miss Tomalin's right hand; on her left was Mrs. Toplady. The humorist of Pont Street, as she listened to the dialogue beside her, smiled very roguishly indeed. Seldom had anything so surprised and entertained her as the progress of intimacy between May and Lord Dymchurch. But she was vexed, as well as puzzled, by Lashmar's recent step, which seemed to deprive the comedy of an element on which she had counted. Perhaps not, however; it might be that the real complication was only just beginning.

"As You Like It " was timed for a couple of hours, intervals included. Miss Tomalin did not fail to whisper to her neighbours at every noteworthy omission from the text, and once or twice she was moved to a pained protest. Her criticism of the actors was largely indulgent; she felt the value of her praise, but was equally aware of the weight of her censure. So the sunny afternoon went by. Here and there a spectator nodded drowsily; others conversed under their breath —not of the bard of Avon. The air was full of that insect humming which is nature's music at high summer-tide.

Upon the final applause followed welcome refreshments. A table laden with dainties gleamed upon the sward. Dymchurch naturally waited upon his ladies; but the elder of them soon wandered off amid the friendly throng, and May, who ate and drank with enjoyment, was able to give her companion the promised description of her activity at Northampton. The listener smiled and smiled; had much ado, indeed, not to exhibit open gaiety; but ever and again his eyes rested on the girl's countenance, and its animation so pleased him that he saw even in her absurdities a spirit of good.

"You never did any work of that sort?" inquired May, regarding him from a good-natured height.

"Never, I'm sorry to say."

"But don't you sometimes feel as if it were a duty?"

"I very often feel I ought to do *something*," answered Dymchurch, in a graver voice. "But whether I could be of any use among the poor is doubtful."

"No, I hardly think you could," said May reflectively. "Your social position doesn't allow of that. Of course you help to make laws, which is more important."

"If I really did so; but I don't. I have no more part in law-making than you have."

"But, why not?" asked May, gazing at him in surprise. "Surely *that* is a duty about which you can have no doubt."

"I neglect *all* duties," he answered.

"How strange! Is it your principle? You are not an anarchist, Lord Dymchurch?"

"Practically, I fancy that's just what I am. Theoretically, no. Suppose," he added, with his pleasantest smile, "you advise me as to what use I can make of my life."

Our Friend the Charlatan

The man was speaking without control of his tongue. He had sunk into a limp passivity; in part, it might be, the result of the drowsily humming air; in part, a sort of hypnotism due to May's talk and the feminine perfume which breathed from her. He understood the idleness of what fell from his lips, but it pleased him to be idle. Therewithal—strange contradiction—he was trying to persuade himself that, more likely than not, this chattering girl had it in her power to make him an active, useful man, to draw him out of his mouldy hermitage and set him in the world's broad daylight. The analogy of Lord Honeybourne came into his mind; Lord Honeybourne, whose marriage had been the turning-point of his career, and whose wife, in many respects, bore a resemblance to May Tomalin.

"I shall have to think very seriously about it," May was replying. "But nothing could interest me more. You don't feel at all inclined for public life ? "

Their dialogue was interrupted by the hostess, who came forward with a gentleman she wished to present to Miss Tomalin. Hearing the name—Mr. Langtoft—Dymchurch regarded him with curiosity, and, moving aside with Lady Honeybourne as she withdrew, he inquired whether this was *the* Mr. Langtoft.

"It is," the hostess answered. "Do you take an interest in his work ? Would you like to know him ? "

Dymchurch declined the introduction for the present, but he was glad to have seen the man, just now frequently spoken of in newspapers, much lauded, and vehemently attacked. A wealthy manufacturer, practically lord of a swarming township in Lancashire, Mr. Langtoft was trying to get into his own hands the education of all the lower-class children growing up around his towering chimneys. He disapproved of the board-school; he looked with still less favour on the schools of the clergy; and, regardless of expense, was establishing schools of his own, where what he called "civic instruction" was gratuitously imparted.

Our Friend the Charlatan

The idea closely resembled that which Dyce Lashmar had borrowed from his French sociologist, and Dyce had lately been in correspondence with Mr. Langtoft. Lashmar's name, indeed, was now passing between the reformer and Miss Tomalin.

"His work," said Dymchurch to himself. "Yes, everybody has his work—except me."

And the impulse to experiment in life grew so strong with him, that he had to go apart under the trees and pace nervously about; idle talk being no longer endurable.

The gathering began to thin. He had noted the train by which he would return to London, and a glance at his watch told him that he must start if he would reach the station in time. Moving towards the group of people about the hostess, he encountered Mrs. Toplady.

"Have you a cab?" she asked. "If not, there's plenty of room in ours."

Dymchurch would have liked to refuse, but hesitation undid him. Face to face with Mrs. Toplady and May, he drove to the station, and, as was inevitable, performed the rest of the journey in their company. The afternoon had tired him; alone, he would have closed his eyes, and tried to shut out the kaleidoscopic sensation which resulted from theatrical costumes, brilliant illustrations of the feminine mode, blue sky and sunny green glades; but May Tomalin was as fresh as if new-risen, and still talked, talked. Enthusiastic in admiration of Lady Honeybourne, she heard with much interest that Dymchurch's acquaintance with the Viscount went back to Harrow days.

"That's what I envy you," she exclaimed, "your public school and university education! They make us feel our inferiority, and it isn't fair."

Admission of inferiority was so unexpected a thing on Miss Tomalin's lips, that her interlocutor glanced at her. Mrs. Toplady, in her corner of the railway-carriage, seemed to be smiling over a newspaper article.

Our Friend the Charlatan

"The feeling must be very transitory," said Dymchurch, with humorous arch of brows.

"Oh, it doesn't trouble me very often. I know I should have done just as much as men do if I had had the chance."

"Considerably more, no doubt, than either Honeybourne or I."

"You have never really put out your strength, I'm afraid, Lord Dymchurch," said May, regarding him with her candid smile. "Never in anything—have you?"

"No," he responded, in a like tone. "A trifler—always a trifler!"

"But if you *know* it——"

Something in his look made her pause. She looked out of the window before adding:

"Yet I don't think it's quite true. The first time I saw you, I felt you were very serious and that you had thought much. You rather over-awed me."

Dymchurch laughed. In her corner, Mrs. Toplady still found matter for ironic smiling as she rustled over the evening journal; and the train swept on towards London.

CHAPTER XVI.

For a week after Lady Ogram's return, Dr. Baldwin called daily at Rivenoak. His patient, he said, was suffering from over-exertion; had she listened to his advice, she would never have gone to London; the marvel was that such an imprudence had had no worse results. Lady Ogram herself, of course, refused to take this view of the matter; she was perfectly well, only a little tired, and, as the hot nights interfered with her sleep just now, she rested during the greater part of the day, seeing Lashmar for half-an-hour each afternoon in the little drawing-room up-stairs. Her friendliness with Dyce had much increased; when he entered the room she greeted him almost affectionately, and their talk was always of his brilliant future.

"I want to see you safely in Parliament," she said one day. "I can't expect to live till you've made your name; that isn't done so quickly. But I shall see you squash Robb, and that's something."

Of his success at Hollingford she seemed never to entertain a doubt, and Lashmar, though by no means so sanguine, said nothing to discourage her. His eye noted ominous changes in her aspect and her way of talking, even the sound of her voice made plain to him that she was very rapidly losing the reserve of force which kept her alive. Constance, who was on friendly terms with the doctor, learnt enough of the true state of things to make her significantly grave after each visit; she and Dyce, naturally, exchanged no remark on the subject.

Our Friend the Charlatan

"What do your parents say about it?" Lady Ogram asked of Lashmar, during one of their conversations.

"They are delighted. Especially my mother, who has always been very ambitious for me."

"But I mean about your engagement."

Dyce had, of course, omitted all mention of Constance in his letters to Alverholme.

"They give their approval," he replied, "because they have confidence in my judgment. I fancy," he added, with a modest smile, "that their ambition, in this respect, is not altogether satisfied, but— Of course, I have said nothing whatever to them about the peculiarity of Constance's position; I didn't feel justified in doing so."

"You may tell them what you like," said Lady Ogram graciously.

She one day received a letter from Mrs. Toplady, which gave her great satisfaction. It seemed to re-establish her vigour of mind and body; she came down-stairs, lunched with her young friends, and talked of going to Wales.

"May is enjoying herself greatly; she must stay a little longer. The day before yesterday she was at a garden-party at Lady Honeybourne's, where they acted 'As You Like It' in the open air."

"There was mention of it yesterday in the papers," remarked Lashmar.

"Yes, yes; I saw. And May's name among the guests—of course, of course. I notice that Lord Dymchurch was there too." She ended with a quavering laugh, unexpected and rather uncanny.

"And the much-discussed Mr. Langtoft," put in Constance, after a keen look at the mirthful hippocratic face.

"Langtoft, yes," said Dyce. "I don't quite know what to think of that fellow. There seems to me something not quite genuine about him. What is he doing at Lady Honeybourne's garden-party? It looks like tuft-hunting, don't you think, Constance?"

Our Friend the Charlatan

Dyce was secretly annoyed that an idea of his own (that is to say, from his own French philosopher) should be put into practice by some one else before he could assert his claim to it. Very vexatious that Langtoft's activity was dragged into public notice just at this moment.

"I don't at all like the tone of his last letter to you," said Constance. "He writes in a very flippant way, and not a bit like a man in earnest."

Not long ago Miss Bride's opinion of Langtoft would have been quite different. Now she was disposed to say things that Dyce Lashmar liked to hear. Dyce had remarked the change in her; it flattered him, but caused him at the same time some uneasiness.

Inevitably, they passed much time together. On the journey from London Constance had asked him whether he would not like to begin cycling. He took the suggestion with careless good-humour. At Rivenoak Constance returned to it, insisted upon it, and, as he had little to do, Dyce went into Hollingford for lessons; in a week's time he could ride, and, on a brand-new bicycle of the most approved make, accompanied his nominally betrothed about the country ways. Constance evidently enjoyed their rides together. She was much more amiable in her demeanour, more cheerful in mind; she dropped the habit of irony, and talked hopefully of Lashmar's prospects.

"What's the news from Breakspeare?" she inquired, as they were pedalling softly along an easy road one afternoon, Dyce having spent the morning in Hollingford.

"Oh, he's a prancing optimist," Dyce replied. "He sees everything rose-colour, or pretends to, I'm not quite sure which. If Dobbin the grocer meets him in the street, and says he's going to vote Liberal at next election, Breakspeare sings the pæan."

"I notice that you seem rather doubtful, lately," said Constance, her eyes upon him.

"Well, you know, there *is* a good deal of doubt. It

depends so much on what happens between now and the dissolution."

He entered into political detail, showing the forces arrayed against him, dwelling on the ill-grained Toryism of Hollingford, or, as he called it, the burgess' *Robbish* mind.

" There's no use, is there, in blinking facts ? "

" Of course not. It's what I never do, as I think you are aware. We must remember that to contest the seat is something. It makes you known. If you don't win we will wait for the next chance—not necessarily here."

Dyce had observed that the pronoun "we" was rather frequently on Constance's lips. She was identifying their interests.

" That's true," he admitted. " Look at that magnificent sycamore ! "

" Yes ; but I shouldn't have known it was a sycamore. How is it you know trees so well ? "

" That's my father's doing," replied Dyce. " He used to teach me them when I was a youngster."

" Mine was thinking more about social statistics. I knew the number of paupers in London before I had learnt to distinguish between an ash and an oak. Do you ever hear from your father ? "

" Now and then," said Lashmar, his machine wobbling a little, for he was not yet in perfect command of it, and fell into some peril if his thoughts strayed. " They want me to run over to Alverholme presently. Perhaps I may go next week."

Constance was silent. They wheeled on without speaking for some minutes. Then Dyce asked :

" How long does Lady Ogram wish me to stay here ? "

" I don't quite know. Are you in any hurry to get away? "

" Not at all. Only, if I'm soon going back to London, I should take Alverholme on the journey. Would you probe our friend for me ? "

" I'll try."

Our Friend the Charlatan

At this time they were both reading a book of Nietzsche. That philosopher had only just fallen into their hands, though, of course, they had heard much of him. Lashmar found the matter considerably to his taste, but he ridiculed the form. Nietzsche's individualism was, up to a certain point, in full harmony with the tone of his mind; he enjoyed this frank contempt of the average man, persuaded that his own place was in the seat of the lofty, and that disdain of the hum-drum, in life or in speculation, had always been his strong point. To be sure he counted himself Nietzsche's superior as a moralist; as a thinker, he imagined himself much more scientific. But, having regard to his circumstances and his hopes, this glorification of unscrupulous strength came opportunely. Refining away its grosser aspects, Dyce took the philosophy to heart, much more sincerely than he had taken to himself the humanitarian bio-sociology on which he sought to build his reputation.

And Constance, for her part, was hardly less interested in Nietzsche. She, too, secretly liked this insistence on the right of the strong, for she felt herself one of them. She, too, for all her occupation with social reform, was at core a thorough individualist, desiring far less the general good than her own attainment of celebrity as a public benefactress. Nietzsche spoke to her instincts, as he does to those of a multitude of men and women, hungry for fame, avid of popular applause. But she, like Lashmar, criticized her philosopher from a moral height. She did not own to herself the intimacy of his appeal to her.

" He'll do a great deal of harm in the world," she said, this same afternoon, as Dyce and she drank tea together. " The jingo impulse, and all sorts of forces making for animalism, will get strength from him, directly or indirectly. It's the negation of all we are working for, you and I."

" Of course it is," Dyce replied, in a voice of conviction. " We have to fight against him." He added,

# Our Friend the Charlatan

after a pause, "There's a truth in him, of course, but it's one of those truths which are dangerous to the generality of men."

Constance assented with a certain vagueness.

" Of course. And he delivers his message so brutally."

" That, no doubt, increases its chance of acceptance. The weak, who don't know how else to assert themselves, tend naturally to brutality. Carlyle taught pretty much the same thing at bottom; but his humour and his puritanism made the effect different. Besides, the time wasn't ripe then for the doctrine of irresponsible force; religion hadn't utterly perished in the masses of men as it has now. Given a world without religious faith, in full social revolution, with possibilities of wealth and power dangled before every man's eyes, what can you expect but the prevalence of a more or less ferocious egoism ? We, who are *not* egoists,"— he looked into his companion's eyes—" yet are conscious of unusual strength, may, it seems to me, avail ourselves of the truth in Nietzsche, which, after all, is very much the same as my own theory of the selection of the fit for rule. The difference is, that *we* wish to use our power for the common good, whilst Nietzsche's teaching results in a return to sheer barbarism, the weak trampled because of their weakness."

Constance approved. Yes, their aim, undoubtedly, was the common good, and, whilst keeping this in view, they need not, perhaps, be over-fastidious as to the means they employed. She had for years regarded herself as at war with society, in the narrower sense of the word; its creeds, great or small, had no validity for her; she had striven for what she deemed her rights— the rights of a woman born with intellect and will and imagination, yet condemned by poverty to rank among subordinates. The struggle appeared to have brought her within view of triumph, and was it not to herself, her natural powers and qualities, that she owed all ? At this moment she felt her right to pursue any object

236

which seemed to her desirable. What was good for *her* was good for the world at large.

The next morning they started at the usual hour for their ride, but the sky was cloudy, and, as they were leaving the park, spots of rain fell. It was not by the lodge gates that they usually set forth ; more convenient for their purpose was a postern in the wall which enclosed the greater part of Rivenoak ; the approach to it was from the back of the house, across a paddock, and through a birch copse, where stood an old summer-house, now rarely entered. Constance, with her own key, had just unlocked the door in the wall ; she paused and glanced cloudward.

" I think it'll be a shower," said Lashmar. " Suppose we shelter in the summer-house."

They did so, and stood talking under the roof of mossy tiles.

" What have you worked at this morning ? " asked Constance.

" Nothing particular. I've been thinking."

" I wish you would try to tell me how you worked out your bio-sociology. You must have had a great deal of trouble to get together your scientific proofs and illustrations."

" A great deal, of course," answered Dyce modestly. " I had read for years all sorts of scientific and historical books."

" I rather wonder you didn't write a book of your own. Evidently you have all the material for one. Don't you think it might be well ? "

" We have spoken of that, you know," was Dyce's careless reply. " I prefer oral teaching."

" Still, a solid book, such an one as you could easily write, would do you a great deal of good. Do think about it, will you ? "

Her voice had an unusual quality ; it was persuasive and almost gentle. In speaking, she looked at him with eyes of unfamiliar expressiveness, and all the lines of her face had softened.

Our Friend the Charlatan

"Of course, if you really think—" began Lashmar, affecting to ponder the matter.

"I should so like you to do it," Constance pursued, still with the markedly feminine accent which she certainly did not assume. "Will you—to please me?"

Her eyes fell before the other's quick, startled look. There was a silence; rain pattered on the tiles.

"I'll think about it," Dyce replied at length, moving and speaking uneasily. "It's raining quite hard, you know," he added, moving into the doorway. "The roads will be no good after this."

"No. We had better go in," said Constance, with sudden return to dry, curt speech.

It was evident that, in his anomalous situation, Lashmar's method with women could not have fair play. He was in no small degree beholden to Constance, and her odd behaviour of late kept him in mind of his obligation. Doubtless, he thought, she intended that; and his annoyance at what he considered a lack of generosity outweighed the satisfaction his vanity might have found in her new manner towards him. That manner, especially this morning, reminded him of six years ago. Was Constance capable of exacting payment of a debt which she imagined him to have incurred at Alverholme? Women think queerly, and are no less unaccountable in their procedure.

His curiosity busied itself with the vaguely indicated compact between Constance and Lady Ogram, but no word on the subject, not even a distant allusion to it, ever fell from his nominally betrothed, and the old lady herself, however amiable, spoke not at all of the things he desired to know. Was it not grossly unjust to him? Until he clearly understood Constance's future position, how could he decide upon his course with regard to her? Conceivably, the proposed marriage might carry advantages which it behoved him to examine with all care; conceivably, also, it might at a given moment be his sole rescue from

238

Our Friend the Charlatan

embarrassment, or worse. Meanwhile, ignorance of the essential factors of the problem put him at a grave disadvantage. Constance was playing a game (so Dyce saw it) with all the cards visible before her, and, to such a profound observer as he, it was not unnatural to suppose that she played for something worth the while. Curiously enough, Dyce did not presume to believe that he himself, his person, his mind, his probable career, were gain sufficient. A singular modesty ruled his meditations at this juncture.

Other things were happening which interfered with the confident calm essential to his comfort. Since the vexatious little incident at Mrs. Toplady's, he had not seen Iris Woolstan. On the eve of his departure for Rivenoak, he wrote to her a friendly letter in the usual strain, just to acquaint her with his movements, and to this letter there came no reply. It was unlikely that Iris' answer had somehow failed to reach him; of course, she would address to Rivenoak. No doubt she had discovered his little deception, and took it ill. Iris was quite absurd enough to feel jealousy, and to show it. Of all the women he knew, she had the most essentially feminine character. Fortunately, she was as weak as foolish; at any time he could get the upper hand of her in a private interview. But his sensibility made him restless in the thought that she was accusing him of ingratitude—perhaps of behaviour unworthy a gentleman. Yes, there was the true sting. Dyce Lashmar prided himself on his intellectual lucidity, but still more on his possession of the instincts, of the mental and moral tone, which are called gentlemanly. It really hurt him to think that any one could plausibly assail his claims in this respect.

When he had been a week at Rivenoak, he again wrote to Mrs. Woolstan. Of her failure to answer his last letter he said nothing. She had, of course, received the *Hollingford Express*, with the report of his speech on the 20th. How did she like it? Could she suggest any improvement? She knew that he valued her

239

opinion. "Write," he concluded, "as soon as you have leisure. I shall be here, I think, for another week or so. By the bye, I have taken to cycling, and I fancy it will be physically good for me."

To this communication Mrs. Woolstan replied. She began with a few formal commendations of his speech. "You are so kind as to ask if I can suggest any way in which it could have been improved, but, of course, I know that that is only a polite phrase. I should not venture to criticize anything of yours *now*, even if I had the presumption to think that I was capable of saying anything worth your attention. I am sure you need no advice from me, nor from any one else, now that you have the advantage of Miss Bride's counsels. I regret very much that I have so slight an acquaintance with that lady, but Mrs. Toplady tells me that she is admirably suited to be your companion, and to encourage and help you in your career. I shall have the pleasure of watching you from a distance, and of sincerely wishing you happiness as well as success."

The tortuous style of this letter, so different from Iris' ordinary effusions, made sufficient proof of the mood in which it was written. Dyce bit his lips over it. He had foreseen that Mrs. Woolstan would hear of his engagement, but had hoped it would not be just yet. There was for the present no help; in her eyes he stood condemned of something more than indelicacy. Fortunately, she was not the kind of woman, he felt sure, to be led into any vulgar retaliation. All he could do was to write a very brief note, in which he expressed a hope of seeing her very soon. "I shall have much to tell you," he added, and tried to think that Iris would accept this as a significant promise.

After all, were not man and woman, disguise the fact as one might, condemned by nature to mutual hostility? Useless to attempt rational methods with beings to whom reason was fundamentally repugnant. Dyce fell from mortification into anger, and cursed the poverty which forbade him to act in full accordance with his ideal of conduct.

He had spent nearly a fortnight at Rivenoak, when Lady Ogram, now seemingly restored to her ordinary health, summoned him at eleven in the morning to the green drawing-room.

"I hope I didn't disturb your work," she began kindly. "As you are leaving so soon"—Dyce had said nothing whatever about departure—"I should like to have a quiet word with you, whilst Constance is in the town. All goes well at Hollingford, doesn't it ? "

"Very well indeed, I think. Breakspeare gets more hopeful every day."

Lady Ogram nodded and smiled. Then a fit of abstraction came upon her; she mused for several minutes, Dyce respectfully awaiting her next words.

"What are your own wishes about the date ? "

Imagining that she referred to the election, and that this was merely another example of failing intelligence, Dyce answered that, for his own part, he was ready at any time ; if a dissolution——

"Pooh!" Lady Ogram interrupted, "I'm talking about your marriage."

"Ah! Yes—yes. I haven't asked Constance——"

"Suppose we say the end of October ? You could get away for a month or two."

"One thing is troubling me, Lady Ogram," said Dyce, in tone of graceful hesitancy. "I feel that it will be a very ill return for all your kindness to rob you of Constance's help and society, which you prize so."

The keen old eyes were fixed upon him.

"Do you think I am going to live for ever ? " sounded abruptly and harshly, though, it was evident, with no harsh intention.

"I'm sure I hope——"

"Well, we won't talk about it. I must do without Constance, that's all. You'll, of course, have a house in London, but both of you will often be down here. It's

settled. About the end of October. Time enough to
make arrangements. I'll settle it with Constance. So
to-morrow morning you leave us, on a visit to your
parents. I suppose you'll spend a couple of days
there ? "

In his confused mind, Dyce could only fix the
thought that Constance had evidently told Lady Ogram
of his intention to go to Alverholme. It was plain
that those two held very intimate colloquies.

"A couple of days," he murmured in reply.

"Good. Of course you'll write to me when you're
in town again."

At luncheon Lady Ogram talked of Lashmar's
departure. Constance, he felt sure, already knew
about it. Really, he was treated with somewhat scant
ceremony. An obstinate mood fell upon him; he
resolved that he would say not a word to Constance of
what had passed this morning. If she wished to speak
of the proposed date of their marriage, let her broach
the subject herself. Through the meal he was taciturn.

Miss Bride and he dined alone together that evening.
They had not met since midday. Dyce was still dis-
inclined for talk; Constance, on the other hand, fell
into a cheerful vein of chat, and seemed not at all to
notice her companion's lack of amiability.

"I shall go by the 8.27," said Dyce, abruptly,
towards the end of the meal.

"Yes, that's your best train. You'll be at Alverholme before ten o'clock."

After dinner they sat together for scarcely a quarter
of an hour; Constance talking of politics, Dyce
absolutely silent. Then Miss Bride rose and offered
her hand.

"So, good-bye ! "

She spoke so pleasantly, and looked so kindly, that
Lashmar for a moment felt ashamed of himself. He
pressed her hand, and endeavoured to speak cordially.

"Shall I hear from you ? " Constance asked, trying to
meet his eyes.

Our Friend the Charlatan

" Why, of course, very soon."

" Thank you.   I shall be very glad."

Thus they parted.   And Dyce for a couple of hours sat smoking and brooding.

On the morrow, at luncheon, Lady Ogram mentioned to Constance that May Tomalin would arrive on the following afternoon.   She added, presently, that Lord Dymchurch had accepted an invitation to Rivenoak for a day or two in the ensuing week.

This same day the post brought Constance a letter and a packet.   The letter was from Mrs. Toplady, who wrote thus :

" DEAR MISS BRIDE,

" This morning I came across an article in an American magazine which it struck me would interest you.   The subject is ' Recent Sociological Speculations.' It reviews several books, among them one by a French author, which seems to be very interesting.   When I showed the article to Miss Tomalin, she agreed with me that there seemed a striking resemblance between the theories of this French sociologist and those which Mr. Lashmar has independently formed.   Probably Mr. Lashmar would like to see the book.   In any case, you and he will, I am sure, be interested in reading this article together, so I am posting you the magazine.

" To my great regret, Miss Tomalin—or May, as I have come to call her—leaves me the day after to-morrow.   But the advantage is yours at Rivenoak. Please give my love to dear Lady Ogram, who I hope is now quite well again.   With kindest regards,

" Sincerely yours,

" GERALDINE TOPLADY."

Constance read the magazine article in question, and, immediately after doing so, despatched an order to London for the French sociological work therein discussed.

CHAPTER XVII

PILLOW-PROPPED at her morning studies, the humorist of Pont Street, as she glanced rapidly over the close-printed pages of a trans-Atlantic monthly, had her eye caught by the word "bio-sociological." Whom had she heard using that sonorous term? It sounded to her with the Oxford accent, and she saw Lashmar. The reading of a few lines in the context seemed to remind her very strongly of Lashmar's philosophic eloquence. She looked closer; found that there was question of a French book of some importance recently published, and smilingly asked herself whether it could be that Lashmar knew this book. That he was capable of reticence regarding the source of his ideas, she had little doubt; and what would be more amusing than to see "the coming man" convicted of audacious plagiarism? She wished him no harm; none whatever. It delighted her to see a man make his way in the stupid world by superiority of wits, and Dyce Lashmar was a favourite of hers; she had by no means yet done with him. All the same, this chance of entertainment must not be lost.

Having gone down rather earlier than usual, she found Miss Tomalin also studiously engaged, a solid tome open before her.

"My dear May, what waste of time that is! If you would only believe me that all the substance of big books is to be found in little ones! One gets on so much more quickly, and has a much clearer view of things. Why, no end of poor people now-a-days make their living by boiling down these monsters to essence. It's really a social duty to make use of their work.

244

Our Friend the Charlatan

Look, for instance, at this article I have just been reading—'Recent Sociological Speculations.' Here the good man gives us all that is important in half-a-dozen expensive and heavy volumes. Here's all about bio-sociology. Haven't I heard you talk of bio-sociology?"

"But," cried May, "that's Mr. Lashmar's theory! Has he been publishing it?"

"No. Some one else seems to have got hold of the same idea. Perhaps it's like Darwin and Wallace—that kind of thing."

May took the periodical, and read.

"Why, this is astonishing!" she exclaimed. "There's a passage quoted which is exactly like Mr. Lashmar—almost the very words I have heard him use!"

"Yet, you see, it's from a French book. This would certainly interest him. Perhaps he doesn't see the American reviews. Suppose I sent it to Miss Bride? They can read it together, and it will amuse them."

May assented, and the periodical was addressed to Rivenoak.

Friends came to lunch with them. In the afternoon they made three calls. At dinner some score of persons were Mrs. Toplady's guests. Only as the clock pointed towards midnight did they find an opportunity of returning to the subject of bio-sociology. Mrs. Toplady wished for an intimate chat with her guest, who was soon to leave her; she reclined comfortably in a settee, and looked at the girl, who made a pretty picture in a high-backed chair.

"I hear that Mr. Lashmar leaves Rivenoak to-morrow," she said, referring to a letter that had arrived from Lady Ogram this evening. "I hope he won't be gone when the magazine arrives."

"Indeed? He comes back to-morrow?" said May.

"Not to London. He goes to spend a day or two with his people, it seems. You don't know them?"

"Not at all. I only know that his father is a rural clergyman."

Mrs. Toplady had observed that May's tone in speaking

245

of Lashmar lacked something of its former vivacity. The change had been noticeable since the announcement of the philosopher's betrothal. More than that: the decline of interest was accompanied by a tendency to speak of Lashmar as though pityingly, or, perhaps, even slightingly; and this it was that manifested itself in May's last remark.

"I don't think it's very common," Mrs. Toplady let fall, "for the country clergy—or indeed the clergy anywhere—to have brilliant sons."

"It certainly isn't," May agreed. And, after reflecting, she added: "I suppose one may call Mr. Lashmar brilliant?"

Miss Tomalin had continued to profit by her opportunities. Before coming to London, it would have been impossible for her to phrase a thought thus, and so utter it. That easy superciliousness smacked not at all of provincial breeding.

"On the whole, I think so," was Mrs. Toplady's modulated reply. "He has very striking ideas. How odd that somebody else should have hit upon his theory of civilization! He ought to have written a book, as I told him."

"But suppose," suggested May, with some uneasiness, "that he knew about that French book?"

"Oh, my dear, we can't suppose that! Besides, we haven't read the book. It may really be quite different in its—its tendency from Mr. Lashmar's view."

"I don't see how it *can* be, Mrs. Toplady. Judging from those quotations and the article, it's Mr. Lashmar from beginning to end."

"Then it's a most curious case of coincidence. Poor Mr. Lashmar will naturally be vexed. It's hard upon him, isn't it?"

May did not at once respond. The friend, watching her with the roguish smile, let fall another piece of intelligence.

"I hear that his marriage is to be in the autumn."

"Indeed?" said May indifferently.

Our Friend the Charlatan

"Between ourselves," pursued the other, "didn't you feel just a little surprised?"

"Surprised?"

"At his choice. Oh, don't misunderstand me. I quite appreciate Miss Bride's cleverness and seriousness. But one couldn't help thinking that a man of Mr. Lashmar's promise— Perhaps you don't see it in that way?"

"I really think they are rather well suited," said May, again calmly supercilious.

"It may be so. I had almost thought that—how shall I express it?" Mrs. Toplady searched for a moment. "Perhaps Lady Ogram might have made a suggestion, which Mr. Lashmar, for some reason, did not feel able to disregard. He has quite a chivalrous esteem for Lady Ogram, haven't you noticed? I like to see it. That kind of thing is rare now-a-days. No doubt he feels reason for gratitude; but how many men does one know who can be truly grateful? That's what I like in Mr. Lashmar; he has character as well as intellect."

"But how do you mean, Mrs. Toplady?" inquired May, losing something of her polish in curiosity. "Why should my aunt have wanted him to marry Miss Bride?"

"Ah, that I don't know. Possibly she thought it, knowing him as she does, really the best thing for him. Possibly—one could make conjectures. But one always can."

May puzzled over the hint, her brow knitted; Mrs. Toplady regarded her with veiled amusement, wondering whether it would really be necessary to use plainer words. The girl was not dull, but perhaps her small experience of life, and her generally naïve habit of mind, obscured to her what to the more practised was so obvious.

"Do you mean," said May diffidently, "that she planned it out of kindness to Miss Bride? Of course, I know that she likes Miss Bride very much. Perhaps she thought there would never be a better opportunity."

"It might be so," replied the other absently.

"Miss Bride is very nice and very clever," pursued May, sounding the words on the thinnest possible note. "But one didn't think of her as very likely to marry."

"No; it seemed improbable."

There was a pause. As if turning to quite another subject, Mrs. Toplady remarked:

"You will have visitors at Rivenoak next week. Sir William Amys is to be there for a day or two, and Lord Dymchurch——"

"Lord Dymchurch?"

The girl threw off her air of cold concentration, and shone triumphantly.

"Does it surprise you, May?"

"Oh, I hadn't thought of it—I didn't know my aunt had invited him——"

"The wonder is that Lord Dymchurch should have accepted," said Mrs. Toplady, with a very mature archness. "Did he know, by the bye, that you were going down?"

"I fancy he did."

Their eyes met, and May relieved her feelings with a little laugh.

"Then perhaps the wonder ceases. And yet, in another way——" Mrs. Toplady broke off, and added in a lower voice: "Of course you know all about his circumstances?"

"No, indeed I don't. Tell me about him, please."

"But haven't you heard that he is the poorest man in the House of Lords?"

"I had no idea of it," cried May. "How should I have known? Really? He is so poor?"

"I imagine he has barely enough to live upon. The family was ruined long ago."

"But why didn't you tell me? Does my aunt know?"

May's voice did not express resentment, nor, indeed, strong feeling of any kind. The revelation seemed merely to surprise her. She was smiling, as if at the amusingly unexpected.

Our Friend the Charlatan

"Lady Ogram certainly knows," said Mrs. Toplady.

"Then, of course, that's why he does nothing," May exclaimed. "Fancy!" Her provincialism was becoming very marked. "A lord with hardly enough to live upon! But I'm astonished that he seems so cheerful."

"Lord Dymchurch has a very philosophical mind," said the elder lady, with gravity humorously exaggerated.

"Yes, I suppose he has. Now I shall understand him better. I'm glad he's going to be at Rivenoak. You know that he asked me to advise him about what he should do. It'll be rather awkward, though. I must get him to tell me the truth."

"You'll probably have no difficulty in that. It's pretty certain that he thinks you know all about him already. If he hadn't, I feel sure he wouldn't go to Rivenoak."

The girl mused, smiling self-consciously.

"I had better tell you the truth, Mrs. Toplady," were her next words, in a burst of confidence. "I think Lord Dymchurch is very nice—as a friend. But only as a friend."

"Thank you for your confidence, May. Do you know that I suspected something of the kind?"

"I want to be friends with him," pursued May impulsively. "I shall get him to tell me, all about himself, and we shall see what he can do. Of course, there mustn't be any misunderstanding."

Mrs. Toplady had not been prepared for this tranquil reasonableness. May was either more primitive, or much more sophisticated, than she had supposed. Her interest waxed keener.

"Between ourselves, my dear," she remarked, "that is exactly what I should have anticipated. You are very young, and the world is at your feet. Of money you have no need, and, if Lord Dymchurch *had* had the good fortune to please you— But you are ambitious. I quite understand; trust me. Poor Dymchurch will

Our Friend the Charlatan

never do anything. He is merely a bookish man. But, whilst we are talking of it, there's no harm in telling you that your aunt doesn't quite see the matter with our eyes. For some reason—I don't know exactly what it is—Lady Ogram is very favourable to poor Lord Dymchurch."

"I have noticed that," said May quietly. "Of course, it makes no difference."

"You think not?" asked Mrs. Toplady, beginning to be genuinely impressed by this young woman's self-confidence.

"I mean that my aunt couldn't do more than suggest," May answered, slightly throwing back her head. "I have only to let her know how I think about anything."

"You are sure of that?" asked the other sweetly.

"Oh, quite!"

May's smile was ineffable. The woman of the world, the humorist and cynic, saw it with admiration.

"Ah, that puts my mind at ease!" murmured Mrs. Toplady. "To tell the truth, I have been worrying a little. Sometimes elderly people are so very tenacious of their ideas. Of course, Lady Ogram has nothing but your good at heart."

"Of course!" exclaimed the girl.

"Shall I confess to you that I almost fancied *this* might be the explanation of Miss Bride's engagement?"

"Miss Bride—? How?"

"I only tell you for your amusement. It occurred to me that, having set her heart on a scheme which had reference to Lord Dymchurch, your aunt was perhaps a little uneasy with respect to a much more brilliant and conspicuous man. Had that been so—it's all the merest supposition—she might have desired to see the brilliant and dangerous man made harmless— put out of the way."

A gleam of sudden perception illumined the girl's face. For a moment wonder seemed tending to mirth; but it took another turn, and became naïve displeasure.

Our Friend the Charlatan

"You think so?" broke from her impetuously. "You really think that's why she wanted them to be engaged?"

"It's only what I had fancied, my dear."

"But I shouldn't wonder if you were right! Indeed, I shouldn't! Now that you put it in that way— I remember that my aunt didn't care for me to see much of Mr. Lashmar. It amused me, because, to tell you the truth, Mrs. Toplady, I should never have thought of Mr. Lashmar as anything but a friend. I feel quite sure I shouldn't."

"I quite understand *that*," replied the listener, the corners of her lips very eloquent.

"Such a thing had never entered my mind," pursued May, volubly and with emphasis. "Never!"

"It may have entered some one else's mind, though," interposed Mrs. Toplady, again maturely arch.

"Oh, do you think so!" exclaimed the girl, with manifest pleasure. "I'm sure I hope not. But, Mrs. Toplady, how could my aunt oblige such a man as Mr. Lashmar to engage himself against his will?"

"You must remember, May, that, for the moment at all events, Mr. Lashmar's prospects seem to depend a good deal on Lady Ogram's good-will. She has a great deal of local influence. And then—by the bye, is Mr. Lashmar quite easy in his circumstances?"

"I really don't know," May answered, with an anxious fold in her forehead. "Surely he, too, isn't quite poor?"

"I hardly think he is wealthy. Isn't it just possible that something may depend upon the marriage—— ?"

Mrs. Toplady's voice died away in a considerate vagueness. But May was not at all disposed to leave the matter nebulous.

"If he is really poor," she said, in a clear-cut tone, "it's quite natural that he should want to marry some one who can help him. But why didn't he choose some one really suitable?"

"Poor Mr. Lashmar!" sighed the other humorously. "If he had no encouragement, my dear May!"

251

Our Friend the Charlatan

"But he didn't wait to see whether he had any or not!"

"What if he had very good reason for knowing that Lady Ogram would never, never, never consent to—something we won't mention?"

"But," May ejaculated, "surely he needn't take it for granted that my aunt would never change her mind. If it's as you say, how foolishly he must have behaved! It doesn't concern me in the least. You see I can speak quite calmly about it. I'm only sorry and astonished that he should be going to marry—well, after all, we muss agree that Miss Bride isn't quite an ideal for him, however one looks at it. Of course, it's nothing to me. If it *had* been, I think I should feel more offended than sorry."

"Offended?"

"That he had taken for granted that I had no will of my own, and no influence with my aunt."

"It seems rather faint-hearted, I admit."

The dialogue lasted but a few minutes longer. May repeated once or twice that she had no personal interest in Lashmar's fortunes, but her utterance grew mechanical, and she was evidently withdrawing into her thoughts. As a clock in the room told softly the first hour of the morning Mrs. Toplady rose; she spoke a few words about her engagements for the day which had nominally begun, then kissed her friend on the cheek.

"Don't think any more of it, May. It mustn't interfere with your sleep."

"That indeed it won't, Mrs. Toplady!" replied the girl, with a musically mocking laugh.

Appearances notwithstanding, May told the truth when she declared that she had never thought of marrying Lashmar. This, however, did not necessarily involve an indifference to Lashmar's homage. That the coming man should make his court to her, she saw as a natural and agreeable thing; that he should recognize her intellectual powers, and submit to her personal charm, was only what she had hoped and expected from the first. After their conversation in the supper-room, she counted him a conquest, and looked forward with no little pleasure to the development of this romance. Its sudden extinction astonished and mortified her. Had Lashmar turned away to make some brilliant alliance, her pique would only have endured for a moment; Lord Dymchurch's approach would have more than compensated the commoner's retirement. But that she should merely have amused his idle moments, whilst his serious thoughts were fixed on Constance Bride, was an injury not easy to pardon. For she disliked Miss Bride, and she knew the sentiment was mutual.

Seeing the situation in the new light shed by Mrs. Toplady's ingenious conjectures, her sense of injury was mitigated; the indignant feeling that remained she directed chiefly against Lady Ogram, who seemed inclined to dispose of her in such a summary way. Constance, naturally, she disliked more than ever, but Lashmar she viewed with something of compassion, as a victim of circumstances. Were those circumstances irresistible? Was there not even now a possibility of defeating them?—not with a view to taking Miss Bride's place, but for the pleasure of asserting herself against a plot, and reassuring her rightful position as arbitress of destinies. Lady Ogram was a kind old woman, but decidedly despotic, and she had gone too far. If indeed Lashmar were acting in helpless obedience to her, it would be the merest justice to make an attempt at rescuing him and restoring his liberty.

Not without moral significance was the facial likeness between Lady Ogram in her youth and May Tomalin. One who had seen the girl as she sat to-night in her bedroom, brooding deeply, without the least inclination for repose, must have been struck by a new vigour in the lines of her countenance. Thus—though with more of obstinate purpose—had Arabella

Our Friend the Charlatan

Tomalin been wont to look, at moments of crisis in her adventurous youth.

The clock was pointing to two when May rose from her velvet-seated chair, and went to the little writing-table which stood in another part of the room. She took a plain sheet of note-paper, and, with a hand far from steady, began, not writing, but printing certain words, in large, ill-formed capitals.

"HAVE MORE COURAGE. AIM HIGHER. IT IS NOT TOO LATE."

At this achievement she gazed smilingly. The ink having dried, she folded the paper and put it into an envelope, which she closed. Then her face indicated a new effort. She could think of only one way of disguising her hand in cursive—the common device of sloping it backwards. This she attempted. The result failing to please her, she tried again on a second envelope, and this time with success; the writing looked masculine, and in no respect suggested its true authorship. She had addressed the letter to Dyce Lashmar, Esq., at Rivenoak.

Nine o'clock next morning saw her out-of-doors. In Sloane Street she found a hansom, and was driven to a remote post-office. Before ten she sat in her own room again, glowing with satisfaction.

CHAPTER XVIII

"At last," declared Mrs. Lashmar, "it really looks as if Dyce was going to do something. I've just been writing to Lady Susan, and I have let her see unmistakably what I think of her friendship. But I'm very glad Dyce isn't indebted to her, for a more unendurable woman, when she thinks she has done any one a kindness, doesn't exist. If she gets a place for a servant-girl, all the world is told of it, and she expects you to revere her saintly benevolence. I am *very* glad that she never did anything for Dyce. Indeed, I always felt that she was very little use. I doubt whether she has the slightest influence with respectable people."

It was just after breakfast, and the day promised to be the hottest of the year. The vicar, heavy-laden man, had sat down in his study to worry over some parish accounts. When the door opened to admit his wife, he quivered with annoyance. Mrs. Lashmar had a genius for the malapropos. During breakfast, when her talk would have mattered little, she had kept silence; now that her husband particularly wished to be alone with his anxieties, she entered with an air foreboding long discourse.

"Twenty-three pounds, four shillings and sixpence," muttered the vicar, as he passed a handkerchief over his moist forehead. "Dear me! how close it is! Twenty-three——"

"If Dyce is elected," pursued the lady, "we must celebrate the occasion in some really striking way. Of course, there must be a dinner for all our poor——"

"What I want to know," interrupted Mr. Lashmar,

255

with mild irritableness, "is, how he proposes to meet his expenses, and what he is going to live upon. If he is still looking to *me*—I trust you haven't encouraged him in any hope of that kind?"

"Of course not. In my last letter I expressly reminded him that our affairs were getting into a lamentable muddle. Of course, if *I* had had the management of them, this wouldn't have come about. Do you know what I have been thinking? It might be an advantage to Dyce if you made friends with the clergy at Hollingford. Couldn't you go over one day, and call on the rector? I see he's a Cambridge man, but——"

"Really," cried Mr. Lashmar, half distraught, "I must beg you to let me get this work done in quietness. By some extraordinary error——"

A knock sounded at the door, followed by a man's voice.

"May I come in?"

"There you are!" Mrs. Lashmar exclaimed. "It's Dyce himself. Come in! Come in! Why, who could have thought you would get here so early!"

"I chose the early train for the sake of coolness," answered Dyce, who shook hands with his parents. "The weather is simply tropical. And two days ago we were shivering. What is there to drink, mother?"

Mrs. Lashmar took her son to the dining-room, and, whilst he was refreshing himself, talked of the career before him. Her sanguine mind saw him already at Westminster, and on the way to high distinction.

"There's just one thing I'm anxious about," she said, sinking her voice. "You know the state of your father's affairs. It happens most unfortunately, just when a little help would be so important to you. For years I have foreseen it, Dyce. Again and again I have urged prudence; but you know your father, the most generous of men, but a mere child in matters of business. I feared; but it was only the other day that I discovered the real state of things. I shouldn't be at all surprised, Dyce, if some day we have to look to *you* for succour."

"Don't worry," answered her son. "Things'll come right, I think. Just go on as prudently as you can for the present. Is father really in a hobble?"

"My dear, he doesn't know where to turn for a five-pound note!"

Dyce was sincerely troubled. He seldom thought of his parents; none the less they represented his only true affection, and he became uncomfortable at the prospect of disaster befalling their latter years.

"Well, well, don't bother about it more than you can help. Things are going pretty well with me, I fancy."

"So I supposed, Dyce. But your father is afraid— you know how he looks on the dark side of everything —lest you should be incurring liabilities. I have told him that that was never your habit."

"Of course not," said Dyce confidently. "You may be sure that I haven't taken such serious steps without seeing my way clear before me."

"I knew it! I have always had the fullest faith in you. And, Dyce, how you are improving in looks! You must go to a photographer again——"

"I've just been sitting at Hollingford. The local people wanted it, you know. But I'll send you one from London presently."

"And you assure me that there is no money difficulty?" asked Mrs. Lashmar, with inquisitive eyes.

"None whatever. The fact of the matter is that I am standing to please Lady Ogram, and, of course—" he waved an explanatory hand. "Things are not finally arranged yet, but all will be smooth."

His smile made dignified deprecation of undue insistence on trivial detail.

"I'm delighted to hear it!" exclaimed his mother. "It's just what I had supposed. What could be more natural? Do you think, by the bye, that I ought to go and see Lady Ogram? It might seem to her a right and natural thing. And, from what you tell me of her, I feel sure we should have a good deal in common."

"I've thought of that too," Dyce answered, averting his look. "But wait a little. Just now Lady Ogram isn't at all well; she sees hardly anybody."

"Of course I shall be guided by your advice. A little later, then. And, Dyce, you haven't told me anything about Miss Bride. Is she still with Lady Ogram?"

"Oh yes. Still acting as secretary."

"Of course you don't see much of her?"

"Why, to tell you the truth, we have to see each other a good deal, owing to her duties."

"Ah, yes, I understand. She writes to dictation, and that kind of thing. Strange that Lady Ogram should have engaged such a very unpleasant young woman. I've seldom known any one I disliked so much."

"Really? She's of the new school, you know; the result of the emancipation movement." Dyce laughed, as if indulgently. "Lady Ogram thinks a great deal of her and, I fancy, means to leave her money."

"Gracious! You don't say so!"

Mrs. Lashmar put the subject disdainfully aside, and Dyce was glad to speak of something else.

Throughout the day the vicar was too busy to hold conversation with his son. But after dinner they sat alone together in the study, Mrs. Lashmar being called forth by some parochial duty. As he puffed at his newly-lighted pipe, Dyce reflected on all that had happened since he last sat here, some three months ago, and thought of what might have been his lot had not fortune dealt so kindly with him. Glancing at his father's face, he noted in it the signs of wearing anxiety; it seemed to him that the vicar looked much older than in the spring, and he was impressed by the pathos of age, which has no hopes to nourish, which can ask no more of life than a quiet ending. He could not imagine himself grey-headed, disillusioned; the effort to do so gave him a thrill of horror. Thereupon he felt reproach of conscience. For all the care and kindness he had received from his father, since the days when he used to come into this very room to show how well he could read a page of some child's story, what return had he made? None whatever in words, and little enough in conduct. All at once he felt a desire to prove that he was not the insensible egoist his father perhaps thought him.

"I'm afraid you're a good deal worried, father," he began, looking at the paper-covered writing-table.

"I'm putting my affairs in order, Dyce," the vicar replied, running fingers through his beard. " I've been foolish enough to let them get very tangled; let me advise you never to do the same. But it'll all be straight before long. Don't trouble about me; let me hear of your own projects. I heartily wish it were in my power to help you."

"You did that much longer than I ought to have allowed," returned Dyce. "I feel myself to a great extent the cause of your troubles——"

"Nothing of the kind," broke in his father cheerily. "Troubles be—excommunicated! This hot weather takes it out of me a little, but I'm very well and not at all discouraged; so don't think it. To tell you the truth, I've been feeling anxious to hear more in detail from you about this Hollingford enterprise. Have you serious hopes?"

"I hardly think I shall be elected the first time," Dyce answered, speaking with entire frankness. " But it'll be experience, and may open the way for me."

"Parliament," mused the vicar, "Parliament! To be sure, we must have Members; it's our way of doing things, of governing the country. And if you really feel apt for that——"

He paused dreamily. Dyce, still under the impulse of softened feelings, spoke, as he seldom did, very simply, quietly, sincerely.

" I believe, father, that I am not *unfit* for it. Politics, it's true, don't interest me very strongly, but I have brains enough to get the necessary knowledge, and I feel that I shall do better work in a prominent position of that kind than if I went on tutoring or took to journalism. As you say, we must have representatives, and I should not be the least capable, or the least honest. I find I can speak fairly well; I find I can inspire people with confidence in me. And, without presumption, I don't think the confidence is misplaced."

"Well, that's something," said the vicar absently. " But you talk as if politics were a profession one could live by. I don't yet understand——"

" How I'm going to live. Nor do I. I'll tell you that frankly. But Lady Ogram knows my circumstances, and none the less urges me on. It may be taken for granted that she has something in view; and, after giving a good deal of thought to the matter, I see no valid reason why I should refuse any assistance she chooses to offer me. The case would not be without precedent. There is nothing dishonourable——"

Dyce drifted into verbosity. At the beginning he had lost from sight the impossibility of telling the whole truth about his present position and the prospects on which he counted; he spoke with relief, and would gladly have gone on unbosoming himself. Strong and deep-rooted is the instinct of confession. Unable to ease his conscience regarding outward circumstances, he turned at length to the question of his intellectual attitude.

" Do you remember when I was here last I spoke to you of a French book I had been reading, a sociological work? As I told you, it had a great influence on my mind. It helped to set my ideas in order. Before then, I had only the vaguest way of thinking about political and social questions. That book supplied me with a scientific principle, which I have since been working out for myself."

" Ha !" interjected the vicar, looking up oddly. " And you really feel in need of a scientific principle ? "

Our Friend the Charlatan

"Without it I should have remained a mere empiric, like the rest of our politicians. I should have judged measures from the narrow, merely practical point of view; or rather, I should pretty certainly have guided myself by some theory in which I only tried to believe."

"So you have now a belief, Dyce? Come, that's a point to have reached. That alone should give you a distinction among the aspiring men of to-day. And *what* do you believe?"

After drawing a meditative puff or two, Dyce launched into his familiar demonstration. He would very much rather have left it aside; he felt that he was not speaking as one genuinely convinced, and that his father listened without serious interest. But the theory had all to be gone through; he unwound it, like thread off a reel, rather mechanically and heavily towards the end.

"And that's what you are going to live for?" said his father. "That is your faith necessary to salvation?"

"I take it to be the interpretation of human history."

"Perhaps it is; perhaps it is," murmured the vicar abstractedly. "For my own part," he added, bestirring himself to refill his pipe, "I can still see a guiding light in the older faith. Of course, the world has rejected it; I don't seek to delude myself on that point; I shrink with horror from the blasphemy which would have us pretend that our civilization obeys the spirit of Christ. The world has rejected it. Now as ever 'despised and rejected of men.' The world, very likely, will do without religion. Yet, Dyce, when I think of the Sermon on the Mount——"

He paused again, holding his pipe in his hand unlit, and looking before him with wide eyes.

"I respect that as much as any one can," said Dyce gravely.

"As much as any one can—who doesn't believe it?"

Our Friend the Charlatan

His father took him up with gentle irony. "I don't expect the impossible. You *cannot* believe in it; for you were born a post-Darwinian. Well now, your religion is temporal; let us take that for granted. You do not deny yourself; you believe that self-assertion to the uttermost is the prime duty."

"Provided that self-assertion be understood aright. I understand it as meaning the exercise of all my civic faculties."

"Which, in your case, are faculties of command, faculties which point you to the upper seat, Dyce. Tom Bullock, my gardener, is equally to assert himself, but with the understanding that *his* faculties point to the bottom of the table, where the bread is a trifle stale, and butter sometimes lacking. Yes, yes; I understand. Of course, you will do your very best for Tom; you would like him to have what the sweet language of our day calls a square meal. But still he must eat below the salt; there you can't help him."

"Because nature itself cannot," explained Dyce. "One wants Tom to acknowledge that, without bitterness, and at the same time to understand that, but for *him*, his honest work, his clean life, the world couldn't go on at all. If Tom *feels* that, he is a religious man."

"Ah! I take your point. But, Dyce, I find as a painful matter of fact that Tom Bullock is by no means a religious man. Tom, I have learnt, privately calls himself 'a hagnostic,' and is obliging enough to say among his intimates that, if the truth were told, I myself am the same. Tom has got hold of evolutionary notions, which he illustrates in his daily work. He knows all about natural selection, and the survival of the fittest. Tom ought to be a very apt disciple of your bio-sociological creed. Unhappily, a more selfish mortal doesn't walk the earth. He has been known to send his wife and children supperless to bed, because a festive meeting at a club to which he belongs demanded all the money in his pocket. Tom, you see, feels himself one of the Select; his wife and children, holding an inferior place in great nature's scheme, must be content to hunger now and then, and it's their fault if they don't feel a religious satisfaction in the privilege."

"Why on earth do you employ such a man?" cried Dyce.

"Because, my dear boy, if I did not, no one else would, and Tom's wife and children would have still greater opportunities of proving their disinterested citizenship."

Dyce laughed.

"Speaking seriously again, father, Tom is what he is just because he hasn't received the proper education. Had he been rightly taught, who knows but he would, in fact, have been an apt disciple of the civic religion?"

"I fear me, Dyce, that no amount of civic instruction, or any other instruction, would have affected Tom's ethics. Tom is representative of his age. Come, come; I have every wish to be just to you. A new religion must have time; its leaven must work amid the lump. You, my dear boy, are convinced that the leaven is, though a new sort, a very sound and sufficient yeast; let that be granted. I, unfortunately, cannot believe anything of the kind. To me your method of solution seems a deliberate insistence on the worldly in human nature, sure to have the practical result of making men more and more savagely materialist. I see no hope whatever that you will inspire the world with enthusiasm for a noble civilization by any theory based on biological teaching. From my point of view, a man becomes noble *in spite* of the material laws which condition his life, never in consequence of them. If you ask me how and why— I bow my head and keep silence."

"Can you maintain," asked Dyce respectfully, "that Christianity is still a civilizing power?"

"To all appearances," was the grave answer, "Christianity has failed—utterly, absolutely, glaringly failed. At this moment, the world, I am convinced, holds more potential barbarism than did the Roman Empire under the Antonines. Wherever I look, I see a monstrous contrast between the professions and the practice, between the assumed and the actual aims, of so-called Christian peoples. Christianity has failed to conquer the human heart."

"It must be very dreadful for you to be convinced of that."

"It is. But more dreadful would be a loss of belief in the Christian spirit. By belief, I don't mean faith in its ultimate triumph; I am not at all sure that I can look forward to *that*. No; but a persuasion that the Sermon on the Mount is good—is the best. Once upon a time, multitudes were in that sense Christian. Now-a-days, does one man in a thousand give his mind's allegiance (lips and life disregarded) to that ideal of human thought and conduct? Take your newspaper writer, who speaks to and for the million; he simply scorns every Christian precept. How can he but scorn a thing so unpractical? Nay, I notice that he is already throwing off the hypocrisy hitherto thought decent. I read newspaper articles which sneer and scoff at those who venture to remind the world that, after all, it is nominally in the service of a Christian ideal. Our prophets begin openly to proclaim that self-interest and the hardest materialism are our only safe guides. Now and then such passages amaze, appal me—but I am getting used to them. So I am to the same kind of declaration in every-day talk. Men in most respectable coats, sitting at most orderly tables, hold the language of pure barbarism. If you drew one of them aside, and said to him, ' But what about the fruits of the spirit ?'—what sort of look would he give you ? "

"I agree entirely," exclaimed Dyce. "And for that very reason I want to work for a new civilizing principle."

Our Friend the Charlatan

"If you get into the House, shall you talk there about bio-sociology?"

"Why no," answered Dyce, with a chuckle. "If I were capable of that, I should have very little chance of getting into the House at all, or of doing anything useful anywhere."

"In other words," said his father, still eyeing an unlit pipe, "one must be practical—eh, Dyce?"

"In the right way."

"Yes, yes; one must be practical, practical. If you know which *is* the right way, I am very glad—I congratulate you. For my own part, I seek it vainly; I seek it these forty years and more; and it grows clear to me that I should have done much better not to heed that question at all. 'Blessed are the merciful—blessed are the pure in heart—blessed are the peacemakers.' It is strikingly unpractical, Dyce, my boy; you can't, again in to-day's sweet language, 'run' the world on those principles. They are utterly incompatible with business; and business is life."

"But they are not at all incompatible with the civilization I have in view," Dyce exclaimed.

"I am glad to hear it; very glad. You don't, however, see your way to that civilization by teaching such axioms."

"Unfortunately not."

"No. You have to teach 'Blessed are the civic-minded, for they shall profit by their civism.' It has to be profit, Dyce, profit, profit. Live thus, and you'll get a good deal out of life; live otherwise, and you *may* get more, but with an unpleasant chance of getting a good deal less."

"But isn't it unfortunately true that Christianity spoke also of rewards?"

"Yes, it is true. The promise was sometimes adapted to the poorer understanding. More often, it was nobler, and by that I take my stand. 'Blessed are the pure in heart, for they shall see God. Blessed are the peacemakers, for they shall be called the children of God.'

Our Friend the Charlatan

The words, you know, had then a meaning. Now they have none. To see God was not a little thing, I imagine, but the vision, probably, brought with it neither purple nor fine linen. For curiosity's sake, Dyce, read Matthew v. to vii. before you go to sleep. You'll find the old Bible in your bedroom."

The door was thrown open, and Mrs. Lashmar's voice broke upon the still air of the study.

"Dyce, have you seen to-day's *Times?* Mrs. Hoyle has lent it me. There's a most interesting article on the probable duration of Parliament. Take it up to your room with you, and read it before you go to sleep."

CHAPTER XIX

"THERE'S a letter for you, Dyce; forwarded from Rivenoak, I see."

It lay beside his plate on the breakfast-table, and Dyce eyed it with curiosity. The backward-sloping hand was quite unknown to him. He tapped at an egg, and still scrutinized the writing on the envelope; it was Constance who had crossed out the Rivenoak address, and had written beside it "The Vicarage, Alverholme."

"Have you slept well?" asked his mother, who treated him with much more consideration than at his last visit.

"Very well indeed," he replied mechanically, taking up his letter and cutting it open with a table-knife.

"HAVE MORE COURAGE. AIM HIGHER. IT IS NOT TOO LATE."

Dyce stared at the oracular message, written in printer's capitals on a sheet of paper which contained nothing else. He again examined the envelope, but the post-mark in no way helped him. He glanced at his mother, and finding her eye upon him, folded the sheet carelessly. He glanced at his father, who had just laid down a letter which evidently worried him. The meal passed with very little conversation. Dyce puzzled over the anonymous counsel so mysteriously conveyed to him, and presently went apart to muse unobserved.

He thought of Iris Woolstan. Of course, a woman had done this thing, and Iris he could well believe

267

capable of it. But what did she mean? Did she really imagine that, but for lack of courage, he would have made suit to *her*? Did she really regard herself as socially his superior? There was no telling. Women had the oddest notions on such subjects, and perhaps the fact of his engaging himself to Constance Bride, a mere secretary, struck her as deplorable. "Aim higher." The exhortation was amusing enough. One would have supposed it came at least from some great heiress.

He stopped in his pacing about the garden. An heiress? Miss Tomalin?

Shaking of the head dismissed this fancy. Miss Tomalin was a matter-of-fact young person; he could not see her doing such a thing as this. And yet—and yet —when he remembered their last talk, was it not conceivable that he had made a deeper impression upon her than, in his modesty, he allowed himself to suppose? Had she not spoken, with a certain enthusiasm, of working on his behalf at Hollingford? The disturbing event which immediately followed had put Miss Tomalin into the distance; his mind had busied itself continuously with surmises as to the nature of the benefit he might expect if he married Constance. After all, Lady Ogram's niece *might* have had recourse to this expedient. She, at all events, knew that he was staying at Rivenoak, and might easily not have heard on what day he would leave. Or, perhaps, knowing that he left yesterday, she had calculated that the letter would reach him before his departure; it had possibly been delivered at Rivenoak by the midday post.

Amusing, the thought that Constance had herself readdressed this communication!

Another possibility occurred to him. What if the writer were indeed Iris Woolstan, and her motive quite disinterested? What if she did not allude to herself at all, but was really pained at the thought of his making an insignificant marriage, when, by waiting a little, he was sure to win a wife suitable to his ambition? Of this, too, Iris might well be capable. Her last letter to him had had some dignity, and, all things considered, she had always shown herself a devoted, unexacting friend. It seemed more likely, it seemed much more likely, than the other conjecture.

Nevertheless, suppose Miss Tomalin *had* taken this romantic step? The supposition involved such weighty issues that he liked to harbour it, to play with it. He pictured himself calling in Pont Street; he entered the drawing-room, and his eyes fell at once upon Miss Tomalin, in whose manner he remarked something unusual—a constraint, a nervousness. Saluting, he looked her fixedly in the face; she could not meet his regard; she blushed a little.

Why, it was very easy to determine whether or not she had sent that letter. In the case of Iris Woolstan, observation would have no certain results, for she must needs meet him with embarrassment. But Miss Tomalin would be superhuman if she did not somehow betray a nervous conscience.

Dyce strode into the house. His father and mother stood talking at the foot of the stairs, the vicar ready to go out.

"I must leave you at once," he exclaimed, looking at his watch. "Something I had forgotten—an engagement absurdly dropped out of mind. I must catch the next train—10.14, isn't it?"

Mrs. Lashmar sang out protest, but, on being assured that the engagement was political, urged him to make haste. The vicar all but silently pressed his hand, and with head bent walked away.

He just caught the train. It would bring him to town by midday in comfortable time to lunch and adorn himself before the permissible hour of calling in Pont Street. Rapid movement excited his imagination; he clung now to the hypothesis which at first seemed untenable; he built hopes upon it. Could he win a confession from May Tomalin, why should it be hopeless to sway the mind of Lady Ogram? If that were deemed impossible, they had but to wait. Lady Ogram

would not live till the autumn. To be sure, she looked
better since her return to Rivenoak, but she was frail,
oh, very frail, and sure to go off at a moment's notice.
As for Constance—oh, Constance!

At his lodgings he found unimportant letters. Every
letter would have seemed unimportant, compared with
that he carried in his pocket. Roach, M.P., invited
him to dine. The man at the Home Office wanted
him to go to a smoking-concert. Lady Susan Harrop
sent a beggarly card for an evening ten days hence.
Like the woman's impudence! And yet, as it had been
posted since her receipt of his mother's recent letter, it
proved that Lady Susan had a sense of his growing
dignity, which was good in its way. He smiled at a
recollection of the time when a seat at those people's
table had seemed a desirable and agitating thing.

Before half-past three he found himself walking in
Sloane Street. After consulting his watch several
times in the course of a few minutes, he decided that,
early as it was, he would go on at once to Mrs. Toplady's. Was he not privileged? Moreover, light rain
began to fall, with muttering of thunder; he must seek
shelter.

At a door in Pont Street stood two vehicles, a
brougham and a cab. Was it at Mrs. Toplady's? Yes,
so it proved; and, just as Dyce went up to the house,
the door opened. Out came a servant, carrying luggage;
behind the servant came Mrs. Toplady, and, behind her,
Miss Tomalin. Hat in hand, Lashmar faced the familiar
smile, at this moment undisguisedly mischievous.

"Mr. Lashmar!" exclaimed the lady, in high good-
humour, "we are just going to St. Pancras. Miss
Tomalin leaves me to-day. Why, it is raining! Can't
we take you with us? Yes, yes, come into the carriage,
and we'll drop you where you like."

Lashmar's eye was on the heiress. She said nothing
as she shook hands, and, unless he mistook, there was
a tremor about her lips, her eyelids, an unwonted suggestion of shyness in her bearing. The ladies being

seated, he took his place opposite to them, and again perused Miss Tomalin's countenance. Decidedly, she was unlike herself; manifestly, she avoided his look. Mrs. Toplady talked away in the gayest spirits; and the rain came down heavily and thunder rolled. Half the distance to St. Pancras was covered before May had uttered anything more than a trivial word or two. Of a sudden she addressed Lashmar, as if about to speak of something serious.

" You left all well at Rivenoak ? "

" Quite well."

" When did you come away ? "

" Early yesterday morning," Dyce replied.

May's eyebrows twitched, her look fell.

" I went to Alverholme," Dyce continued, " to see my people."

May turned her eyes to the window. Uneasiness appeared in her face.

" She wants to know," said Dyce to himself, " whether I have received that letter."

" Do you stay in town ? " inquired Mrs. Toplady.

" For a week or two, I think," he added carelessly. " A letter this morning, forwarded from Rivenoak, brought me back."

There was a nervous movement on the part of Miss Tomalin, who at once exclaimed:

" I suppose your correspondence is enormous, Mr. Lashmar ? "

" Enormous—why no. But interesting, especially of late."

" Of course—a public man——"

Impossible to get assurance. The signs he noticed might mean nothing at all; on the other hand, they were perhaps decisive. More about the letter of this morning he durst not say, lest, if this girl had really written it, she should think him lacking in delicacy, in discretion.

" Very kind of you to come to me at once," said Mrs. Toplady. " Is there good news of the campaign ?

Our Friend the Charlatan

Come and see me to-morrow, can you? This afternoon I have an engagement. I shall only just have time to see Miss Tomalin safe in the railway-carriage."

Dyce made no request to be set down. After this remark of Mrs. Toplady's, a project formed itself in his mind. When the carriage entered Euston Road, rain was still falling.

"This'll do good," he remarked. "The country wants it."

His thoughts returned to the morning, a week ago, when Constance and he had been baulked of their ride by a heavy shower. He saw the summer-house among the trees; he saw Constance's face, and heard her accents.

They reached the station. As a matter of course Dyce accompanied his friends on to the platform, where the train was already standing. Miss Tomalin selected her seat. There was leave-taking. Dyce walked away with Mrs. Toplady, who suddenly became hurried.

"I shall only just have time," she said, looking at the clock. "I'm afraid my direction, northward, would only take you more out of your way."

Dyce saw her to the brougham, watched it drive off. There remained three minutes before the departure of Miss Tomalin's train. He turned back into the station; he walked rapidly, and on the platform almost collided with a heavy old gentleman whom an official was piloting to a carriage. This warm-faced, pompous-looking person he well knew by sight. Another moment, and Dyce stood on the step of the compartment where May had her place. At sight of him she half rose.

"What is it? Have I forgotten something?"

The compartment was full. Impossible to speak before these listening people. In ready response to Lashmar's embarrassed look, May alighted.

"I'm so sorry to have troubled you," said Dyce, with laughing contrition. "I thought it might amuse you to know that *Mr. Robb* is in the train!"

"Really? How I should have liked to be in the
272

Our Friend the Charlatan

same carriage. Perhaps I should have heard the creature talk. Oh, and this compartment is so full, so hot! Is it impossible to find a better?"

Dyce rushed at a passing guard. He learnt that, if Miss Tomalin were willing to change half-way on her journey, she could travel at ease; only the through carriages for Hollingford were packed. To this May at once consented. Dyce seized her dressing-bag, her umbrella; they sped to another part of the train, and sprang, both of them, into an empty first-class.

"This is delightful!" cried the girl. "I *am* so much obliged to you!"

"Tickets, please."

"Shown already," replied May. "Change of carriage."

The door was slammed, locked. The whistle sounded.

"But we're starting!" May exclaimed. "Quick! Jump out, Mr. Lashmar."

Dyce sat still, smiling calmly.

"It's too late. I'm afraid I mustn't try to escape by the window."

"Oh, and you have sacrificed yourself just to make me more comfortable! How inconvenient it will be for you! What a waste of time!"

"Not at all. The best thing that could have happened."

"Well, we have papers at all events." May handed him one. "Pray don't feel obliged to talk."

"As it happens, I very much wish to talk. Queer thing that I should owe my opportunity to Robb. I shall never again feel altogether hostile to that man. I wish you had seen him. He looked apoplectic. This weather must try him severely."

"You never spoke to him, I suppose?" asked May.

"I never had that honour. Glimpses only of the great man have been vouchsafed to me. Once seen, he is never forgotten. To-day he looks alarmingly apoplectic."

"But really, Mr. Lashmar," said the girl, settling herself in her corner, "I do feel ashamed to have given you this useless journey—and just when you are so busy."

She was pretty in her travelling costume. Could Lashmar have compared her appearance to-day with that she had presented on her first arrival at Rivenoak, he would have marvelled at the change wrought by luxurious circumstance. No eye-glasses now; no little paper-cutter hanging at her girdle. Called upon to resume the Northampton garb, May would have been horrified. .The brown shoes which she had purchased expressly for her visit to Lady Ogram would have seemed impossibly large and coarse. Exquisite were her lavender gloves. Such details of attire, formerly regarded with some contempt, had now an importance for her. She had come to regard dress as one of the serious concerns of life.

"I went to Pont Street this afternoon," said Dyce, "with a wish that by some chance I might see you alone. It was very unlikely, but it has come to pass."

May exhibited a slight surprise, and by an imperceptible movement put a little more dignity into her attitude.

"What did you wish to speak about?" she asked, with an air meant to be strikingly natural.

"Don't let me startle you; it was about my engagement to Miss Bride."

This time Dyce felt he could not be mistaken. She was confused; he saw colour mounting on her neck; the surprise she tried to convey in smiling was too obviously feigned.

"Isn't that rather an odd subject of conversation?"

"It seems so, but wait till you have heard what I have to say. It is on Miss Bride's account that I speak. You are her friend, and I feel that, in mere justice to her, I ought to tell you a very strange story. It is greatly to her honour. She couldn't tell you the

274

truth herself, and, of course, you will not be able to let her know that you know it. But it will save you from possible misunderstanding of her, enable you to judge her fairly."

May hardly disguised her curiosity. It absorbed her self-consciousness, and she looked the speaker straight in the face.

"To come to the point at once," pursued Lashmar, "our engagement is not a genuine one. Miss Bride has not really consented to marry me. She only consents to have it thought that she has done so. And very generous, very noble, it is of her."

"What a strange thing!" the girl exclaimed, as ingenuously as she had ever spoken in her life.

"Isn't it? I can explain in a word or two. Lady Ogram wished us to marry; it was a favourite project of hers. She spoke to me about it—putting me in a very difficult position, for I felt sure that Miss Bride had no such regard for me as your aunt supposed. I postponed, delayed as much as possible, and the result was that Lady Ogram began to take my behaviour ill. The worst of it was, her annoyance had a bad effect on her health. I think you know that Lady Ogram cannot bear contradiction."

"I know that she doesn't like it," said May, her chin rising a little.

"You, of course, are favoured. You have exceptional influence. But I can assure you that it would have been a very unpleasant thing to have to tell Lady Ogram either that I couldn't take the step she wished, or that Miss Bride rejected me."

"I can believe that," said May indulgently.

"When I saw that she was making herself ill about it, I took the resolve to speak frankly to Miss Bride. The result was—our pretended engagement."

"Was it your suggestion?" inquired the listener.

"Yes, it came from me," Dyce answered, with half-real, half-affected embarrassment. "Of course, I felt it to be monstrous impudence, but, as some excuse for me, you must remember that Miss Bride and I have known each other for many years, that we were friends almost in childhood. Perhaps I was rather a coward. Perhaps I ought to have told your aunt the truth, and taken the consequences. But Miss Bride, no less than I, felt afraid of them."

"What consequences?"

"We really feared that, in Lady Ogram's state of health——"

He broke off significantly. May dropped her eyes. The train roared through a station.

"But," said May at length, "I understand that you are to be married in October."

"That is Lady Ogram's wish. Of course, it's horribly embarrassing. I needn't say that when our engagement is announced as broken off, I shall manage so that all the fault appears to be on my side. But I am hoping that Lady Ogram may somehow be brought to change her mind. And I even dare to hope that you will help us to that end."

"I? How could I possibly?"

"Indeed, I hardly know. But the situation is so awkward, and you are the only person who has really great influence with Lady Ogram."

There was silence amid the noise of the train. May looked through one window, Dyce through the other.

"In any case," exclaimed Lashmar, "I have discharged what I felt to be a duty. I could not bear to think that you should be living with Miss Bride, and totally misunderstanding her. I wanted you to do justice to her noble self-sacrifice. Of course, I have felt ashamed of myself ever since I allowed her to get into such a false position. You, I fear, think worse of me than you did."

He regarded her from under his eyelids, as if timidly. May sat very upright. She did not look displeased; a light in her eyes might have been understood as expressing satisfaction.

"Suppose," she said, looking away, "that October

comes, and you haven't been able to—to put an end to this situation?"

"I'm afraid—very much afraid—that we shall have to do so at any cost."

"It's very strange, altogether. An extraordinary state of things."

"You forgive me for talking to you about it?" asked Dyce, leaning respectfully forward.

"I understand why you did. There was no harm in it."

"Do you remember our talk in the supper-room at Mrs. Toplady's?—when we agreed that nothing was more foolish than false modesty? Shall I venture to tell you, now, that if this marriage came about it would be something like ruin to my career? You won't misunderstand. I have a great respect, and a great liking, for Miss Bride; but think how all-important it is, this question of marriage for a public man."

"Of course, I understand that," May replied.

He enlarged upon the topic, exhibiting his hopes.

"But I rather thought," said May, "that Miss Bride was just the sort of companion you needed. She is so intelligent, and——"

"Very! But do you think she has the qualities which would enable her to take a high position in society? There's no unkindness in touching upon that. Admirable women may fall short of these particular excellencies. A man chooses his wife according to the faith he has in his future."

"I understand; I quite understand," said May, with a large air. "No; it has to be confessed that Miss Bride— I wonder my aunt didn't think of that."

They turned aside to discuss Lady Ogram, and did so in such detail, with so much mutual satisfaction, that time slipped on insensibly, and, ere they had thought of parting, the train began to slacken down for the junction where Miss Tomalin would have to change carriages.

"How annoying that I shan't be able to see you again!" cried Lashmar.

"But shan't you be coming to Rivenoak?"

"Not for some time, very likely. And when I do——"

The train stopped. Dyce helped his companion to alight, and moved along to seek a place for her in the section which went to Hollingford. Suddenly an alarmed voice from one of the carriage-doors shouted: "Guard! Station-master!" People turned in that direction; porters ran; evidently something serious had happened.

"What's the matter?" asked May, at her companion's side.

"Somebody taken ill, I think," said Dyce, moving towards the door whence the shout had sounded.

He caught a glimpse of a man who had sunk upon the floor of the carriage, and was just being lifted on to the seat by other passengers. Pressing nearer, he saw a face hideously congested, with horrible starting eyes. He drew back, and whispered to May:

"It's Robb! Didn't I tell you that he looked apoplectic?"

The girl shrank in fear.

"Are you sure?"

"Perfectly. Stand here a minute, and I'll ask how it happened."

From the talk going on he quickly learnt that Mr. Robb, complaining that he felt faint, had risen, just as the train drew into the station, to open the door and descend. Before any one could help him, he dropped, and his fellow-travellers shouted. Dyce and May watched the conveyance of the obese figure across the platform to a waiting-room.

"I must know the end of this," said Lashmar, his eyes gleaming.

"You wouldn't have gone further, should you?"

"I suppose not—though I had still a great deal to tell you. Quick! we must get your place."

"I could stop for the next train," suggested May.

"Better not, I think. The carriage will be waiting

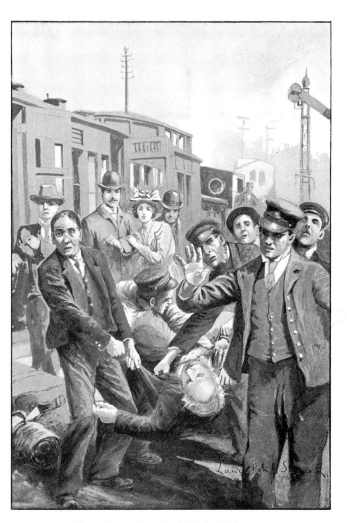

"I must know the end of this," said Lashmar.

for you at Hollingford. No, better not. I have another idea."

They found a seat. Dyce threw in the dressing-bag, and alighted again.

"There's still a minute or two," he said, keeping May beside him on the platform. "This affair may be tremendously important for me, you know."

"It would mean an election at once," said the girl excitedly.

"Of course." He approached his face to hers, and added in low, rapid tones: "You know the park door into the Wapham road?"

"Yes."

"You have a key. Could you be there at eight to-morrow morning? If it's fine take your bicycle, as if you were going for a spin before breakfast. Miss Bride never goes out before breakfast, and no one else is likely to pass that way."

"You mean you would be there?"

"If there's anything important to tell—yes. From a quarter to eight. I shall stay here till I know the state of things. If there's recovery I will go back to town, and wire to-morrow to Lady Ogram that I have heard a rumour of Robb's serious illness, asking for information. Do you agree?"

Doors were slamming; porters were shouting. May had only just time to spring into the carriage.

"Yes," she exclaimed, with her head at the window.

Dyce doffed his hat. They smiled at each other, May's visage flushed and agitated, and the train whirled away.

In the carriage awaiting Miss Tomalin at Hollingford station sat Constance Bride.

"A horrible journey!" May exclaimed, taking a seat beside her. "No seat in a through carriage at St. Pancras. Had to change at the junction. Somebody in the train had a fit, or something—no wonder, with such heat! But it's cooler here. Have you had a storm?"

Our Friend the Charlatan

The footman, who had been looking after luggage, stepped up to the carriage-door and spoke to Miss Bride. He said there was a rumour in the station that Mr. Robb, travelling by this train, had been seized with apoplexy on the way.

"Mr. Robb!" exclaimed Constance. "Then he was the person you spoke of?"

"I suppose so," May answered. "Queer thing!"

They drove off. Constance gazed straight before her, thinking intently.

"If the attack was fatal," said May, "we shall have an election at once."

"Yes," fell from her companion's lips mechanically.

"Who will be the Conservative candidate?"

"I have no idea," answered Constance, still absorbed in her thoughts.

May cast a glance at her, and discovered emotion in the fixed eyes, the set lips. There was a short silence, then Miss Tomalin spoke as if an amusing thought had struck her.

"You received that American magazine from Mrs. Toplady? Isn't it an odd coincidence—the French book, you know?"

"It didn't seem to me very striking," replied Constance coldly.

"No? Perhaps not." May became careless. "I hadn't time to read it myself; I only heard what Mrs. Toplady said about it."

"There was a certain resemblance between the Frenchman's phraseology and Mr. Lashmar's," said Constance; "but nothing more. Mr. Lashmar's system isn't easy to grasp. I doubt whether Mrs. Toplady is quite the person to understand it."

"Perhaps not," May smiled, raising her chin. "I must read the article myself."

"Even then," rejoined her companion, in a measured tone, "you will hardly be able to decide as to the resemblance of the two theories."

"Why not?" asked May sharply.

Our Friend the Charlatan

" Because you have had no opportunity of really studying Mr. Lashmar's views."

" Oh, I assure you he has made them perfectly clear to me—perfectly."

" In outline," said Constance, smiling as one who condescends to a childish understanding.

" Oh no, in detail."

Miss Bride contented herself with a half-absent " Indeed ! " and seemed to resume her meditations. Whereupon May's eyes flashed, and her head assumed its most magnificent pose.

They exchanged not another word in the drive to Rivenoak.

CHAPTER XX

MAY awoke very early next morning. It was broad daylight, however, and she hastened to look at her watch. Reassured as to the time, her next thought regarded the weather; she stepped to the window, and saw with vexation a rainy sky. An hour later she again lifted the blind to look forth. No sun was shining, but rain had ceased. She began to dress.

At a quarter to eight, equipped for walking, she quietly left her room and tripped down-stairs. A housemaid met her in the hall; she asked whether the great door was unlocked, and the servant went before to open for her. Following a path which led to the rear of the house, she was soon out in the park; in some ten minutes she passed the old summer-house among the trees, and, with quickened pace, came to the door which opened into the Wapham road. Before using her key, she tapped lightly on the wood; from without there sounded immediately an answering knock. Then she opened.

" Do you know ? " asked Lashmar eagerly, as he gave his hand, forgetting the formal salute.

" Yes. We had the news after dinner. Mr. Breakspeare sent a message."

" He lived for about an hour. I came on to Hollingford late, and have passed the night at the Saracen's Head. It's to be understood, of course, that I got the news in town just in time for the last train."

Whilst exchanging rapid sentences they stood, one within, one outside, the park wall. May held the door, as if uncertain what to do next.

Our Friend the Charlatan

"You can spare me a few minutes?" said Dyce, glancing this way and that along the public way.

"Come in. I didn't bring my bicycle, as it's so wet."

"Of course not. You needn't be anxious. Nobody comes this way."

He closed the door. May was looking behind her into the trees and bushes, which hid them from the park. The sky had begun to brighten; a breeze shook drops from the shining leafage.

"How does Lady Ogram take the news?" Lashmar inquired, trying to speak with his wonted calm, but betraying a good deal of nervousness.

"I haven't seen her. She was in her room when it came."

"I shouldn't wonder if she's sorry. She had set her mind on our beating Robb at the poll. No one seems to know who will stand for the Conservatives. I saw Breakspeare after midnight; he was in the wildest excitement. He thinks it's good for us."

"Of course you'll see Lady Ogram to-day?"

"I shall come at lunch-time. That'll be best, won't it?"

May nodded. Her eyes kept turning in the direction of the house.

"How very kind of you to have come out so early!" said Dyce. "All night I've been reproaching myself for giving you the trouble, and when I saw the rain I didn't think for a moment you would be here. I'm delighted to be able to talk to you before seeing any one else. Don't you think this event has happened very luckily? Whether I am elected or not, it'll be easier for me to get out of my false position."

"Why? How?"

"In this way. During the excitement of the election, I shall find opportunities of speaking more freely with Lady Ogram, and who knows but I may bring her to see that the plan she made for me was not altogether to my advantage? Miss Bride, of course, will speak whenever she has a chance, in the same sense——"

"Are you sure of that?" asked May, casting a furtive glance at him. She stood boring the path with the point of her slim umbrella.

"Do you feel any doubt?" asked Dyce in turn.

"I really can't judge. It's such a very curious situation—and," she added, "Miss Bride is so peculiar."

"Peculiar?—I understand. You don't find her very communicative. But I'm sure you'll make allowance for the difficulty of——"

"Oh, I make all allowances," interrupted May, with her smile of superiority. "And, of course, Miss Bride's affairs don't in the least concern me."

"Except, I hope, in so far as they concern *me*."

Dyce spoke with insinuating humour. Both hands resting on his umbrella-handle, he held himself very upright, and looked May steadily in the face. She, as though challenged, straightened herself and met his look.

"I should be sorry to see your career spoilt," she said, with rather excessive dignity. "But you will admit that you have acted, to say the least, imprudently."

"It looks so. You think I should have had *more courage*. But you will see that it's *not too late*."

Speaking, he watched her face. He saw her lips twitch, and her eyes stray.

"You know," he pursued, "that I *aim high*."

Her look fell.

"But no man can do without help. The strong man is he who knows how to choose his helper, and at the right moment. I am at a crisis of my life, and—it is to you that I turn."

"I, of course, feel that to be a great compliment, Mr. Lashmar," said May, recovering her grand air. "I promise you to do what I can. But you mustn't count on me for impossibilities."

"I count on nothing that isn't easy for *you*—with your character, your influence."

"Thank you again. My first piece of advice to you is to win the election."

Our Friend the Charlatan

"I shall do my best. If I am beaten in this, I shall win another; you are aware of that. Are you easily discouraged? I think not."

He smiled at her with admiration. That it was genuine, May easily perceived; how much, or how little, it implied, she did not care to ask. These two, alike incapable of romantic passion, children of a time which subdues everything to interest, which fosters vanity and chills the heart, began to imagine that they were drawn to each other by all the ardours of sex and youth. Their minds remarkably lucid, reviewing the situation with coolest perspicuity, calculating each on the other's recognized weaknesses, and holding themselves absolutely free if contingency demanded freedom, they indulged, up to a certain point, the primitive impulse, and would fain have discovered in it a motive of the soul. May, who had formed her opinion as to Miss Bride's real attitude regarding Lashmar, took a keen pleasure in the treacherous part she was playing; she remembered the conversation last evening in the carriage, and soothed her wounded self-esteem. Dyce, gratified by yet another proof of his power over womankind, felt that in this case he had something to be really proud of; Miss Tomalin's beauty and her prospects spoke to the world at large. She was in love with him, and he detected in himself a reciprocal emotion. Interesting and agreeable state of things!

May, instead of directly answering his last question, allowed her eyes to meet his for a second. Then she said:

"Some people are coming to us this afternoon."

"To stay? Who are they?"

"Sir William and Lady Amys—and Lord Dymchurch——"

"Dymchurch! Lady Ogram has invited him?"

"He would hardly come to stay without being invited," said May archly. "But I thought you most likely knew. Didn't Lady Ogram mention it to you?"

"Not a word," answered Dyce. "No doubt she had

285

Our Friend the Charlatan

a reason for saying nothing. You, possibly, could suggest it?"

His face had changed. There was cold annoyance in his look and in his voice.

"It must have been mere accident," said May.

"That it certainly wasn't. How long will Dymchurch stay?"

"I have no idea, Mr. Lashmar.—I must leave you. Many thanks for taking so much trouble to bring me the news."

She held out her hand. Dyce took and detained it.

"I am going to stay on at Hollingford," he said, "at the hotel. I shall run up to town this evening, but be back to-morrow. At lunch-time to-day I shall see you, but, of course, that doesn't count; we shan't be able to talk. Wednesday, to-morrow; on Thursday morning meet me here again, will you?"

"I'm afraid I can't do that, Mr. Lashmar," she answered with self-possession, trying, unobtrusively, to withdraw her hand.

"I beg you to! Indeed, you must."

He tried the power of a smile meant to be at once virile and tender. But May was steadily drawing away her hand; he had not the courage to hold it forcibly.

"We shall find other opportunities of talking about the things that interest us," she said, moving a step back.

"It surprises me that you came this morning!" Dyce exclaimed, with a touch of sarcasm.

"Then," May answered loftily, "you will be spared a second surprise."

She turned and left him. Dyce, after watching for a moment her graceful figure, strode in pursuit. The were near the summer-house.

"You were forgetting," he said, "that you have left the key in the door."

May uttered an exclamation of alarm.

"How foolish of me! Thank you so much!"

"I fear I must give you the trouble of walking back to let me out."

" Why, of course."

They returned to the door, and Dyce again took the offered hand.

"I shall be here at eight on Tuesday," he said, "unless it rains. In that case, on the first fine morning."

" I don't promise to meet you."

" I will come without a promise."

" As you like," said May, slowly closing the door upon him. " But don't prepare for yourself another surprise."

She regained the house, having met no one but a gardener. Within, she encountered no one at all. Safe in her room, she reflected on the morning's adventure, and told herself that it had been, in a double sense, decidedly dangerous. Were Constance Bride or Lady Ogram to know of this clandestine rendezvous, what a storm would break ! On that account alone she would have been glad of what she had done. But she was glad, also, of Lashmar's significant behaviour and language. He perceived, undoubtedly, that the anonymous letter came from her, and, be the upshot what it might, their romantic intimacy gave life a new zest. May flattered herself that she knew the tremors of amorous emotion. "If I liked, I *could* be really, really in love ! " This was delightful experience; this was living ! Dangerous, yes; for how did she mean to comport herself in the all but certain event of her receiving an offer of marriage from Lord Dymchurch ? Mrs. Toplady was right; Lady Ogram had resolved upon this marriage, and would it be safe to thwart that strong-willed old woman ? Moreover, the thought was very tempting. A peeress ! Could she reasonably look for such another chance if this were lost ? Was she prepared to sacrifice it for the sake of Dyce Lashmar, and the emotional joys he represented ?

She thought of novels and poems. Browning was much in her mind. She saw herself as the heroine of psychological drama. How interesting ! How thrilling! During her life at Northampton she had dreamed of such things, with no expectation of their ever befalling her. Truly, she was Fortune's favourite. Destiny had raised her to the sphere where her powers and sensibilities would have full play.

So it was with radiant face that she appeared at the breakfast-table. Constance and she shook hands as usual, with everyday words. It seemed to her that she saw disquiet in the secretary's countenance—after all, what was Miss Bride but a salaried secretary? Lashmar's betrothed might well suffer uneasiness, under the circumstances; *she*, it was obvious, did not regard the engagement as a mere pretence. No, no; Constance Bride was ambitious, and thought it a great thing to marry a man with a parliamentary career before him. She was of a domineering, jealous nature, and it would exasperate her to feel that Lashmar merely used her for his temporary purposes. Noble self-sacrifice, indeed! Lashmar himself did not believe that. Best of all things, at this moment, May would have liked to make known her power over Lashmar, and to say: "Of course, dear Miss Bride, he is nothing whatever to me. In my position, you understand——"

There had been a few moment's silence, when Constance asked:

"Do you ever hear of Mr. Yabsley?"

Was the woman a thought-reader? At that instant May had been thinking—the first time for weeks, perhaps—of her admirable Crichton in the old Northampton days, and reflecting with gratification on the vast change which had come upon her life and her mind since she followed Mr. Yabsley's spiritual direction. Startled, she gazed at the speaker.

"How odd that you should have remembered his name!"

"Not at all. I heard it so often when you first came here."

"Did you?" said May, pretending to be amused. "Mr. Yabsley is a remarkable man, and I still value

Our Friend the Charlatan

his friendship. You remind me that I really ought
to write to him."

Constance seemed to lose all her interest in the
matter, and spoke of something trivial.

In the course of the morning there happened a
singular thing.

Lady Ogram rose earlier than usual. Before leaving
her room, she read in the *Hollingford Express* all about
the sudden death of Mr. Robb. The event had kept
her awake all night. Though on the one side a disappointment, for of late she had counted upon Robb's
defeat at the next election as an all but certain thing,
the fact that she had outlived her enemy, that he lay,
as it were, at her feet, powerless ever again to speak
an insulting word, aroused all the primitive instincts
of her nature. With the exultation of a savage she
gloated over the image of Robb stricken to the ground.
Through the hours of darkness she now and then sang
to herself, and the melodies were those she had known
when a girl or a child, common songs of the street.
It was her chant of victory and revenge.

Having risen, she went into the drawing-room on
the same floor as her bedchamber, and summoned two
men-servants. After her first serious illness, she had
for a time been carried up and down-stairs in a chair
made for that purpose; she now bade her attendants
fetch the chair, and convey her to the top storey of
the house. It was done. In her hand she had a key,
and with this she unlocked the door of that room
which had been closed for half-a-century. Having
stood alone within the garret for a few minutes, she
called to the men, who, on entering, looked with
curiosity at dust-covered forms in clay and in marble.
Their mistress pointed to a bust which stood on a
wooden pedestal some three feet high.

"You are to clean that. Bring water and soap.
I will wait here whilst you do it."

The task was quickly performed; the marble shone
once more, and its pedestal of lustrous black looked

little the worse for long seclusion. Lady Ogram sat
with her eyes fixed upon the work of art, and for a
minute or two neither moved nor spoke.

"Who is that?" she inquired suddenly, indicating
the head, and turning her look upon the two men.

"I think it is yourself, my lady," answered the
bolder of the two.

Lady Ogram smiled. That use of the present
tense was agreeable to her.

"You are to take it down to the green drawing-
room. Carry me there first, and I will show you
where to place it."

Arrived at the ground-floor, she quitted her chair
and walked into the drawing-room with step which was
almost firm. Here, among the flowers and leafage, sat
May Tomalin, who, surprised at her aunt's early appearance, rose with an exclamation of pleasure.

"How well you look this morning, aunt!"

"I'm glad you think so, my dear," was the pleased
and dignified reply. "Be so kind, May, as to go into
the library and wait there until I send for you."

The girl turned pale. For a moment she thought
her escapade of this morning had been discovered, and
that terrible things were about to happen. Her alarm
could not escape Lady Ogram's observation.

"What, have I frightened you? Did it remind you
of being sent into the corner when you were a little
girl?"

She laughed with discordant gaiety.

"Really, for the moment I thought I was being
punished," replied May. And she, too, laughed a
melodious trill.

A quarter of an hour passed. Lady Ogram presented
herself at the library door and saw May reading,
whilst Constance Bride sat writing at the table.

"Come, both of you!"

Surprised at the look and tone with which they
were summoned, the two followed into the drawing-
room, where, guided by Lady Ogram's glance, they

"Who is that?" she inquired suddenly.
"I think it is yourself, my lady," answered the bolder of the two.
Frontispiece.

became aware of a new ornament. They approached; they gazed; they wondered.

"Who is that?" asked their conductress, turning to Miss Bride.

Constance felt no doubt as to the person whom the bust was supposed to represent, and her disgust at what she thought the shameless flattery practised by the sculptor hardly allowed her to reply.

"Of course," she said, in as even a voice as possible, "it is a portrait of Miss Tomalin."

Lady Ogram's eyes shone; on the point of laughing she restrained herself, and looked at her niece.

"May, what do *you* think?"

"Really, aunt, I don't know what to think," answered the girl, in a happy confusion. "If Miss Bride is right—it's very, very kind of you. But how was it done without my sitting?"

This time the old lady's mirth had its way.

"How, indeed! There's a mystery for you both, my dears! May, it's true you are like me, but don't let Constance make you conceited. Go near, and look at the date carved on the marble."

"Why, aunt, of course it is you yourself!" exclaimed the girl, her averted face long-drawn in mortification; she saw the smile with which Miss Bride had received this disclosure. "How wonderful!"

"You can hardly believe it?"

Some incredulity might have been excused in one who turned from that superb head, with its insolent youth and beauty, to the painted death-mask grinning there before it. Yet the marble had not flattered, and, looking closely enough, you saw a reminiscence of its contour in the bloodless visage which, since that proud moment, had chronicled the passions of three-score years.

"How stupid not to have understood at once," said May, the epithet directed towards Constance.

"It's a magnificent bust!" declared Miss Bride, examining it now with sincere interest. "Who was the sculptor, Lady Ogram?"

Our Friend the Charlatan

"My husband," answered the old lady, with pride. "Sir Quentin had much talent, and this was the best thing he ever did."

"And it has just come into your possession?" asked May.

"No, my dear. But I thought you would like to see it."

An hour later Dyce Lashmar presented himself at Rivenoak. He was conducted at once to the drawing-room, where Lady Ogram still sat with May and Constance.

"I expected you," cried the senile voice, on a high note.

"I heard the news at dinner-time yesterday," said Lashmar. "Just caught the last train, and sat up half the night with Breakspeare."

"I sent out a telegram for you the first thing this morning," said Lady Ogram. "Had you left Alverholme before it arrived?"

"I was in town," answered Dyce, only now remembering that he had to account for his movements. "A letter called me up yesterday morning."

The old autocrat was in no mood for trifling explanations. She passed the point, and began to ask the news from Hollingford. Who would be the Conservative candidate? They talked, said Dyce, of a stranger to the town, a man named Butterworth, one of Robb's private friends.

"It's Butterworth of the hoardings—Butterworth's jams and pickles, you know. He's made a million out of them, and now thinks of turning his energies to the public service. Robb, it seems, didn't mean to face another election, and of late had privately spoken here and there of Butterworth."

"Jams and pickles!" cried Lady Ogram, with a croaking laugh. "Will the Hollingford Tories stand that?"

"Why not? Robb evidently thought they would, and he knew them. Butterworth is a stout Unionist, I'm told, and if he makes another million he may look

Our Friend the Charlatan

for a peerage. Jam has not hitherto been thought
so respectable as ale or stout, but that's only a prejudice.
Robb's enlightened mind saw the budding aristocrat.
Breakspeare is thinking out an article on the deceased
champion of aristocratic traditions, to be followed by
another on the blazonry of the jam-pot and pickle-jar.
We shall have merry reading when decorum releases
our friend's pen."

As his eye stole towards May Tomalin, Dyce perceived the marble bust. He gazed at it in silent
surprise. The looks of all were upon him; turning,
he met smiles of inquiry.

" Well ? " said Lady Ogram bluntly.

" Who is that ? Is it a new work ? " he inquired,
with diffidence.

" It looks new, doesn't it ? "

" I should have thought," said Dyce reflectively,
" that it represented Lady Ogram at about the same
age as in the painting."

" Constance," exclaimed the old lady, vastly pleased,
" congratulate Mr. Lashmar."

" Then I am right," cried Dyce, encountering Constance's look. " What a fine bit of work ! What a
magnificent head ! "

He moved nearer to it, and continued freely to
express his admiration. The resemblance to May
Tomalin had struck him ; he thought it probable that
some sculptor had amused himself by idealizing the
girl's suggestive features ; but at this juncture it
seemed to him more prudent, as in any case it would
be politic, to affect to see only a revival of Lady
Ogram's youth. It startled him to find that his tact
had guided him so well.

He continued to behave with all prudence, talking
through luncheon chiefly with the hostess, and directing
hardly a remark to May, who, on her side, maintained
an equal discretion. Afterwards, he saw Lady Ogram
in private.

" You mean to stay on at the hotel, no doubt," she

Our Friend the Charlatan

said. "Yes, it'll be more convenient for you than if you came here. But look in and let us know how things go on. Let me see, to-morrow is Wednesday; don't come to-morrow. On Thursday I may have something to tell you; yes, come and lunch on Thursday. You understand—on Thursday. And there's something else I may as well say at once; the expenses of the election are my affair."

Dyce began grateful protests, but was cut short.

"I say that is my affair. We'll talk about it when the fight is over. No petty economies! In a day or two, when things are in order, we must have Breakspeare here. Perhaps you had better go away for the day of Robb's funeral. Yes, don't be seen about on that day. Spare no useful expense; I give you a free hand. Only win; that's all I ask of you. I shan't like it if you're beaten by jams and pickles. And lunch here on Thursday—you understand?"

Dyce had never known the old autocrat so babblingly iterative. Nor had he ever beheld her in such a mood of gaiety, of exultation.

"Go, and have a word with Constance," she said at length; "I rather think she's going into the town; if so, you can go together. She's in great spirits. It isn't her way to talk much, but I can see she feels very hopeful. By the bye, I'm expecting Sir William before dinner—Sir William Amys, you know. He may be here still when you come on Thursday."

Why Lady Ogram should be so careful to conceal the fact that Lord Dymchurch was expected, Dyce found it difficult to understand. But it was clear that Dymchurch had been invited in the hope, perhaps the certainty, that he would propose to May Tomalin. That he was coming at all seemed, indeed, decisive as to his intentions. Plainly, the old schemer had formed this project at the time of her visit to London, and, improbable as the thing would have appeared to any one knowing Dymchurch, she was carrying it successfully through. On the one side; but how about May?

Our Friend the Charlatan

Dyce tried to assure himself that, being in love with *him*, May would vainly be wooed by any one else. But had she the courage to hold out against her imperious aunt? Could she safely do so? The situation was extremely disquieting. He wished it were possible to see May alone, even for a minute. But he did not see her at all, and, as Lady Ogram had suggested, he found himself obliged to return to Hollingford in Constance's company. They drove in the landau. On the way, Dyce made known to his companion Lady Ogram's generous intentions.

"I knew she would do that," said Constance, regarding him with the smile which betrayed her inmost thoughts.

Because of the proximity of their coachman, they talked in subdued tones, their heads close together. To Lashmar this intimacy meant nothing at all; Constance, in his busy thoughts, was as good as non-existent. He had remarked with vexation the aspect of renewed vigour presented by Lady Ogram, and would have spoken of it, but that he felt ashamed to do so.

"Don't you think," asked his companion, "that everything is going wonderfully well with you?"

"It looks so, for the present."

"And, after all, whom have you to thank for it?"

"I don't forget," Dyce replied, wondering whether she alluded to the fact of her having introduced him to the mistress of Rivenoak, or to the terms of their engagement.

"If you win the election, don't you think it would be graceful not only to feel, but to show, a little gratitude?"

She spoke in a voice which once more reminded him of the summer-house on that rainy morning, a voice very unlike her ordinary utterance, soft and playfully appealing.

"Don't be so severe on me," answered Dyce, with a laugh. "I am not *all* self-interest."

He added what was meant for a reassuring look, and began to talk of electioneering details.

CHAPTER XXI

LADY OGRAM's life had been much guided by super-
stition. No one knew it, or suspected it, for this was
among the tokens of her origin which she carefully
kept out of sight. Through all the phases of her
avowed belief, she remained subject to a private
religion of omens and auspices, which frequently in-
fluenced her conduct. Thus she would long ago have
brought forth and displayed that marble visage of her
beauty in its prime, but for a superstitious fear which
withheld her. On the night before Sir Quentin's
death, she dreamt that she ascended to the garret,
took the bust in her arms, and carried it down-stairs.
Many years went by, and again she had the same
dream; the next day her first serious illness fell upon
her, and remembering the vision, she gave herself up
for lost; but the sign this time had less than fatal
significance. Now once more, on the Sunday night of
the present week, she seemed to enter the locked
garret, and to carry away the marble. All Monday she
lived in a great dread, but at evening came the news
that her arch-enemy was no more, and behold the
vision explained!

On Monday night she dreamt not at all; being kept
awake by exultation in what had happened and forecast of triumphs soon to be enjoyed. But her thoughts
turned constantly to the graven image which she
longed to see, and by a process of reasoning natural to
such a mind as hers, she persuaded herself that now
was the moment to fulfil her desire. The bust once
brought down, she would not again dream of going to

Our Friend the Charlatan

seek it, and, consequently, it could not serve again to augur evil. Not without tremors, she executed her resolve, and, the thing once done, her joy was boundless. Looking on that marble face, she seemed to recover something of the strength and spirit it had immortalized. Notwithstanding her restless night, she felt so clear in mind, so well in body, that the forebodings which had perturbed her since her exhausting visit to London were joyously dismissed. To-day Lord Dymchurch was coming; to-morrow May's betrothal would be a fact to noise abroad. She would then summon Kerchever, and, in the presence of Sir William Amys, the trusty friend sure to outlive her, would complete that last will and testament which was already schemed out. Twice already had she executed a will, the second less than a year ago. When in town she had sufficiently discussed with her man of law the new situation brought about by her discovery of May Tomalin; but the hope which she connected with Dymchurch bade her postpone awhile the solemn signature. All had come to pass even as she desired, as she resolved it should. To the end she was supreme in her own world.

When her guests arrived—all travelled from London by the same train—she received them royally. She had clad herself with unusual magnificence; on the shrivelled parchment of her cheeks shone an audacious bloom; her eyes gleamed as if in them were concentrated all the proud life which still resisted age and malady. Rising from her bowered throne in the drawing-room, she took a step towards Lady Amys, pressed her hand cordially—not at all feebly—and welcomed her with affectionate words. The baronet she addressed as " Willy," but with such a dignity of kindness in the familiar name that it was like bestowal of an honour. Towards the peer her bearing was marked with grave courtesy, softening to intimate notes as their conversation progressed. Scarce a touch of senility sounded in her speech; she heard perfectly, indulged in no

characteristic brusquerie of phrase, fulfilled every
formality proper to the occasion.

Sir William and his wife were the only people of
their world who had always seen the lady of Rivenoak
in her better aspect; who, whilst appreciating the
comedy of her life, regarded her with genuine friendship. They understood the significance of Lord Dymchurch's visit, and like Mrs. Toplady, though in a much
more human spirit, awaited with amusement the successful issue of Lady Ogram's scheme. They saw no
harm in it. Dymchurch, it might well be, had fallen
in love with the handsome girl, and it was certain that
her wealth would be put to much better use in his
hands than in those of the ordinary man who weds
money. Lady Ogram's deliberate choice of this land-
less peer assuredly did her credit. She wanted the
peerage for her niece; but it would not have been
difficult to gratify her ambition in a more brilliant
way, had she cared less for the girl's welfare. Society
being what it is, they did not see how their energetic
old friend could have acted more prudently and kindly.

At dinner there was much pleasant talk. The
baronet's vein of humorous criticism flowed freely.
Walking through London streets this morning, his eye
had caught sight of a couple of posters which held him
long in meditation.

"One was a huge picture of an ox, and beneath it
one read in great letters that sixty thousand bullocks
are annually slaughtered for the manufacture of Noke's
beef-tea. The other advertised Stoke's pills, and informed the world, in still bigger lettering, that every
minute of the day seven of these pills 'reach their
destination.' Delightful phrase! 'Reach their destination.' And this, you see, is how we adorn the
walls of our cities. It is not only permitted, but
favoured. I am quite sure that a plebiscite, if some
more civilized alternative were offered, would pronounce
in favour of the bullocks and the pills, as much more
interesting. Yet to my mind, spoilt by pottering

Our Friend the Charlatan

among old pictures, that bit of wall was so monstrous
in its hideousness that I stood moon-stricken, and even
yet I haven't got over it. I shall dream to-night of
myriads of bullocks massacred for beef-tea, and of an
endless procession of pills—reaching their destination.
I ask myself, in my foolish theoretic way, what earthly
right we have to lay claim to civilization. How much
better it would be always to speak of ourselves as
barbarians. We should then, perhaps, make some endeavour to improve. The barbarian who imagines
himself on the pinnacle of refinement is in a parlous
state—far more likely to retrogade than to advance."

"There should be a league of landowners," said Miss
Tomalin, "pledged to forbid any such horror on their
own property."

"I don't know that I have much faith in leagues,"
returned Sir William. "I am a lost individualist. Let
every one try to civilize himself; depend upon it, it's
the best work he can do for the world at large."

"And yet," put in Dymchurch, "the world can't do
without apostles. Do you think mere example has
ever availed much?"

"Perhaps not. I would say that I don't care. Do
you really believe that the world ever *will* be much
more civilized than it is? In successive epochs, there
are more or fewer persons of liberal mind—that's all;
the proportion rises and falls. Why should we trouble
about it? Let those of us who really dislike the ox
and pill placards, keep as much out of sight of them
as possible, that's all. It doesn't do to think over
much about the problems of life. Now-a-days almost
everybody seems to feel it a duty to explain the
universe, and with strange results. For instance, I
read an article last night, a most profound article,
altogether too much for my poor head, on the question
of right and wrong. Really, I had supposed that I
knew the difference between right and wrong; in my
blundering way, I had always tried to act on the knowledge. But this writer proves to me that I shall have

to begin all over again. 'Morality,' he says, 'depends upon cerebral oxidation.' That's a terrible dictum for a simple-minded man. If I am not cerebrally oxidized, or oxidally cerebrized, in the right degree, it's all over with my hopes of leading a moral life. I'm quite sure that a large number of people are worrying over that article, and asking how they can oxidize if not their own cerebellum, at all events that of their off-spring."

"Man and nature," said Dymchurch presently, "have such different views about the good of the world."

"That," exclaimed the baronet, "is a very striking remark. Let me give you an illustration of its truth. Years ago I had an intimate friend, a wonderfully clever man, who wrote and published a delightful little book. Few such books have ever been written; it was a marvel of delicate thought and of exquisite style. The half-dozen readers who could appreciate it cried aloud that this man had a great future, that his genius was a jewel which the world would for ever prize—and so on. Well, my friend married, and since then he has written nothing, nor will he ever again. I know people who lament his fate, who declare that marriage was his ruin, and a crime against civilization. The other day I called upon him—not having seen him for ages. I found a rather uncomfortable little house, a pretty, dull little wife, and three beautiful children in the most vigorous health. 'Alas!' said my friend to me in private, 'I try to work, but I can do nothing. I need absolute tranquillity, such as I had when I wrote my book. I try, but domestic life is fatal to me.' Now, what better example of what you say, Lord Dym-church? To *us* it seems a misfortune to the world that this man didn't live on in bachelorhood and write more exquisite books. But nature says, 'What do I care for his *books*? Look at his *children!*' That's what she meant him for, and from nature's point of view he is a triumphant success."

Dymchurch seemed not only amused, but pleased.

Our Friend the Charlatan

He grew thoughtful, and sat smiling to himself whilst others carried on the conversation.

The evening passed. Lady Amys gave the signal of retirement; May and Constance followed; Sir William and Lord Dymchurch chatted for yet a few minutes with their hostess, then bade her good-night. But, just as he was leaving the room, Dymchurch heard Lady Ogram call his name; he stepped back towards her.

"I forgot to tell you," she said, "that Mr. Lashmar will lunch with us the day after to-morrow. Of course, he is very busy at Hollingford."

"I shall be glad to see him," Dymchurch replied cordially. "I wish I could help him in any way."

Lady Ogram resumed her seat. She was looking at the marble bust, and Dymchurch, following the direction of her eyes, also regarded it.

"Until this morning," she said, "I hadn't seen that for more than fifty years. I would tell you why—but I should only send you to sleep."

Dymchurch begged to hear the story, and sat down to listen. Though her day had been so unusually long and fatiguing, Lady Ogram seemed to feel no effect of it; her eyes were still lustrous; she held herself with as much dignity as when the guests arrived. She began a narrative of such clearness and vigour that the listener never thought of doubting its truth; yet the story of her youth, as the lady of Rivenoak wished Lord Dymchurch to receive it, differed in very important points from that which her memory preserved. Not solely, nor indeed chiefly, on her own account did Arabella thus falsify the past; it was as the ancestress of May Tomalin that she spoke, and on behalf of May's children. Dymchurch, looking back into years long before he was born, saw a beautiful maiden of humble birth loyally wooed and wedded by a romantic artist— son of a proud baronet. Of course she became the butt of calumny, which found its chief support in the fact that the young artist had sculptured her portrait,

301

Our Friend the Charlatan

and indiscreetly shown it to friends before their
marriage. Hearing these slanderous rumours, she
wished all the work which represented her to be
destroyed, and her husband led her to believe that this
was done; but on succeeding to the title, and coming
to live at Rivenoak, Sir Quentin confessed that he had
not been able to destroy that marble bust which was
his joy and his pride; he undertook, however, to keep
it hidden under lock and key, and only this day, this
very day, had it come forth again into the light.

"I am an old, old woman," she said, not without
genuine pathos in her utterance. "I have long outlived the few who were my enemies and spoke ill of me,
as well as those who knew the truth and held me in
respect. I fear no one. I wanted to see how I looked
when I was a girl, and I confess I am glad for others
to see it too."

Dymchurch murmured that nothing could be more
natural.

"I was almost as good-looking as May, don't you
think?" she asked, with a not very successful affectation of diffidence.

"There is a likeness," answered Dymchurch.
"But——"

She interrupted his effort to describe the points of
difference.

"You very much prefer the other face. That doesn't
surprise me, and you needn't be afraid to confess it.
May is much better tempered than I was, and she
looks it. Did I ever tell you how she is related to
me? I call her my niece, but she is really the grand-
daughter of my brother, who emigrated to Canada."

Thereupon Lady Ogram sketched a portrait of that
brother, depicting him as a fine specimen of the
colonizing Briton, breezy, sturdy, honest to the core.
She traced the history of the Canadian family, which
in the direct line had now no representative but May.
Of her long search for the Tomalins she did not think
it necessary to speak; but, turning back to her own

302

history, she told of the son she had lost, and how all
her affections were now bestowed upon this young girl,
who in truth had become to her as a daughter. Then,
discreetly, with no undue insistence, she made known
her intention to endow May Tomalin with the greater
part of her fortune.

"I have lived long enough to know that money is
not happiness, but in the right hands it is a great and
good thing. I have no fear of the use May will make
of it, and you can't know what a pleasure it is to be
able to give it to her, to one of my own blood, my own
name, instead of leaving it to strangers, as I once
feared I must. But," she broke off suddenly in a
changed voice, "here I keep you listening to my
old tales when you ought to be asleep. Good-night,
Lord Dymchurch. To-morrow you must see Rivenoak.
Good-night."

For her there was again no sleep. The weather had
changed; through the open window breathed a cool,
sweet air, very refreshing after the high temperature of
the last few days; but Lady Ogram in vain closed her
eyes and tried to lull her thoughts to rest. It disappointed her that Dymchurch, in reply to her confidences, had spoken no decisive word. Of course, he
would declare himself on the morrow; he would have
every opportunity for private talk with May, and of
the issue there could be no serious doubt. But Lady
Ogram's nerves were tortured with impatience. In the
glimmer of dawn she wished to rise and walk about,
but found herself unequal to the effort. Her head
ached, her blood was feverish. Though it was a thing
she hated to do, she summoned the attendant, who lay
in an adjoining room.

At midday she was able to descend. At the foot of
the stairs she encountered Constance Bride, who stood
glancing over a book.

"What are they all doing?" was her first question.
And, before Constance could reply, she asked: "Where
is Lord Dymchurch?"

Our Friend the Charlatan

"I saw him not long ago in the garden."

"Alone?"

"No, with Miss Tomalin."

"Why didn't you say so at once? Where are the others? Tell them I am down."

Constance delayed replying for a moment, then said with cold respectfulness:

"You will find Sir William and Lady Amys in the drawing-room."

"I shall find them there, shall I? And what if I don't wish to go into the drawing-room?"

Constance looked into the angry face. In the book she was carrying, a French volume arrived by post this morning, she had found things which troubled her mind and her temper; she was in no mood for submitting to harsh dictatorship. But those blood-shot eyes and shrivelled lips, the hollow and drawn muscles which told of physical suffering, stilled her irritation.

"I will tell them at once, Lady Ogram."

Dymchurch and May Tomalin had strayed from the garden into the park. They were sitting on a bench which encircled a great old tree. For some minutes neither had spoken. Dymchurch held in his hand a last year's leaf, brown, crisp, but still perfect in shape; he smiled dreamily, and, as his eyes wandered to the girl's face, said in a soft undertone:

"How easily one loses oneself in idle thoughts! I was asking myself where this grew—on which branch, which twig; and it seemed strange to me that by no possibility could any one discover it."

May had not a very high opinion of her companion's intelligence, but it struck her that this morning he was duller than usual. She humoured him, replying with her philosophical air:

"Yet we try to find out how life began, and what the world means."

Dymchurch was pleased. He liked to find her capable of such a reflection. It encouraged the movement of vague tenderness which had begun to justify

Our Friend the Charlatan

a purpose formed rather in the mind than in the heart.

"Yes! Amusing, isn't it? But you, I think, don't trouble much about such questions?"

"It seems to me waste of time."

She was thinking of Dyce Lashmar, asking herself whether she would meet him, or not, to-morrow morning. Certainly she wished to do so. Lashmar at a distance left her coolly reasonable; she wanted to recover the emotional state of mind which had come about during their stolen interview. With Lord Dymchurch, though his attentions were flattering, she could not for a moment imagine herself touched by romantic feeling.

"So it is," he was saying. "To waste time in that way has always been one of my bad habits—but I am going to get rid of it."

He seemed on the point of adding more significant words. May heard the sound fail in his throat; saw —without looking at him—his sudden embarrassment. When the words came, as surely they would, what was to be her answer? She hoped for inspiration. Why should it be necessary for her to make precise reply? No! She would not. Freedom, and the exercise of power were what she wanted. Enough to promise her answer a month, or half-a-year, hence. If the old lady didn't like it, let her learn patience.

Dymchurch sat bending forward. The dry leaf crackled between his fingers; he was crushing it to powder.

"Who," he asked, "is the lady Miss Bride was speaking of, in connection with the servants' training-school?"

"Mrs. Gallantry. A very good, active sort of woman at Hollingford."

"That scheme doesn't interest you much?"

"Not very much, I confess. I quite approve of it. It's just the kind of thing for people like Miss Bride, plodding and practical; no doubt, they'll make it very useful. But I have rather lost my keenness for work of that sort. Perhaps I have grown out of it. Of course, I wish as much as ever for the good of the lower classes, but I feel that my own work will lie in another direction."

" Tell me what you have in mind," said Dymchurch, meeting her look with soft eyes.

" What I really care about now is the spirit of the educated class. There's such a great deal to be done among people of our own kind. Not, of course, by direct teaching and preaching, but by personal influence, exerted in all sorts of ways. I should like to—to set the intellectual tone in my own circle. I should like my house to—as it were, to radiate light."

The listener could not but smile. Yet his amusement had no tincture of irony. He himself would not have used these phrases, but was not the thought exactly what he had in mind ? He, too, felt his inaptitude for the ordinary forms of " social " usefulness; in his desire and his resolve to " do something," he had been imagining just this sort of endeavour, and May's words seemed to make it less vague.

" I quite understand you," he exclaimed, with some fervour. " There's plenty of scope for that sort of influence. You would do your best to oppose the tendencies of vulgar and selfish society. If only in a little circle one could set the fashion of thought, of living for things that are worth while ! And I see no impossibility. It has been done before now."

" I'm very glad you like the idea," said May graciously.

Again—without looking at him—she saw his lips shaping words which they could not sound; she saw his troubled, abashed smile, and his uneasy movement which ended in nothing at all.

" We have some fine trees at Rivenoak," fell from her, as her eyes wandered.

" Indeed you have !"

" You like trees, don't you ? "

"Very much. When I was a boy, I once saw a great many splendid oaks and beeches cut down, and it made me miserable."

"Where was that?"

"On land that had belonged to my father, and, which, for a year or two, belonged to me."

He spoke with an uneasy smile, again crushing a brown leaf between his fingers. May's silence compelled him to proceed.

"I have no trees now." He tried to laugh. "Only a bit of a farm which seems to be going out of cultivation."

"But why do you let it do so?"

"It's in the hands of a troublesome tenant. If I had been wise, I should have learnt to farm it myself years ago. Perhaps I shall still do so."

"That would be interesting," said May. "Tell me about it, will you? It's in Kent, I think."

The impoverished peer spoke freely of the matter. He had been seeking this opportunity since the beginning of their talk. Yet, before he had ceased, moral discomfort took hold upon him, and his head drooped in shame. The silence which followed—May was saying to herself that now, now the moment had come—did but increase his embarrassment. He wished to speak of his sisters, to hint at their circumstances, but the thing was impossible. In desperation, he broke into some wholly foreign subject, and for this morning, all hope of the decisive step had passed.

The day brought no other opportunity. Towards midnight Dymchurch sat at the open window of his chamber, glad to be alone, anxious, self-reproachful; to-morrow he must discharge what had become an obvious duty, however difficult it might be.

He had received a long letter from the younger of his sisters. It spoke of the other's ill-health, a subject of disquiet for the past month, and went on to discuss a topic which frequently arose in this correspondence— the authority of the Church of Rome. A lady who had

just been passing a fortnight at the house in Somerset
was a Catholic, and Dymchurch suspected her of
proselytism; from the tone of the present letter it
appeared that her arguments had had considerable
success. Though impartial in his judgment of the old
faith, Dymchurch felt annoyed and depressed at the
thought that one of his sisters, or both, might turn in
that direction; he explained their religious unrest by
the solitude and monotony of their lives, for which it
seemed to him that he himself was largely to blame.
Were he to marry May Tomalin, everything would at
once, he thought, be changed for the better; his sisters
might come forth from their seclusion, mingle with
wholesome society, and have done with more or less
morbid speculation.

He had gone so far that honour left him no alternative. And he had gone thus far because it pleased
him to do a thing which broke utterly with his habits
and prejudices, which put him into a position such as
he had never foreseen. He was experimenting in life.

May, he told himself, behaved very well. Never for
a moment had she worn the air of invitation; a smirk
was a thing unknown to her; the fact of his titular
dignity she seemed wholly to disregard. Whatever her
faults—he saw most of them—she had the great virtue
of unaffectedness. Assuredly he liked her; he could
not feel certain that even a warmer sentiment did not
breathe within him. As for May's willingness to
marry him, why, at all events, it appeared a probability.
They had some intellectual sympathies, which were
likely to increase rather than diminish. And, if the
marriage would be for him a great material benefit, he
hoped that May also might profit by it.

Lady Ogram desired their union, that was clear.
That she should have made choice of *him* was not easy
to explain, for surely she might have wedded her niece
more advantageously. But then, Lady Ogram was no
mere intriguer; he thought her, on the whole, a woman
of fine character, with certain defects so obvious that

Our Friend the Charlatan

they could never be the means of misleading any one. She was acting, undoubtedly, in what she deemed the best interests of her young relative—and *he* could hardly accuse her of having made a mistake.

Pacing the room, he took up a review, opened at a philosophical article, and tried to read.

"Why does man exist? Why does *anything* exist? Manifestly because the operations of the energies of nature, under the particular group of conditions, compel it, just in the same way that they cause everything else to happen."

He paused, and re-read the passage. Was it satire or burlesque? No, he saw that the writer meant it for a serious contribution to human knowledge. In disgust he flung the periodical aside. This was the kind of stuff that people feed upon now-a-days, a result of the craze for quasi-scientific phraseology, for sonorous explanations of the inexplicable. Why does man exist—forsooth! To guard his lips against the utterances of foolishness, and to be of what use in the world he may.

Before midday on the morrow he would offer May Tomalin his heart and hand—offer both with glad sincerity, disregarding all else but the fact that to this point had destiny brought him.

He thought of her humble origin, and rejoiced in it. His own family history was an illustration of how a once genuinely noble house might fall into decay if not renewed by alliances with more vigorous blood. May Tomalin had perfect health; she represented generations of hardy, simple folk, their energy of late recruited in the large air of Canada. Why, had he gone forth deliberately to seek the kind of wife best suited to him, he could not have done better than chance had done for him in his indolent shirking existence. If he had children, they might be robust and comely. In May's immediate connections, there was nothing to produce embarrassment; as to her breeding, it would compare more than favourably with that of many high-born young ladies whom society delights to honour. Of such young ladies he had always thought with a peculiar dread. If ever he allowed himself to dream of love and marriage, his mind turned to regions where fashion held no sway, where ambitions were humble. May Tomalin stood between the two worlds, representing a mean which would perchance prove golden.

So determined and courageous was his mood when he fell asleep that it did not permit him long slumbers. A bright sunrise, gleaming on a sky which in the night had shed cool showers, tempted him to rise much before his usual time. He turned over a volume or two from the shelves in the bedroom, seeking thus to keep his nerves steady and to tune his mind. Presently, he thought he would take a stroll before breakfast. It was nearly eight o'clock; servants would be about and the door open. He left his room.

Passing a great window at the end of the corridor, he glanced out upon the garden lying behind the house. Some one was walking there—why, it was no other than May herself! She moved quickly in the direction of the park; evidently bent on a ramble before her friends were stirring. Better chance could not have befallen him. He went quickly down-stairs.

But, when he had made his way to that part of the grounds where May had appeared, she was no longer discoverable. He strode on in what seemed the probable direction, taking, as a matter of fact, the wrong path; it brought him into the park, but at a point whence he looked in vain for the girl's figure. This was vexatious. Should he linger here for her return, or step out at a venture? He strolled vaguely for some minutes, coming at length into a path which promised pleasant things. Perhaps May had gone to the bosky hollow yonder. If he missed her, they were sure of meeting after breakfast. He walked towards the clustered trees.

CHAPTER XXII

PIQUED by the uneventfulness of the preceding day, May Tomalin stole forth this morning in a decidedly adventurous frame of mind. She scorned danger; she desired excitement. Duplicity on her part was no more than Lord Dymchurch merited after that deliberate neglect of opportunity under the great tree. Of course, nothing irrevocable must come to pass; it was the duty of man to commit himself, the privilege of woman to guard an ambiguous freedom. But, within certain limits, she counted on dramatic incidents. A brisk answer to her tap on the door in the park wall made her nerves thrill delightfully. No sooner had she turned the key than the door was impatiently pushed open from without.

" Quick ! " sounded Lashmar's voice. " I hear wheels on the road.—Ha ! Just in time ! It might be someone who would recognize me."

He had grasped May's hand. He was gazing eagerly, amorously into her face. His emotions had matured since the meeting two days ago.

" Tell me all the news," he went on. " Is Dymchurch here ? "

" Yes. And the others. You come to lunch to-day, of course. You will see them."

She recovered her hand, though not without a little struggle, which pleased her. For all her academic modernism, May belonged to the class which has primitive traditions, unsophisticated instincts.

" And what has happened ? " asked Dyce, advancing

as she stepped back. He spoke like one who has a right to the fullest information.

"Happened? Nothing particular. What could have happened?"

"I have been tormenting myself. Of course, I know why Dymchurch has come, and so do you. I can't go away in a horrible uncertainty. If I do, I shall betray myself when I come to luncheon, so I give you warning."

"What do you mean?" exclaimed the girl, with an air of dignity surprised.

"Tell me the truth. Has Dymchurch spoken?"

"Many times," answered May, smiling with excessive ingenuousness. "He is not very talkative, but he doesn't keep absolute silence. I hear that you have been to see Mrs. Gallantry."

"What do I care about Mrs. Gallantry? I've seen no end of people, but all the time I was thinking of you. Yesterday morning I all but wrote to you."

"What about?"

"All sorts of things. Of course, I should have disguised my handwriting in the address."

May avoided his look, and shaped her lips to severity.

"If you had done such a thing—I should have been very greatly displeased. I'm very glad you didn't so far forget yourself."

"So am I, now. Won't you tell me if anything has happened? Won't you put my mind at ease?"

"I can stay only for a few minutes. There's really nothing to tell—nothing. But *you* must have plenty of news. How are things going on?"

Lashmar hurriedly told of two or three circumstances which seemed to favour him in the opening campaign. There was now no doubt that Butterworth would be the Conservative candidate, and, on the whole, his name appeared to excite but moderate enthusiasm. He broke off with an impatient gesture.

"I can't talk about that stuff! It's waste of time whilst I am with you."

Our Friend the Charlatan

"But it interests me very much," said May, who seemed to grow calmer as Dyce yielded to agitation. "Lord Dymchurch says he would gladly help you, if it were in his power. Don't you think he *might* be of some use?"

"No, I don't. Dymchurch is a dreaming nobody."

"What a strange way to speak of him!" said May, as if slightly offended. "You used to have quite a different opinion."

"Perhaps so. I didn't know him so well. There's nothing whatever in the man, and he'll never do anything as long as he lives. You know that as well as I do."

"I think you are mistaken," May answered, in an absent voice, her look betraying some travail of the mind, as if she were really debating with herself the question of Dymchurch's prospects.

"Do you mean that?" cried Lashmar, with annoyance.

"I certainly shouldn't call him a 'dreaming nobody,'" replied May, in the tone of dignified reproof. "Lord Dymchurch is very thoughtful, and very well informed, and has very high principles."

"One may admit all that. All I meant was that there is no career before him. Would any one think of comparing him, for instance, with me? You needn't smile. You remember the talk we had at Mrs. Toplady's that evening. I know my own qualities, and see no use in pretending that I don't. But what are we talking about! Of course you care nothing for Dymchurch. I know that very well. If you did, you wouldn't be here."

He ended in a little laugh of triumph, and therewith, catching hold of both her hands, he drew her gently forward, looked close into her face, murmured "May! My beautiful May!" In that moment there came the strangest look upon May's countenance—a look of alarm, almost of terror. Her eyes were turned to a spot among the trees, some ten yards away. Dyce,

313

seeing the sudden change of her expression, turned in the direction of her gaze. He was just in time to perceive the back of a retreating figure, which disappeared behind bushes.

"Who was that?" he asked, in a startled voice.

May could only whisper.

"It was Lord Dymchurch."

"I thought so. Confound that fellow! What is he doing here at this time of the morning?"

"He saw us," said May, her cheeks burning. "Oh, who could have expected—! He saw us distinctly. I shouldn't wonder if he heard what you were saying. Why," she added angrily, "did you speak so loud?"

"Nonsense! He couldn't hear at that distance."

"But he had been nearer."

"Then the fellow is a sneak! What right has he to steal upon us?"

"He didn't!" cried the girl. "I saw him as he stopped. I saw his face, and how astonished he looked. He turned away instantly."

"Well, what does it matter?" exclaimed Dyce, who was quivering with excitement. "What do I care? What need you care? Haven't we perfect liberty to meet? After all, what *does* it matter?"

"But you forget," said May, "that he knows of your engagement."

"My engagement! Let him know, and let him think what he likes! My engagement, indeed! Why, I haven't once thought of it since I left London—not once! There'll have to be an end to this intolerable state of things. Dymchurch isn't likely to tell any one what he sees; he's a gentleman."

"I must go in at once," cried May, losing her head. "Somebody else may come. Go away, please! Don't stay another minute."

"But it's impossible. We have to come to an understanding. Listen to me, May!"

He grasped her hand, passed his other arm around her. There was resistance, but Dyce used his strength

in earnest. The girl's beauty fired him; he became
the fervent lover, leaving her no choice between high
resentment and frank surrender. Indignation was
rapidly dying out of May's look. She ceased to
struggle; she bent her head to his shoulder.

"Isn't that much better?" he whispered laughingly;
"isn't that the way out of our difficulties?"

May allowed him to breathe a few more such soothing
sentences, then spoke with troubled accent.

"But you don't understand. What must Lord
Dymchurch think of me—believing that you are
engaged?"

"I'll tell him the truth. I'll go and tell him at
once."

"But still you don't understand. My aunt wants
me to marry him."

"I know she does, and know she'll be disappointed,"
cried Dyce exultantly.

"But do you suppose that Lord Dymchurch will
stay here any longer? He will leave this very morning, I'm sure he will. My aunt will want to know
what it means. There'll be dreadful explanations."

"Keep calm, May. If we lose our courage, it's all
over with us. We have to deal boldly with Lady
Ogram. Remember that she is very old and weak;
I'm perfectly sure she can't resist you and me if we
speak to her in the proper way—quietly and reasonably
and firmly. We have made up our minds, haven't we?
You are mine, dearest May! There's no more doubt
about *that!*"

"Miss Bride will be our deadly enemy," said May,
again yielding to his caresses.

"Enemy!" Dyce exclaimed. "Why?"

"Surely you don't need to be told. She dislikes me
already (as I do her), and now she will hate me. She'll
do her best to injure us with Lady Ogram."

"You're mistaken. I have only to see her and talk
to her—as I will, this morning. Before luncheon she
shall be firmly on our side, I promise you! Don't have

the least anxiety about *her*. The only serious difficulty is with Lady Ogram."

" You mean to tell Miss Bride the truth ? " exclaimed May. " You mean to tell her what has happened this morning ? I forbid you to do so ! I *forbid* you ! "

" I didn't mean anything of the kind," replied Lashmar. " To Dymchurch, of course, I shall speak quite freely ; there's no choice. To Miss Bride I shall only say that I want our sham engagement to come to an end, because I am in love with *you*. The presence of Dymchurch here will be quite enough to explain my sudden action—don't you see ? I assure you, she must be made our friend—and I can do it."

" If you do, it'll be a miracle," said May, with a face of utter misgiving.

" It would be, perhaps, for any other man. Now, we have no time to lose. I must see Dymchurch immediately. I shall hurry round inside the park wall, and come up to the front of the house, like an ordinary visitor. Election business will account for the early hour, if Lady Ogram hears about it; but she isn't likely to be down before eleven, is she ? Don't let us lose any more time, May. Go back quietly, and let no one see that anything has happened. Don't worry; in a quarter of an hour Dymchurch shall know that there's not a shadow of blame upon you."

" He won't believe that story. If he does, he'll think it very dishonourable."

Dyce checked the words in amorous fashion, but they conveyed an unpleasant truth, which he turned about in his mind as he hastened towards the interview with Dymchurch. For once in his life, however, he saw a clear course of action before him, indicated alike by interest and by honour. He was roused by supreme impulse and necessity. Seeing him as he strode along, you might have supposed him bent on some high purpose, so gallantly did he hold his head, and so radiant was his visage. There are men capable of viewing themselves as heroes in very unheroic situations, and Lashmar was one of them. Because his business with Dymchurch and with Constance would be distinctly disagreeable, and yet he faced it without hesitation, his conscience praised him aloud. Nothing less than brilliant issue could be the reward of such brave energy.

Meanwhile, May had begun to retrace her steps through the little wood. She wished to go quickly, yet was afraid, if she did so, of overtaking Lord Dymchurch. In her, too, the self-approving mind was active; she praised herself for having given the preference to love over ambition. With the choice of becoming a peeress, she had bestowed her beauty, intellect, wealth upon a man who had nothing but hopes to offer. Was not this nobler than any nobility of rank ? The sentimentality of a hundred novels surged within her; verses of Browning chanted in her brain. " Love is best ! " She walked a heroine of passion. All obstacles would fall before her burning resolve. This was life ! This was high romance !

She passed from among the trees into the open park —and there before her stood the man she least wished to see. He had evidently been waiting; he began to move towards her. A score of more or less ingenious lies rose to her tongue; this was instinct; but she remembered that deceit was not called for. Lord Dymchurch had raised his hat. He looked very grave, but not at all ill-tempered. May did not offer her hand. After the " good-morning," he walked beside her, and at once began to speak.

" I find I must leave Rivenoak this morning, Miss Tomalin."

His voice was low, gentle, not unkind.

" Must you indeed, Lord Dymchurch ? "

" I'm afraid I must," he answered quietly.

" I am *so* sorry. But you will be able to see Lady Ogram ? "

" I fear not. I wish to leave almost at once."

They were drawing near to the garden. Dymchurch

paused, glanced at his companion with sad eyes, and, his look cast down, again spoke.

"Miss Tomalin, I came to Rivenoak hoping to ask you to be my wife. Only a foolish shyness prevented me from doing so yesterday. This morning, I know that it would be too late. Pray forgive me for speaking of the matter at all. I feel obliged to explain myself. Perhaps I had better make the explanation complete by saying that I saw you go through the garden, and followed in the same direction, hoping for an opportunity of speaking with you alone."

May felt that a man in this position could not well have conducted himself more kindly and delicately. No hint in look or voice that he thought her behaviour extraordinary; he had been defeated by a rival, that was all; his tone begged excuse for unwilling intrusion upon her privacy. But for the hopelessly compromising moment at which he had arrived, probably he would have given her all benefit of the doubt, and, in one way or another, would still have prosecuted his wooing. Very nervous and confused, she made what seemed to her an appropriate answer.

"Thank you very much, Lord Dymchurch. I had so hoped we could be friends—simply friends. Do let me think of you still in that way."

"Will you give me a proof of friendship," said the other, smiling nervously, "by permitting me to tell Lady Ogram, in a note I shall leave for her, that you have declined my offer of marriage?"

This, thought May, was indeed a smoothing of her difficulties. She glanced at the speaker with gratitude.

"You will really do that? How generous of you, Lord Dymchurch!"

"Allow me to leave you now, Miss Tomalin. I must get ready."

May offered her hand. Dymchurch just perceptibly pressed it, saluted with the gravest politeness, and walked away.

On the terrace before the house he encountered

Our Friend the Charlatan

Lashmar, who came up to him with glowing countenance.

"I hoped I should find you here. Nothing could be better. Just a moment's talk."

Dyce had thrust out a hand, but as the other appeared not to see it, he drew it back again as naturally as he could. Dymchurch stood waiting in an attitude of cold civility.

"It's rather a delicate matter. Accident has obliged me to speak; otherwise I shouldn't, of course, have troubled you about my private affairs. I wish to tell you that the engagement which once existed between Miss Bride and myself is at an end."

"I presumed so," was the reply, spoken with unmoved features.

"Also, that Miss Tomalin has for some days been aware of this state of things."

"I took it for granted."

"So that," Dyce continued, in a stumbling way, "you won't retain any disagreeable impressions from this morning's incident? I am very glad indeed to have been able to see you at once. It puts an end to a natural uneasiness on both sides."

"I am obliged to you," said Dymchurch.

With a bow and a look past his interlocutor, he turned to enter the house.

As soon as he had disappeared Lashmar followed, and rang the door-bell. Of the servant who came, he asked whether Miss Bride was down yet. The domestic went to inquire. Waiting in the hall, Dyce heard a footstep behind him; he turned and saw May, who, with features discomposed, just met his eyes and hurried away up the staircase. When the servant returned, it was with a request that Mr. Lashmar would step into the library. There, in a few minutes, Constance joined him.

"You are early!" she exclaimed. "No bad news, I hope?"

"No. But I want a little quiet talk with you. Of

319

course, it's absurd to come at this hour. You know I
lunch here to-day, and I couldn't have gone through it
without seeing you in private. I'm in a queer state of
mind; very much upset; in fact, I never felt such need
of a true friend to consult."

Constance kept her eyes fixed upon him. She had
been up for a couple of hours, reading in the French
book which had reached her yesterday. The same
volume had occupied her till long after midnight. Her
face showed the effects of over-study.

"Tell me all about it," she said, with voice subdued
to the note of intimacy, and look in which there shone
an indulgent kindliness.

"You have often said that you wished me well, that
you desired to help me in my career."

"Have I not done more than say it?" returned the
other softly.

"Indeed you have! Few women would have been
capable of such self-sacrifice on a friend's behalf. You
know the law of human nature; we always make old
kindness a reason for demanding new. Again I am
come to ask your help, and again it involves heroism
on your part."

The listener's face grew troubled; her lips lost their
suavity. Lashmar's eyes fell before her look.

"I feel ashamed," he went on, with an uneasy movement of his hands. "It's too bad to expect so much of
you. You have more pride than most people, yet I
behave to you as if you didn't know the meaning of the
word. Do, I beg, believe me when I say that I am
downright ashamed, and that I hardly know how to
tell you what has happened."

Constance did not open her lips; they were sternly
compressed.

"I want you," Dyce continued, "first of all to consent
to the termination of our formal engagement. Of
course," he hastened to add, "that step in itself is
nothing to you. Indeed, you will be rather glad of it
than otherwise; it relieves you from an annoying and

embarrassing situation—which only your great good-nature induced you to accept. But I ask more than that. I want it to be understood that our engagement had ended when I last left Rivenoak. Can you consent to this? Will you bear me out when I break the news to Lady Ogram?"

"You propose to do that yourself?" asked Constance, with frigid sarcasm.

"Yes, I shall do it myself. I am alone responsible for what has happened, and I must face the consequences."

"Up to a certain point, you mean," remarked the same pungent voice.

"It's true; I ask your help in that one particular."

"You say that something has happened. Is it within my privilege to ask what, or must I be content to know nothing more?"

"Constance, don't speak like that!" pleaded Dyce. "Be generous to the end. Haven't I behaved very frankly all along? Haven't we talked with perfect openness of all I did? Don't spoil it all, now at the critical moment of my career. Be yourself, generous and large-minded!"

"Give me the opportunity," she answered, with an acid smile. "Tell what you have to tell."

"But this is not like yourself," he remonstrated. "It's a new spirit. I have never known you like this."

Constance moved her foot, and spoke sharply.

"Say what you have to say, and never mind anything else."

Lashmar bent his brows.

"After all, Constance, I am a perfectly free man. If you are annoyed because I wish to put an end to what you yourself recognize as a mere pretence, it's very unreasonable and quite unworthy of you."

"You are right," answered the other, with sudden change to ostentatious indifference. "It's time the farce stopped. I, for one, have had enough of it. If you like, I will tell Lady Ogram myself this morning."

"No!" exclaimed Dyce, with decision. "That I certainly do *not* wish. Are you resolved, all at once, to do me as much harm as you can?"

"Not at all. I thought I should relieve you of a disagreeable business."

"If you really mean that, I am very grateful. I wanted to tell you everything, and talk it over, and see what you thought best to be done. But, of course, I shouldn't dream of forcing my confidence upon you. It's a delicate matter, and only because we were such intimate friends——"

"If you will have done with all this preamble," Constance interrupted, with forced calm, "and tell me what there is to be told, I am quite willing to listen."

"Well, I will do so. It's this. I am in love with May Tomalin, and I want to marry her."

Their eyes met. Dyce was smiling—an uneasy, abashed smile. Constance wore an expression of cold curiosity, and spoke in a corresponding voice.

"Have you asked her to do so?"

"Not yet," Lashmar replied.

For a moment Constance gazed at him; then she said quietly:

"I don't believe you."

"That's rather emphatic," cried Dyce, affecting a laugh.

"It conveys my meaning. I don't believe you, for several reasons. One of them is——" She broke off, and rose from her chair. "Please wait; I will be back in a moment."

Lashmar sat looking about the room. He began to be aware that he had not breakfasted—a physical uneasiness added to the various forms of disquiet from which his mind was suffering. When Constance re-entered he saw she had a book in her hand, a book which, by its outward appearance, he at once recognized.

"Do you know this?" she asked, holding the volume to him. "I got it yesterday, and have already gone through most of it. I find it very interesting."

Our Friend the Charlatan

"Ah, I know it quite well," Dyce answered, fingering the pages. "A most suggestive book. But—what has it to do with our present conversation?"

Constance viewed him wonderingly. If he felt at all disconcerted, nothing of the kind appeared in his face, which wore, indeed, a look of genuine puzzlement.

"Have you so poor an opinion of my intellect?" she asked, with subdued vehemence. "Do you suppose me incapable of perceiving that all the political and social views you have been living upon were taken directly from this book? I admire your audacity. Few educated men now-a-days would have ventured on so bold a—we call it plagiarism."

Dyce stared at her.

"You are very severe," he exclaimed, on the note of deprecation. "Views I have been 'living upon'? It's quite possible that now and then something I had read there chanced to come into my talk; but who gives chapter and verse for every conversational allusion? You astound me. I see that, so far from wishing me well, you have somehow come to regard me with positive ill-feeling. How has it come about, Constance?"

"You dare to talk to me in this way!" cried Constance passionately. "You dare to treat me as an imbecile! This is going too far! If you had shown ever so little shame I would have thrown the book aside, and never again have spoken of it. But to insult me by supposing that force of impudence can overcome the testimony of my own reason! Very well. The question shall be decided by others. All who have heard you expatiate on your—*your* 'bio-sociological' theory shall be made acquainted with this French writer, and form their own opinion as to your originality."

Lashmar drew himself up.

"By all means." His voice was perfectly controlled. "I have my doubts whether you will persuade any one to read it—people don't take very eagerly to philosophical works in a foreign language—and I think it very unlikely that any one but yourself has troubled to keep in mind

the theories and arguments which you are so kind as
to say I stole. What's more, will it be very dignified
behaviour to go about proclaiming that you have
quarrelled with me, and that you are bent on giving
me a bad character? Isn't it likely to cause a smile?"

As she listened, Constance shook with anger.

"Are you so utterly base," she cried, "as to stand
there and deny the truth of what I say?"

"I never argue with any one in a rage. Why such
a thing as this—a purely intellectual matter, a question
for quiet reasoning—should infuriate you, I am at a
loss to understand. We had better talk no more for
the present. I must hope for another opportunity."

He moved as though to withdraw, but by no means
with the intention of doing so, for he durst not have
left Constance in this mood of violent hostility. Her
outbreak had astonished him; he knew not of what
she might be capable. There flashed through his mind
the easy assurance he had given to May—that Constance
Bride should be persuaded to friendly offices on their
behalf, and he had much ado to disguise his consternation. For a moment he thought of flattering her pride
by unconditional surrender, by submissive appeal; but
to that he could not bring himself. Her discovery, her
contempt and menaces, had deeply offended him; the
indeterminate and shifting sentiments with which he
had regarded her crystallized into dislike—that hard
dislike which commonly results, whether in man or
woman, from trifling with intimate relations. That
Constance had been—perhaps still was—tenderly disposed to him, served merely to heighten his repugnance.
To stand in fear of this woman was a more humiliating
and exasperating sensation than he had ever known.

"Do as you think fit," he added, in a stern voice,
pausing at a little distance. "It is indifferent to me.
In any case, Lady Ogram will soon know how things
stand, and the result must be what it will. I have
chosen my course."

Constance was regarding him steadily. Her wrath

Our Friend the Charlatan

had ceased to flare, but it glowed through her countenance.

"You mean," she said, "that just at the critical moment of your career you are bent on doing the rashest thing you possibly could? And you ask me to believe that you are acting in this way before you even know whether you have a chance of gaining anything by it?"

"It had occurred to me," Lashmar replied, "that when you understood the state of things, you might be willing to exert yourself to help me. But that was before I learnt that you regarded me with contempt, if not with hatred. How the change has come about in you I am unable to understand. I have behaved to you with perfect frankness——"

"When, for instance, you wished me to admire you as a sociologist!"

"It's incredible," cried Dyce, "that you should harp on that paltry matter! Who, in our time, is an original thinker? Ideas are in the air! Every man uses his mind—if he has any—on any suggestion which recommends itself to him. If it was worth while, I could point out most important differences between the bio-sociological theory as matured by me and its crude presentment in that book you have got hold of. —By the bye, how did it come into your hands?"

After an instant's reflection, Constance told him of Mrs. Toplady's letter and the American magazine.

"And," he asked, "does Mrs. Toplady regard me as a contemptible plagiarist?"

"It is probable that she has certain thoughts."

Lashmar's eyes fell. He saw that Constance was watching him. In the confusion of his feelings all he could do was to jerk out an impatient laugh.

"It's no use," he exclaimed. "You and I have come to a deadlock. We no longer understand each other. I thought you were the kind of woman whom a man can treat as his equal, without fear of ridiculous misconceptions and hysterical scenes. One more disillusion!"

325

"Don't you think," asked Constance, with a bitter smile, "that you are preparing a good many others for yourself?"

"Of course, I know what you mean. There are certain things it wouldn't be easy to discuss with you at any time; you can't expect me to speak of them at present. Suppose it an illusion. I came to you, in all honesty, to tell you what had happened. I thought of you as my friend, as one who cared about my happiness."

"Why this morning?"

"For the reason I began by explaining. I have to come here to lunch."

"Would it surprise you, when you do come, to be met with the news that Lord Dymchurch has proposed to Miss Tomalin and been accepted?"

"Indeed," Dyce answered, smiling, "it would surprise me very much."

"Which is as much as to say that I was right, just now, in refusing to believe you. Do you know," Constance added, with fresh acerbity, "that you cut a very poor figure? As a diplomatist, you will not go very far. As an ordinary politician, I doubt whether you can make your way with such inadequate substitutes for common honesty. Perhaps you *do* represent the coming man. In that case, we must look anxiously for the coming woman to keep the world from collapse. Be so good, now, as to answer a plain question. You will do so, simply because you know that I have but to speak half-a-dozen words to Lady Ogram, and you would be spared the trouble of coming here to lunch. What is your scheme? If I had been as pliant as you expected, what would you have asked of me?"

"Merely to use your influence with Lady Ogram when she is vexed by learning that May Tomalin is not to marry Dymchurch. What could be simpler and more straightforward? Scheme there is none. I have done with that kind of thing. I wish to marry this girl for her own sake, but if I can keep Lady Ogram's

326

good-will at the same time, I suppose there's nothing very base in wishing to do so ? "

" You speak of 'vexation.' Do you really imagine that that word will describe Lady Ogram's state of mind if she learns that Lord Dymchurch is rejected ? "

" Of course there will be an uproar. We can't help that. We must face it, and hope in Lady Ogram's common-sense."

" Answer another question. How do you *know* that May Tomalin will refuse Lord Dymchurch ? "

" I had better refuse to answer. You talk much of honour. If you know what it means, you will accept my refusal as the only thing possible under the circumstances."

Constance stood in hesitation. It seemed as if she might concede this point, but at the critical moment jealous wrath again seized her, extinguishing the better motive.

" You will answer my question. You will tell me what has passed."

She glared at him, and it was Lashmar's turn to betray indecision.

" You are at my mercy," Constance exclaimed, "and you will do as I bid you."

Lashmar yielded to exasperation.

" I have enough of this," he cried angrily. " Go and do as you please ! Take your silly feminine revenge, and much good may it do you ! I have no more time to waste."

He caught up his hat and left the room.

Passing the foot of the staircase, he saw some one descending. It was May; involuntarily he stopped; the girl's gesture of alarm, bidding him be off, was disregarded. He waved to her, and she joined him.

" I've seen them both. It's all right. Keep up your courage ! "

" Go ! Go !" whispered May in fright. " Some one will see us."

" At lunch !"

Our Friend the Charlatan

He pressed her hand, smiled like a general in the thick of battle, and hurried away. Scarcely had he vanished through the portal when Constance, issuing from the library, encountered Miss Tomalin. May uttered an unnaturally suave "Good-morning!" The other looked her in the eyes, and said, in a voice of satisfaction:

"Mr. Lashmar has just been here. Didn't you see him?"

"Mr. Lashmar?—No."

Still gazing full at the confused face, Constance gave a little laugh, and passed on.

CHAPTER XXIII

At the door of the breakfast-room Constance was approached by Lady Ogram's maid, who in an undertone informed her that Dr. Baldwin had been sent for. Lady Ogram had passed a very bad night, but did not wish it to be made known to her guests, whom she hoped to meet at luncheon. Of the possibility of this, the maid declared herself very doubtful; she did not think the doctor would allow her mistress to get up.

"Let me know when the doctor is leaving," said Constance. "I should like to see him."

Sir William and his wife breakfasted with the two young ladies. Lord Dymchurch did not appear. When the others had left the room, Constance asked a servant if his lordship was down yet, and learnt that he had this morning gone away, leaving a note for Lady Ogram. At this moment word was brought to Miss Bride that Dr. Baldwin waited in the library. Constance replied that she would see him. Then, turning to the other attendant, she asked whether Lord Dymchurch's note had been delivered to Lady Ogram. It lay, she learnt, with the rest of the morning's letters, which the maid had not yet taken up. Thereupon Constance sought and found it, and carried it with her as she entered the library.

"How do you find your patient, doctor?" she inquired, in her usual tone.

"Quite unfit to get up to-day, though I fear she is determined to do so," replied Dr. Baldwin. "Wonderful, the influence of her mind upon her physical state. I found her alarmingly weak, but, as usual, she insisted
329

on hearing the news of the town, and something I was able to tell her acted with more restorative force than any drug in the pharmacopœia."

" What was that ? "

" Mr. Robb's will. I hear on good authority that he leaves not a penny to our hospital. Lady Ogram was delighted. He leaves the field clear for her. She declares that she will buy the site on Burgess Hill immediately. The will is dated fifteen years ago, they say ; no doubt he purposed making another."

" That, I am sure, was a cordial," exclaimed Constance. " Impossible for Mr. Robb to have done Lady Ogram a greater kindness."

After a few more inquiries concerning the patient, she let the doctor take his leave. Then she stood looking at the outside of Lord Dymchurch's letter, and wondering what might be its contents. Beyond a doubt they were of an explosive nature. Whatever his excuse, Lord Dymchurch's abrupt departure would enrage Lady Ogram. Had he been refused by May ? Or had something come to pass which made it impossible for him to offer marriage—something connected with Lashmar's early visit this morning ? That he had intended a proposal, Constance could not doubt. Meanwhile, she felt glad of the outbreak in prospect ; her mood desired tumultuous circumstances. What part she herself would play in to-day's drama she had not yet decided ; that must largely depend upon events. Her future was involved in the conflict of passions and designs which would soon be at its height. How much it would have helped her could she have read through the envelope now in her hand !

There came a knock at the door. Lady Ogram wished to speak with Miss Bride.

It was the rarest thing for the secretary to be summoned to her ladyship's bedroom. In the ante-chamber the maid encountered her.

" My lady means to get up," whispered this discreet attendant. " She thinks herself very much better, but

I am sure she is very ill indeed. I know the signs. The doctor forbade her to move, but I dursn't oppose her."

"Does she know that Lord Dymchurch has gone?" asked Constance.

"No, miss. I thought it better to say nothing just yet. Everything excites her so."

"You were very wise. Keep silence about it until Lady Ogram leaves her room."

"My lady has just asked for her letters, miss."

"Bring up those that have come by post. I will deliver the other myself."

Constance entered the bedroom. With cheeks already touched into ghastly semblance of warm life, with her surprising hair provisionally rolled into a diadem, the old autocrat lay against upright pillows. At sight of Constance, she raised her skeleton hand, and uttered a harsh croak of triumph.

"Do you know the news?" followed in scarce articulate utterance. "Robb's will! Nothing to the hospital—not a penny for town charities."

Constance affected equal rejoicing, for she knew how the singular old philanthropist had loathed the thought that Hollingford's new hospital might bear Robb's name instead of her own.

"But I beg you not to excite yourself," she added. "Try to think quietly——"

"Mind your own business!" broke in the thick voice, whilst the dark eyes flashed with exultation. "I want to know about Lord Dymchurch. What are the plans for this morning?"

"I don't think they are settled yet. It's still early."

"How is May this morning?"

"Very well, I think."

"I shall be down at midday, if not before. Tell Lord Dymchurch that."

The morning's correspondence was brought in. Lady Ogram glanced over her letters, and bade Constance reply to two or three of them. She gave, also,

Our Friend the Charlatan

many instructions as to matters which had been occupying her lately; her mind was abnormally active and lucid; at times her speech became so rapid that it was unintelligible.

"Now go and get to work," she said at length, coming to an abrupt close. "You've enough to occupy you all the morning."

Constance had paid little attention to these commands, and, on returning to the library, she made no haste to begin upon her secretarial duties. For more than an hour she sat brooding. Only as a relief to her thoughts did she at length begin to write letters. It was shortly before midday when again there came a summons from Lady Ogram; obeying it, Constance took Lord Dymchurch's letter in her hand.

Lady Ogram had risen. She was in the little drawing-room up-stairs, reclining upon a sofa; the effort of walking thus far had exhausted her.

"I hear that Mr. Lashmar has called this morning," she began, half-raising herself, but at once sinking back again. "What did he come about? Can't he come to lunch?"

"Yes, he will be here at one o'clock," Constance replied.

"Then why did he come? It was before nine. What had he to say?"

"He wanted to speak to me in private."

"Oh, I suppose that's privileged," returned the autocrat, smiling. "What have you got there? Something just come?"

"It's a note for you from Lord Dymchurch."

"From Lord Dymchurch? Give it me at once, then. Where is he? Why couldn't he wait till I came down?"

She tore the envelope with weak, trembling hands. Constance watched her as she read. Of a sudden the shrunk, feeble figure sprang upright, and stood as though supported with the vigorous muscles of youth.

"Do you know what this contains?" sounded a

clear, hard voice, strangely unlike that which had just been speaking.

"I have no idea."

"But you knew that he had left?"

"Yes, I knew. I kept it from you till now, because I feared you were not well enough to bear the agitation."

"And who," cried the other fiercely, "gave you authority to detain letters addressed to me? What have *you* to do with my health? When did Lord Dymchurch leave?"

"Whilst we were at breakfast," Constance answered, with a great effort at self-command. "He saw nobody."

"Then you lied to me when you came up before?"

"I think, Lady Ogram," said Constance, standing rigid and with white face, "you might give me credit for good intentions. It was nothing to me whether you heard this news then or later; but I knew that you had passed a sleepless night, and that the doctor had been sent for."

"You knew—you knew!" cried the listener, with savage scorn. "Did you know why Lord Dymchurch had gone?"

"I took it for granted that it had something to do with Miss Tomalin."

"Answer me in plain words, without a lie, and without shiftiness. Do you know that Lord Dymchurch has proposed to May and been refused?"

"I did not know it."

"You suspected as much."

"I thought it possible. But the business was none of mine, and I gave very little heed to it."

Lady Ogram had begun to totter. She let herself sink upon the sofa, and re-read the letter that shook in her hand.

"He says he has a sister ill. Did you hear anything of that?"

"Nothing at all."

The autocrat stared for a moment, as though trying to read Constance's thoughts; then she waved her hand.

"Go back to your work. Stay in the library till you hear from me again."

Constance quivered with the impulse to make indignant reply, but prudence prevailed. She bent her head to conceal wrathful features, and in silence went from the room.

Five minutes later May Tomalin entered by the awful door. She knew what was before her, and had braced her nerves, but at the first sight of Lady Ogram a sinking heart drew all the blood from her cheeks. Encountering the bloodshot glare from those fleshless eye-caverns, she began to babble a "Good-morning, aunt!" But the words failed, and her frightened simper, meant for a smile, passed into mere blankness of visage.

"Come here, May. Is it true that you have refused Lord Dymchurch?"

The voice was less terrifying than her aunt's countenance had led her to expect. She was able to recover her wits sufficiently to make the reply she had spent all the morning in preparing.

"Refused him? I didn't mean that. He must have misunderstood me."

"What *did* you mean, then?"

"I hardly knew what Lord Dymchurch meant," answered May, trying to look playfully modest.

"Let us have no nonsense," sounded in stern accents. "Lord Dymchurch writes me a letter, saying distinctly that he has proposed to you, and that you have refused him, and then he goes off without a word to any one. Did you know he was leaving this morning?"

"Certainly not," answered the girl, with a bold plunge into mendacity. "I expected to see him at breakfast. Then I was told he was gone. I don't understand it at all."

From the moment of entering the room, she had put

away all thought of truthfulness. This, plainly, was no time for it. As soon as possible, she would let Dyce Lashmar know that they must feign and temporize; the policy of courage looked all very well from a distance, but was quite another thing in the presence of the mistress of Rivenoak enraged. Lashmar must caution Constance, who seemingly (much to May's surprise) had submitted to his dictation at this juncture. For a time nothing could be done beyond cloaking what had really happened, and soothing Lady Ogram's wrath with apparent submission.

" When did you see him last ?" pursued the questioner.

" This morning, before breakfast, for a few minutes in the garden."

Better to be veracious so far, thought May. She might otherwise fall into self-contradiction.

" Was it an appointment ?"

" No. By chance. I never thought of meeting him."

" And what did he say to you ? Tell me his words."

" I couldn't possibly recall them," said May, who had seated herself and was becoming all but calm. " Lord Dymchurch has a very vague way of talking. He rambles from one subject to another."

" But didn't he say anything at all about marriage ?" cried Lady Ogram, in exasperation.

" He spoke of his position and his prospects. Perhaps he hoped I should understand—but it was all so vague."

" Why, then, the man is a scoundrel ! He never proposed to you at all, and he runs away, leaving a lying letter behind him. Yet I should never have thought that of Lord Dymchurch."

She fixed her eyes on May, and added fiercely :

" Are you telling me the truth ?"

The girl bridled, staring straight before her with indignant evasiveness of look.

" My dear aunt ! How can you ask me such a ques-

tion! Of course, I may have misunderstood Lord
Dymchurch, but, if it hadn't been for what you have
once or twice said to me, I really shouldn't ever have
supposed that he meant anything. He talks in such a
rambling way——"

She grew voluble. Lady Ogram listened awhile,
then cut her short.

"Very well. There has been some queer sort of
mistake, that's plain. I should like to know what
Lord Dymchurch means. Why couldn't he see me,
like an honest man? It's very extraordinary, this
running away before breakfast, saying good-bye to
nobody."

She mused stormily, her eye ever and again turning
upon the girl.

"Look here, May; do you think Constance knows
anything about it?"

"I really can't say—I don't see how——"

"It was she that brought me his letter. Do you
think he spoke to her?"

"About me?" exclaimed May uneasily. "Oh! I
don't think so—I never noticed that they were
friendly."

"Ring the bell."

Constance Bride was sent for. Some moments
passed; Lady Ogram stamped impatiently. She
ordered May to ring again, and demanded why Miss
Bride kept her waiting. Considerably more than five
minutes had elapsed before the figure of the secretary
appeared; her face wore an expression of proud indifference, and at the sight of May's subdued, timid
air, she smiled coldly.

"Why have you been so long?" cried Lady Ogram.

"I came as soon as I could," was the clear reply.

"Now, listen to me, Constance," broke vehemently
from the bloodless lips. "I'll have no nonsense! You
understand that? I'll not be played with. Deceive
me, or treat me in any way unbecomingly, and you
shall remember it the longest day you live. I want to

know whether Lord Dymchurch said anything to you
to explain his sudden departure."

" To me ?   Certainly not."

" Now mind !   I'll get at the truth of this.   You
know me !   May says that Lord Dymchurch never
proposed to her at all.   What do you make of that ? "

Constance glanced at Miss Tomalin, whose eyes fell.
Again she smiled.

" It's very strange," she answered, with a certain air
of sympathy.   " That's really all I can say.   It's
impossible to have any opinion about such a personal
matter, which doesn't in the least concern me."

" Please remember, aunt," put in May, " that I only
said I didn't *understand* Lord Dymchurch in that
sense."

" Are you a fool, girl ! " croaked the autocrat
violently.   " I never thought you so, and if he had said
anything that was meant for an offer of marriage, you
would have understood it quickly enough.   Either
you're telling me the truth, or you're lying.   Either he
proposed to you, or he didn't."

May caught the look of Constance turned upon her ;
it suggested amusement, and this touched her feelings
far more deeply than the old lady's strong language.

" I am obliged to remind you, aunt," she said, her
cheek flushing, " that I have no experience of—of this
kind of thing.   If I made a mistake, I think it excusable.   I see that Miss Bride thinks it funny, but she
has the advantage of me in age, and in—in several
other ways."

Even whilst speaking, May knew that she committed
an imprudence ; she remembered all that depended
upon Constance's disposition towards her.   And, indeed,
she could not have spoken more unwisely.   In the
enflamed state of Constance's pride, a feminine slap
such as this sent such a tingling along her nerves
that she quivered visibly.   It flashed into her mind
that Dyce Lashmar had all but certainly talked of her
to May, with significant look and tone, whatever his

words. How much had he told her? Lady Ogram's voice was again heard.

"Well, that's true. You're only a child, and perhaps you said something which sounded as you didn't mean it."

Constance was gazing at the speaker. Her lips moved, as if in a nervously ineffectual effort to say something.

"Miss Bride can go back to her work again," said Lady Ogram, as if dismissing a servant.

May smiled, openly and disdainfully. She could not resist the pleasure of showing her superiority. The smile had not died away when Constance spoke.

"I will ask your permission to stay for a few minutes longer, Lady Ogram. As Miss Tomalin has so satis-factorily explained her part in this unfortunate affair, I think I had better use this opportunity for making known to you something which concerns her, and which, I am sure, will interest you very much. It won't take me long—if you feel able to listen."

"What is it?" asked the autocrat sharply.

"You are aware that Mr. Lashmar called very early this morning. He came, as I said, on private business. He had something of importance to tell me, and he asked my help in a great difficulty."

"Something about the election?"

"It had nothing whatever to do with that. I'll put it in the fewest possible words, not to waste your time and my own. Mr. Lashmar began by saying that if I didn't mind, he would be glad to be released from his engagement to me."

"What!"

"Pray don't let there be any misunderstanding—this time," said Constance, whose grave irony was, perhaps, somewhat too fine for the intelligence of either of her hearers. "Mr. Lashmar behaved like a man of honour, and I quite approve of the way in which he expressed himself. His words would have been per-fectly intelligible—even to Miss Tomalin. Admitting

his right to withdraw from the engagement if he had
conscientious objections to it, I ventured to ask Mr.
Lashmar whether there was any particular reason for
his wish to be released. He paid me the compliment
of perfect frankness. His reason was, that he wished
to marry some one else."

"And who is that?" came hoarsely from Lady
Ogram.

"Miss Tomalin."

May had lost her natural colour. She could not take
her eyes from the speaker; her lips were parted, her
forehead was wrinkled into a strange expression of
frightened animosity. Until the utterance of her
name she had hoped against hope that Constance did
not intend the worst. For the first time in her life
she felt herself struck without pity, and the mere fact
of such stern enmity affected her with as much surprise
as dread. She would have continued staring at
Constance, had not an alarming sound, a sort of moaning snarl, such as might proceed from some suddenly
wounded beast, caused her to turn towards her aunt.
The inarticulate sound was followed by words which
seemed to be painfully forced out.

"Go on—what else?—go on, I tell you!"

The speaker's breath came with difficulty. She was
bent forward, her eyes starting, her scraggy throat
working as if in anguish. Constance had stepped
nearer to her.

"Are you ill, Lady Ogram? Shall I call help?"

"Go on! Go *on*, I tell you!" was the hoarse reply.
"I hadn't thought of that. I see, now. What next
did he say?"

"Mr. Lashmar," pursued Constance, in a voice somewhat less under control, "did me the honour to say
that he felt sure I had only his interests and his
happiness at heart. He knew that there might be
considerable difficulties in his way, even after it had
been made known that he was free to turn his attention
to Miss Tomalin, and he was so good as to request my

assistance. It had occurred to him that I might be able to present his case in a favourable light to you, Lady Ogram. Naturally, I was anxious to do my best. Perhaps this is hardly the moment to pursue the subject. Enough for the present to have made known Mr. Lashmar's state of mind."

Lady Ogram seemed to have overcome her physical anguish. She sat upright once more, and, looking at May, asked in voice only just above a whisper :

"What have you to say to this ?"

"What can I say," exclaimed the girl, with high-voiced vehemence. "I know nothing about it. Of course, it's easy enough to believe that Mr. Lashmar wants to get out of his engagement to Miss Bride." She laughed scornfully. "He——"

She stopped, checking in her throat words which she suddenly remembered would be fatal to the attitude she had assumed.

"Go on !" cried Lady Ogram. "He—what ?"

"I was only going to say that Mr. Lashmar might easily have thought that he had made a mistake. Well, that's my opinion; if it isn't pleasant to Miss Bride, I can't help it. I tell the truth, that's all."

"And that I will have !" said her aunt, with new self-command. "The very last word of it, mind you ! Constance, why are you standing all this time ? Sit down—here, on this chair. Now I want you to repeat what you have told me. First of all, at what o'clock did this happen ?"

"At about half-past eight this morning."

Had it been possible, Constance would have rolled oblivion over all she had spoken. Already she found her vengeance a poor, savourless thing ; she felt that it belittled her. The fire of her wrath burnt low, and seemed like to smoulder out under self-contempt. She spoke in a dull, mechanical voice, and gazed at vacancy.

"May," Lady Ogram resumed, "when did you get up this morning ?"

"At about—oh, about half-past seven, I think."

"Did you go out before breakfast?"

"I have told you that I did, aunt. I saw Lord Dymchurch in the garden."

"I remember," said her aunt, with a lowering, suspicious look. "And you saw Mr. Lashmar as he was coming to the house?"

"No. I didn't see him at all."

"How was that? If you were in the garden?"

May glibly explained that her encounter with Lord Dymchurch took place not before, but behind, the house. She had a spot of red on each cheek; her ears were scarlet; she sat with clenched hands, and stared at the lower part of her aunt's face.

"Constance," pursued the questioner, whose eyes had become small and keen as her utterance grew more sober, "tell it me all over again. It's worth hearing twice. He began——"

The other obeyed, reciting her story in a curt, lifeless way, so that it sounded less significant than before.

"And you promised to help him?" asked Lady Ogram, who repeatedly glanced at May.

"No, I didn't. I lost my temper, and said I don't know what foolish things."

This was self-punishment, but it, too, sounded idle in her ears as soon as she had spoken.

"But you consented to release him?"

"Of course."

"Now, look at me. Have you told me all he said?"

"All."

"Look at me! If I find that you are keeping any secret—! I shall know everything, you understand that. I won't sleep till I know everything that has been going on. Deceive me, if you dare!"

"I am not deceiving you," answered Constance wearily. "You have heard all I know."

"Now, then, for what you suspect," said Lady Ogram, leaning towards her. "Turn your mind inside out. Tell me what you *think!*"

Our Friend the Charlatan

"That is soon done. I suspect—indeed, I believe—that Mr. Lashmar's behaviour is that of a man with an over-excited mind. He thinks everything is within his reach, and everything permitted to him. I believe he spoke to me quite honestly, seriously thinking I might somehow plead his cause with you."

"That isn't what I want. Do you suspect that he had any hopes to go upon?"

"I care so little about it," answered Constance, "that I can't form any conjecture. All I can say is, that such a man would be quite capable of great illusions —of believing anything that flattered his vanity."

Lady Ogram was dissatisfied. She kept a brief silence, with her eyes on May's countenance.

"Ring the bell," were her next words.

Constance rose and obeyed. A servant entered.

"When Mr. Lashmar arrives," said Lady Ogram, "you will bring him at once to me here."

"Mr. Lashmar has this moment arrived, my lady."

CHAPTER XXIV

"Ask him to come— No! Stay!"

Lady Ogram stood up, not without difficulty. She took a step or two forwards, as if trying whether she had the strength to walk. Then she looked at her two companions, who had both risen.

"Constance, give me your arm. I will go down-stairs."

They left the room, May slowly following and watching them with anxiety she vainly endeavoured to disguise. The descent was slow. Constance held firmly the bony arm which clung to her own, and felt it quiver at every step. Just before they reached the bottom, Lady Ogram ordered the servant who came after them to pass before and conduct Mr. Lashmar into the library. At the foot of the stairs she paused; on her forehead stood little points of sweat, and her lips betrayed the painful effort with which she continued to stand upright.

"May,"—she looked into the girl's face—"if I don't come when the luncheon-bell rings, you will excuse me to Sir William and Lady Amys, and take my place at table."

Slowly she walked on, still supported by Constance, to the library door. When it was opened, and she saw Lashmar awaiting her within (he had passed into the library by the inner door which communicated with the drawing-room), she spoke to her companion.

"Thank you, Constance. If I don't come, sit down with the others. I hope your meal will not be disturbed, but I may have to send for you."

"Lady Ogram——"

343

Constance began in a low, nervous voice. She was looking at Lashmar, who, with an air of constraint, moved towards them.

"What is it?"

"Will you let me speak to you for a moment before——"

"No!"

With this stern monosyllable, Lady Ogram dismissed her, entered the room, and closed the door.

Then her face changed. A smile, which was more than half a grin of pain, responded to Lashmar's rather effusive salutation; but she spoke not a word, and, when she had sunk into the nearest chair, her eyes, from beneath drooping lids, searched the man's countenance.

"Sit down," were her first words.

Lashmar, convinced that Constance Bride had sought to avenge herself, tried to screw up his courage. He looked very serious; he sat stiffly; he kept his eye upon Lady Ogram's.

"Well, what have you to tell me?" she asked, with a deliberation more disconcerting than impatience would have been.

"Everything goes on pretty well."

"Does it? I'm glad you think so."

"What do you allude to, Lady Ogram?" Lashmar inquired, with grave respectfulness.

"What do *you*?"

"I was speaking of things at Hollingford."

"And I was thinking of things at Rivenoak."

Lashmar's brain worked feverishly. What did she know? If Constance had betrayed him, assuredly May also must have been put to the question, and with what result? He was spared long conjecture.

"Let us understand each other," said the autocrat, who seemed to be recovering strength as the need arose. "I hear that you want to break off with Constance Bride. She is no bride for you. Is that the case?"

Our Friend the Charlatan

" I am sorry to say it is the truth, Lady Ogram."

Having uttered these words, Dyce felt the heroic mood begin to stir in him. He had no alternative now, and would prove himself equal to the great occasion. She smiled.

" You want to marry some one else ? "

" I'm sure you will recognize," Dyce replied, rather in his academic tone, " that I am doing my best to act honourably, and without giving any unnecessary pain. Under certain circumstances a man is not entirely master of himself."

There sounded the luncheon-bell. It rang a vague hope to Lashmar, whose voice dropped.

" Are you hungry ? " asked the hostess, with impatience.

" Not particularly, thank you."

" Then I think we had better get our little talk over and done with. We shan't keep the others waiting."

Dyce accepted this as a good omen. " Our little talk ! " He had not dreamt of such urbanity. Here was the result of courage and honesty. Evidently his bearing had made a good impression upon the old despot. He began to look cheerful.

" Nothing could please me better."

" Go on, then," said Lady Ogram dryly. " You were saying——"

" I wish to use complete frankness with you," Dyce resumed. " As I think you know, I always prefer the simple, natural way of looking at things. So, for instance, in my relations with women; I have always aimed at fair and candid behaviour; I have tried to treat women as they themselves, justly enough, wish to be treated, without affectation, without insincerity. Constance knew my views, and she approved them. When our friendship developed into an engagement of marriage, we both of us regarded the step in a purely reasonable light; we did not try to deceive ourselves, and, less still, to deceive each other. But a man cannot always gauge his nature. To use the

Our Friend the Charlatan

common phrase, I did not think I should ever fall in
love; yet that happened to me, suddenly, unmistakably.
What course had I to follow ? Obviously I must act
on my own principles; I must be straightforward,
simple, candid. As soon as my mind was made up, I
came to Constance."

He broke off, observed the listener's face, and added
with an insinuating smile :

"There was the *other* course—what is called the
unselfish, the heroic. Unfortunately, heroism of that
kind is only another name for deliberate falsehood, in
word and deed, and I confess I hadn't the courage for
it. Unselfishness, which means calculated deception,
seems to me by no means admirable. It was not an
easy thing to go to Constance and tell her what I had
to tell; but I knew that she herself would much prefer
it to the sham-noble alternative. And I am equally
sure, Lady Ogram, what your own view will be of the
choice that lay before me."

The listener made no sort of response to this appeal.

"And what had Constance to say to you ?" she
asked.

Lashmar hesitated, his embarrassment half-genuine,
half-feigned.

"Here," he replied, in a thoughtfully suspended
voice, "I find myself on very delicate ground. I hardly
feel that I should be justified in repeating what passed
between us. I hoped you had already heard it. Was
it not from Constance that you learnt ?"

"Don't begin to question *me*," broke in Lady Ogram,
with sudden severity. "What I know, and how I
know it, is none of your business. You'll have the
goodness to tell me whatever I ask you."

Dyce made a gesture of deprecating frankness.

"Personally," he said, in a low voice, "I admit your
right to be kept fully informed of all that comes to
pass in this connection. Will it be enough if I say
that Constance accepted my view of what had
happened ?"

346

Our Friend the Charlatan

"Did you tell her everything that *had* happened?" asked Lady Ogram, looking him in the eyes.

"Not in detail," Dyce replied, rather nervously, for he could not with certainty interpret that stern look. "You will understand that—that I was not at liberty —that I had to respect——"

He came near to losing himself between the conflicting suggestions of prudence and hopefulness. At the sight of his confusion, Lady Ogram smiled grimly.

"You mean," she said, in a voice which seemed to croak indulgence, "that you had no right to tell Constance anything about Miss Tomalin?"

Lashmar's courage revived. He suspected that the old autocrat knew everything, that both girls had already gone through the ordeal of a private interview with her, and had yielded up their secrets. If so, plainly the worst was over, and nothing would now serve but sincerity.

"That is what I mean," he answered, quietly and respectfully, admiring his own dignity as he spoke.

"We are beginning to understand each other," said Lady Ogram, the grim smile still on her face. "I don't mind telling you now that I have spoken both with Constance and with May."

Lashmar manifested his relief. He moved into an easier posture; his countenance brightened; he said within himself that destiny was bearing him on to glorious things.

"I'm very glad indeed to hear that, Lady Ogram! It puts my mind at rest."

"I have talked with them both," continued the reassuring voice, which struggled with hoarseness. "That they told me the truth, I have no doubt; both of them know me too well to do anything else. Constance, I understand, had your authority for speaking to me, so her part was easy."

"She has a fine, generous spirit!" exclaimed Dyce, with the glow of genuine enthusiasm.

Our Friend the Charlatan

"Well for you that she has. As for May, you had put her into a more difficult position."

"I fear so. But I am sure, Lady Ogram, that you dealt with her very kindly."

"Exactly." The smile was very grim indeed, and the voice very hoarse. "But the things I couldn't ask May to tell me, I expect to hear from you. Begin with this morning. You met her, I understand, before you came to the house to see Constance."

Dyce fell straight into the trap. He spoke almost joyously.

"Yes; we met at eight o'clock."

"Of course by appointment."

"Yes, by appointment."

"The best will be for you to begin at the beginning and tell the story in your own way. I've heard all my niece cared to tell me; now I give you the chance of telling your own tale. All I ask is the truth. Tell me the truth, from point to point."

At the pass he had reached, Lashmar asked nothing better. He was befooled and bedazzled. Every trouble seemed of a sudden to be lifted from his mind. Gratitude to Constance, who had proved so much better than her word, romantic devotion to May, who had so bravely declared her love, filled him with fervours such as he had never known. He saw himself in a resplendent light; his attitude was noble, his head bent with manly modesty, and, when he began to speak, there was something in his voice which he had never yet been able to command, a virile music, to which he listened with delighted appreciation.

"I obey you, Lady Ogram; I obey you frankly and gladly. I must go back to the day of Miss Tomalin's return from London. You will remember I told you that on that day I was in town, and in the afternoon, early, I called at Mrs. Toplady's."

Omitting the fact of his having told May about the relations between Miss Bride and himself, he narrated all else with perfect truth. So pleasant was the sense of veracity, that he dwelt on unimportant particulars, and lengthened out the story in a way which would have made it intolerably tedious to any other hearer. Lady Ogram, however, found it none too long. The smile had died from her face; her lips were compressed, and from time to time her eyes turned upon the speaker with a fierce glare; but Lashmar paid no heed to these trifles. He ended at length with beaming visage, his last sentences having a touch of emotion which greatly pleased him.

"Ring the bell," said Lady Ogram, pointing to the electric-button.

Glad to stand up and move, Dyce did her bidding. Only a few moments elapsed before Constance Bride and May Tomalin entered the room.

"Constance, come here," said Lady Ogram. "You" —she glared at May—"stand where I can have a good view of you."

Lashmar had welcomed their entrance with a smile. The voice and manner of the autocrat slightly disturbed him, but he made allowance for her brusque ways, and continued to smile at May, who looked pale and frightened.

"Constance, did you know, or did you not, that these two had a meeting this morning in the park before Mr. Lashmar came to see you?"

"No, I knew nothing of it," answered Miss Bride coldly.

"And did you know that they had met before at the same place and time, and that they came from town together by the same train, and that there was a regular understanding between them to deceive you and me?"

"I knew nothing of all this."

"Look at her!" exclaimed Lady Ogram, pointing at the terrified girl. "This is her gratitude; this is her honesty. She has lied to me in every word she spoke! Lord Dymchurch offered her marriage, and she tried to make me believe that he hadn't done so at all, that he was a dishonourable shuffler——"

Our Friend the Charlatan

"Aunt!" exclaimed May, coming forward with hurried step. "He did *not* offer me marriage! I'll tell you everything. Lord Dymchurch saw me by chance this morning—Mr. Lashmar and me—saw us together in the park, and he understood, and spoke to me about it, and said that the only thing he could do was to tell you I had refused him——"

"Oh, that's it, is it?" broke in the hoarse voice, all but inarticulate with fury. "Then he, too, is a liar; that makes one more."

Lashmar stood in bewilderment. He caught May's eye, and saw that he had nothing but hostility to expect from her.

"*There* is the greatest of all!" cried the girl, with a violent gesture. "He has told you all about *me*, but has he told all about himself?"

"Lady Ogram," said Dyce, with offended dignity, "you should remember by what means you obtained my confidence. You told me that Miss Tomalin had already confessed everything to you. I naturally believed you incapable of falsehood."

"Being yourself such a man of honour!" Lady Ogram interrupted, with savage scorn. "Constance, you are the only one who has not told me lies, and you have been shamefully treated."

"You think she has told you no lies?" cried May, her voice at the high pitch of exasperation. "Wait a moment. This man has told you that he came down from London in the train with me; but did he tell you what he talked about? The first thing he disclosed to me was that the engagement between him and Miss Bride was a mere pretence. Finding you wished them to marry, they took counsel together, and plotted to keep you in good-humour by pretending to be engaged. This he told me himself."

Lady Ogram turned upon Lashmar, who met her eyes defiantly.

"You believe that?" he asked, in a contemptuous tone.

Our Friend the Charlatan

She turned to Constance, whose face showed much the same expression.

" Is that true ? "

" I shall answer no charge brought by Miss Tomalin," was the cold reply.

"And you are right." Lady Ogram faced to May. "I give you half-an-hour to pack your luggage and leave the house! Be off!"

The girl burst into an hysterical laugh, and ran from the room. For some moments Lady Ogram sat looking towards the door; then, sinking together in exhaustion, she let her eyes move from one to the other of the two faces before her. Lashmar and Constance had exchanged no look; they stood in sullen attitude, hands behind them, staring at vacancy.

" I have something to say to you." The voice that broke the silence was so faint as to be but just audible. " Come nearer."

The two approached.

" That girl has gone. She is nothing to me, and nothing to you. Constance, are you willing to marry Mr. Lashmar ? "

There was no reply.

"Do you hear?" whispered Lady Ogram, with a painful effort to speak louder. " Answer me."

" How can you expect me to be willing to marry him ? " exclaimed Constance, in whom a great struggle was going on. Her cheeks were flushed, and tears of humiliation stood in her eyes.

" You!' Lady Ogram addressed Lashmar. " Will you marry her ? "

" How is it possible, Lady Ogram," replied Dyce, in an agony of nervousness, " to answer such a question under these circumstances ? "

"But you *shall* answer!" sounded in a choked sort of scream. " I give you the choice, both of you. Either you are married in three days from now, or you go about your business, like that lying girl. You can get a licence, and be married at once. Which

Our Friend the Charlatan

is it to be? I give you three days, not an hour more."

Lashmar had gone very pale. He looked at his partner in the dilemma.

"Constance," fell from his lips, "will you marry me?"

There came an answer which he could just hear, but which was inaudible to Lady Ogram.

"Speak, girl! Yes or no!" croaked their tormentor.

"She has consented," said Dyce.

"Then be off and get the licence! Don't lose a minute. I suppose you'll have to go to London for it? Constance, give me your arm. I must go and excuse myself to my guests."

Constance bent to her, and Lady Ogram, clutching at the offered arm, endeavoured to rise. It was in vain; she had not the strength to stand.

"Mr. Lashmar!" She spoke in a thick mumble, looking with wild eyes. "Come—other side—arm——"

She was drooping, falling. Lashmar had only just time to catch and support her.

"What is it?" he asked, staring at Constance as he supported the helpless form. "Has she fainted?"

"Lay her down, and I'll call for help."

A moment, and Sir William Amys came hastening into the room, followed by his wife and two or three servants. Lady Ogram gave no sign of life, but the baronet declared that her pulse was still beating. Silent, still, with half-closed eyes, the old autocrat of Rivenoak lay stretched upon a sofa awaiting the arrival of Dr. Baldwin.

CHAPTER XXV

Sir William Amys drew Lashmar aside.

"What brought this about?" he asked. "What has been going on?"

Dyce, whose nerves were in a tremulous state, did not easily command himself to the quiet dignity which the occasion required. He saw that the baronet regarded him with something of suspicion, and the tone in which he was addressed seemed to him rather too much that of a superior. With an effort of the muscles he straightened himself and looked his questioner in the face.

"There has been a painful scene, Sir William, between Lady Ogram and her niece. Very much against my will, I was made a witness of it. I knew the danger of such agitation, and did my best to calm Lady Ogram. Miss Tomalin had left the room, and the worst seemed to be over. We were talking quietly when the blow fell."

"That is all you have to say?"

"I am not sure that I understand you, Sir William," Lashmar replied coldly. Being slightly the taller, he had an advantage in being able to gaze at the baronet's forehead instead of meeting his look. "You would hardly wish me to speak of circumstances which are purely private."

"Certainly not," said the other, and abruptly moved away.

Lady Amys and Constance stood together near the couch on which Lady Ogram was lying. With a glance in that direction Lashmar walked towards the

353

door, hesitated a moment, went out into the hall. He had no wish to encounter May; just as little did he wish for a private interview with Constance; yet it appeared to him that he was obliged by decorum to remain in or near the house until the doctor's arrival. Presently he went out into the terrace, and loitered in view of the front windows. That Lady Ogram was dying he felt not the least doubt. Beneath his natural perturbation there stirred a joyous hope.

Nearly an hour passed before Dr. Baldwin's carriage rolled up the drive. Shortly after came another medical man, who had been summoned at the same time. Whilst waiting impatiently for the result of their visits, Lashmar mused on the fact that May Tomalin certainly had not taken her departure; it was not likely now that she would quit the house; perhaps at this moment she was mistress of Rivenoak.

Fatigue compelled him at length to enter, and in the hall he saw Constance. Involuntarily, she half-turned from him, but he walked up to her, and spoke in a low voice, asking what the doctors said. Constance replied that she knew nothing.

" Are they still in the library ? "

" No. Lady Ogram has been carried up-stairs."

" Then I'll go in and wait."

He watched the clock for another half-hour, then the door opened, and a servant, evidently sent to him, brought information that Lady Ogram remained in the same unconscious state.

" I will call this evening to make inquiry," said Lashmar, and thereupon left the house.

Reaching his hotel at Hollingford, he ordered a meal and ate heartily. Then he stepped over to the office of the *Express*, and made known to Breakspeare the fact of Lady Ogram's illness; they discussed the probabilities with much freedom, Breakspeare remarking how odd it would be if Lady Ogram so soon followed her old enemy. At about nine in the evening Dyce inquired at Rivenoak lodge; he learnt that there

Our Friend the Charlatan

was still no change whatever in the patient's condition;
Dr. Baldwin remained in the house. Dyce walked
back to Hollingford, and, in spite of his anxious
thoughts, slept particularly well. Immediately after
breakfast he drove out to Rivenoak, and had no sooner
alighted from the cab than he saw that the blinds were
down at the lodge windows. Lady Ogram, he was
informed, had died between two and three o'clock.

He dismissed his vehicle, and walked along the roads
skirting the wall of the park. Now, indeed, was his
life's critical moment. How long must elapse before
he could know the contents of Lady Ogram's will? In
a very short time he would have need of money; he
had been disbursing freely, and could not face the
responsibilities of the election without assurance that
his finances would soon be on a satisfactory footing.
He thought nervously of Constance Bride, more
nervously still of May Tomalin. Constance's position
was doubtless secure; she would enter upon the " trust "
of which so much had been said; but what was her
state of mind with regard to *him?* Had not the
consent to marry him simply been forced from her?
May, who was now possessor of a great fortune, might
perchance forget yesterday's turmoil, and be willing to
renew their amorous relations; he felt such a thing to
be by no means impossible. Meanwhile, ignorance
would keep him in a most perplexing and embarrassing position. The Amyses, who, of course, knew nothing
of the rupture of his ostensible engagement, would be
surprised if he did not call upon Miss Bride, yet it
behoved him, for the present, to hold aloof from both
the girls, not to compromise his future chances with
either of them. The dark possibility that neither one
nor the other of them would come to his relief he
resolutely kept out of mind; that would be immediate
ruin, and a certain buoyancy of heart assured him that
he had no such catastrophe to fear. Prudence only
was required; perhaps in less than a week all his
anxieties would be over, for once and all.

Our Friend the Charlatan

He decided to call, this afternoon, upon Lady Amys. The interview would direct his future behaviour.

It was the day of Robb's funeral, and he had meant to absent himself from Hollingford. He shut himself in his private sitting-room at the Saracen's Head, wrote many letters, and tried to read. At four o'clock he drove out again to Rivenoak, only to learn that Lady Amys could receive no one. He left a card. After all, perhaps, this was the simplest and best way out of his difficulty.

As he turned away from the door another cab drove up, and from it alighted Mr. Kerchever. Dyce had no difficulty in recognizing Lady Ogram's solicitor, but discretion kept his head averted, and Mr. Kerchever, though observing him, did not speak.

By the post next morning he received a formal announcement of Lady Ogram's death, with an invitation to attend her funeral. So far, so good. He was now decidedly light-hearted. Both Constance and May, he felt sure, would appreciate his delicacy in holding aloof, in seeking no sort of communication with them. Prudence! Reserve! The decisive day approached.

Meanwhile, having need of a black suit, he had consulted Breakspeare as to the tailor it behoved him to patronise. Unfortunately, the only good tailor at Hollingford was a Conservative, who prided himself on having clad the late M.P. for many years. Lashmar of necessity applied to an inferior artist, but in this man, who was summoned to wait upon him at the hotel, he found a zealous politician, whose enthusiasm more than compensated for sartorial defects.

"I have already been canvassing for you, sir," declared the tailor. "I can answer for twenty or thirty votes in my neighbourhood——"

"I am greatly obliged to you, Mr. Bingham," Dyce replied, in his suavest tone. "We have a hard fight before us, but if I find many adherents such as you——"

Our Friend the Charlatan

The tailor went away and declared to all his acquaintances that if they wished their borough to be represented by a *gentleman*, they had only to vote for the
Liberal candidate.

As a matter of policy Dyce had allowed it to be
supposed that he was a man of substantial means.
With the members of his committee he talked in a
large way whenever pecuniary matters came up. Every
day some one dined with him at the hotel, and the little
dinners were as good as the Saracen's Head could
furnish; special wines had been procured for his table.
Of course, the landlord made such facts commonly
known, and the whole establishment bowed low before
this impressive guest. All day long the name of Mr.
Lashmar sounded in bar and parlour, in coffee-room
and commercial-room. Never had Dyce known such
delicious thrills of self-respect as under the roof of this
comfortable hostelry. If he were elected he would
retain rooms, in permanence, at the hotel.—Unless, of
course, destiny made his home at Rivenoak!

Curiosity as to what was going on at the great house
kept him in a feverish state during these days before
the funeral. Breakspeare, whom he saw frequently,
supposed him to be in constant communication with
Rivenoak, and at times hinted a desire for news, but
Lashmar's cue was a dignified silence, which seemed
to conceal things of high moment. Sir William and
Lady Amys he knew to be still in the house of mourning; he presumed that May Tomalin had not gone
away, and it taxed his imagination to picture the
terms on which she lived with Constance. At the
funeral, no doubt, he would see them both; probably
would have to exchange words with them—an embarrassing necessity.

Hollingford, of course, was full of gossip about the
dead woman. The old, old scandal occupied tongues
malicious or charitable. Rivenoak domestics had
spread the news of the marble bust, to which some of
them attached a superstitious significance; Breakspeare

heard, and credited, a rumour that the bust dated from the day when its original led a brilliant, abandoned life in the artist world of London; but, naturally, he could not speak of this with Lashmar. Highly imaginative stories, too, went about concerning Miss Tomalin, who, every one took for granted, was the heiress of Lady Ogram's immense wealth. By some under-current, no doubt of servants'-hall origin, the name of Lord Dymchurch had come into circulation, and the editor of the *Express* ventured to inquire of Lashmar whether it was true that Miss Tomalin had rejected an offer of marriage from this peer. Perfectly true, answered Dyce, in his discreet way; and he smiled as one who, if he would, could expatiate on the interesting topic.

He saw Mrs. Gallantry, and from her learnt—without betraying his own ignorance—that callers at Rivenoak were received by Lady Amys, from whom only the barest information concerning Lady Ogram's last illness was obtainable. Neither Miss Tomalin nor Miss Bride had been seen by any one.

The day of the funeral arrived; the hour appointed was half-past two. All the morning rain fell, and about midday began a violent thunderstorm, which lasted for an hour. Then the sky began to clear, and as Lashmar started for Rivenoak he saw a fine rainbow, across great sullen clouds, slowly breaking upon depths of azure. The gates of the park stood wide open, and many carriages were moving up the drive. Afterwards, it became known that no member of the Ogram family had been present on this occasion. Half-a-dozen friends of the deceased came down from London, but the majority of the funeral guests belonged to Hollingford and the immediate neighbourhood. In no sense was it a distinguished gathering; mere curiosity accounted for the presence of nearly all who came.

Lashmar had paid his respects to Lady Amys, who received him frigidly, and was looking about for faces that he knew when a familiar voice spoke at his shoulder; he turned, and saw Mrs. Toplady.

"Have you come down this morning?" he asked, as they shook hands.

"Yesterday. I want to see you, and we had better arrange the meeting at once. Where are you staying in Hollingford? An hotel, isn't it?"

She spoke in a low voice. Notwithstanding her decorous gravity, Lashmar saw a ghost of the familiar smile hovering about her lips. He gave his address, and asked at what hour Mrs. Toplady thought of coming.

"Let us say half-past five. There's an up-train just before eight, which I must catch."

She nodded, and moved away. Again Lashmar looked about him, and he met the eye of Mr. Kerchever who came forward with friendly aspect.

"Dreadfully sudden, the end, Mr. Lashmar!"

"Dreadfully so, indeed," Dyce responded, in mortuary tones.

"You were present at the seizure, I understand?"

"I was."

"A good age," remarked the athletic lawyer, with obvious difficulty subduing his wonted breeziness. "The doctor tells me that it was marvellous she lived so long. Wonderful woman! Wonderful!"

And he, too, moved away, Lashmar gazing after him, and wishing he knew all that was in his legal mind at this moment. But that secret must very soon become common property. Perhaps the contents of Lady Ogram's will would be known at Hollingford this very evening.

He searched vainly for Constance and for May. The former he did not see until she crossed the hall to enter one of the carriages; the latter appeared not at all. Had she, then, really left Rivenoak? Seated in his hired brougham, in dignified solitude, he puzzled anxiously over this question. Happily, he would hear everything from Mrs. Toplady.

In the little church of Shawe his eyes wandered as

much as his thoughts. Surveying the faces, most of them unknown to him, he noticed that scarcely a person present was paying any attention to the ceremony, or made any attempt to conceal his or her indifference. At one moment it vexed him that no look turned with interest in his direction; was he not far and away the most important of all the people gathered here? A lady and a gentleman who sat near him frequently exchanged audible whispers, and he found that they were debating a trivial domestic matter with some acerbity of mutual contradiction. He gazed now and then at the black-palled coffin, and found it impossible to realize that there lay the strange, imperious old woman who for several months had been the centre of his thoughts, and to whom he owed so vast a change in his circumstances. He felt no sorrow, yet thought of her with a certain respect, even with a slight sensation of gratitude, which was chiefly due, however, to the fact that she had been so good as to die. Live as long as he might, the countenance and the voice of Lady Ogram would never be less distinct in his memory than they were to-day. He, at all events, had understood and appreciated her. If he became master of Rivenoak, the marble bust should always have an honoured place under that roof.

Dyce saw himself master of Rivenoak. He fell into a delightful dream, and, when the congregation suddenly stirred, he found with alarm that he had a broad smile on his face.

Rather before the hour she had named, Mrs. Toplady presented herself at the Saracen's Head. Lashmar was impatiently expectant; he did his best to appear gravely thoughtful, and behaved with the ceremonious courtesy which, in his quality of Parliamentary candidate, he had of late been cultivating. His visitor, as soon as the door was closed, became quite at her ease.

"Nice little place," she remarked, glancing about the room. "You make this your head-quarters, of course?"

Our Friend the Charlatan

"Yes; I am very comfortable here," Dyce answered, in melodious undertone.

"And all goes well? Your committee at work, and all that?"

"Everything satisfactory, so far. The date is not fixed yet."

"But it'll be all over, no doubt, in time for the partridges," said Mrs. Toplady, scrutinizing him with an amused look. "Do you shoot?"

"Why no, Mrs. Toplady. I care very little for sport."

"Like all sensible men.—I wanted to hear what you think about Lady Ogram's will."

Lashmar was disconcerted. He had to confess that he knew nothing whatever about the will.

"Indeed? Then I bring you news."

They were interrupted by a waiter who appeared with tea. The visitor graciously accepted a cup.

"Funerals exhaust one so, *don't* they?" she remarked. "I don't know your opinion, but I think people should be married and buried far more quietly. For my own part, I grieve sincerely for the death of Lady Ogram. It's a great loss to me. I liked her, and I owed her gratitude for very much kindness. But I certainly shouldn't have gone to her funeral if it hadn't been a social duty. I should have liked to sit quietly at home, thinking about her."

"I thoroughly agree with you," replied Dyce absently. "You came down yesterday?"

"In the evening.—You know that Miss Tomalin is at my house?"

"I had no idea of it."

"Yes. She arrived the day before yesterday. She left Rivenoak as soon as she knew about Lady Ogram's will. I'm very glad indeed that she came to me; it was a great mark of confidence. Under the circumstances, she could hardly remain here."

"The circumstances?"

"Lady Ogram's will does not mention her."

Lashmar felt a spasm in his breast. The expression

361

of his features was so very significant that Mrs.
Toplady's smile threatened to become a laugh.

"It's rather startling, isn't it?" she continued.
"The will was made a year ago. Lady Ogram didn't
mean it to stand. When she was in town she talked
over her affairs with her solicitor; a new will was to be
made, by which Miss Tomalin would have come into
possession of Rivenoak, and of a great deal of money.
You can probably guess why she put off executing it.
She hoped her niece's marriage-settlement would come
first. But the old will remains, and is valid."

"Will you tell me its provisions?" asked Lashmar
deliberately.

"In confidence. It won't be made public till the
executors—Sir William Amys and Mr. Kerchever—
have proved it. I never knew a more public-spirited
will. Hollingford gets a hospital, to be called the Lady
Ogram; very generously endowed. Rivenoak is to be
sold, and the proceeds to form a fund for a lot of Lady
Ogram scholarships. A working-girls' home is to be
founded in Camden Town (it seems she was born
there), and to be called Lady Ogram House. A lady
named Mrs. Gallantry, here at Hollingford, becomes
trustee for a considerable sum to be used in founding
a training-school for domestic servants—to be named
the Lady Ogram. Then there's a long list of minor
charitable bequests. All the servants are most liberally
treated, and a few friends in humble circumstances
receive annuities. There is not much fear of Lady
Ogram being forgotten just yet, is there?"

"No, indeed," said Lashmar, with studious control of
his voice. "And"—he paused a moment—"is that all?"

"Let me see. Oh, I was forgetting. Some money
is left to Miss Bride; not to her absolutely, but in
trust for certain purposes not specified."

Mrs. Toplady's smile had never been more eloquent
of mischievous pleasure. She was watching Lashmar
as one watches a comedian on the stage, without the
least disguise of her amusement.

"I had heard something of that," said Dyce, the tension of whose feelings began to show itself in a flush under the eyes. "Can you tell me——"

"Oh," broke in the other, "I've forgotten a detail that will interest you. In the entrance hall of the Lady Ogram Hospital is to be preserved that beautiful bust which you have seen at Rivenoak. By the bye, there are odd stories about it. I hear that it was brought out of concealment only the day before her death."

"Yes. I don't know any more about it. With regard to Miss Bride's trusteeship——"

"Oh, and I forgot that Hollingford is to have a fine market-hall, on condition that the street leading to it is called Arabella Street—her name, you know."

"Oh, indeed!" murmured Dyce, and became mute.

Mrs. Toplady amused herself for a moment with observation of the play of his muscles. She sipped her tea.

"I'll have another cup, if you please. Oh yes, we were speaking of Miss Bride. Naturally, that interests you. An odd bequest, isn't it? She is spoken of as a trustee, but evidently the disposal of the money is quite at her own discretion. If I remember, there are words to the effect that Lady Ogram wishes Miss Bride to use this money, just as she herself would have done, for the purposes in which they were both particularly interested. By the bye, it isn't money only; Miss Bride becomes owner of the paper-mill at the village by Rivenoak."

"I had heard of this," said Lashmar, with a brusque movement as though he felt cramp in his leg. He had begun to look cheerful. "I knew all about Lady Ogram's intentions. You don't remember," he added carelessly, "the amount of the bequest?"

"Mr. Kerchever tells me it represents about seventy thousand pounds."

Lashmar involuntarily heaved a sigh. Mrs. Toplady watched him over the rim of her teacup, the hand which held it shaking a little with subdued mirth.

"As you say," he observed, "it's a most remarkable

will. But it seems rather too bad that the poor lady's real wishes should be totally neglected."

"Indeed it does. I have been wondering what Miss Bride will think about it. Of course, I couldn't speak to her on the subject. One almost feels as if she ought at all events to give half that money to Miss Tomalin, considering the terms on which she receives it."

"But," objected Dyce, "that wouldn't be fulfilling the conditions of the bequest, which, I happen to know, were very specific. Really, it's a most unfortunate thing that Lady Ogram died so suddenly, most unfortunate. What a serious injustice is done to that poor girl!"

"After all, Mr. Lashmar," fell sweetly from the other's lips, "her position might be worse."

"How? Has she an income of her own?"

"Oh, a trifling annuity, not worth mentioning. But I didn't speak of that. I meant that, happily, her future is in the hands of an honourable man. It would have been sad indeed if she had owed this calamity to the intrigues of a mere fortune-hunter. As it is, a girl of her spirit and intelligence will very soon forget the disappointment. Indeed, it is much more on another's account than on her own that she grieves over what has happened."

Lashmar was perusing the floor. Slowly he raised his eyes until they met Mrs. Toplady's. The two looked steadily at each other.

"Are you speaking of me?" Dyce inquired, in a low voice.

"Of whom else could I be speaking, Mr. Lashmar?"

"Then Miss Tomalin has taken you entirely into her confidence?"

"Entirely, I am happy to say. I am sure you won't be displeased. It goes without saying that she does not know I am having this conversation with you."

"I think, Mrs. Toplady," said Dyce, with deliberation, "that you had better tell me, if you will, exactly what you have heard from Miss Tomalin. We shall be more sure of understanding each other."

Our Friend the Charlatan

"That's easily done. She told me of your railway journey together, of your subsequent meetings, of what happened with Lord Dymchurch, and, last of all, what happened with Lady Ogram."

"Probably," said Dyce, "not of all that happened with Lady Ogram. Did she mention that, instead of remaining loyal to me, as I was all through to her, she did her best to injure me with Lady Ogram by betraying a secret I had entrusted to her?"

"I know what you refer to. Yes, she told me of that unfortunate incident, and spoke of it with deep regret. The poor girl simply lost her head; for a moment she could think of nothing but self-preservation. Put yourself in her place. She saw utter ruin before her, and was driven almost crazy. I can assure you that she was not responsible for that piece of disloyalty. I am afraid not many girls would have been more heroic in such a terrible situation. You, a philosopher, must take account of human weakness."

"I hope I can do that," said Lashmar, with a liberal air. "Under other circumstances I should hardly have mentioned the thing. But it convinced me at the time that Miss Tomalin had deceived herself as to her feeling for me, and now that everything is necessarily at an end between us, I prefer to see it still in the same light, for it assures me that she has suffered no injury at *my* hands."

"But, pray, why should everything be necessarily at an end?"

"For two or three reasons, Mrs. Toplady. One will suffice. After Miss Tomalin had left the room, Lady Ogram insisted on my making offer of immediate marriage to Miss Bride. Being plainly released from the other obligation, I did so—and Miss Bride gave her consent."

Mrs. Toplady arched her eyebrows, and rippled a pleasant laugh.

"Ah! That, of course, May could not know. I may presume that, *this* time, the engagement is serious?"

365

" Undoubtedly," Lashmar replied, grave yet bland.

" Then I can only ask you to pardon my interference."

" Not at all. You have shown great kindness, and, under other circumstances, we should not have differed for a moment as to the course it behoved me to follow."

Dyce had never heard himself speak so magnanimously; he smiled with pleasure, and continued in a peculiarly suave voice.

" I am sure Miss Tomalin will find in you a steadfast friend."

" I shall do what I can for her, of course," was the rather dry answer. " At the same time, I hold to my view of Miss Bride's responsibility. The girl has really nothing to live upon; a miserable hundred a year; all very well when she belonged to the family at Northampton, but useless now she is adrift. To tell you the truth, I shall wait with no little curiosity for Miss Bride's—and your—decision."

" Need I say that Miss Bride will be absolutely free to take any step she likes ? "

" How could I doubt it ? " exclaimed the lady, with her most expressive smile. " Do you allow me to make known the—the renewal of your engagement ? "

" Certainly," Dyce answered, beaming upon her.

Mrs. Toplady rose.

" I am so happy to have been the first to bring you the news. But it a little surprises me that you had not learnt it already from Miss Bride, who knew all about the will two days ago."

" Why should it surprise you ? " said Lashmar gently, as he took her hand. " Naturally I have kept away from Rivenoak, supposing Miss Tomalin to be still there; and Miss Bride was not likely to be in haste to communicate a piece of news which, strictly speaking, hardly concerns me at all."

" Be sure you come to see me when you are in town," were Mrs. Toplady's last words.

And her eyes twinkled with appreciation of Lashmar's behaviour.

CHAPTER XXVI

Dyce walked about the room. Without knowing it, he sang softly to himself. His countenance was radiant.

So, after all, Constance would be his wife. One moment's glimpse of a dread possibility that neither she nor May Tomalin benefited by Lady Ogram's will had sufficed to make him more than contented with the actual issue of the late complications. He had seen himself overwhelmed with sheer disaster, reduced to the alternative of withdrawing into ignominious obscurity or of again seeking aid from Mrs. Woolstan, aid which might or might not be granted, and in any case would only enable him to go through with the contest at Hollingford—a useless effort, if he had nothing henceforth to live upon. As it was, he saw Constance and seventy thousand pounds, with the prosperous little paper-mill to boot. He did not love Constance, but the feeling of dislike with which he had recently come to regard her had quite passed away. He did not love Constance, but what a capable woman she was!—and what a help she would be to him in his career! Her having detected his philosophic plagiarism seemed to him now rather a good thing than otherwise; it spared him the annoyance of intellectual dishonesty in his domestic life, and put him in a position to discuss freely with her the political and social views by which he was to stand. After all, she was the only woman he knew whose intelligence he really respected. After all, remembering their intimacy long ago at Alverholme, he felt a fitness in this fated sequel. It gave him the pleasant sense of honourable conduct.

He smiled at the thought that he had fancied himself in love with May Tomalin. The girl was a half-educated simpleton, who would only have made him ridiculous. Her anonymous letter pointed to a grave fault of breeding; it would always have been suggestive of disagreeable possibilities. May was thoroughly plebeian in origin, and her resemblance to Lady Ogram might develop in a way it made him shudder to think of. Constance came of gentlefolk, and needed only the favour of circumstances to show herself perfectly at ease in whatever social surroundings. She had a natural dignity, which, now he came to reflect upon it, he had always observed with pleasure. What could have been more difficult than her relations with Lady Ogram? Yet she had always borne herself with graceful independence.

Poor girl! She had gone through a hard time these last four weeks, and no wonder if she broke down under the strain of a situation such as that which ended in Lady Ogram's death. He would make up to her for it all. She should understand him, and rest in perfect confidence. Yes, he would reveal to her his whole heart and mind, so that no doubt of him, no slightest distrust, could ever disturb her peace. Not only did he owe her this complete sincerity; to him it would be no less delightful, no less tranquilizing.

He sat down to write a note.

"Dear Constance"—yes, that sufficed. "When can I see you? Let it be as soon as possible. Of course, you have understood my silence. Do you stay at Rivenoak a little longer? Let me come to-morrow, if possible."

After a little reflection he signed himself, "Ever yours, D. L."

Having despatched this by private messenger, he went out and took a walk, choosing the direction away from Rivenoak. As he rambled along an uninteresting road, it occurred to him that he ought to write to Mrs. Woolstan. No need, of course, to say anything about the results of Lady Ogram's decease, but he really owed Iris a letter, just to' show that he was not unmindful of her kindness. The foolish little woman had done her best for him; indeed, without her help, where would he have been now? He must pay his debt to her as soon as possible, and it would, of course, be necessary to speak of the matter to Constance. Not, perhaps, till after their marriage. Well, he would see; he might possibly have an impulse. Happily this was the very last of the unpleasant details he would have to dismiss. The luxury of living without concealment, unembarrassed, and unafraid!

By the bye, how would Constance understand the duties of her trusteeship? What portion of her income would she feel at liberty to set apart for personal uses? In all likelihood, she had spoken of that with Lady Ogram; at their coming interview she would fully explain her position.

He returned to the hotel, and dined alone. To his disappointment, there came no answer from Rivenoak. Was it possible that Constance had already gone away? Very unlikely, so soon after the funeral. She would reply, no doubt, by post; indeed, there was no hurry, and a little reserve on her part would be quite natural.

Morning brought him the expected letter. "Dear Mr. Lashmar," wrote Constance. Oh, that was nothing; merely the reserve he had anticipated; he liked her the better for it. "I shall be at home all to-morrow, busy with many things. Could you come about three o'clock? Sincerely yours——" What could be in better taste? How else could she write, under the circumstances? His real wooing had not yet begun, and Constance merely reminded him of that, with all gentleness.

So, in the afternoon, he once more presented himself at Rivenoak, and once more followed the servant into the drawing-room. Constance sat there; she rose as he approached, and silently gave her hand. He thought she looked rather pale; that might be the effect of black attire, which made a noticeable change in her appearance. But a certain dignity of which the visitor was very sensible, a grace of movement and of bearing which seemed new to her, could not be attributed to the dress she wore. In a saddened voice, he hoped that she was well, that she had not suffered from the agitations of the past week, and, with courtesy such as she might have used to any one, Constance replied that she felt a little tired, not quite herself. They talked for some minutes in this way. Lashmar learnt that the Amyses had returned to London.

"For the present you stay here?" he said, the interrogative accent only just perceptible.

"For a day or two. My secretaryship goes on, of course. I have a good deal of correspondence to see to."

On his way hither Lashmar had imagined quite a different meeting; he anticipated an emotional scene, beginning with pronounced calmness on Constance's side, leading on to reproaches, explanations, and masculine triumph. But Constance was strangely self-possessed, and her mind seemed to be not at all occupied with agitating subjects. Lashmar was puzzled by the calm which had fallen upon her; he felt it wise to imitate her example, to behave as quietly and naturally as possible, taking for granted that she viewed the situation even as he did.

He turned his eyes to the marble bust, on its pedestal behind Constance. The scorn in its fixed smile caught his attention.

"So that is to stand in the hospital," he murmured.

"Yes, I believe so," replied Constance absently, with a glance towards the white face.

"What strange stories it will give rise to in days to come! She will become a legendary figure. I can hardly believe that I saw and talked with her only a few days ago. Have you the same feeling at all?

Our Friend the Charlatan

Doesn't she seem to you more like some one you have read of, than a person you really knew?"

"I understand what you mean," said Constance, smiling thoughtfully. "It's certain one will never again know any one like her."

"Are all the provisions of her will practicable?"

"Perfectly, I think. She took great trouble to make them so. By the bye, from whom did you get your information?"

It was asked in a disinterested voice, the speaker's look resting for a moment on Lashmar with unembarrassed directness.

"Mrs. Toplady told me about the will."

Dyce paused for a moment; then continued, with an obvious effort, indeed, but in an even voice.

"She came to see me after the funeral. Mrs. Toplady has a persevering curiosity; she wanted to know what had happened, and, I have no doubt, had recourse to me after finding that you were not disposed to talk as freely as she wished. I was able to enlighten her on one point."

"May I ask what point?"

"She began by telling me that Miss Tomalin was at her house. She had heard Miss Tomalin's story, with the result that she supposed me in honour bound to marry that young lady. I explained that this was by no means the case."

"How did you explain it?" asked Constance, still in her disinterested tone.

"By telling the simple truth, that Miss Tomalin had herself cancelled the engagement existing between us."

"I see."

Constance leaned back in her chair. She looked like one who is sitting alone, occupied with tranquil reflection. Dyce allowed a moment to elapse before he again spoke; he was smiling to himself.

"How strange it all is!" he at length resumed, as though starting from a reverie. "This past fortnight seems already as dim and vague to me as the recollec-
371

tion of something that happened long years ago. I never believed myself capable of such follies. Tell me frankly"—he leaned towards Constance, smiling at her in an amused, confidential way—"could *you* have imagined that I should ever lose my head like that, and run off into such vagaries?"

Constance also smiled, but very faintly. Her eyebrows rose ever so little. Her lips just moved, but uttered no sound.

"You know me better than any one else ever did or ever will," he went on. "It is quite possible that you know me better than I know myself. Did you ever foresee such a possibility?"

"I can't say that it astonished me," was the deliberate reply, without any ironic note.

"Well, I am glad of that," said Dyce, with a little sigh of relief. "It's much better so. I like to think that you read me with so clear an eye. For years I have studied myself, and I thought I knew how I should act in any given circumstances; yet it was mere illusion. What I regret is that I hadn't talked more to you about such things; you would very likely have put me on my guard. I always felt your power of reading character; it seemed to me that I concealed nothing from you. We were always so frank with each other—yet not frank enough, after all."

"I'm afraid not," assented the listener absently.

"Well, it's an experience; though, as I say, more like a bit of delirium than actual life. Happily, you know all about it; I shall never have to tell you the absurd story. But I mustn't forget that other thing which really did surprise and vex you—my bit of foolish plagiarism. I have so wanted to talk to you about it. You have read the whole book?"

"Very carefully."

"And what do you think of it?" he asked, with an air of keen interest.

"Just what I thought of the large quotations I had heard from you. The theory seems plausible; I should think there is a good deal of truth in it. In any case, it helps one to direct one's life."

"Ah, you feel that? Now *there*," exclaimed Lashmar, his eye brightening, "is the explanation of what seemed to you very dishonourable behaviour in me. You know me, and you will understand as soon as I hint at the psychology of the thing. When that book fell into my hands, I was seeking eagerly for a theory of the world by which to live. I have had many glimpses of the truth about life—glimpses gained by my own honest thought. This book completed the theory I had been shaping for myself; it brought me mental rest, and a sense of fixed purpose such as I had never known. Its reconciliation of the aristocratic principle with a true socialism was exactly what I had been striving for; it put me at harmony with myself, for you know that I am at the same time aristocratic and socialist. Well, now, I spoke of the book to my father, and begged him to read it. It was when we met at Alverholme in the spring; you remember? How long ago does that seem to you? To me, several years. Yes, I had the volume with me, and showed it to my father; sufficient proof that I had no intention of using it dishonestly. But—follow me, I beg—I had so absorbed the theory, so thoroughly made it the directing principle of my mind, that I very soon ceased to think of it as somebody else's work. I completed it with all sorts of new illustrations, confirmations, which had been hanging loose in my memory, and the result was that I one day found myself talking about it as if it had originated with me. If I'm not mistaken, I was talking with Dymchurch— yes, it was Dymchurch. When I had time to reflect, I saw what I had unconsciously done—quite unconsciously, believe me. I thought it over. Ought I to let Dymchurch know where I had got my central idea? And I decided at length that I would say nothing."

Constance, leaning back in her chair, listened attentively, with impartial countenance.

"You see why, don't you?" His voice thrilled with

earnestness; his eyes shone as if with the very light of truth. "To say calmly: by the bye, I came across that bio-sociological theory in such and such a book, would have been a flagrant injustice to myself. I couldn't ask Dymchurch to listen whilst I elaborately expounded my mental and spiritual history during the past year or two, yet short of that there was no way of making him understand the situation. The thing had become *mine*—I thought by it, and lived by it; I couldn't bear to speak of it as merely an interesting hypothesis discovered in the course of my reading. At once it would have seemed to me to carry less weight; I should have been thrown back again into uncertainty. This, too, just at the moment when a principle, a conviction, had become no less a practical than a subjective need to me; for, thanks to you, I saw a new hope in life, the possibility of an active career which would give scope to all my energies. Do you follow me ? Do I make myself clear ? "

"Perfectly," replied Constance, with a slight inclination of her head. She seemed at the same time to listen and to be absorbed in thought.

"From that moment I ceased to think of the book. I had as good as forgotten its existence. Though, on the whole, it had done me so great a service, there were many things in it I didn't like, and these would now have annoyed me much more than at the first reading. I should have felt as if the man had got hold of *my* philosophy, and presented it imperfectly. You will understand now why I was so astonished at your charge of plagiarism. I really didn't know what to say; I couldn't perceive your point of view; I don't remember how I replied; I'm afraid my behaviour seemed only to confirm your suspicion. In very truth, it was the result of genuine surprise. Of course, I had only to reflect to see how this discovery must have come upon you, but then it was too late. We were in the thick of extraordinary complications, no hope of quiet and reasonable talk. Since the tragic end, I

Our Friend the Charlatan

have worried constantly about that misunderstanding.
Is it quite cleared up? We must be frank with each
other now or never. Speak your thought as honestly
as I have spoken mine."

"I completely understand you," was the meditative
reply.

"I was sure you would! To some people, such an
explanation would be useless; Mrs. Toplady, for instance.
I should be sorry to have to justify myself by psychological reasoning to Mrs. Toplady. And, remember,
Mrs. Toplady represents the world. A wise man does
not try to explain himself to the world; enough if, by
exceptional good luck, there is one person to whom he
can confidently talk of his struggles and his purposes.
Don't suppose, however, that I lay claim to any great
wisdom; after the last fortnight, that would be rather
laughable. But I am capable of benefiting by experience, and very few men can truly say as much. It
is on the practical side that I have hitherto been most
deficient. I see my way to correcting that fault.
Nothing could be better for me, just now, than
electioneering work. It will take me out of myself,
and give a rest to the speculative side of my mind.
Don't you agree with me?"

"Quite."

"There's another thing I must make clear to you,"
Dyce pursued, now swimming delightedly on the flood
of his own eloquence. "For a long time I seriously
doubted whether I was fit for a political career. My
ambition always tended that way, but my conscience
went against it. I used to regard politics with a good
deal of contempt. You remember our old talks at
Alverholme?"

Constance nodded.

"In one respect, I am still of the same opinion.
Most men who go in for a Parliamentary career regard
it either as a business by which they and their friends
are to profit, or as an easy way of gratifying their
personal vanity and social ambitions. That, of course,

is why we are so far from ideal government. I used to think that the man in earnest should hold aloof from Parliament, and work in more hopeful ways—by literature, for instance. But I see now that the fact of the degradation of Parliament is the very reason why a man thinking as I do should try to get into the House of Commons. If all serious minds hold aloof, what will the government of the country sink to? The House of Commons is becoming in the worst sense democratic; it represents, above all, newly-acquired wealth, and wealth which has no sense of its responsibilities. The representative system can only be restored to dignity and usefulness by the growth of a new Liberalism. What I understand by that you already know. One of its principles—that which for the present must be most insisted upon—is the right use of money. Irresponsible riches threaten to ruin our civilization. What we have first of all to do is to form the nucleus of a party which represents money as a civilizing, instead of a corrupting, power."

He looked into Constance's eyes, and she, smiling as if at a distant object, met his look steadily.

"I have been working out this thought," he continued, with vigorous accent. "I see it now as my guiding principle in the narrower sense—the line along which I must pursue the greater ends. The possession of money commonly says very little for a man's moral and intellectual worth, but there is the minority of well-to-do people who have the will to use their means rightly, if only they knew how. This minority must be organized, it must attract intellect and moral force from every social rank. Money must be used against money, and in this struggle it is not the big battalions will prevail. Personally, I care very little for wealth, as I think you know. I have no expensive tastes; I can live without luxuries. Oh, I like to be comfortable, and to be free from anxiety; who doesn't? But I never felt the impulse to strive to enrich myself. On the other hand, money as a civilizing force has great value in my eyes. Without it, one can work indeed, but with what slow results! It is time to be up and doing. We must organize our party, get our new Liberalism to work. In this also, do you agree with me?"

"It is certain," Constance replied, "that the right use of money is one of the great questions of our day."

"I know how much you have thought of it," said Dyce. Then, after a short pause, he added, in his frankest tone, "And it concerns you especially."

"It does."

"Do you feel"—he softened his voice to respectful intimacy—"that, in devoting yourself to this cause, you will be faithful to the trust you have accepted?"

Constance answered deliberately.

"It depends upon what you understand by devoting myself. Beyond a doubt, Lady Ogram would have approved the idea as you put it."

"And would she not have given me her confidence as its representative?" asked Dyce, smiling.

"Up to a certain point. Lady Ogram desired, for instance, to bear the expenses of your contest at Hollingford, and I should like to carry out her wish in the matter."

A misgiving began to trouble Lashmar's sanguine mood. He searched his companion's face; it seemed to him to have grown more emphatic in expression; there was a certain hardness about the lips which he had not yet observed. Still Constance looked friendly, and her eyes supported his glance.

"Thank you," he murmured, with some feeling. "And, if by chance I should be beaten, you wouldn't lose courage? We must remember——"

"You have asked me many questions," Constance interrupted quietly. "Let me use the privilege of frankness which we grant each other, and ask you one in turn. Your private means are sufficient for the career upon which you are entering?"

"My private means?"

Our Friend the Charlatan

He gazed at her as if he did not understand, the smile fading from his lips.

"Forgive me if you think I am going too far."

"Not at all!" Dyce exclaimed eagerly. "It is a question you have a perfect right to ask. But I thought you knew I had *no* private means."

"No, I wasn't aware of that," Constance replied, in a voice of studious civility. "Then how do you propose—— ?"

Their eyes encountered. Constance did not for an instant lose her self-command; Lashmar's efforts to be calm only made his embarrassment more obvious.

"I had a small allowance from my father till lately," he said; "but that has come to an end. It never occurred to me that you misunderstood my position. Surely I have more than once hinted to you how poor I was? I had no intention of misleading you. Lady Ogram certainly knew——"

"She knew you were not wealthy, but she thought you had a competence. I told her so when she questioned me. It was a mistake, I see, but a very natural one."

"Does it matter now?" asked Dyce, his lips again curling amiably.

"I should suppose it mattered very much. How shall you live?"

"Let us understand each other. Do you withdraw your consent to Lady Ogram's last wish?"

"That wish, as you see, was founded on a misunderstanding."

"But," exclaimed Lashmar, "you are not speaking seriously?"

"Quite. Lady Ogram certainly never intended the money she had left in trust to me to be used for your private needs. Reflect a moment, and you will see how impossible it would be for me to apply the money in such a way."

"Reflection," said Dyce, with unnatural quietness, "would only increase my astonishment at your in-
378

Our Friend the Charlatan

genuity. It would have been much simpler and better to say at once that you had changed your mind. Can you for a moment expect me to believe that this argument really justifies you in breaking your promise?"

"I assure you," replied Constance, also in a soft undertone, "it is much sounder reasoning than that by which you excuse your philosophical plagiarism."

Lashmar's eyes wandered. They fell upon the marble bust; its disdainful smile seemed to him more pronounced than ever.

"Then," he said, on an impulse of desperation, "you really mean to take Lady Ogram's money, and to disregard the very condition on which she left it to you?"

"You forget that her will was made before she had heard your name."

He sat in silence, a gloomy resentment lowering on his features. After a glance at him, Constance began to speak in a calm, amiable voice.

"It is my turn to confess. I, too, seem to myself to have been living in a sort of dream, and my awaking is no less decisive than yours. At your instigation, I behaved dishonestly; I am very much ashamed of the recollection. Happily, I see my way to atone for the follies, and worse, that I committed. I can carry out Lady Ogram's wishes—the wishes she formed while still in her sound mind—and to that I shall devote my life."

"Do you intend, then, to apply none of this money to your personal use? Do you mean to earn your own living still?"

"That would defeat Lady Ogram's purpose," was the calm answer. "I shall live where and how it seems good to me, guided always by the intention which I know was in her mind."

Dyce sat with his head bent forward, his hands grasping his knees. After what seemed to be profound reflection, he said gravely:

"This is how you think to-day. I won't be so unjust to you as to take it for your final reply."

Our Friend the Charlatan

"Yet that's what it is," answered Constance.

"You think so. The sudden possession of wealth has disturbed your mind. If I took you at your word" —he spoke with measured accent—"I should be guilty of behaviour much more dishonourable than that of which you accuse me. I can wait." He smiled with a certain severity. "It is my duty to wait until you have recovered your natural way of thinking."

Constance was looking at him, her eyes full of wonder and amusement.

"Thank you," she said. "You are very kind, very considerate. But suppose you reflect for a moment on your theory of the equality of man and woman. Doesn't it suggest an explanation of what you call my disordered state of mind? Let us use plain words. You want money for your career, and, as the need is pressing, you are willing to take the encumbrance of a wife. I am to feel myself honoured by your acceptance of me, to subject myself entirely to your purposes, to think it a glorious reward if I can aid your ambition. Is there much equality in this arrangement?"

"You put things in the meanest light," protested Lashmar. "What I offer you is a share in all my thoughts, a companionship in whatever I do or become. I have no exaggerated sense of my own powers, but this I know, that, with fair opportunity, I can attain distinction. If I thought of you as in any sense an encumbrance, I shouldn't dream of asking you to marry me; it would defeat the object of my life. I have always seen in you just the kind of woman who would understand me and help me."

"My vanity will grant you that," replied Constance. "But for the moment I want you to inquire whether you are the kind of man who would understand and help *me*— You are surprised. That's quite a new way of putting the matter, isn't it? You never saw *that* as a result of your theory?"

"Stay!" Dyce raised his hand. "I know perfectly well that you are ambitious. If you were not, we

380

Our Friend the Charlatan

should never have become friends. But you must remember that, from my point of view, I am offering you such a chance of gratifying your ambition as you will hardly find again."

"That is to say, the reflection of *your* glory. As a woman, what more can I ask? You can't think how this amuses me, now that I have come to my senses. Putting aside the question of whether you are likely to win glory at all, have you no suspicion of your delightful arrogance? I should like to know how far your contempt of women really goes. It went far enough, at all events, to make you think that I believed your talk about equality of the sexes. But really, I am not quite such a simpleton. I always knew that you despised women, that you looked upon them as creatures to be made use of. If you ask: why, then, did I endure you for a moment?—the answer must be that I am a woman. You see, Mr. Lashmar, we females of the human species are complex. Some of us think and act very foolishly, and all the time, somewhere in our curious minds, are dolefully aware of our foolishness. You know that of *men;* let me assure you that women share the unhappy privilege in a high degree."

Lashmar was listening with knitted brows. No word came to his lips.

"You interest me," pursued Constance. "I think you are rather a typical man of our time, and it isn't at all impossible that you may become, as you say, distinguished. But, clothed and in my right mind, I don't feel disposed to pay the needful price for the honour of helping you on. You mustn't lose heart; I have little doubt that some other woman will grasp at the opportunity you so kindly wish to reserve for me. But may I venture a word of counsel? Don't let it be a woman who holds the equality theory. I say this in the interest of your peace and happiness. There are plenty of women, still, who like to be despised, and some of them are very nice indeed. They are the only good wives; I feel sure of it. We others—women

381

cursed with brains—are not meant for marriage. We grow in numbers, unfortunately. What will be the end of it, I don't know. Some day you will thank your stars that you did not marry a woman capable of understanding you."

Dyce stood up and took a few steps about the floor, his eye fixed on the marble bust.

" When can I see you again ? " he asked abruptly.

" I shall be going to London in a day or two. I don't think we will meet again—until your circumstances are better. Can you give me any idea of what the election expenses will be ? "

"Not yet," Dyce answered, in an undertone. "You are going to London ? Will you tell me what you mean to do ? "

" To pursue my career."

" Your career ? "

" That surprises you, of course. It never occurred to you that I also might have a career in view. Yet I have. Let us enter upon a friendly competition. Five years hence, which of us will be better known ? "

" I see," remarked Dyce, his lip curling. " You will use your money to make yourself talked about ? "

" Not primarily; but it is very likely that that will result from my work. It offends your sense of what is becoming in a woman ? "

" It throws light upon what you have been saying."

" So I meant. You will see, when you think about it, that I am acting strangely like a male creature. We females with minds have a way of doing that. I'll say more, for I really want you to understand me. ' The sudden possession of wealth ' has not, as you suppose, turned my head, but it has given my thoughts a most salutary shaking, and made me feel twice the woman that I was. At this moment, I should as soon think of taking a place as kitchen-maid as of becoming any man's wife. I am free, and have power to assert myself—the first desire, let me assure you, of modern women no less than of modern men. That I shall assert myself for the good of others is a peculiarity of mine, a result of my special abilities; I take no credit for it. Some day we shall meet again, and talk over our experiences; for the present let us be content with corresponding now and then. You shall have my address as soon as I am settled."

She rose, and Lashmar gazed at her. He saw that she was as little to be moved by an appeal, by an argument, as the bust smiling behind her.

"I suppose," he said, "you will appear on platforms?"

"Oh dear, no!" Constance replied, with a laugh. "My ambition doesn't take that form. I leave that to you, who are much more eloquent."

"How you have altered!" He kept gazing at her with a certain awe. "I hardly know you."

"I doubt whether you know me at all. Never mind," —she held out her hand—"we may be friends yet— when you have come to understand that you are not so very, very much my superior."

CHAPTER XXVII

LASHMAR walked back to Hollingford, and reached the hotel without any consciousness of the road by which he had come. He felt as tired as if he had been walking all day. When he had dropped into an easy-chair, he let his arms hang, and, with head drooping forward, stared at his feet stretched out before him; the posture suggested a man half overcome with drink.

He had a private meeting to attend to-night. Should he attend it or not? His situation had become farcical. Was it not his plain duty to withdraw at once from the political contest, that a serious candidate might as soon as possible take his place? Where could he discern even the glimmer of a hope in this sudden darkness? His heart was heavy and cold.

He went through the business of the evening, talking automatically, seeing and hearing as in a dream. He had no longer the slightest faith in his electioneering prospects, and wondered how he could ever have been sanguine about them. Of course, the Conservative would win. Breakspeare knew it; every member of the committee knew it; they pretended to hope because the contest amused and occupied them. No Liberal had a chance at Hollingford. To-morrow he would throw the thing up, and disappear.

Never in his life had he passed such a miserable night. At each waking from hag-ridden slumbers, the blackest despondency beset him; once or twice his tortured brain even glanced towards suicide, temptation lurking in the assurance that, by destroying himself, he

384

would become, for a few days at all events, the subject
of universal interest.

He found no encouragement even in the thought of
Iris Woolstan. Not only had he deeply offended her
by his engagement to Constance Bride, but almost
certainly she would hear from her friend Mrs. Toplady
the whole truth of his disaster, which put him beyond
hope of pardon. He owed her money; with what face,
even if she did not know the worst, could he go to her
and ask for another loan? In vain did he remember
the many proofs he had received of Mrs. Woolstan's
devotion; since the interview with Constance, all belief
in himself was at an end. He had thought his
eloquence, his personal magnetism, irresistible; Constance had shown him the extent of his delusion. If
he saw Iris, the result would be the same.

At moments, so profound was his feeling of insignificance that he hid his face even from the darkness
and groaned.

Not only had he lost faith in himself; there remained
to him no conviction, no trust, no hope of any kind.
Intellectually, morally, he had no support; shams,
insincerities, downright dishonesties, had clothed him
about, and these were now all stripped away, leaving
the thing he called his soul to shiver in shamed naked-
ness. He knew nothing; he believed nothing. But
death still made him fearful.

With the first gleam of daylight, he flung himself
out of his hot, uncomfortable bed, and hastened to be
a clothed mortal once more. He felt better as soon as
he had dressed himself and opened the window. The
night with its terrible hauntings was a thing gone by.

At breakfast he thought fixedly of Iris Woolstan.
Perhaps she had not seen Mrs. Toplady yet. Perhaps,
at heart, she was not so utterly estranged from him as
he feared; something of his old power over her might
even now be recovered. It was the resource of desperation; he must try it.

The waiter's usual respect seemed, this morning,

covert mockery. The viands had no savour; only the draught of coffee that soothed his throat was good. He had a vague headache, and a tremor of the nerves. In any case, it would have been impossible to get through the day in the usual manner, and his relief when he found himself at the railway-station was almost a return of good spirits.

On reaching London, he made straight for West Hampstead. As he approached Mrs. Woolstan's house, his heart beat violently. Without even a glance at the windows, he rang the bell. He heard it sound distinctly, but there came no response. He rang again, and again listened to the far-off tinkling. Only then did he perceive that the blinds at the lower windows were drawn. The house was vacant.

Paralyzed for a moment, he stared about, as if in search of some one who could give him information. Then, with sweat on his forehead, he stepped up to the next door, and asked if anything was known of Mrs. Woolstan; he learnt only that she had been absent for about ten days; where she was, the servant with whom he spoke could not tell him. Were the other neighbours likely to know, he asked. Encouraged by a bare possibility, he inquired at the house beyond; but in vain.

Fate was against him. He might as well go home and write a letter to Hollingford.

Stay, could he not remember the school to which Leonard Woolstan had been sent? Yes, it was noted in his pocket-book; for he had promised to write to the boy.

He sought the nearest post-office, and despatched a telegram to Leonard: "Please let me know immediately your mother's present address." The reply was to be sent to his rooms in Devonshire Street, and thither he straightway betook himself, hoping that in an hour or so he would have news. An extempore lunch was put before him; never had he satisfied his hunger with less gusto. Time went on; the afternoon brought him no telegram. At seven o'clock he lay on his sofa, exhausted by nervous strain, anticipating a hideous night. Again his thoughts had turned to suicide. It would be easier to obtain poison here than at Hollingford. But he must leave behind him something in writing, something which would excite attention when it appeared in all the newspapers. Addressed to the coroner ? No ; to his committee at Hollingford. He would hint to them of a tragic story, of noble powers and ambitions frustrated by the sordid difficulties of life. The very truth, let malice say what it would. At his age, with his brain and heart, to perish thus for want of a little money ! As he dwelt on the infinite pathos of the thing, tears welled to his eyes, trickled over his cheek.

Of a sudden he started up, and shouted " Come in !" Yes, it was a telegram ; he took it from the servant's hand with an exclamation of joy. Leonard informed him that Mrs. Woolstan was staying at Gorleston, near Yarmouth, her address "Sunrise Terrace." He clutched at a railway-guide. Too late to get to Yarmouth to-night, but that did not matter. "Sunrise Terrace !" In his sore state of mind a name of such good omen brought him infinite comfort. He rushed out of the house, and walked at a great rate towards Regent Street, impelled by the joy of feeling himself alive once more. Sunrise ! Iris Woolstan would save him. Already he warmed with gratitude to her ; he thought of her with a tender kindness. She might be richer than he supposed ; at all events, she was in circumstances which would allow him to live independently. And was she not just the kind of woman Constance Bride had advised him to marry ? Advice given in scorn, but, his conscience told him, thoroughly sound. A nice, gentle, sufficiently intelligent little woman. Pity that there was the boy ; but he would always be at school. Suppose she had only four or five hundred a year ? Oh, probably more than that, seeing that she could economize such substantial sums. He was saved; the sun would rise for him, literally and in metaphor.

A rainy morning saw him at Liverpool Street. The squalid roofs of north-east London dripped miserably under a leaden sky. Not till the train reached the borders of Suffolk did a glint of sun fall upon meadow and stream; thence onwards the heavens brightened; the risen clouds gleamed above a shining shore. Lashmar did not love this part of England, and he wondered why Mrs. Woolstan had chosen such a retreat, but in the lightness of his heart he saw only pleasant things. Arrived at Yarmouth, he jumped into a cab, and was driven along the dull flat road which leads to Gorleston. Odour of the brine made amends for miles of lodgings, for breaks laden with boisterous trippers, for tram-cars and piano-organs. Here at length was Sunrise Terrace, a little row of plain houses on the top of the cliff, with sea-horizon vast before it, and soft green meadow-land far as one could see behind. Bidding his driver wait, Lashmar knocked at the door, and stood tremulous. It was half-past twelve; Iris might or might not have returned from her morning walk; he prepared for a brief disappointment. But worse awaited him. Mrs. Woolstan, he learnt, would not be at home for the midday meal; she was with friends who had a house at Gorleston.

"Where is the house?" he asked impatiently, stamping as if his feet were cold.

The woman pointed his way.

"Who are the people? What is their name?"

He heard it, but it conveyed nothing to him. After a moment's reflection, he decided to go to the hotel, and there write a note. Whilst he was having lunch the reply came, a dry missive, saying that, if he would call at three o'clock, Mrs. Woolstan would have much pleasure in presenting him to her friends the Barkers, with whom she was spending the day.

Lashmar fumed, but obeyed the invitation. In a garden on the edge of the cliff he found half-a-dozen persons: an elderly man, who looked like a retired tradesman, his wife, of suitable appearance, their son, their two daughters, and Iris Woolstan. Loud and mirthful talk was going on; his arrival interrupted it only for a moment.

"So glad to see you!" was Mrs. Woolstan's friendly, but not cordial, greeting. "I didn't know you ever came to the east coast."

Introductions were carelessly made; he seated himself on a camp-stool by one of the young ladies, and dropped a few insignificant remarks. No one paid much attention to him.

"Seventy-five runs!" exclaimed Mrs. Woolstan, addressing herself as though with keen interest to the son of the family, a high-coloured, large-limbed young man of about Lashmar's age. "That was splendid! But you did better still against East Croydon, didn't you?"

"Made my century there," answered Mr. Barker, jerking out a leg in self-satisfaction.

"How conceited you're making him, Mrs. Woolstan!" cried one of his sisters, with a shrill laugh. "It's a rule in this house to put the stopper on Jim when he begins to talk about cricket. If we didn't, there'd be no living with him."

"Are you a cricketer, Mr.—Mr. Lasher?" asked materfamilias, eyeing the visitor curiously.

"It's a long time since I played," was the reply, uttered with scarcely veiled contempt.

Mrs. Woolstan talked on in the highest spirits, exhibiting her intimacy with the Barker household, and her sympathy with their concerns. Lashmar waited for her to question him about Hollingford, to give him an opportunity of revealing his importance; but her thoughts seemed never to turn in that direction. As soon as a movement in the company enabled him to rise, he stepped up to her, and said, in a voice audible to those standing by:

"I want to speak to you about Leonard. Shall you be at home this evening?"

Our Friend the Charlatan

Iris gave him a startled look.

" You haven't bad news of Len ? "

" Oh no; nothing of the kind."

" Can you call at six o'clock ? "

He looked into her eyes, and nodded.

" What do you say to a boat, Mrs. Woolstan ? " shouted Barker the son.

This suggestion was acclaimed, and Lashmar was urged to join the party, but he gladly seized this chance of escape. Wandering along the grassy edge of the cliffs, he presently descried the Barkers and their friend putting forth in two little boats. The sight exasperated him. He strode gloomily on, ever and again turning his head to watch the boats, and struggling against the fears that once more shaped themselves.

In a hollow of dry sand, where the cliffs broke, he flung himself down, and lay for an hour or two. Below him, on the edge of the tide, children were playing; he watched them sullenly. Lashmar disliked children; the sound of their voices was disagreeable to him. He wondered whether he would ever have children of his own, and heartily hoped not.

Six o'clock seemed very long in coming. But at length he found himself at Sunrise Terrace again, and was admitted to an ordinary lodging-house parlour, where, with tea on the table, Mrs. Woolstan awaited him. The sea air had evidently done her good; she looked younger and prettier than when Dyce last saw her, and the tea-gown she wore became her well.

" How did you know where I was ? " she began by asking, rather distantly.

Lashmar told her in detail.

" But why were you so anxious to see me ?—Sugar, I think ? "

" It's a long story," he replied, looking at her from under his eyebrows, " and I don't much care for telling it in a place like this, where all we say can be heard by any one on the other side of the door."

Iris was watching his countenance. The cold polite-

ness with which she had received him had become a
very transparent mask; beneath it showed eager
curiosity and trembling hope.

"We can go out, if you like," she said.

"And most likely meet those remarkable friends of
yours. Who on earth are they?"

"Very nice people," replied Mrs. Woolstan, holding
up her head.

"They are intolerably vulgar, and you must be aware
of it. I felt ashamed to see you among them. What
are you doing at a place like this? Why have you
shut up your house?"

"Really," exclaimed Iris, with a flutter, "that is my
business."

Lashmar's nervous irritation was at once subdued.
He looked timidly at the indignant face, let his eyes
fall, and murmured an apology.

"I've been going through strange things, and I'm
not quite master of myself. The night before last"—
his voice sunk to a hollow note—"I very nearly took
poison."

"What do you mean? Poison?"

Mrs. Woolstan's eyes widened in horror. Lashmar
regarded her with a smile of intense melancholy.

"One thing only kept me from it. I remembered
that I was in your debt, and I felt it would be too
cowardly."

"What has happened?—Come and sit near the
window; no one could hear us talking here. I have
been expecting to read of your election. Is it something to do with Lady Ogram's death? I have wanted
so much to know about that, and how it affected
you."

A few questions gave Dyce the comfortable assurance
that Iris had not seen Mrs. Toplady for a long time.
Trouble with servants, she said, coming after a slight
illness, had decided her to quit her house for the rest
of the summer, and the Barkers persuaded her to
come to Gorleston. When Leonard left school for

his holidays, she meant to go with him to some nice place.

"But do tell me what you mean by those dreadful words? And why have you come to see *me*?"

She was her old self, the Iris Woolstan on whom Lashmar had first tried his "method," who had so devoutly believed in him and given such substantial proof of her faith. The man felt his power, and began to recover self-respect.

"Tell me, first of all," he said, bending towards her, "may I remain your debtor for a little longer? Will it put you to inconvenience?"

"Not at all!" was the impulsive reply. "I told you I didn't want the money. I have more than six hundred pounds a year, and never spend quite all of it."

Lashmar durst not raise his eyes lest a gleam of joy should betray him. He knew now what he had so long desired to know. Six hundred a year; it was enough.

"You are very kind. That relieves me. For two or three days I have been in despair. Yes, you shall hear all about it. I owe you the whole truth, for no one ever understood me as you did, and no one ever gave me such help—of every kind. First of all, about my engagement to Miss Bride. It's at an end. But more than that—it wasn't a real engagement at all. We tried to play a comedy, and the end has been tragic."

Iris drew a deep breath of wonder. Her little lips were parted, her little eyebrows made a high arch; she had the face of a child who listens to a strange and half-terrifying story.

"Don't you see how it was?" he exclaimed, in a subdued voice of melodious sadness. "Lady Ogram discovered that her niece—you remember May Tomalin?—thought rather too well of me. This did not suit her views; she had planned a marriage between May and Lord Dymchurch. You know what her temper was. One day she gave me the choice; either

392

Our Friend the Charlatan

I married Constance Bride, or I never entered her house again. Imagine my position. Think of me, with my ambitions, my pride, and the debt I had incurred to you. Can you blame me much if, seeing that Lady Ogram's life might end any day, I met her tyranny by stratagem? How I longed to tell you the truth! But I felt bound in honour to silence. Constance Bride, my friend and never anything more, agreed to the pretence of an engagement. Wasn't it brave of her? And so things went on until the day when Dymchurch came down to Rivenoak and proposed to May. The silly girl refused him. There was a terrible scene, such as I hope never to behold again. May was driven forth from the house, and Lady Ogram, just as she was bidding me take steps for my immediate marriage, fell to the ground unconscious—dying."

He paused impressively. The listener was panting as if she had run a race.

"And the will?" she asked.

"It dates from a year ago. May Tomalin is not mentioned in it. I, of course, have nothing."

Iris gazed at the floor. A little sound as of consternation had passed her lips; but she made no attempt to console the victim of destiny who sat with bowed head before her. After a brief silence, Lashmar told of the will as it concerned Constance Bride, insisting on the fact that she was a mere trustee of the wealth bequeathed to her. With a humorously doleful smile, he spoke of Lady Ogram's promise to defray his election expenses, and added that Miss Bride, in virtue of her trusteeship, would carry out this wish. Another exclamation sounded from the listener, this time one of joy.

"Well, that's something! I suppose the expenses are heavy, aren't they?"

"Oh, not very. But what's the use? Of course I withdraw."

He let his hand fall despondently. Again there was silence.

"And that is why you thought of taking poison?" asked Iris, with a quick glance at his lowering visage.

"Isn't it a good reason? All is over with me. If Lady Ogram had lived to make her new will, I should have been provided for. Now I am penniless and hopeless."

"But, if she had lived, you would have had to marry Miss Bride."

Dyce made a sorrowful gesture.

"No. She would never have consented, even if I could have brought myself to such a sacrifice. In any case, I was doomed."

"But——"

Iris paused, biting her lip.

"You were going to say?"

"Only—that I suppose you would have been willing to marry that girl, the niece."

"I will answer you frankly." He spoke in the softest tone, and his smile had a touching candour. "You, better than any one, know the nature of my ambition. You know it is not merely personal. One doesn't like to talk grandiloquently, but, alone with you, there is no harm in saying that I have a message for our time. We have reached a point in social and political evolution where all the advance of modern life seems to be imperilled by the growing preponderance of the multitude. Our need is of men who are born to guide and rule, and I feel myself one of these. But what can I do as long as I am penniless? And so I answer you frankly: yes, if May Tomalin had inherited Lady Ogram's wealth, I should have felt it my duty to marry her."

Iris listened without a smile. And Lashmar had never spoken with a more convincing show of earnestness.

"What is she going to do?" asked the troubled little woman, her eyes cast down.

Dyce told all that he knew of May's position. He was then questioned as to the state of things political at Hollingford; his replies were at once sanguine and disconsolate.

"Well," he said at length, "I have done my best, but fortune is against me. In coming to see you, I discharged what I felt to be a duty. Let me again thank you for your generous kindness. Now I must work, work——"

He stood, an image of noble sadness, of magnanimity at issue with cruel fate. Iris glanced timidly at him; her panting showed that she wished to speak, but could not. He offered his hand; Iris took it, but only for an instant.

"I want you to tell me something else," broke from her lips.

"I will tell you anything."

"Are you in love with that girl—Miss Tomalin?"

With sorrowful dignity he shook his head; with proud self-consciousness he smiled.

"Nor with Miss Bride?"

"I think of her exactly as if she were a man."

"If I told you that I very much wished you to do something, would you care to do it?"

"Your wish is for me a command," Dyce answered gently. "If it were not, I should be grossly ungrateful."

"Then promise to go through with the election. Your expenses are provided for. If you win, I am *sure* some way can be found of providing you with an income—I am *sure* it can!"

"It shall be as you wish," said Lashmar, seeming to speak with a resolute cheerfulness. "I will return to Hollingford by the first train to-morrow."

They talked for a few minutes more. Lashmar mentioned where he was going to pass the night. He promised to resume their long-interrupted correspondence, and to let his friend have frequent reports from Hollingford. Then they shook hands, and parted silently.

After dinner Dyce strayed shorewards. He walked

down to the little harbour, and out on to the jetty. A clouded sky had brought night fast upon sunset, green and red lamps shone from the lighthouse at the jetty head, and the wash of the rising tide sounded in darkness on either hand. Not many people had chosen this spot for their evening walk, but, as he drew near to the lighthouse, he saw the figure of a woman against the grey obscurity; she was watching a steamboat slowly making its way through the harbour mouth. He advanced, and at the sound of his step on the wooden flooring the figure faced to him. There was just light enough to enable him to recognize Iris.

"You oughtn't to be here alone," he said.

"Oh, why not?" she replied, with a laugh. "I'm old enough to take care of myself."

The wind had begun to moan; waves tide-borne against the pier made a hollow booming, and at moments scattered spray.

"How black it is to-night!" Iris added. "It will rain. There! I felt a spot."

"Only a splash of sea-water, I think," replied Lashmar, standing close beside her.

Both gazed at the dark vast of sea and sky. A pair of ramblers approached them; a young man and a girl, talking loudly the tongue of lower London.

"I know a young lady," sounded in the feminine voice, "as 'as a keeper set with a di'mond and a hamethyz—lovely!"

"Come away," said Dyce. "What a hateful place this is! How can you bear to live among such brutes?"

Iris moved on by him, but said nothing.

"I felt ashamed," he added, "to find you with people like the Barkers. Do you mean to say they don't disgust you?"

"They are not so bad as that," Iris weakly protested. "But you mustn't think I regard them as intimate friends. It's only that—I've been rather lonely lately. Len away at school—and several things——"

" Yes, yes, I understand. But they're no company for you. Do get away as soon as possible."

Another couple went by them talking loudly the same vernacular.

" If I put it down for a day," said the young woman, " I forget all I've read. I've a hawful bad memory for readin'."

" How I loathe that class ! " Lashmar exclaimed. " I never came to this part of the coast, because I knew it was defiled by them. For heaven's sake, get away ! Go to some place where your ears won't be perpetually outraged. I can't bear to think of leaving you here."

" I'll go as soon as ever I can—I promise you," murmured Iris. " There ! It really is beginning to rain. We must walk quickly."

" Will you take my arm ? "

She did so, and they hurried on.

" That's the democracy," said Lashmar. " Those are the people for whom we are told that the world exists. They get money, and it gives them power. Meanwhile, the true leaders of mankind, as often as not, struggle through their lives in poverty and neglect."

Iris's voice sounded timidly.

" You would feel it of no use to have just enough for independence ? "

" For the present," he replied, " it would be all I ask. But I might just as well ask for ten thousand a year."

The rain was beating upon them. During the ascent to Sunrise Terrace, neither spoke a word. At the door of her lodgings Iris looked into her companion's face, and said, in a tremulous voice :

" I am sure you will be elected ! I'm certain of it ! "

Dyce laughed, pressed her hand, and, as the door opened, walked away through the storm.

CHAPTER XXVIII

LORD DYMCHURCH went down into Somerset. His younger sister was in a worse state of health than he had been led to suppose; there could be no thought of removing her from home. A day or two later her malady took a hopeless turn, and by the end of the week she was dead.

A month after this, the surviving daughter of the house, seeking solace in the ancient faith to which she had long inclined, joined a religious community. Dymchurch was left alone.

Since his abrupt departure from Rivenoak he had lived a silent life, spending the greater part of every day in solitude. Grief was not sufficient to account for the heaviness and muteness which had fallen upon him, or for the sudden change by which his youthful-looking countenance had become that of a middle-aged man. He seemed to shrink before eyes that regarded him, however kind their expression; one might have thought that some secret shame was harassing his mind. He himself, indeed, would have used no other word to describe the ill under which he suffered. Looking back on that strange episode of his life which begun with his introduction to Mrs. Toplady and ended in the park at Rivenoak, he was stung almost beyond endurance by a sense of ignominious folly. On his lonely walks, and in the silence of sleepless nights, he often gesticulated and groaned like a man in pain. His nerves became so shaken that at times he could hardly raise a glass or cup to his lips without spilling the contents. Poverty and loneliness he had known, and had learnt to bear them with equanimity ; he was tasting for the first time of humiliation.

A thousand times he reviewed the stages of his foolishness and, as he deemed it, of his dishonour. But he had lost the power to understand that phantasm of himself which pranked so grotesquely in the retrospect. Was it the truth that he had reasoned and taken deliberate step after step in the wooing of Lady Ogram's niece ? Might he not urge in his excuse, to cloak him from his own and the world's contempt, some unsuspected calenture, for which, had he known, he ought to have taken medical advice ? When, in self-chastisement, he tried to summon before his mind's eye the image of May Tomalin, he found it quite impossible; the face no longer existed for him; the voice was as utterly forgotten as any he might have chanced to hear for a few minutes on that fatal evening in Pont Street. And this was what he had seen as an object of romantic tenderness—this vaporous nothing, this glimmer in a dazed eye !

Calm moments brought a saner self-reproach. " I simply yielded to the common man's common temptation. I am poor, and it was wealth that dazzled and lured me. Pride would explain more subtly: that is but a new ground of shame. I fell a prey to the vulgarest and basest passion ; better to burn that truth into my mind, and to make the brand a life-long warning. I shall the sooner lift up my head again."

He seemed to palliate his act by remembering that he wished to benefit his sisters. Neither of them— the poor dead girl, and she who lived only for self-forgetfulness—would have been happier at the cost of his disgrace. How well it was, indeed, that he had been saved from that debasement in their eyes.

He lived on in the silent house, quite alone and desiring no companionship. Few letters came for him, and he rarely saw a newspaper. After a while he was able to forget himself in the reading of books which tranquilized his thought, and held him far from the

noises of the passing world. So sequestered was the
grey old house that he could go forth when he chose
into lanes and meadows without fear of encountering
any one who would disturb his meditation and his enjoyment of nature's beauty. Through the mellow days of
the declining summer he lived amid trees and flowers,
slowly recovering health and peace in places where a
bird's note, or the ripple of a stream, or the sighing of
the wind, were the only sounds under the ever-changing
sky.

His thoughts were often of death, but not on that
account gloomy. Reading in his Marcus Aurelius, he
said to himself that the Stoic Emperor must, after all,
have regarded death with some fear: else, why speak of
it so persistently, and with such marshalling of arguments to prove it no matter for dread? Dymchurch
never wished to shorten his life, yet, without other logic
than that of a quiet heart, came to think more than
resignedly of the end towards which he moved. He
was the last of his family, and no child would ever
bear his name. Without bitterness, he approved this
extinction of a line which seemed to have outlived its
natural energies. He, at all events, would bear no
responsibility for suffering or wrong-doing in the days
to come.

The things which had so much occupied him during
the last year or two, the state of the time, its perils
and its needs, were now but seldom in his mind; he
felt himself ripening to that " wise passiveness," which,
through all his intellectual disquiet, he had regarded
as the unattainable ideal. When, as a very young
man, he exercised himself in versifying, the model he
more or less consciously kept before him was Matthew
Arnold; it amused him now to recall certain of the
compositions he had once been rather proud of, and to
recognize how closely he had trodden in Arnold's foot-
prints; at the same time, he felt glad that the aspiration of his youth seemed likely to become the settled
principle of his maturity. Now-a-days he gave much of

his thought to Wordsworth, content to study without the desire of imitating. Whether he could *do* anything, whether he could bear witness in any open way to what he held the truth, must still remain uncertain; sure it was that a profound distrust of himself in every practical direction, a very humble sense of follies committed and dangers barely escaped, would for a long time make him a silent and solitary man. He hoped that some way might be shown him, some modest yet clear way, by following which he would live not wholly for himself; but he had done for ever with schemes of social regeneration, with political theories, all high-sounding words and phrases. It might well prove that the work appointed him was simply to live as an honest man. Was that so easy, or such a little thing?

Walking one day a mile or two from home, in one of those high-bowered Somerset lanes, he came within sight of a little cottage, which stood apart from a hamlet hidden beyond a near turning of the road. Before it moved a man, white-headed, back-bent, so crippled by some ailment that he tottered slowly and painfully with the aid of two sticks. Just as Dymchurch drew near, the old fellow accidentally let fall his pipe, which he had been smoking as he hobbled along. For him this incident was a disaster; he stood staring helplessly at the pipe and the little curl of smoke which rose from it, utterly unable to stoop for its recovery. With a timid smile, he turned to the stranger who approached, and Dymchurch, seeing the state of things, at once stepped to his assistance.

"I thank you, sir; I thank you, sir," said the hobbler, with pleasant frankness. "A man isn't much use when he can't even keep his pipe in his mouth, to say nothing of picking it up when it drops; what do *you* think, sir?"

Dymchurch talked with him. The man had spent his life as a gardener, and now for a couple of years, invalided by age and rheumatism, had lived in this cottage on a pension. His daughter, a widow, dwelt

with him, but was away working nearly the whole of
the day. He got along very well, but one thing there
was that grieved him, the state of his little garden.
Through the early summer he had been able to look
after it as usual, pottering among the flowers and the
vegetables for an hour or two each day ; but there came
rainy weather, and with it one of his bad attacks, and
the garden was now so overgrown with weeds that it
"hurt his eyes," it really did, to look that way. The
daughter dug potatoes and gathered beans as they
were wanted, but she had neither time nor strength to
do more.

Interested in a difficulty such as he had never
imagined, Dymchurch went up to the garden wall, and
viewed the state of things. Indeed, it was deplorable.
Thistles, docks, nettles, wild growths innumerable, were
choking the flowers in which the old man so delighted.
But the garden was such a small one that little trouble
and time would be needed to put it in order.

"Will you let me do it for you ? " he asked good-
naturedly. "It's just the kind of job I should like."

"You, sir ! " cried the old fellow, all but again losing
his pipe in astonishment. "Ho, ho ! That's a joke
indeed ! "

Without another word Dymchurch opened the
wicket, flung off his coat, and got to work. He
laboured for more than an hour, the old man leaning
on the wall and regarding him with half-ashamed, half-
amused countenance. They did not talk much, but,
when he had begun to perspire freely, Dymchurch
looked at his companion, and said:

"Now here's a thing I never thought of. Neglect
your garden for a few weeks, and it becomes a wilderness ; nature conquers it back again. Think what that
means ; how all the cultivated places of the earth are
kept for men only by ceaseless conflict with nature,
year in, year out."

"And that's true, sir, that's true. I've thought of
it sometimes, but then I'm a gardener, you see, and

Our Friend the Charlatan

it's my business, as you may say, to have such thoughts."

"It's every man's business," returned Dymchurch, supporting himself on his hoe, and viewing the up-rooted weeds. "I never realized as in this half-hour at the cost of what incessant labour the earth is kept at man's service. If I have done you a good turn, you have done me a better."

And he hoed vigorously at a root of dandelion.

Not for years had he felt so well in body and mind as during his walk home. There, there was the thought for which he had been obscurely groping! What were volumes of metaphysics and of sociology to the man who had heard this one little truth whispered from the upturned mould? Henceforth he knew *why* he was living, and *how* it behoved him to live. Let theories and poesies follow if they would: for him, the prime duty was that nearest to him, to strive his best that the little corner of earth which he called his should yield food for man. At this moment there lay upon his table letters informing him of the unsatisfactory state of his Kentish farm; the tenant was doing badly in every sense of the word, and would willingly escape from his lease if opportunity was given. Very well; the man should go.

"I will live there myself. I will get some practical man to live with me, until I understand farming. For profit I don't care; all will be well if I keep myself alive and furnish food for a certain number of other mortals. This is the work ready to my hand. No preaching, no theorizing, no trying to prove that the earth should be parcelled out and every man turn delver. I will cultivate this ground because it is mine, and because no other way offers of living as a man should—taking some part, however humble, in the eternal strife with nature."

The idea had before now suggested itself to him, but not as the result of a living conviction. If he had then turned to farming, it would have been as an

403

experiment in life; more or less vague reflections on
the needs of the time would have seemed to justify
him. Now he was indifferent to all "questions" save
that prime solicitude of the human race, how to hold
its own against the hostile forces everywhere leagued
against it. Life was a perpetual struggle, and, let
dreamers say what they might, could never be anything
else; he, for one, perceived no right that he had to
claim exemption from the doom of labour. Had he telt
an impulse to any other kind of work, well and good,
he would have turned to it; but nothing whatever
called to him with imperative voice save this task of
tilling his own acres. It might not always satisfy
him; he took no vow of one sole vocation; he had no
desire to let his mind rust whilst his hands grew horny.
Enough that for the present he had an aim which he
saw as a reality.

On his return home he found a London letter
awaiting him. It was with a nervous shrug that he
saw the writing of Mrs. Toplady. Addressing him at
his club, she invited him to dine on an evening a
fortnight hence, if he chanced to be in town.

"You heard, of course," she added, "of the defeat of
Mr. Lashmar at Hollingford. It seems to have been
inevitable."

So Lashmar had been defeated. The Hollingford
election interested Dymchurch so little that he had
never inquired as to its result; in truth, he had
forgotten all about it.

"I fear Mr. Lashmar was in every respect rather
disappointing. Rumour says that the philosophical
theory of life and government which he put before us
as original was taken word for word from a French
book which he took for granted no one would have
read. I hope this is not true; it has a very unpleasant
sound."

Quite as unpleasant, thought Dymchurch, was Mrs.
Toplady's zeal in spreading the rumour. He found no
difficulty in crediting it. The bio-sociological theory

had occupied his thoughts for a time, and, in reflecting upon it now, he found it as plausible as any other; but it had no more power to interest him. Lashmar, perhaps, was mere sophist, charlatan, an unscrupulous journalist who talked instead of writing. Words, words! How sick he was of the universal babble! The time had taken for its motto that counsel of Mephisto: *Vor allem haltet euch an Worte!* And how many of these loud talkers believed the words they uttered, or had found them in their own minds?

And how many preachers of socialism—in this, that, or the other form, had in truth the socialistic spirit? Lashmar, with his emphasis on the universal obligation of social service—was he not simply an ambitious struggler and intriguer, careless of everything but his own advancement? Probably enough. And, on the whole, was there ever an age so rank with individualism as this of ours, which chatters ceaselessly of self-subdual to the common cause?

"I, too," thus he thought, "am as much an individualist as the others. If I said that I cared a rap for mankind at large, I should be phrase-making. Only, thank Heaven! I don't care to advertise myself, I don't care to make money. I ask only to be left alone, and to satisfy in quiet my sense of self-respect."

On the morrow he was gone.

CHAPTER XXIX

" When you receive this letter you will have already
seen the result. I knew how it would be, but tried to
hope because you were hoping. My poll is better than
that of the last Liberal candidate, but Hollingford
remains a Tory stronghold. Shall I come to see you?
I am worn out, utterly exhausted, and can scarcely
hold the pen. Perhaps a few days at the seaside would
do me good, but what right have I to idle? If you
would like me to come, please wire to Alverholme
Rectory. Possibly you would rather I didn't bring my
gloom, now you have Len with you and are enjoying
yourself. Above all, be quite frank. If you are too
disappointed to care to see me, in heaven's name, say
so! You needn't fear its effect upon me. I should be
glad to have done with the world, but I have duties to
discharge. I wish you could have heard my last
speech, there were good things in it. You shall see
my address of thanks to those who voted for me; I
must try to get it widely circulated, for, as you know,
it has more than local importance Breakspeare, good
fellow, says that I have a great career before me; I
grin, and can't tell him the squalid truth. There are
many things I should like to speak about; my brain is
feverishly active. I must try to rest; another twenty-
four hours of this strain, and the results would be
serious. In any case, wire to me—yes or no. If it is
no, I shall say 'so be it,' and begin at once to look out
for some way of earning bread and cheese. We shall
be friends all the same."

Mrs. Woolstan was at Eastbourne. Having read

Lashmar's letter she brooded for a few minutes, then betook herself to the post-office, and telegraphed "Come at once." A few hours later she received a telegram informing her that Lashmar would reach Eastbourne at eleven o'clock on the next morning. At that hour she waited in her lodgings on the sea-front. A cab drove up; Lashmar was shown into the room.

He looked, indeed, much the worse for his agitations. His hand was hot; he moved heavily, and seemed to be too tired to utter more than a few words.

"Are you alone?"

"Quite. Len is down on the shore, and won't be back till half-past one."

"Would you—mind—if I lay down—on the sofa?"

"Of course not," replied Iris, regarding him anxiously. "You're not ill, I hope?"

He took her hand and pressed it against his forehead with the most melancholy of smiles. Having dropped on to the couch, he beckoned Iris to take a chair beside him.

"What can I get for you?" she asked. "You must have some refreshment——"

"Sleep, sleep!" he moaned musically. "If I could but sleep a little!—But I have so much to say. Don't fuss; you know how I hate fuss. No, no, I don't want anything, I assure you. But I haven't slept for a week. —Give me your hand. How glad I am to see you again! So you still have faith in me? You don't despise me?"

"What nonsense!" said Iris, allowing him to hold her hand against his breast as he lay motionless, his eyes turned to the ceiling. "You must try again, that's all. At Hollingford it was evidently hopeless."

"Yes. I made a mistake. If I could have stood as a Conservative, I should have carried all before me. It was Lady Ogram's quarrel with Robb which committed me to the other side."

Iris was silent, panting a little as if she suppressed words which had risen to her lips. He turned his head to look at her.

Our Friend the Charlatan

"Of course you understand that party names haven't the least meaning for me. By necessity I wear a ticket, but it's a matter of total indifference to me what name it bears. My object has nothing to do with party politics. But for Lady Ogram's squabble I should at this moment be Member for Hollingford."

"But would it be possible," asked Iris, with a flutter, "to call yourself a Conservative next time?"

"I have been thinking about that." He spoke absently, his eyes still upwards. "It is pretty certain that the Conservative side gives me more chance. It enrages me to think how I should have triumphed at Hollingford! I could have roused the place to such enthusiasm as it never knew! The great mistake of my life—but what choice had I? Lady Ogram was fatal to me." He groaned, and let his eyelids droop. "It is possible that, at the General Election, a Liberal constituency may invite me. In that case, of course"— He broke off with a weary wave of the hand. "But what's the use of thinking about it? I must look for work. Do you know, I have thoughts of going to New Zealand."

"Oh, that's nonsense!"

"Try to realize my position." He raised himself on his elbow. "After my life of the last few months, will it be very enjoyable to become a subordinate, to work for wages, to sink into obscurity? Does it seem to you natural? Do you think I shall be able to bear it?"

He had begun to quiver with excitement. As Iris kept silence, he rose to a sitting position, and continued more vehemently.

"Don't you understand that death would be preferable, a thousand times? Imagine me—*me* at the beck and call of paltry every-day people! Does it seem to you fitting that I should pay by such degradation for one or two trivial errors? How I shall bear it, I don't know; but bear it, I must. I keep reminding myself that I am not a free man. If once I could pay my debt——"

Our Friend the Charlatan

"Oh, *don't* talk about that!" exclaimed Iris, on a note of distress. "What do *I* care about the money?"

"No, but *I* care about my honour!" cried Lashmar. "If I had won the election, all would have been different; my career would have begun. Do you know what I should have done in that case? I should have come to you, and have said: 'I am a Member of Parliament. It is to you that I owe this, more than to any one else. Will you do yet more for me? Will you be my companion in the life upon which I am entering —share all my hopes—help me to conquer?'—That is what I meant to do. But I am beaten, and I can only ask you to have patience with your miserable debtor."

He let his face fall on to the head of the sofa, and shook with emotion. There was a short silence, then Iris, her cheeks flushing, lightly touched his hair. At once he looked up, gazed into her face.

"What! You still believe in me? Enough for that?"

"Yes," replied Iris, her eyes down and her bosom fluttering. "Enough for that."

"Ah! but be careful—think—!" He looked at her with impressive sadness. "Your friends will tell you that you are marrying a penniless adventurer. Have you the courage to face all that kind of thing?"

"I know you better than my friends do," replied Iris, taking in both her own the hand he held to her. "My fear," she added, again dropping her eyes and fluttering, "is that you will some day repent."

"Never! Never! It would be the blackest ingratitude!"

He spoke so fervently that the freckled face became rosy with joy. It was so near to his, that the man in him claimed warmer tribute, and Iris grew rosier still.

"Haven't you always loved me a little?" she whispered.

"If I had only known it!" answered Lashmar, the victorious smile softened with self-reproach. "My ambition has much to answer for. Forgive me, Iris."

Our Friend the Charlatan

"There's something else I must say, dear," she murmured. "After all, I have so little—and there is Len, you know——"

"Why, of course. Do you imagine I should wish to rob him?"

"No, no, no!" she panted. "But it *is* such a small income, after all. I'm afraid we ought to—to be careful, at first——"

"Of course we must. We shall live as simply as possible. And then you mustn't suppose that I shall never earn money. It's only waiting for one's opportunity."

A silence fell between them. Lashmar's amorous countenance had an under-note of thoughtfulness; Iris, smiling blissfully, none the less reflected.

"What are you thinking of?" he asked gently.

"Only how happy I am. I haven't the slightest fear. I know you have great things before you. Of course we must make use of our friends. May I write to Mrs. Toplady and tell her?"

She spoke without looking at him, and so was spared the interpretation of muscular twitches.

"Certainly. Do you know whether she is still in London?"

"I don't know, but probably not. Don't you think she may be very useful to us? I have always found her very nice and kind, and she knows such hosts of people."

Lashmar had his own thoughts about Mrs. Toplady, but the advantage of her friendship was undeniable. Happily, he had put it out of her power to injure him by any revelations she might make concerning May Tomalin; his avowal to Iris that May had been undisguisedly in love with him would suffice to explain anything she might hear about the tragi-comedy at Rivenoak. Whether the lady of Pont Street could be depended upon for genuine good-will, was a question that must remain unsettled until he had seen her again. She had bidden him to call upon her, at all

410

events, and plainly it would be advisable to do so as soon as possible.

"Yes," he answered reflectively. "She is a person to be reckoned with. It's possible her advice might be worth something in the difficulty about Liberal or Conservative. She is intelligent enough, I think, to understand me on that point. Yes, you might write to her at once. If I were you, I would speak quite frankly. You know her well enough for that, don't you?"

"Frankly? How?"

"Oh, I mean that you might say we have really been fond of each other for a long time—and that—well, that fate has brought us together in spite of everything—that kind of thing, you know."

"Yes, yes!" exclaimed Iris. "That's just what I should like to say."

Their talk grew calmly practical; the last half-hour of it was concerned with pecuniary detail. Her eye on the clock—for Leonard was sure to enter very soon—Mrs. Woolstan gave a full account of her income, enumerating the securities which were in the hands of her trustee, Mr. Wrybolt, and those which she had under her own control. In the event of her re-marriage Mr. Wrybolt's responsibility came to an end, a circumstance very pleasing to Lashmar. When the school-boy interrupted them, their conversation was by no means finished. After a cheerful lunch they resumed it on the sea-shore, Leonard being sent off to amuse himself as he would. By tea-time, it had been agreed that Lashmar should at once give up his expensive London rooms, and come down to Eastbourne, to recruit his health and enjoy Iris' society, until Leonard went back to school. The house at West Hampstead should be their home for the first twelve-month; by that time they would see how things were going, and be able to make plans. Early in the evening Lashmar took a train for town.

At his lodgings he found several letters: two of

411

them were important. Constance Bride's handwriting indicated the envelope to be first torn open. She wrote concisely and with her usual clearness. The ill news from Hollingford had been a grief to her, but it was very satisfactory to see that Lashmar had reduced the Conservative majority. "You have gained some very useful experience, which I hope you may before long have an opportunity of using. Please send me a statement of the election expenses as soon as you can; you remember the understanding between us in that matter. I am soon leaving England for a few weeks, but a letter directed as above will always reach me." The address referred to was that of a well-known society for Social Reform in the west of London.

His hand tremulous with the anger which this curt epistle had excited, Lashmar broke an envelope on the flap of which was printed in red letters the Pont Street address so familiar to him. Mrs. Toplady wrote more at length; she took the trouble to express her disappointment at the result of the Hollingford election in courteously rounded terms: "Our dear old friend of Rivenoak would have found some apt phrase to describe such a man as Butterworth. Wasn't she good at that kind of thing! How I have laughed to hear her talk of the late lamented Robb! You have the satisfaction of knowing that you got more votes than any Liberal has done at Hollingford for many years—so the papers tell me. In fact, you have made a very good start indeed, and I am sure the eye of the party will be on you."

Lashmar glowed. He had not expected such words from Mrs. Toplady. After all, Iris had given him good advice. Who knew but this woman might be more useful to him than Lady Ogram had been?

"Do you care for news of Miss Tomalin?" the latter continued. "After spending two or three days with me, she grew restless, and took rooms for herself. I am afraid, to tell you the truth, that she is a little disappointing; it is perhaps quite as well that a certain

Our Friend the Charlatan

romantic affair which was confided to me came to nothing. A week after she left my house, I received a very stiff (not to say impertinent) letter, in which the young lady informed me that she was about to marry a Mr. Yabsley, of Northampton, a man (to quote her words) 'of the highest powers, and with a brilliant ·future already assured to him.' This seemed to me, I confess, a little sudden, but at least it had the merit of being amusing. Perhaps I may venture to hope that you are already quite consoled. Remember me, I beg, to Miss Bride. Are you likely to be in this part of the world during the holidays? If anywhere near, do come and see me, and we will talk about that striking philosophical theory of yours."

Lashmar bit his lip. All at once he saw Mrs. Toplady's smile, and it troubled him. None the less did he ponder her letter, re-reading it several times. Presently he mused with uneasiness on the fact that Iris might even now be writing to Mrs. Toplady. Would her interest in him—she seemed, indeed, to be genuinely interested—survive the announcement that, after all, he was not going to marry Constance Bride, but had declined upon an insignificant little widow with a few hundreds a year? Was not this upshot of his adventures too beggarly? Had Mrs. Toplady been within easy reach, he would have gone to see her, but she wrote from the north of Scotland. He could only await the result of Iris's letter.

To the news concerning May Tomalin, he gave scarcely a thought. Mr. Yabsley, of Northampton!

Exceeding weariness sank him for a few hours in sleep; but before dawn he was tossing again on the waves of miserable doubt. Why had he not waited a little before going to see Iris? If only he had received this letter of Mrs. Toplady in time, it would have checked him—or so he thought. Was it the malice of fate which had ordained that, on his way to Eastbourne, he should not have troubled to look in at his lodgings? How many such wretched accidents he could recall!

Our Friend the Charlatan

Was he, instead of being fortune's favourite, simply a poor devil hunted by ill-luck, doomed to lose every chance? Why not he as well as another? Such men abound.

He had not yet taken the irretrievable step. Until he was actually married, a hope remained to him. He might postpone the fatal day; his purse was not yet empty. Why should he be too strict in the report of his election expenses to Constance? Every pound in his pocket meant a prolongation of liberty, a new horizon of the possible.

Two days later he was back again at Eastbourne. He had taken a cheap little lodging, and yielded himself to seaside indolence. A week passed, then Iris heard from Mrs. Toplady. She did not at once show Lashmar the letter; she awaited a moment when he was lulled by physical comfort into a facile and sanguine humour.

"Mrs. Toplady must have been in a hurry when she wrote this," was her remark, as, with seeming carelessness, she produced the letter. "Of course, she has an enormous correspondence. I shall hear again from her, no doubt, before long."

But one side of the note-paper was covered. In formal phrase, the writer said that she was glad to hear of her friend's engagement, and wished her all happiness. Not a word about their future meeting; not an allusion to Lashmar's prospects. If Iris had announced her coming marriage with some poor clerk, Mrs. Toplady could not have written less effusively.

"There's an end of her interest in *me*," Dyce remarked, with a nervous shrug.

Iris protested, and did her best to put another aspect on the matter, but without success. For twenty-four hours Lashmar kept away from her; she, offended, tried to disregard his absence, but at length sped to make inquiries, fearful lest he should be driven to despair. At the murky end of a wet evening they paced the esplanade together.

Our Friend the Charlatan

" You don't love me," said Iris, on a sob.

" It is because I love you," he replied, glooming, " that I can't bear to think of you married to such a luckless fellow as I am."

" Dearest ! " she whispered ; " am I ruining you ? Do you wish to be free again ? Tell me the truth ; I think I can bear it."

The next day saw them rambling in sunshine, Lashmar amorous and resigned, Iris flutteringly hopeful. And with such alternations did the holiday go by. When Leonard returned to school, their marriage was fixed for ten days later.

Shortly before leaving Eastbourne, Iris had written to Mr. Wrybolt. Already they had corresponded on the subject of her marriage ; this last letter, concerning a point of business which required immediate attention, remained without reply. Puzzled by her trustee's silence, Iris, soon after she reached home, went to see him at his City office. She learnt that Mr. Wrybolt was out of town, but would certainly return in a day or two.

Again she wrote. Again she waited in vain for a reply. On a dull afternoon near the end of September, as she sat thinking of Lashmar and resolutely seeing him in the glorified aspect dear to her heart and mind, the servant announced Mr. Barker. This was the athletic young man in whose company she had spent some time at Gorleston before Lashmar's coming. His business lay in the City ; he knew Mr. Wrybolt, and through him had made Mrs. Woolstan's acquaintance. The face with which he entered the drawing-room portended something more than a friendly chat. Iris had at one time thought that this young man felt disposed to offer her marriage ; was that his purpose now, and did it account for his odd look ?

" I want to ask you," Mr. Barker began, abruptly, " whether you know anything about Wrybolt ? Have you heard from him lately ? "

Iris replied that she herself wished to hear of that

gentleman, who did not answer her letters, and was said to be out of town.

"That's so, is it?" exclaimed the young man, with a yet stranger look on his face. "You really have no idea where he is?"

"None whatever. And I particularly want to see him!"

"So do I," said Mr. Barker, smiling grimly. "So do several people. You'll excuse me, I hope, Mrs. Woolstan. I knew he was a friend of yours, and thought you might perhaps know more about him than we did in the City. I mustn't stay."

Iris stared at him as he rose. A vague alarm began to tremble in her mind.

"You don't mean that anything's wrong?" she panted.

"We'll hope not, but it looks queer."

"Oh!" cried Iris. "He has money of mine. He is my trustee."

"I know that. Please excuse me; I really mustn't stay."

"Oh, but tell me, Mr. Barker!" She clutched at his coat-sleeve. "Is my money in danger?"

"I can't say, but you certainly ought to look after it. Get some one to make inquiries at once; that's my advice. I really must go."

He disappeared, leaving Iris motionless in amazement and terror.

CHAPTER XXX

THE wedding was to be a very quiet one. Lashmar
would have preferred the civil ceremony, at the table of
the registrar, with musty casuals for witnesses; but
Iris shrank from this. It must be at a church, and with
a few friends looking on, or surely people would gossip.
Had he been marrying an heiress, Dyce would have
called for pomp and circumstance, with portraits in the
fashion papers, and every form of advertisement which
society has contrived. As it was, he desired to slink
through the inevitable. He was ashamed; he was
confounded; and only did not declare it. To the very
eve of the wedding-day his mind ferreted elusive
hopes. Had men and gods utterly forsaken him?
In solitude he groaned and gnashed his teeth. And
no deliverance came.

Physical reaction made him at times the fervent
lover, and these amorous outbreaks supported Iris's
courage. "Let it once be over!" she kept saying to
herself. She trusted in her love and in her womanhood.

"At all events," cried the bridegroom, "we needn't
go through the foolery of running away to hide ourselves. It's only waste of money."

But Iris pleaded for the honeymoon. People would
think it so strange if they went straight from church
to their home at West Hampstead. And would not a
few autumn weeks of Devon be delightful? Again he
yielded.

The vicar of Alverholme and his wife, when satisfied that Dyce's betrothed was a respectable person,

Our Friend the Charlatan

consented to be present at the marriage. Not easily did Mrs. Lashmar digest her bitter disappointment, which came so close upon that of Dyce's defeat at Hollingford; but she was a practical woman, and, in the state of things at Alverholme, seven hundred a year seemed to her not altogether to be despised.

"My fear was," she remarked one day to her husband, "that Dyce would be tempted to marry money. I respect him for the choice he has made; it shows character."

The vicar just gave a glance of surprise, but said nothing. Every day made him an older man in look and bearing. His head was turning white. He had begun to mutter to himself as he walked about the parish. Not a man in England who worried more about his own affairs and those of the world.

In an obscure lodging Dyce awaited the day of destiny. One evening he went to dine at West Hampstead; though he was rather late, Iris had not yet come home, and she had left no message to explain her absence. He waited a quarter of an hour; when at length his betrothed came hurrying into the room, she wore so strange a countenance that Dyce could not but ask what had happened. Nothing, nothing—she declared. It was only that she had been obliged to hurry so, and was out of breath, and—and— Whereupon she tottered to a chair, death-pale, all but fainting.

"What the devil is the matter with you?" cried Lashmar, whose over-strung nerves could not endure this kind of thing.

His violence had an excellent effect. Iris recovered herself, and came towards him with hands extended.

"It's nothing at all, dearest. I couldn't bear to keep you waiting, and fretted myself into a fever when I saw what time it was. Don't be angry with me, will you?"

Dyce was satisfied. It seems to him a very natural explanation, and caresses put him into his gracious mood. "After all, you know," he said, "you're a very

418

womanly woman. I think we shall have to give up pretending that you're not."

"But I've given it up long since!" Iris exclaimed, with large eyes. "Didn't you know that?"

"I'm not sure"—he laughed—"that I'm not glad of it."

And they passed a much more tranquil evening than usual. Iris seemed tired; she sat with her head on Dyce's shoulder, thrilling when his lips touched her hair. He had assured her that her hair was beautiful —that he had always admired its hue of the autumn elm leaf. Her face, too, he was beginning to find pretty, and seldom did he trouble to reflect that she was seven years older than he.

Already he regarded this house as his own. His books had been transferred hither, and many of his other possessions. Very carefully had Iris put out of sight, or got rid of, everything which could remind him of her former marriage. Certain things (portraits and the like) which must be preserved for Leonard's sake were locked away in the boy's room. Of course Lashmar had given her no presents; she, on the other hand, had been very busy in furnishing a study which should please him, buying the pictures and ornaments he liked, and many expensive books of which he said that he had need. Into this room Dyce was not allowed to peep; it waited as a surprise for him on the return from the honeymoon. Drawing-room and dining-room he trod as master, and often felt that, after all, a man could be very comfortable here for a year or two. A box of good cigars invited him after dinner. A womanly woman, the little mistress of the house; and, all things considered, he wasn't sure that he wasn't glad of it.

One more day only before that of the wedding. Dyce had been on the point of asking whether all the business with Wrybolt was satisfactorily settled; but delicacy withheld him. Really, there was nothing to do; Iris's money simply passed into her own hands on the event of her marriage. It would be time enough to talk of such things presently. They spent nearly all the last day together. Iris was in the extremity of nervousness; she looked as if she had not slept for two or three nights; often she hid her face against Dyce's shoulder, and shook as if sobbing, but no tears followed.

"Do you love me?" she asked, again and again. "Do you really, really love me?"

"But you know I do," Dyce answered, at length irritably. "How many times must I tell you? It's all very well to be womanly, but don't be womanish."

"You're not sorry you're going to marry me?"

"You're getting hysterical, and I can't stand that."

Hysterical she became as soon as Lashmar had left her. One of the two servants, looking into the dressing-room before going to bed, saw her lying, half on the floor, half against the sofa, in a lamentable state. She wailed incoherent phrases.

"I can't help it—too late—I can't, *can't* help it—oh! oh!"

Unobserved, the domestic drew back, and went to gossip with her fellow-servant of this strange incident.

The hours drove on. Lashmar found himself at the church, accompanied by his father, his mother, his old friend the Home Office clerk. They waited the bride's coming; she was five minutes late, ten minutes late; but came at last. With her were two ladies, kinsfolk of hers. Had Iris risen from a sick-bed to go through this cere-mony, she could not have shown a more disconcerting visage. But she held herself up before the altar. The magic books were opened, the words of power were uttered; the golden circlet slipped on to her trembling hand; and Mrs. Dyce Lashmar passed forth upon her husband's arm to the carriage that awaited them.

A week went by. They were staying at Dawlish, and Lashmar, who had quite come round to his wife's opinion on the subject of the honeymoon, cared not how long these sunny days of contented indolence lulled his ambitious soul: at times he was even touched by the

Our Friend the Charlatan

devotion which repaid his sacrifice. A certain timidity which clung to Iris, a tremulous solicitude which marked her behaviour to him, became her, he thought, very well indeed. Constance Bride was right; he could not have been thus at his ease with a woman capable of reading his thoughts, and of criticizing them. He talked at large of his prospects, which took a hue from the halcyon sea and sky. One morning they had strolled along the cliffs, and, in a sunny hollow, they sat down to rest. Dyce took from his pocket a newspaper he had bought on coming forth.

"Let us see what fools are doing," he said genially.

Iris watched him with uneasy eye. The sight of a newspaper was dreadful to her: yet she always eagerly scanned those that came under her notice. Lying now on the dry turf, she was able to read one page whilst Dyce occupied himself with another. Of a sudden she began to shake; then a half-stifled cry escaped her.

"What is it?" asked her husband, startled.

"Oh, look, Dyce! Look at this!"

She pointed him to a paragraph headed: "Disappearance of a City Man." When Lashmar had read it, he met his wife's anguished look with surprise and misgiving.

"You've had a precious narrow escape. Of course, this is nothing to *you*, now?"

"Oh, but I'm afraid it is—I'm afraid it is, Dyce——"

"What do you mean? Didn't you get everything out of his hands?"

"I thought it was safe—I left it till we were back at home——"

Lashmar started to his feet, pale as death.

"What? Then all your money is lost?"

"Oh, surely not? How can it be? We must make inquiries at once——"

"Inquiries? Inquiries enough have been made, you may depend upon it, before this got into the papers. The fellow has bolted; the police are after him; he has robbed and swindled right and left. Do you imagine *your* money has escaped his clutches?"

They stood face to face.

"Dear, don't be angry with me!" sounded from Iris in a choking voice. "I am not to blame—I couldn't help it—oh, don't look at me like that, dear husband!"

"But you have been outrageously careless. What right had you to expose us to this danger? Ass that I was—ass, *ass* that I was! I wanted to speak of it, and my cursed delicacy prevented me. What right had you to behave so idiotically?"

He set off at a great speed towards Dawlish. Iris ran after him, caught his arm, clung to him.

"Where are you going? You won't leave me?"

"I'm going to London, of course," was his only reply as he strode on.

Running by his side, Iris told with broken breath of the offer of marriage she had received from Wrybolt not long ago. She understood now why he wished to marry her; no doubt he already found himself in grave difficulties, and saw this as a chance either of obtaining money, or of concealing a fraud he had already practised at her expense.

"Why didn't you tell me that before?" cried Lashmar savagely. "What right had you to keep it from me?"

"I ought to have told you. Oh, do forgive me! Don't walk so quickly, Dyce! I haven't the strength to keep up with you. You know that he hadn't everything—most fortunately not everything——"

With an exclamation of wrathful contempt the man pursued his way. Iris fell back; she tottered; she sank to her knees upon the grass, moaning, sobbing. Only when he was fifty yards ahead did Dyce pause and look back. Already she was running after him again. He turned, and walked less quickly. At length there was a touch upon his arm.

"Dear — dear — don't you love me?" panted a scarce audible voice.

"Don't be a greater idiot than you have been

already," was his fierce reply. "I have to get to London, and look after your business; that's enough to think about just now."

In less than an hour they had taken train. By early evening they reached Paddington Station, whence they set forth to call upon the person whom Iris mentioned as most likely to be able to inform them concerning Wrybolt. It was the athletic Mr. Barker, who dwelt with his parents at Highgate. An interview with this gentleman, caught at dinner, put an end to the faint hopes Lashmar had tried to entertain. Wrybolt, said Barker, was not a very interesting criminal; the frauds he had perpetrated were not great enough to make his case sensational; but there could be no shadow of doubt that he had turned his trusteeship to the best account.

"He has nothing but his skin to pay with," added the young City man, "and I wouldn't give much for that. Don't distress yourself, Mrs. Lashmar; I know a lady who is let in worse than you—considerably worse."

The newly-married couple made their way to West Hampstead. The servant who had been left in charge of the house did not conceal her surprise as she admitted them. It was nearly ten o'clock.

"I suppose we must have something to eat," said Dyce sullenly.

"You must be very hungry," Iris answered, regarding him like a frightened but affectionate dog that eyes its master. "Jane shall get something at once."

They sat down to such a supper as could be prepared at a moment's notice. By good fortune, a bottle of claret had been found, and, excepting one glass, which his wife thankfully swallowed, Lashmar drank it all. At an ordinary time, this excess would have laid him prostrate: in the present state of his nerves, it did him nothing but good; a healthier hue mantled on his cheeks, and he began to look furtively at Iris with eyes which had lost their evil expression. She, so exhausted that she could scarce support herself on the chair, timidly met these glances, but as yet no word was spoken.

"Why haven't you eaten anything?" asked Dyce at length, breaking the silence with a voice which was almost natural.

"I have, dear."

"Yes, a bit of bread. Come, eat! You'll be ill if you don't."

She tried to obey. Tears began to trickle down her face.

"What's the use of going on like that?" Lashmar exclaimed, petulantly rather than in anger. "You're tired to death. If you really can't eat anything, better go to bed. We shall see how things look in the morning."

Iris rose and came towards him.

"Thank you, dear, for speaking so kindly. I don't deserve it."

"Oh, we won't say anything about that," he replied, with an air of generosity. Then, laughing, "Aren't you going to show me the study?"

"Dyce! I haven't the heart."

She began to weep in earnest.

"Nonsense! Let us go and look at it. I'll carry the lamp."

They left the room, and Iris, struggling with her tears, led the way to the study door. As he entered Dyce gave an exclamation of pleasure. The little room was furnished and adorned very tastefully; book-shelves, with all Lashmar's own books carefully arranged, and many new volumes added, made an appetizing show; a handsome writing-table and a revolving-chair seemed to invite to pen-work.

"I could have done something here," he remarked, with a nodding of the head.

Iris came nearer. Timidly she laid a hand upon his shoulder; appealingly she gazed into his face.

"Dear"—it was a just audible whisper—"you are so clever—you are so far above ordinary men——"

Our Friend the Charlatan

Lashmar smiled. His arm fell lightly about her waist.

"We have still more than two hundred pounds a year," the whisper continued. "There's Len—but I must take him from school——"

"Pooh! We'll talk about that."

A cry of gratitude escaped her.

"Dyce! How good you are! How bravely you bear it, my own dear husband. I'll do anything, anything! We needn't have a servant. I'll work—I don't care— anything if you still love me. Say you still love me!"

He kissed her hair.

"It's certain I don't hate you.—Well, we'll see how things look to-morrow. Who knows? It may be the real beginning of my career!"

THE END.

Notes to the Text

Page 1, line 1:
As he waited for his breakfast, never served to time . . . Gissing refers
in several other works to the unpleasantness of having to wait for a
meal. Alfred Yule, in *New Grub Street,* is made impatient by the
slightest delay. Henry Ryecroft rejoices at the punctuality of his
housekeeper with regard to meals.

Page 3, line 1:
She could not brook a semblance of disregard . . .The same remark
occurs frequently in Gissing's books. In his *Commonplace Book* (ed.
Jacob Korg, 1962, p. 50) he observes: 'Most men are in a degree capable of quiet authority, but most women are hopelessly incapable of
anything of the kind, and the exceptional instances give one a high
idea of all that is implied in rank and education. The last thing to be
looked for in a woman of low social standing is the power of ruling
subordinates, and I suppose it is rare even among the highly placed.'
This was written in 1891; it reflects his own domestic experience. In
the American edition of *Our Friend the Charlatan,* Gissing wrote:
'Yet, like women in general, had no idea of how to rule.' On p. 105,
line 13 of the present edition, we read that Lady Ogram's servants
respected 'her power of ruling, the rarest gift in women of whatever
rank.'

Page 5, line 14:
Sweet are the uses of disappointment. An adaptation of 'Sweet are the
uses of adversity', *As You Like It,* II, 1, 12.

Page 39, line 9:
The Temple of the Winds at Athens. A tower built in white marble in
the first century B.C., about three hundred yards north of the Acropo-
lis.

Page 40, line 36:
Charles Mudie founded his famous circulating library in 1842. For some 50 years Mudie's was the single most important distributor of fiction in England, exercising a virtual dictatorship over the literary world.

Page 42, line 13:
Gissing's use of the Greek word, *demos*, for the people, is significant of both the influence of classical culture upon him and of his attitude towards the masses. He uses the word in other works—in particular *Demos* and *The Private Papers of Henry Ryecroft*.

Page 43, line 31:
Herbert Spencer (1820-1903) published *The Man versus The State* in 1884. Gissing read the book on February 20, 1896, and transcribed this sentence in his *Commonplace Book* (p. 26): 'There is no political alchemy by which you can get golden conduct out of leaden instincts.' He commented: 'Precisely. And the whole answer to Socialism is: that if Society were ready for pure Socialism, *it would not be such as it is now*.' The distinction between *l'Elite* and *la Foule* is made by Izoulet in his preface to *La Cité Moderne* (Paris, 1894): 'Le grand probleme social ... c'est d'équilibrer justement l'Elite et la Foule dans la Cité. Or, il faut en convenir, le Passé ne nous montre guère que *l'eviction de la Foule par l'Elite*. Qui sait si l'Avenir, par un ostracisme inverse, ne s'apprête pas à nous montrer *l'éviction de l'Elite par la Foule?*' (p.vii).

Page 47, line 32:
Fruges consumere arti. From Horace, *Epistles*, I, II, 27. 'Nos numerus sumus et fruges consumere arti': we are the ciphers, fit for nothing but to eat our share of earth's fruits.

Page 48, line 23:
Loving the life of the country ... and leave the world aside. This is the ideal expounded in the *Private Papers of Henry Ryecroft*, and adumbrated in *New Grub Street*. Edwin Reardon dreams of 'a life of scholarly self-indulgence' (ch. XXVI), but his hopes are frustrated.

Page 49, line 17:
What is not good for the beehive cannot be good for the bee. Marcus Aurelius, *Meditations*, Book VI, 54.

Page 78, line 2:
It's what I've been preaching in season and out of season, for the last ten years: 'be instant in season, out of season.' The Second Epistle of Paul to Timothy, IV, 2.

Page 79, line 15:
Nunc dimittis. From Evening Prayer in *The Book of Common Prayer*.

Page 82, line 7:
Hoc signo vinces! Eusebius, *Life of Constantine*, I, 28. 'In hoc signo vinces': in this sign shalt thou conquer.

Page 83, line 32:
Sat prata biberunt. From Virgil, Eclogue, III, iii. 'The meadows have drunk enough.'

Page 84, line 21:
We shall soon be fighting the good fight together. 'Fight the good fight of faith'. The First Epistle of Paul to Timothy, VI, 12.

Page 88, line 34:
Lombard Street: a financial centre of the City. In the thirteenth century Lombard merchants came to England and were employed to help in collecting the dues payable to the popes.

Page 102, line 11:
The rule that low-born English girls cannot rise above their native condition. A remark which Gissing doubtless felt justified in making when he looked back on his two disastrous matrimonial ventures. Neither Nell nor Edith showed any capacity for self-improvement.

Page 104, line 7:
Robb the Grinder. Lady Ogram's pun is based on the nickname of Robin Toodle, a character in *Dombey and Son*. Toodle is also called Biler and Rob the Grinder. He was educated at the Charitable Grinders' establishment.

Page 105, line 25:
From the sublime to the ridiculous: Napoleon is reported to have first used the phrase when addressing De Pradt, Polish ambassador, after the retreat from Moscow in 1812. By Gissing's time the phrase had become common property.

Page 110, line 8:
The man of hope. 'A man of hope and forward-looking mind', Wordsworth, *The Excursion*, Book VII, 276.

Page 119, line 17:
the tools to him who can use them. 'To the very last, he [Napoleon] had a kind of idea; that, namely, of *La carriere ouverte aux talents*, The tools to him who can handle them.' Carlyle, *Critical and Miscellaneous Essays*, vol. IV, 'Sir Walter Scott'.

Page 121, line 5:
Sedet in oeternumque sedebit. Virgil, *Aeneid*, 6, 617. 'He sits and will sit through eternity.'

Page 121, line 20:
No armed Pallas leaping to sudden life. Pallas, or Athene, the Greek goddess of wisdom, daughter of Zeus and Metis. She sprang fully grown and armed from the brain of her father, who had swallowed Metis when pregnant, fearing that her child would be mightier than he *(Oxford Companion to English Literature).*

Page 135, line 29:
Meminisse juvabit. 'Forsan et haec olic meminisse juvabit.' Virgil, *Aeneid*, 1, 203. 'The day may dawn when this plight shall be sweet to remember.'

Page 136, line 28:
I have heard of thee . . . 'I have even heard of thee, that the spirit of the gods is in thee, and that light and understanding and excellent wisdom are found in thee.' Daniel, V, 14.

Page 137, line 9:
Mundungus: bad-smelling tobacco—from Spanish mondongo = tripe, black-pudding. One Mundungus in Sterne's *Sentimental Journey* stands for Dr. S. Sharp, author of *Letters from Italy* (1766).

Page 138, line 9:
The monstrous regiment of women. The full title of John Knox's pamphlet is *The First Blast of the Trumpet Against the Monstrous Regiment of Women* (1558).

Page 138, line 26:
As a jewel of gold in a swine's snout, so is a fair woman which is without discretion. Proverbs, XI, 22.

Page 138, line 31:
One man among a thousand have I found . . . Ecclesiastes, VII, 28.

Page 139, line 16:
She will do him good and not evil all the days of her life. Proverbs, XXXI, 12. The same quotation appears in Gissing's short story 'Out of the Fashion'.

Page 139, line 19:
Give her of the fruit of her hands . . . Proverbs, XXXI, 31.

Page 139, line 30:
Thou art the sophist of our time, and list how the wise men spoke of

thy kind. Plato's sophist is described by Plato as 'a charlatan, a hireling, a disputant, no true teacher.' The passage quoted on pp. 139-40 is apparently not to be found in Plato's *Sophist*.

Page 140, line 9:
Comes it not something near? Shakespeare, *The Winter's Tale*, V, III, 23.

Page 140, line 13:
Yeoman's service. 'It did me yeoman's service.' Shakespeare, *Hamlet*, V, II, 36.

Page 140, line 29:
Honest water which ne'er left man i' the mire. Shakespeare, *Timon of Athens*, I, II, 61.

Page 159, line 17:
A gentleman of Northampton, a man of light and leading. In *Denzil Quarrier* (ch. XV) Mr. Chown, the radical Polterham draper, reads aloud Disraeli's public letter to the Duke of Marlborough, in which the country is warned against the perils of Home Rule. 'It is to be hoped that all men of light and leading will resist this destructive doctrine.'

Page 173, line 24:
The exciting tenor of his life. 'The noiseless tenor of their way.' Gray's *Elegy Written in a Country Churchyard*, XIX. This phrase was often quoted or adapted by Gissing, especially in *Born in Exile* and *The Private Papers of Henry Ryecroft*.

Page 191, line 9:
He exchanged phrases of such appalling banality . . . confusion of perfumes. The inanity of social gatherings is a recurrent theme in Gissing's novels. See in particular *Isabel Clarendon*, *Born in Exile* and the largely autobiographical *Ryecroft Papers*, Summer XIII. Austin Harrison described his tutor's misery under such circumstances in 'George Gissing', *Nineteenth Century and After*, September 1906, pp. 453-63.

Page 203, line 35:
Lashmar must have been of much sterner stuff. 'Ambition should be made of sterner stuff.' Shakespeare, *Julius Caesar*, III, II, 98.

Page 213, line 3:
Discontent, the malady of the age, had taken hold upon him. Matthew Arnold, a poet admired by Dymchurch (see p. 400), wrote in 'Youth's Agitations' that 'one thing only has been lent/To youth and age in common—discontent.'

Page 214, line 18:
When thou art ... do require. Marcus Aurelius, *Meditations*, Book V, 1.

Page 215, line 23:
Earning bread in the sweat of his brow. 'In the sweat of thy face shalt thou eat bread.' *Genesis*, III, 19.

Page 216, line 2:
His uselessness in the scheme of things. Doubtless an echo from Fitzgerald's translation of *Omar Khayyám*, I, LXXIII: 'To grasp this sorry Scheme of Things entire.'

Page 223, line 3:
The murdering of Shakespeare. Gissing wrote from experience: the liberties taken with Elizabethan plays by Victorian producers shocked the more intellectual portion of the public. His diary for April 25, 1894 records his going to a matinee of *Twelfth Night* at Daly's Theatre: 'The most offensive performance I ever sat through. Only 3 acts were given, and then, to fill up the time, a concert followed!'

Page 233, line 17:
Bicycling was extremely popular in the 1890s, and 'new women' regarded the bicycle as an instrument of emancipation. Gissing wrote a short story, 'The Schoolmaster's Vision', which foreshadows the bicycling sections of the present novel.

Page 233, line 34:
Dobbin the grocer. Captain, afterwards Colonel, William Dobbin is a character in Thackeray's *Vanity Fair*.

Page 235, line 1:
At this time they were both reading a book of Nietzsche. It is interesting to note that Gissing discussed Nietzsche in his correspondence with Eduard Bertz. Bertz published two articles on the German philosopher about the time Gissing was writing *Our Friend the Charlatan*. See *The Letters of George Gissing to Eduard Bertz*, ed. A.C. Young (1961), pp. 228, 230, 283 and 288. The dangers of Nietzsche's philosophy were apprehended in a truly prophetic spirit.

Page 236, line 9:
Gissing's complex response to Carlyle's philosophy can be seen in his correspondence with his family, with Eduard Bertz and Edward Clodd. Carlyle is mentioned in *Demos* (ch. XXIX), *Isabel Clarendon* (vol. II, ch. VI and XV), *Thyrza* (ch. XXXV), *New Grub Street* (ch. II), *In the Year of Jubilee* (Part I, ch. VII) and *The Private Papers of Henry Ryecroft* (Winter, XVIII).

Page 245, line 9:
Charles Darwin (1809-82) and Alfred Russel Wallace (1823-1913) hit upon the idea of natural selection as the solution to the problem of evolution at about the same time. They made a joint communication to the Linnean Society on the theory of evolution in 1858.

Page 253, line 22:
A victim of circumstances. This is the title of a well-known short story by Gissing. In both cases the phrase has an ironical flavour. The word 'circumstances' recurs frequently in his fiction, often with a dramatic or pathetic meaning, as in *Born in Exile.*

Page 261, line 32:
Despised and rejected of men. Isaiah, LII, 3. As P.F. Kropholler remarks, 'quotations from the Bible and the Prayer Book have been skilfully woven into the Rev. Mr. Lashmar's speech . . . A thorough knowledge of the Bible is listed as one of Gissing's intellectual ambitions' in his *Commonplace Book,* p. 26.

Page 262, line 18:
A square meal. The expression is of American origin; it has been traced back to 1868. The Rev. Lashmar naturally resents its novelty. Similarly, 'to run', with the sense of 'to direct' (p. 265, line 18) is of American origin, its first use being traced back to 1864.

Page 264, line 34:
But what about the fruits of the spirit? 'To bring forth the fruits of the spirit' occurs in the *Prayer Book* (The Litany).

Page 265, lines 15 and 37:
Blessed are the merciful . . . From the Beatitudes in *St Matthew,* V, 3.

Page 266, line 3:
The vision, probably, brought with it neither purple nor fine linen. 'There was a certain rich man, which was clothed in purple and fine linen, and fared sumptuously every day.' *St Luke,* XVI, 19.

Page 266, line 5:
Matthew V. to VII. contain several condemnations of charlatanism.

Page 287, line 37:
As P.F. Kropholler plausibly suggests, Miss Tomalin may have been intended to think of 'In a Balcony', in which the Queen obliges Constance to give up her lover.

Page 298, line 27:
The anecdote comes from Gissing's *Commonplace Book* (p. 45), where it is dated 1893.

Page 317, line 16:
The sentimentality of a hundred novels surged within her. Two passages in Gissing's works can be readily connected with this statement: that in which Alice Mutimer (*Demos*, ch. XIX) asphyxiates herself with cheap, sentimental fiction, and Rhoda Nunn's onslaught on the depiction of love in novels (*The Odd Women*, ch. VI).

Page 317, line 18:
Love is best! From Browning's 'Love among the Ruins'.

Page 376, line 33:
In this struggle it is not the big battalions will prevail. Voltaire ironically observed: 'On dit que Dieu est toujours pour les gros bataillons', Letter to M. Le Riche, February 6, 1770.

Page 400, line 29:
Wise passiveness. 'That we can feed this mind of ours/In a wise passiveness.' Wordsworth, 'Expostulation and Reply'.

Page 405, line 8:
Vor allem haltet euch an Worte! The original reads: 'Im ganzen—haltet Euch an Worte.' *Faust*, Studierzimmer line 1990. Bayard Taylor translated in 1872: 'On *words* let your attention centre.'

Page 417, line 7:
Pomp and circumstance. 'Pride, pomp and circumstance of glorious war!' Shakespeare, *Othello*, III, III, 355.

The Manuscript

Replying to a query about his methods of work, Gissing once admitted that literary production gave him a great deal of trouble, and that more than half of what he wrote went into the fire—with maledictions (G.B. Burgin, 'How Authors Work', *Idler*, April 1896, pp. 344-48). He might have added that out of professional conscientiousness and so as to facilitate the printers' task he made fair copies of any passage carrying heavy corrections. He did so at least until he decided with *Sleeping Fires* to have the manuscripts of his novels typewritten, with the consequence that, perhaps excepting *Workers in the Dawn*, his most interesting manuscripts are the later ones. Corrections were made on typescripts and also on proofs. As the opportunities to make alterations increased, so did the alterations themselves.

Our Friend the Charlatan is a good illustration of this. Few Gissing novels if any lend themselves better to a textual study. Not only do we have a manuscript which contains many corrections, but also a set of page proofs for the English edition. As usual the typescript, of which several copies were made in September 1900, has disappeared, and it is all the more to be regretted as the typescript for the American edition (which was corrected from March 2 to 8 1901) was revised separately and led to an American version of the story which differs from the English one on a number of minor points. Further complication results from the existence of an annotated copy of the first American edition which bears a few corrections in Gissing's hand. A detailed and exhaustive study of all the variants offered by the half-dozen states available would be a daunting task and would run to the length of a small volume. This is of course out of the question here. The following study, however brief, is nonetheless a comprehensive attempt to record all the types of variants worth noting and to reproduce the passages which were cancelled either on the manuscript or on the typescript.

The title-page of the MS reads: 'The Coming Man/A Novel/by/George Gissing' in the author's handwriting, with the following addition in another hand: 'Title changed to Our Friend the Charlatan/1901'. In the prefatory note, Izoulet's volume so perkily ransacked by Lashmar was at first called a 'most interesting a suggestive book.' It was ultimately styled 'remarkable', an epithet which did not succeed in concealing Gissing's ambivalent attitude to Izoulet's bio-sociological theory. Then the place and date at the bottom of the note varied as the production of the novel advanced: St. Honoré became St. Honoré, Nièvre, then St. Honoré en Morvan; August 29, 1900 was altered to August 1900 on the proofs, and either the printers or the publishers of the English edition made this into 1901.

The changes which any attentive reader would notice on the MS fall into two classes: the changes which were made in the run of the pen before the first draught of a given sentence was actually written and those that occurred at any time between the moment the writer had completed his period and that when he despatched his MS to Pinker to be typed. The first version therefore is only indicative of a transient intention but, as will be seen, it may be significant when it testifies that Gissing's purposes were still comparatively indefinite with regard to some details at the actual moment of writing. Some variants recorded below were cancelled on the MS, others were set down at the typescript stage. The 150 corrections on the proofs are mainly concerned with misprints, punctuation and capitalization, but some last-minute changes were effected, and in such cases Gissing saw to it that the final version did not exceed the preceding one in length. For instance, on p. 2, line 14, 'demanded a generous expenditure' was altered to 'demanded bountiful expenditure', and on p. 39, 'do on a paltry three hundred a year' was changed to 'do on less than three hundred a year.' Or again, at the close of the first paragraph, on p. 71 an unfortunate echo was removed when 'visage' was substituted for 'countenance' in 'circumstance had never yet shown him an austere visage'.

The differences between the manuscript and the printed

text are of greater significance. They range from the obvious
lapse of the pen, which was remedied either silently by the
typist, or by the author on the typescript, to the cancellation
of whole paragraphs or pages. At this stage too, punctuation
and capitalization were rationalized. Hyphens were introduced into the dialogue to indicate interruptions in a given
character's speech: words like Parliament, Civil Servant, Conservative, Liberal and University were ultimately spelt with
the initial capitals which the reader expects in most contexts.
Italics were sometimes cancelled when they could indeed be
dispensed with (p. 134, line 3, *that*), but the reverse process
was more frequent (p. 246, line 26, *can*; p. 316, line 5, *forbid*;
p. 350, line 14, *there*). In the latter part of the story two short
paragraphs in succession were occasionally fused into one.
Other changes made with a view to concentrating, clarifying
or simplifying occur throughout the text. Some personal pro-
nouns were replaced by the names of the characters concerned; an occasional superfluous word, question or
authorial remark was left out. Thus on p. 24, line 3, the MS
reads: 'The son listened [unmoving] to an exposition of his
father's difficulties.' On p. 125, line 11, after remarking to her
solicitor that she could not see why he did not find her grand-
niece ages ago, Lady Ogram asked a question which needlessly emphasized her thoughtlessness: 'Haven't you advertised in Canada?' And the reply was: 'No. We knew that your
brothers went to Australia.' At the end of ch. XVII, May Tomalin originally posted her anonymous exhortatory note to
Lashmar at the Marble Arch; in the book she finds a hansom
and is 'driven to a remote post-office.' On p. 355, line 8, Dyce
Lashmar hears that Lady Ogram 'had died between two and
three o'clock', and the paragraph on the MS ended with
'never having regained consciousness.'
   The names of some characters were altered during the composition. Lady Susan Harrop was at first called Lady Walsh;
the journalist Halliday was renamed Breakspeare; May Tomalin was originally Miss Kickweed and Dr. Wolff became Dr.
Baldwin. On p. 243, Mrs. Toplady signed herself Mercia E.
Toplady, not Geraldine Toplady. Matters of time also
received careful attention at the stage of revision. The Rev.
Lashmar (p. 2, line 7) had seen his income decrease 'for a
good many years'; Constance Bride (p. 11, line 6) had given
up dispensing 'about a year ago', she would be travelling (p.
15, line 34) 'until nine o'clock', not 'for two or three hours';

Dymchurch was appealed to by the tenant of his Kentish farm for a reduction of rent 'not long ago', then 'two years ago', and finally 'some time ago' (p. 215, line 12). Similarly some references to money matters were touched up. The elder Lashmar (p. 2, line 18) still had a small private fortune, 'some hundred and fifty pounds a year—most of it assigned to a special purpose.' This sum was reduced to 'about a hundred pounds a year—devoted to a private purpose.' On pp. 51-52, Dyce's 'little competence' was at first said to amount to 'three hundred a year', and Iris Woolstan's cheque to Dyce was for five, not three, hundred pounds. Here as in many other cases, Gissing aimed at greater plausibility; he also removed unnecessarily accurate details. The characters' psychology, rather than material facts, was in some cases the matter at issue. Of Dyce (p. 14, line 14), it was distinctly better to say that 'sometimes he had the air of a lyric enthusiast' (MS: often). Constance Bride's description of Lady Ogram as 'very rich' rather than 'enormously rich' is more acceptable in view of her guarded answer to Dyce (p. 17, line 11). After listening to Dyce's attack on men's chivalrous attitude to women and to his promise that he will 'never try to please a woman by any other methods than those which would win the regard and friendship of a man', she originally replied: 'If you stick to that you'll be worthy of all respect.' The change to 'you'll be a man worth knowing' better suits the irony of the situation (p. 67, line 3). Similarly Lady Ogram's miscalling the Rookes the Crows (p. 125) is all the more effective and amusing as it occurs once, not twice, as was the case on the MS.

Through the host of slight stylistic improvements, it is possible to follow the many directions in which the novelist's thought was running when he revised his manuscript. He removed some false elegancies, like 'the morning's showers' (p. 71, line 23), 'a critical moment of his *courbe*' (p. 213, line 1), or 'you were born post Darwinium' (p. 262, line 3); he eliminated repetitions of words or ideas and ambiguous or awkward phrasing (p. 307, line 13: 'But you do you let it [do so]?'); he corrected a number of epithets describing his characters' physical or mental features, which doubtless helped the illustrator in his not very remarkable performance. A number of commonplace words were replaced by more felicitous ones (note/chord, p. 3; quietly decisive/soberly decisive, p. 7; talked about/published, p. 149). The quest for the *mot juste* is noticeable on every page (pauperdom/indigence, p, 8; to speak/to complain of an ailment, p. 32; avowal/revelation, p. 75). In one particular instance the shadow of Mrs. Grundy lies across the MS. Gissing had once been taken to task by a reviewer for using the epithet 'sexual', and perhaps he remembered this when on p. 18, line 3, he chose to speak of 'masculine' instead of 'sexual' prejudice.

The improvements extended beyond the scope of style in a few cases: Dymchurch reflects, playing, as he commonly does, with a seal on his watch-guard, not with a button of his waistcoat (p. 44, line 30). At the end of ch. IX, Kerchever replied to Lady Ogram's remarks about Lashmar's brains and their usefulness in the forthcoming electoral campaign: 'I must know him better'. Considering the relations between the solicitor and the old autocrat of Rivenoak as well as his contempt for intellectual activities, we prefer to hear him say: 'I have never heard that they [brains] went for much in politics.' With this example we are on the border-line of a type of alteration which concerned the characters' personalities and the intercourse between the characters. Here is a list of such alterations which are all suggestive of Gissing's hesitations on matters of detail as he wrote his story after making abundant notes on the plot and the characters:

- p. 8, line 16: 'Ogram? I think not/I know the name.' Dyce must be shown to be knowledgeable.
- p. 12, line 14: 'How do you do, Miss Constance/Miss Connie!' Dyce still regards Miss Bride with adolescent eyes. The familiar form happily smacks of condescension.
- p. 101, line 11: 'Sir Quentin had perhaps/doubtless fallen short of entire happiness.' The continuation of the narrative shows that there is no room for doubt.
- p. 111, line 18: 'She cared little for any enterprise/she cared for no enterprise, however laudable, in which she could only be a sharer.' Lady Ogram's autocratic temper requires the negative form.
- p. 114, line 4: 'Necessarily she spoke of him as an old friend.' This remark in brackets was not allowed to stand, and the ambiguity of Constance's attitude to Lashmar in the early chapters gained by it.
- p. 122. In the central paragraph on Kerchever Gissing passed from satire to sarcasm: '... paternal office. You might have pointed to him: behold the kind of man we can produce in England! He rowed, he shot, he played golf or tennis, to universal admiration. At times he read.'

- p. 124, line 24: The brilliant marriage of Joseph's and Thomas's sister was commented upon briefly in the MS version: 'Mrs. Rooke declared that it was a marriage with a nobleman.' This could have led the dialogue into an unprofitable track.
- pp. 139-40: The authorship of the passage quoted by Martin Blaydes to Breakspeare was revealed before Blaydes began to read, not after the lengthy apposite quotation: '...Mr. Blaydes presently reached down a volume, apropos of nothing but his vagrant fancy. He had happened upon a translation of Plato's Republic, and, on opening it, became aware...' The suspense concerning the authorship is an improvement in the narrative technique; it falls in with the personality of the narrator.
- p. 147, line 32, the MS reads: 'Constance had received a letter from Dyce. She assented with all good humour to Lady Ogram's praise.' The suppression of the letter makes the end of the scene more plausible.
- p. 150, line 36: May Tomalin exclaimed with unconscious impertinence and typical delight in facts: 'Oh, yes. It's nothing. Just one change.'
- p. 222. Lord Dymchurch's meditations were extended at the close of the first paragraph as follows: 'Nay, were there not signs that from its ranks might be recruited even the titular aristocracy, as old families—like his own—decayed and disappeared?' This foolish hope of a decadent aristocrat in love showed him in his less resigned mood.
- p. 235, line 12: Dyce's views on Nietzsche took a slightly different course on the MS: 'He counted himself Nietzsche's superior as a thinker; there was a brutal charm in the philosopher which offended him. It preserved, too, his sociological theory—indeed he had come to regard it...' But the sentence was not completed.
- p. 346, line 6: Dyce's self-defence in the presence of Lady Ogram was introduced with a more obvious suggestion of impertinence: 'He broke off, observed the listener's expression, and added in the tone of one who confidently expects a generous interpretation.'
- p. 359, line 39: The burial ceremony took place in the cemetery chapel, not 'in the little church of Shawe.'

More important than these alterations were most of the following which in some cases amounted to fragments of scenes, if not scenes of some length. The three more substantial passages were published by Dr. J.R. Tye in his article on 'Autograph Gissing Material in New Zealand' (see Bibliography). They are those beginning on pp. 129, 141 and 369.

(1). p. 6, line 39: Passage cancelled after 'corner': 'but, when he had discovered the flowers themselves, they were lying half dead, recklessly torn and scattered by some brutal and foolish hand.

"Such a thing could only have happened in our day", said Mr. Lashmar to himself, retiring sadly with a few pale florets upon his palm. "In our day, only." '

(2). p. 21, line 31: Passage cancelled between 'to say that Dymchurch' and 'You'd like Dymchurch, father': 'seems to me the most reasonable man I know. He's very poor, but finds he has just enough to live upon, and mustn't bother to ask anything more by giving his name to company promoters; he might make lots of money but he despises that kind of thing.'

(3). p. 22, line 19, the MS reads: 'Here's a book I picked up second-hand a few days ago. It would interest you, father.' The volume which Dyce has been reading is said on the MS to bear 'the date of two or three years before.' These two changes were made on the typescript.

(4). p. 25: Iris Woolstan's letter read after 'again'' (passage cancelled): 'This note I do not write about Leonard, who goes on all right, but something has happened which makes me wish to see you as soon as possible. Would you do me the great kindness of calling to-morrow afternoon. I am sorry to trouble you.'

(5). p. 69, line 22: A line or so is crossed out on the MS after 'conclusions': 'He imagined, however, that his success as a politician, or even as a statesman, depended merely upon his powerful intellect.'

(6). p. 74, line 1, the MS reads: 'Dyce listened with amusement, surprised at this sprightlier mood of his companion which was like nothing he remembered in her.' The change occurred at the typescript stage.

(7). p. 106, line 22, to p. 106, line 30: This passage, uncancelled on the MS, originally read: 'In the early days of recovery Lady Ogram sent for her solicitor. This gentleman was the son of the legal adviser (long deceased) who had been useful to Sir Quentin in the early days [second version: at the beginning] of his married life; from Mr. Kerchever, the widow had no secrets. Twice already since her husband's death had she made a will; now she revised the document. What to do with her great possessions had long been a harassing subject of thought with Lady Ogram. She wished to use them for some praiseworthy purpose, which, at the same time, would perpetuate her memory. To the Ogram side of the family she saw no need for leaving anything at all; her husband's relatives were well-to-do, and had never been more than decently civil to her. As for kinsfolk of her own, it was doubtful whether any existed. More than twenty years ago she had instructed her solicitor, Mr. Kerchever, to set on foot an inquiry for surviving members of her clan. The name was Tomalin [earlier version: was an odd one—Kickweed].'

Then the following paragraph, beginning after 'offspring of her own' (p. 107, line 32) and left untouched on the MS, was cancelled on the typescript: 'At this time she began to think and talk as never before of the child she had lost. Her talk was with the Hollingford doctor, to whom she narrated all the circumstances of the boy's illness, recalling, with incredible memory, the minutest details of day after day. Why had the child died? He was of sound constitution, and ought to have overcome that attack of scarlet fever. She sought Dr. Wolff's opinion as eagerly as if it concerned a patient lying in the next room. More than that, she procured medical books, and read up the subject, with the result that she convinced herself that her son had been a victim of professional incompetence and raged about it as over an event of to-day. Dr. Wolff had to endure savage sarcasms directed against the whole medical world. How could she tell—Lady Ogram demanded—whether her own case was being intelligently treated? Ten to one she too would perish of crass ignorance and brutal disregard! The doctor, with some dignity, withdrew before this onslaught, and did not appear again until he was sent for, when Lady Ogram began with a handsome apology. They were very good friends, and, at bottom, felt a respect for each other.'

(8). p. 108, line 19: This is another passage which was modified on the typescript: 'Her flowery and leafy drawing-room indicated no particular love of garden growths; the feature was due to a suggestion by her gardener when she converted to her own use the former smoking-room; finding that people admired and thought it original, she made the arrangement a permanence, anxious only that the plants exhibited

should be rarer and finer than those possessed by her neighbours. So, in the purchase of her little Cornwall estate, she
had not been guided by any admiration of beautiful scenery,
but merely by her enjoyment of the mild climate in
winter—for she had a stubborn prejudice against foreign
countries, and could not be induced to seek even change of
atmosphere abroad. On the other hand . . .'

(9). p. 113: The conclusion of the chapter, uncancelled on
the MS, was a little longer:

'"Let us talk about our coming man", were her next
words.

"I hope the dinner won't make you ill with excitement",
said Constance.

"Pooh! Do you take me for an idiot! What is there to excite
me, I should like to know?"

They talked of Dyce Lashmar.'

(10). p. 121, lines 24-27: This passage, deleted in
part—from 'Lady Ogram' to 'lately'—was much longer on
the MS. Changes also occurred at the typescript stage:

'"In outline, yes. The theory is there, and I shouldn't
wonder if it begins to peep out in books and articles before
long. I have no intention of writing, myself; let who will
take the suggestion and use it. Keep my letter, will you? so
that if, some day, I am accused of plagiarism—"

Dyce read the newspapers and walked a little in the
garden. Punctually at eleven, Lady Ogram was ready for
her drive. Face to face with her, the guest listened to a vehement outpouring on the subject of Mrs. Toplady; with
Constance's words in mind, he found it easy to understand
afterwards: to interpret the contemptuous tolerance which
was the upshot of this tirade, and even trusted himself to
point [afterwards: to indicate], delicately, the personal contrast involved. His hostess's eyes shone with pleasure. So
Constance was right. An acute person, Constance Bride;
Lashmar's respect for her had much increased lately.'

(11). p. 126, line 28, to p. 127, line 3: About half this passage
is cancelled on the MS; it is clear that corrections were made
on the typescript:

'Mrs. Toplady was waiting impatiently in the dining-
room, ready to fall upon her mess of shredded flesh; the hostess gave her only a careless nod, and looked about for Lashmar. Dyce and Miss Bride entered together.

"Come along! Come along!" sounded Lady Ogram's

voice, as she seated herself. "Everybody's late this morning. Mr. Kerchever—Mr. Lashmar—I want you to know
each other. Mr. Lashmar, what have you been doing all the
morning? Why, of course you had a drive with me—I had
forgotten. Mr. Kerchever—Mrs. Toplady. Do sit down and
let us eat. If everyone's as hungry as I am! Mrs. Toplady,
how did you sleep?"

The guest began a detailed account of her reaction to
[illegible], but was rapidly cut short.

"Nonsense! You imagine it all. No one every [sic] sleeps
badly at Rivenoak. It's the finest air in England. But if you
would sleep well, you must eat well. Good food and plenty
of it has been my prime rule of health through my life.
Have some lunch, Mrs. Toplady, and throw Salisbury to
the dogs. Ask Mr. Kerchever his opinion of all such fads; *he*
doesn't look much of an invalid."

It was evident that Mrs. Toplady did not relish this jest-
ing; she smiled sourly, and, on the first chance, made her
voice heard [afterwards: and began a voluble self-defence].

"I am the last person in the world to take up a fad. Fads
have always been my abhorrence. I venture to say that I
never do anything without the authority of reason. Do you
know the Salisbury treatment, Mr. Kerchever? Let me
explain the principles—"

The athletic man of law, being seated next to Mrs.
Toplady, had no choice but to lend an ear while she dis-
coursed. But Lady Ogram, who had satisfied her appetite
with one or two mouthfuls, talked on in a joyously excited
way, to the astonishment of Constance, who saw that Mr.
Kerchever must have brought some very important news.
Lashmar, also exhilarated, kept up conversation with the
hostess, and presently succeeded in detaching Mr. Kerchever from Mrs. Toplady. It was a vivacious company, Constance being the only person who spoke little.'

The uncancelled MS version of this passage only differs
from the printed text at the beginning:

'Mrs. Toplady joined them in the dining-room. She and
Mr. Kerchever were already acquainted, having met at Rivenoak once or twice before.

"Come along! Come along!" sounded Lady Ogram's
voice, as she seated herself. "Everybody's late to-day . . ." '
(12). p. 129, line 13 to p. 130, line 31: This passage was

added on p. 36b of the MS. The earlier version, though deleted, is quite legible:

'. . . spirits. The sense of social inferiority did not trouble her; rather, in looking upon the ladies present, she enjoyed the reflection that not one of them had half her intellect or her practical ability.

Even Mrs. Toplady displayed animation and talked of other things than the state of her health. In the privacy of the afternoon, Lady Ogram had made ample amends to her for rudeness at luncheon, had spoken of her troubles with kindliness, and flattered her by seriously asking her opinion of Lashmar's powers. Mrs. Toplady at once declared an enthusiastic faith in the young politician. Her house was open to him; she hoped to see him very often; she would made him acquainted with a world of people, every one of whom was sure to recognize and proclaim his distinction.

"A friend of him," said Lady Ogram, "is Lord Dymchurch. Do you know him?"

"Oh, very well," cried the other mechanically. She added, "That is, I have met him. Friends of mine are very intimate with him."

Mrs. Toplady had never heard Lord Dymchurch's name, but it was a point of pride with her to know everyone who had a place in society.

"If I am in town next month," continued Lady Ogram, "arrange for me to meet him, will you?"

"Of course I will; of course—I thought you had no intention—"

"I may be in town for a week or two presently."' '

(13). p. 135, line 6: Breakspeare's remarks on his maid-servant, undeleted on the MS, were cancelled on the typescript:

'At one of the doors, Breakspeare rang, and it was opened by a very ugly but neat-looking woman, who smiled respectfully and at once disappeared.

"She has been our servant for seventeen years", whispered Breakspeare, "ever since we were married. A good creature. I favour fixity of tenure—don't you?" '

(14). p. 141, lines 16-34: This passage was added on p. 36b of the MS. The earlier version, at the top of p. 39, is perfectly legible:

'They two, as usual, were alone together at breakfast time, and Dyce began a humorous account of the evening he had passed; but, in the middle of his story, to the surprise of both, there entered Mrs. Toplady. Pausing just within the room, she stood with a singular smile, her head sentimentally drooping to one side. To their salutations, she responded with a languorous amiability. Oh, how well she had slept! And what a calm, bright, delicious morning it was! What were their plans? Should she be in the way if she joined them? To this, Constance made curt reply; for her part she had to work as usual. So Mrs. Toplady made an appointment with Lashmar for ten o'clock, in the garden. Dyce prepared himself for infinite boredom, but he was rather surprised than bored by the strain in which his companion talked to him as they paced the alleys. All at once she had become deeply interested in him, almost tenderly anxious about his future. And, as though by natural transition, she began to speak of her married life, which, she declared, had been "a dream of happiness." Had not her husband died whilst still young (fifty-three was Mr. Toplady's age) he would have left a name in the annals of his country, and he used to say that it was to *her* he owed the steady purpose of his existence. Intelligence and earnestness had always characterized her; these were the qualities above all requisite in the wife of an ambitious man. Happily, Mr. Lashmar did not need admonition on this subject; he was not led astray by glittering superficialities; he could read women's characters. And now let her say that she counted on seeing him in Pont Street very soon. He was to come whenever he liked, as one of the intimates, and she would take care that he made useful acquaintances. His career would henceforth be her ceaseless concern; it gave a new object to her declining and woefully burdened life.'

(15). p. 147, line 21: The central paragraph goes on undeleted on the MS: 'She had not dared to grant herself that vision of a past which was her secret pride, her shame if known to all. Thinking of it now, her lips curled, her brows scowled defiance.

    "Well," she said, as if angrily, "you'll see the girl..."

(16). p. 154, line 3: After 'to make', the MS first went on as follows: ' "their homes less ugly. I don't know", she glanced from the one to the other of her listeners, "whether you have any idea how ugly and cheerless they often are. We want to teach these good people how to choose nice wall-papers and

what sort of pictures to put up." ' Here Gissing stopped
abruptly, deleted the passage just transcribed, and linked up
'make' with 'use of the free library.'

(17). p. 174, line 14: A short paragraph occurs here on the
MS; it was cancelled on the typescript: 'Dyce had frequently
felt uneasiness on this subject. But it seemed probable, to the
point of certainty, that Lady Ogram's testamentary disposi-
tions were already made; no doubt her vague talk regarding
Constance Bride had reference to arrangements finally settled. And in that direction he preferred not to speculate for
the present.'

(18). p. 292, lines 12-18: This passage bears heavy corrections. There does not seem to be an original version distinct
from the printed one. Gissing amended his text as he wrote
on:

> 'I expected you,' she exclaimed jubilantly. 'How did you
> get the news?'
> 'Heard it in town at dinner-time yesterday,' answered
> Lashmar '[obscure] had had a telegram. I came down to
> Hollingford by the last train, and sat up half the night
> with Breakspeare.'
> 'Then *my* telegram was no use,' said Constance. 'I sent
> one at eight o'clock this morning.'
> 'Did you? Many thanks.' [These last two cues were cer-
> tainly cancelled before he wrote on.]
> 'I sent out a telegram for you the first thing this morn-
> ing,' said Lady Ogram. But it was addressed at Alv'. Here
> Gissing deleted the unfinished second part of Lady
> Ogram's cue and went on with what was to be the printed
> version: 'Had you left . . .'

(19). p. 298, line 2: The following passage is cancelled on
the MS:

> ' "At ninety", remarked Lady Amys to her husband, as
> they were dressing for dinner, "what a well-bred person
> she will be!"
> They were the only people of their world who had
> always seen Lady Ogram on her best side, and who had a
> genuine friendship for her.'

(20). p. 369, line 37: A long passage is cancelled on the MS,
p. 100:

> 'So, in the afternoon, he once more drove up to Riven-
> oak, and once more followed the servant into the drawing-
> room. There sat Constance Bride, behind her the marble

bust, which shone very white in contrast with her garb of mourning. Lashmar observed that she looked well in this attire; he had never seen her rise with such an easy grace, with such calm dignity. He took her hand, and pressed it. Constance did not smile; her expression was gravely courteous, and when she invited him to be seated, it was with a soft voice perfectly under control.

"I was sorry not to be able to speak a word yesterday," Dyce began, with a constraint for which he had not prepared himself. "At the cemetery, I saw that you didn't feel able—"

"I think it's better not to talk at such times," said Constance.

"Certainly. Are the Amyses still here?"

"No. They returned to London in the evening."

"For the present, you remain?"

"For a little while. Of course there are many things to be seen to—I go on with my secretaryship."

Lashmar smiled. He was holding his resplendent silk hat, and wanted to put it down, but his muscles would not act on the suggestion.

"In a few days, no doubt," he said, "you will be free to make your own plans?"

"Most likely."

Constance betrayed a little nervousness, and Lashmar took courage. He succeeded in laying aside his hat; then, fixing his look on the face before him, he began to say what he had in mind.'

(21). p. 378, line 28: A rather confusing passage, deleted on the MS, occurred here:

' "You surely don't expect that what was a dream, a deliverance, to you should be binding reality for me?" "To tell you the truth, I hardly know [Here another line was begun.]

"The dream ceased when Miss Tomalin left the room. After that, I came back to my senses. But the question itself as you [Here again the line was left unfinished and another one begun.]

"Unfortunately I didn't."

Again they gazed fixedly at each other.'

(22). p. 380, line 10: One more false start can be reconstructed here: "You consider[?]", she said, "that I am losing an opportunity such as I am never likely to have again. It is very considerate of you [afterwards: it is difficult for you to believe] that I can resist the temptation to become the wife of such a man as you." The sentence is unfinished on the MS.

(23). p. 384. The last paragraph reads as follows on the MS:
    'Never in his life had he passed such a miserable night. At each waking from hag-ridden slumber, the black thoughts beset him; his tortured brain formed projects of suicide; by the hour he debated with himself where and how he should die. Temptation lurked in the assurance that by destroying himself, he would become, for a few days at all events, the subject of universal interest. Of course it must be narcotic poison; he had not the courage for any other form of voluntary death. But the details were troublesome; now and then he sat up in bed to think them over.
    So utter a despondency lay upon him that he found . . .'

(24). p. 385, line 34: This sentence, undeleted on the MS, occurs after 'Iris Woolstan': 'He knew no one else from whom he could with shadow of reason expect sympathy or aid.'

(25). p. 405: The last sentence of the chapter, uncancelled on the MS, was: 'Dymchurch went to dinner, and, after his vigorous exercise, ate with appetite.'

The conclusion to be drawn from the variations between the manuscript, the proofs and the novel in its first English edition is clear enough. In revising his story Gissing learned anew an artistic virtue which he had praised in the days of *Isabel Clarendon:* the virtue of restraint. The ultimate version shows a careful avoidance of the obvious, a greater consistency in tone, a removal of some conversational topics which tended to get out of focus. Such characters as Mrs. Toplady and Constance Bride became subtler creations in the process of revision. Their enigmatic nature largely results from Gissing's second thoughts on their personality. The style also benefited from his careful attention: the number of modifications made between the first draft and the despatching of the page proofs to the printers surely amounts to a few thousands. Since no preparatory notes seem to have survived, these alterations show us better than any other document the writer at work, the novelist enjoying the practice of his craft. Gissing once said that when he wrote he always had in mind the better kind of reader. His deliberate choice to let the reader of *Our Friend the Charlatan* read between the lines and make abundant use of his intelligence testifies to a deep artistic sensibility which has too often gone unacknow-ledged.

Bibliography

I - Reviews of the first edition (all published in 1901). * indicates a reprint in *Gissing: The Critical Heritage*

Daily Telegraph, 31 May, p. 11 (by W.L. Courtney).
Spectator, 1 June, p. 809.
Manchester Guardian, 5 June, p. 3.*
Globe, 5 June, p. 4.
Glasgow Herald, 6 June, p. 9.
Pall Mall Gazette, 6 June, p. 4.*
Scotsman, 6 June, p. 2.
Morning Post, 7 June, p. 2.
Daily Chronicle, 10 June, p. 3 (by Henry Harland).*
Guardian (London weekly), 12 June, p. 806.
Literature, 15 June, p. 519.*
St. James's Gazette, 19 June, p. 5.
Birmingham Daily Post, 21 June, p. 9.
Athenaeum, 22 June, pp. 783-84.
Academy, 22 June, pp. 535-36.*
Outlook (New York), 22 June, p. 460.
Daily Mail, 25 June, p. 3.
The Times, 29 June, p. 5.*
Illustrated London News, 29 June, p. 942.
World (London), 3 July, pp. 31-32.
Daily Graphic, 6 July, p. 11.
Saturday Review, 6 July, p. 20.
Outlook (London), 13 July, p. 762.
New York Tribune Illustrated Supplement, 14 July, pp. 11-12.*
Standard, 19 July, p. 4.
Graphic (London weekly), 27 July, pp. 128 and 130.
Fortnightly Review, July, pp. 166-67 (by Stephen Gwynn).
Litterarische Echo, July, p. 1430 (by Elizabeth Lee).
Literary World (Boston), 1 August, p. 115.

Truth (London), 15 August, p. 446 (by Desmond O'Brien).
La Revue (Paris), 15 August, pp. 421-23.
Queen, 21 August, pp. 306-07.
Literary World (London), 23 August, p. 127.
Sphere, 24 August, p. 226 (by C.K. Shorter).
Bookman (London), August, pp. 152-54 (by A. Macdonell).
Literary News (New York), September, p. 260 (reprinted from the New York *Commercial Advertiser*).
Book Lover (Melbourne), September, p. 98 [by H.H. Champion].
Bookman (New York), September, pp. 95-96.
Overland Monthly (San Francisco), October, pp. 314-15 (by Grace Luce Irwin).

II - Books and articles containing material on *'Our Friend the Charlatan'*

Anon., 'An Idealistic Realist', *Atlantic Monthly*, February 1904, pp. 280-82.

Courtney, W.L., 'George Gissing', *English Illustrated Magazine*, November 1903, pp. 188-92.

Coustillas, P. (ed.), *Collected Articles on George Gissing*, London and New York, 1968.

Coustillas, P. and Partridge, C. (eds.), *Gissing: The Critical Heritage*, London and Boston, 1972.

Davis, Oswald H., *George Gissing: a Study in Literary Leanings*, London, 1966.

Donnelly, Mabel Collins, *George Gissing: Grave Comedian*, Cambridge, Mass., 1954.

Gapp, Samuel Vogt, *George Gissing: Classicist*, Philadelphia, 1936.

Gettmann, Royal A., *George Gissing and H.G. Wells*, London and Urbana, Ill., 1961.

Gissing, Algernon and Ellen (eds.), *Letters of George Gissing to Members of His Family*, London, 1927.

Gordan, John D., *George Gissing 1857-1903: An Exhibition from the Berg Collection*, New York, 1954.

Kennedy, J.M., *English Literature 1880-1905*, London, 1912.

Korg, Jacob, *George Gissing, a Critical Biography*, Seattle, 1963; London, 1965.

Leavis, Q.D., "Gissing and the English Novel", *Scrutiny*, June 1938, pp. 73-81.

McKay, Ruth Capers, *George Gissing and his Critic Frank Swinnerton*, Philadelphia, 1933.

Poole, Adrian, *Gissing in Context*, London 1975.

Spiers, J. and Coustillas, P., *The Rediscovery of George Gissing*, London, 1971.

Swinnerton, Frank, *George Gissing: a Critical Study*, London, 1912.

Tindall, Gillian, *The Born Exile: George Gissing*, London and New York, 1974.
Tye, J.R., 'Autograph Gissing Material in New Zealand', *Gissing Newsletter*, July 1972, pp. 1-7. Includes a study of the Ms of *Our Friend the Charlatan.*

III - Other related material

Baker, Ernest A., *The History of the English Novel*, vol. IX, London, 1936.
Gissing, George, *Demos*, edited with introduction and notes by P. Coustillas, Brighton, The Harvester Press, 1972.
Gissing, George, *The Nether World*, edited with an introduction by John Goode, Hassocks, The Harvester Press, 1974.
Izoulet, Jean, *La Cité moderne*, Paris, Felix Alcan, 1894.
Keating, Peter, *The Working Classes in Victorian Fiction*, London 1971.